PARALLEL LIVES

Lena Rotmensz

Cover designed by CREATIVE PRODUCTS, LLC
www.CProducts.com

This book is a work of fiction. Names, characters, places, and incidents either are products of the author's imagination or are used fictitiously. Any resemblance to actual persons, living or dead, events, or locales is entirely coincidental.

Lena Rotmensz
Contact: lrotmensz@gmail.com

Printed in the United States of America

First Printing: Jul 2018
CREATIVE PRODUCTS, LLC
www.CProducts.com

ISBN-13 978-1-9833591-7-0

This book is dedicated to my children and grandchildren.

Heartfelt thanks to my daughter, Rachel, for her help, enthusiasm and encouragement.

CONTENTS

PROLOGUE

The core of this story is true. It was told to me thirty-five years ago. Since then, I knew that one day I would tell it to the world.

This is a unique story that began just before the Second World War in Europe. It is the story of a young Jewish married couple with a baby who get separated as a result of the war.

The young woman assumes a new identity in a concentration camp, falls in love with a German military official, and starts a new life.

Her husband struggles with life, reunites with their young daughter, and tries to deal with the supposed loss of his wife.

This is a story of their gripping survival, and most of all, their separation and "Parallel Lives" thereafter.

The novel takes the reader through the political differences of several countries, emotional struggles, and love. The book demonstrates cowardice, selfishness, heroism, and patriotism. It describes how war could affect families for generations.

That era is very familiar to me.
I too, have lived through it.

* * *

LENA ROTMENSZ

CHAPTER 1

After a week of rain, snow and a lot of speculation at home, Warsaw had its first glorious day!

Family and friends gathered in the evenings to try to understand the German politics of the day and their future events. Liliana had enough of it!

The cold breeze was refreshing after being home for several days. The doctor's office was several blocks away. The beautiful fall day in her beloved Warsaw prompted Liliana to walk instead of taking a taxi. She knew she was with child. She could feel it. However she did not want to say anything to anyone until the doctor confirmed the pregnancy.

She had mixed feelings. She knew it would make her Henry very happy. But was she happy?

Liliana and Henry had been married for over a year, and everyone had been expecting her to be with child, especially Henry. Every month, before her monthly, he questioned, "How do you feel"?

She thought she wanted to be a mother. It would keep her occupied, and in some sense, make her feel useful. Since her marriage, she had not done very much. They had a housekeeper and a cook. The homemaking training Liliana received from her mother had not been put to use. Instead, she studied German and some typing with her tutor.

Nervously she thought a child would bind them together. She found a seat next to a small window and watched the last leaves of the fall season looking like gold and copper dancing on the street.

"Mrs. Kopel," a nurse called. Her heart stopped! Liliana walked away from the window and entered the examination room.

"Yes doctor, yes doctor," she heard herself saying. But because of her excitement, she didn't comprehend his words.

She couldn't wait to see Henry to share the news! The streets were crowded. It was late afternoon and Liliana felt jubilant.

Finally she arrived at the store. It was truly impressive. The store was the most important antique gallery in Warsaw and was located on the most premier street of the city.

The secretary informed Liliana that Mr. Kopel was in conference with a client.

The gallery was full with magnificent collections of artifacts, old silver, rugs, statues and paintings. Much of these treasures decorated the interior of their own home. It took a long time for Liliana to get used to this new life.

Her marriage was arranged by her parents and the Kopels, who lived in a small town near Warsaw, called Gąbin. Henry's father and her father were watchmakers and longtime friends.

At first it was a terrible upset for Liliana. She had just met Joseph, a handsome, shy and delicate boy who was an apprentice at her father's shop. He was from a nearby town called Nowy-Dwor. They managed to see each other a few times, going to the movies and small cafes. She was infatuated with him.

Slowly, her parents convinced her to marry Henry to have a "good marriage" and a "better life" full of comfort and prestige. Henry Kopel was kind, intelligent, and enamored with Liliana. Henry was fifteen years older than her, a little shorter and a little chubby. He was always finely attired and looked impeccable, always wearing custom suits, shirts and ties. Although not handsome, Henry was always elegant.

Finally Henry came from his office. Seeing her, he asked, "Is everything ok?"

"Henry," she answered, "Everything is more than ok! We would have a baby in eight months!"

Henry paled, went down on his knees and kissed her hand. "Thank you, my beautiful Liliana."

That evening they shared the news with her parents. Her father's eyes filled with tears of joy.

The next few months Liliana spent most of her time reading and, at the instance of her mother, her reading was in German. "You never know when you may need it," preached her mother. She was always the driving force for Liliana and her brother's education. A foreign language was a must.

The uneasiness of the Jewish community was very obvious. The reports from Germany were not good. Trying to ignore the bad news, Liliana immersed herself in her readings and tried to remain calm. The change in her body was visible at last.

Since childhood, Liliana always heard, "You don't look like a Jewish girl." Liliana was tall, slender, and blue-eyed with dark blonde hair. Because of her appearance, she never encountered anti-Semitic outbursts. Her father always said, "You're such a shiksa!" She did look different from all her cousins.

Finally it was spring. She loved to sit in the beautiful Lazienki Park. The air was clear, the leaves were filling the trees, the grass was getting green and the flowers would soon appear, transforming the park into a fairytale scene.

She went to the antique store often, trying to learn the business. Each item had a history or a pedigree, but Henry had no patience to teach her at that time. He was moving the most valuable antiques to friends' homes for safekeeping. The mood in the city was of uncertainty; but Liliana thought that would pass.

The day before, two Hassidic Jews came to sell an item that Henry did not want to buy. "Customers are not buying now, especially antiques," Henry explained. Listening to their conversation was an eye opener for Liliana. Hasidic Jews were true believers. They thought God would take care, God would provide at the right time. "Not to worry," they said. How wonderful it must have been to have total belief. But history was teaching us differently. Henry smiled.

Evenings with family were spent in discussions about the future. Henry's parents, Samuel and Helen, came to visit. They were anxiously awaiting the birth of their first grandchild. It would also be the first grandchild for Liliana's parents. Liliana's brother, Daniel, was graduating from high school that May. His father was doing everything possible to send him out of Poland. It was not easy.

The next day Henry and Liliana were invited to their friends' home nearby. Phillip and Sofia Witkowski grew up with Henry in the small town of Gąbin. They were both Catholic. They were both doctors.

The maternity dress Liliana was wearing for dinner was awkward, but she had no choice. The preferred way for Liliana to get to the Witkowskis' home was to walk, but Henry insisted on taking a taxi. The evening was wonderful. Liliana felt at ease and welcomed. The dinner was delicious and beautifully presented.

Philip Witkowski helped Liliana with her coat and quietly said, "Don't worry too much. We would always stand by you and help you in any way we can."

Liliana did not understand. "What help do we need?" she questioned herself.

The weather was getting warmer by the day and the baby was due in two months, sometime in July. Liliana was glad it would be summer for the baby's birth. It would be great if she could talk with a woman who had recently had a baby. Mother was not much help. She said, "Do not worry. You are not the first woman to give birth. It would be all right when the time comes."

Spending time in the park reading her German novels, chaperoned by the housekeeper, was the highlight of Liliana's last months of her pregnancy. Her favorite bench in the park was near the famous statue of Chopin. She loved to close her eyes and hear the music of Chopin and smell the sweetness of the flowers surrounding her.

Henry was interviewing for a nanny. Liliana wished he would allow her to take part in the decision, but he insisted upon doing it himself. Henry had also been busy transferring his antique treasures to Phillip and Sofia Witkowski's home.

The whole world was in turmoil, but somehow Liliana was unfazed. She could not understand her malaise. It was like being in the clouds and watching the world pass by. She was completely untouched by reality. "Is this how depression feels or is this how being pregnant feels?" questioned Liliana. Liliana's last month of pregnancy had been a very impatient time. Every day she woke up thinking, "Is this the day?"

Finally "the day" came at night! She awoke with a sharp pain in the abdomen. Henry called a taxi and they were on the way to the hospital. The doctor was waiting for them as they arrived. After receiving medication for pain, Liliana could hardly remember the following few hours.

Early in the morning, on July 15, 1939, her beautiful daughter was born. They named her Rebecca. The next few days were spent in a private hospital room filled with flowers and well-wishers. Liliana was dazed by all the attention. The only thing she cared about was seeing her daughter at feeding time. Her hands would shake when the nurse placed the baby in her arms, not from fear but from anticipation of holding her little Rebecca.

The day they were going home, the nanny came with Henry. She was a sturdy woman in her 40's named Lola. A likeable, smiley, pleasant individual, she raised a few children from infancy to early childhood. Liliana liked her immediately. Lola held the baby with ease and care. Liliana told her she intended to be a very involved mother. Lola agreed.

The baby's room and adjoining nanny's room were prepared with elegance and good taste. Liliana could never have done that; it was Henry's skill. The days passed in a routine way. Liliana's parents came daily. Henry would stand by the crib staring at Rebecca sleeping. Liliana had to pull him away every night.

The day came for Liliana & Lola to take Rebecca to Liliana's favorite park. It was September 1939. Before they reached the park, they saw people running and crying. Lola asked a woman passing by what was happening.

"The War, the War is happening!" They turned back immediately and were met by Henry who was running to meet them. They arrived home within minutes. Liliana's parents were there already. Rebecca was crying as if she knew what happening. Henry held her to calm her down saying, "Shush, little baby, nothing would happen to you, I would make sure."

But what did it mean, "War"? Liliana read a lot of history novels, but it never gave her the feeling of the true horror of war. Henry's parents did not believe that it would be so horrible. They thought it would be like the First World War. They did not believe it would be a long war.

The decision was made to prepare food that would last for a while. Henry closed the shop, which by then was practically empty.

Henry's cousins came to his house and scared Liliana and him with their prediction of the war. They thought the Jews were in tremendous danger. The cousins were taking their families to Russia. "To Russia? To Communist Russia?" questioned Henry.

The next few weeks passed by in great chaos. Rebecca, oblivious to the commotion, was growing beautifully. She had Liliana's coloring and Henry's features. Blond curls, blue eyes, very fair skin, she had a determined character. She was a healthy child with a sweet smile. The days passed for Liliana by playing and caring for Rebecca, feeling totally helpless with regard to their future.

Some of the family fled from the city and some tried to go abroad. And then there were those, like Liliana and Henry, who thought they could remain right there in Warsaw.

The news out of Germany was very difficult to believe. The Jewish community there was being attacked. The Hasidim were being attacked on the streets of Berlin. Their businesses had been confiscated. The German military was growing out of proportion. No one was able to oppose them. They were doing whatever they wanted, and the world stood by waiting. Waiting for what?

Whenever Liliana dwelled on their situation, she felt a strong pang in her stomach. She could not see how this would "just go away" the way Henry says it would. Liliana's concern was to just keep Rebecca safe, but how could she do so? Henry and Liliana met with Philip and Sofia to discuss the worst case scenario. There had been rumors of the Germans creating a ghetto for the Jewish people in part of Warsaw. And it would be mandatory for all Jews to live there.

Sofia was surprised at Liliana's look of distress. Sofia put her arms around her and said, "Please do not worry. We would make it our priority to keep Rebecca safe." Sofia took out her crystal goblets and poured some wine. After a surprisingly good dinner, they made themselves comfortable in the living room.

"Thank you for the delicious dinner," said Liliana.

Sofia gave her a smile. "If it were not for Henry, we would not even have the food to cook!" Liliana knew food was scarce, but somehow their kitchen was full. The "somehow" was Henry.

Finally they started their conversation about their plans. Philip was the first to speak. He was apologetic for what he was about to say. "If the ghetto is created, I don't believe you should go there. There is no choice for your parents. They are elderly and, forgive me, but they look Jewish. I think you should move to our house and tell your neighbors you're leaving the country. That would be a solution for now. We would see what developments and events occur in the future. The nanny should be let go. All of this had to be done without leaving any traces. Absolutely no one could know where you are. Already, we have started to prepare false documents for you. Our house is pretty secure, with walled-in gardens and an iron gate. The terrible bombarding of the city had subsided a little. We were lucky there was no damage to our neighborhood. You must tell your parents, and no one else. All this had to be done as soon as possible."

The ghetto in Warsaw was being prepared. The Germans were forcing Polish workers to build a tall wall in the district called *The Old City*.

One hundred and thirty thousand Poles were being evacuated to make room for four hundred thousand Jews, which represented thirty percent of the population in Warsaw.

Henry went to the ghetto to find a reasonably comfortable flat for Liliana's parents and brother. Within one month, all Jews had been commanded to be relocated.

Preparation for the move was on its way. Nanny Lola was told the family was leaving for London the following week and that she had to be let go. The house started to feel very sad. The paintings were off the wall. Some furniture had already been removed and clothes were being packed

Jews were forced to wear a yellow star on their outer clothing. Henry was wearing one, but Liliana refused, so she could not leave the house. The next day they were to move to Sofia and Philip's home. They cried saying their goodbyes.

Rebecca would sleep in Henry and Liliana's bed that night.

The taxi came to pick them up in the morning. The unknown was very scary. The taxi came through the gate of the Witkowski house. The gate closed behind them. Their rooms were already prepared for them and were beautifully arranged with all the comforts of home. The help was let go from the Witkowski household. From now on, Liliana and Sofia would do all the cleaning and cooking.

Rebecca just had started to walk, and she was everywhere! She felt safe there. Philip was still going to his office, but soon he would only work in the hospital since no one was paying bills anymore and he no longer had nursing help available.

After putting Rebecca to bed, Philip and Sofia took Henry and Liliana to the basement to show them where everything was. A lot of stored food, water, wine. It looked like a warehouse. They also told them about a small house they own in a quiet suburb of Gdynia, walking distance to the beach of the Baltic Sea.

"Please remember this place," said Philip. "It is located on the so-called Polish Corridor." He handed them a small card with the address. He told them to memorize the address, and throw away the card. If by any chance they got separated and they had to find each other, this would be the place. The next day their new identification papers would be completed.

That evening, Rebecca was asleep. Phillip took out some papers from his desk and started to talk to Liliana in a very calm voice. "From now on your name will be Helena Michalowski. You would be the daughter of Count Michalowski from Krakow, who just left Poland to go to London. He just lost his daughter, about your age. She died at home of tuberculosis very recently and was buried in the family plot. There is no evidence of her death registered anywhere. With all of the commotion of the war, most of the government offices are closed. You have all the documents you need; the photo is of you. I prepared a little bag for you to wear around your neck to hold these documents. You must keep these documents with you at all times. Also, try to memorize the history of Count Michalowski from 1885, when he moved to Krakow, until their recent departure to London."

Liliana was mesmerized as she looked at the documents. All she said was, "Thank you, thank you so much."

"Well, this is not all," said Sofia. "Your daughter, Rebecca, now would be known as Eva Witkowski, a child we just adopted. The old documents with her true identity would be buried next to an oak tree at the summerhouse, for the future.

"Henry would keep his own identity, partly because of his looks and because it's very easy to identify Jewish men because they are circumcised.

"If at any time you or Henry are caught by German police, you cannot return to this house. That is how we would keep Rebecca safe."

Sitting and listening to this proposal was so incredible, Liliana could not process all of it. Her cheeks were wet with tears. Henry hugged her and gave her a handkerchief. "We have such good friends," said Henry.

The bombarding of the city continued. The Jews were forced to relocate to the Ghetto. Liliana and Henry could not help their families with anything. Henry told Liliana's parents to go to a specific flat that he prepared for them.

The Witkowskis were thinking, "Maybe it would be better to go to Gdynia. It is becoming very difficult to travel around. For now, we are home, like in a cocoon, and safe." Besides Philip, they did not go out of the house for weeks. Philip was still going to the hospital. He was being forced to treat the wounded Germans. Philip said, "They are just like us... in pain, hungry and lost."

Henry made the decision not to go to Gdynia. He would stay in Warsaw. Liliana could not imagine being without him. At the time they were living as if they were brother and sister, for fear of getting pregnant. And feeling happy was out of the question. Only Rebecca gave them happiness right now. They did not have fresh milk for Rebecca. They thought they could get a goat and keep it in a shed in the backyard. The only problem would be how to keep the goat quiet.

Philip came home very tired. He had been in the hospital for three days, nonstop. He told them that the Germans gathered several doctors and told them they were needed in other places and that they must be moved. Preparations to leave Warsaw had to take place sooner than later. They would not be safe in Warsaw.

The rumors Philip heard in the hospital were grim. He repeated the news at home. The Ghetto was in chaos. It was crowded, the sanitation trucks were not picking up garbage, it was hard to purchase food, and abandoned children were dying in the streets. Liliana could not imagine the situation. How could her parents and brother have managed to stay alive?

The Germans started bringing Jews from small towns surrounding Warsaw into the Ghetto. Most likely, Henry's parents were among them. Henry was very restless.

He felt he had to do something for his parents, but it was impossible and it made it harder for him to accept.

That night at dinner it was decided that the next week both families would start the journey to Gdynia. They realized the Germans would stop them as they travelled, so they had to remember the details of their new identities. They would travel as far as they could by car, but cars were getting confiscated by the Germans. They would take side roads, not main routes and they would travel mostly at night.

Henry would venture out the next day. He said he couldn't leave without finding out about his parents' wellbeing. Liliana begged him not to go, although she understood how he felt. She couldn't sleep that night. In the morning, at breakfast, she was so anxious she could not even swallow her food.

Henry & Liliana both cried and hugged; Henry showered Rebecca with kisses. There was nothing Liliana could do but wait. It was a somber morning. Henry was gone.

The day had passed, and Henry had not returned. Liliana, Philip and Sofia looked at each other without saying a word. Evening came and Liliana took Rebecca into bed with her. She watched her daughter, breathing evenly, and her heart was aching. "What would happen to us?" she questioned.

In the morning Liliana begged Philip to let her go to find what happened to Henry. Philip tried to explain that it was too dangerous. "The Germans pick up people right in the streets. They force them into closed trucks and transport them directly into concentration camps!" In Polish these were called "Lapanka." This was most likely what happened to Henry.

Liliana felt like she must try to find Henry, whatever might happen. She said her endearing goodbyes to Rebecca and her friends and departed.

CHAPTER 2

The fear of the unknown had taken her breath away. She had her documents in a bag under her blouse, and a few gold coins in her pocket. Looking around, she realized that there were very few people on the streets. She turned the corner onto a street leading to the ghetto. As she walked, she took in the destruction that had happened in Warsaw. How sad and terribly wrong the war was.

Finally she saw the tall wall of the ghetto and stopped in her tracks. She feared entering the ghetto. "What would happen to Rebecca if she couldn't get out? What now? What should I do? How can I find Henry?" She felt helpless and afraid. Her only thought was to run back home.

She retraced her steps and thought that maybe she would find Henry at the antique shop. The shock overwhelmed her. Most of the building was in ruins. The windows in Henry's store were broken and a swastika was painted on the door. She was frozen in place. There were almost no people on the street. She heard the rumble of a truck coming. It was a covered truck and stopped right in front of her. Two German soldiers jumped out, grabbed her under her arms, and heaved her into the truck. The soldiers sat at the gate. Liliana did not cry out or say anything. After adjusting to the darkness of the truck, she saw a woman crying and men sitting with their heads lowered. She was numb. Where was she going? Where were they taking her? What would happen to her?

After a while, the truck stopped. Two Germans from the front cabin, with drawn rifles, forced all the captured off of the truck. They were at a train station. Hundreds of cattle cars were lined up in the darkness of the station. Liliana heard people in the cars begging for water. She and the other occupants of the truck were shoved into the last cattle car, which was half empty. She understood the order from the German officer to start the train. She sat on the bare floor in the corner of the cattle car thinking this was exactly what must have happened to Henry. She thought that maybe she would find him at the end of this journey.

It was not a very long train ride. They arrived in the middle of the night. Everyone was ordered off the train.

"You go there!" "You go here!" The children were crying. The chaos was unbelievable.

After being shoved around and questioned if she was Jewish, which she denied, Liliana found herself with a group of young women in a separate line from all the others. They were kept separate and ordered to wait. Liliana looked at this scene. She saw men in striped garments, more like pajamas. They were following German orders to segregate the new arrivals into different groups. Children were torn from their mothers. The wailing was piercing. Liliana thought of how lucky she was that her little girl was safe.

Liliana touched the bag under her blouse, which was hung from her neck. It contained her false documents. She repeated the information in her head: the false family name, and the false family history. Liliana didn't remember how much time had passed when two German officers walked toward her.

One of them was a tall, sturdy, rowdy man with red cheeks and a red nose. Right behind him stood a slender young officer, with his head tilted down and had the saddest face she ever saw. His eyes were lowered; his hands were clasped behind his back. Liliana almost felt sorry for him, not knowing why. It was a strange feeling that overtook her.

In that split second, she saw a familiar face. "My God!" she thought to herself. It was Joseph! He was wearing those striped pajamas with a jacket that had a yellow star on the sleeve. He was herding the captives. Joseph saw her too. Her first thought was to ask him if maybe he knew where her Henry was. She opened her mouth to speak, but Joseph quickly put his hand over his mouth, signaling her not to talk. He turned away and acted as if he did not know her. Liliana understood not to call out to him. Joseph was hauling the luggage off the train and Liliana quickly lost sight of him in the turmoil.

The rowdy German shouted, "Which of you girls knows the German language, writing, reading and typing? Probably none of you."

"I do," said Liliana. "I can read German, I can write German, I can type," she answered in German.

The slender officer was surprised at the response. He picked up his head to see which girl in the line spoke. With his warm, hazel eyes, almost green, he stared at Liliana. He did not utter a word. The rowdy officer turned and said to him, "Robert, check out this girl. If she is capable, like she says, you've got yourself a secretary!"

A woman took Liliana away from the rest of the group. This woman said in German, "Follow me." They went to a building far away from the noise of the rail yard. Only a few windows were lit. She took Liliana in to a room with two desks, a typewriter, file cabinets and shelves. Obviously this was an office of some sort. The woman introduced herself as a housekeeper. Her name was Frau Ingrid. "And what is your name?" she asked Liliana.

Liliana heard herself answer, in German. "Helena Michalowski."

"Are you Polish?" asked Ingrid.

"Yes, I am." answered Liliana, as sweat dripped down her back.

"Please be seated and wait. I would bring you tea and toast." And Ingrid left the room.

Liliana was exhausted. She sat and waited. For a long time, no one came, and her eyelids became heavy. In the dark, adjoining room, she noticed a couch. She lied down and instantly fell asleep.

When she awoke, the slender officer with the hazel eyes was sitting on a chair staring at her. She sat up instantly and straightened her blouse. The officer, Robert, addressed her in German. "Don't worry about where you are. After you refresh yourself and change your clothes, I would show you what has to be done in the office. Your room would be to the left of this office. There is a small bathroom for your use. I would return in an hour."

Liliana walked into the sparse bedroom. It was very clean. On the bed was a change of clothes. Liliana wondered, "Which Jew did they belong to?" Now, properly dressed, after a long shower, her hair in a braid coiled around the crown of her head, she sat and awaited the return of the officer. She ignored the rumbling of hunger in her stomach and walked to the small window. She pushed aside the curtain to see outside the window. About twenty feet from the building was a barbed wire fence about fifteen feet high. Behind the fence was an enchanted forest!

Liliana wondered if she could open the window, but she did not try. She looked out and saw she was either on the second or third floor of the building. She left the window and continued to wait at the desk. Robert entered the room. He looked very serious, and said, "My name is Robert Van Klaus. I am second in command of the concentration camp. My duties are mainly in the office adjoining this office. I would like to know a little about you."

At that moment, Liliana realized, she must maintain her identity as Helena, and she respond, "I am Helena Michalowski. My father is Count Michalowski from Krakow. My parents left Poland and are now in England. I came to Warsaw to see a distant relative who lives on the street where I was picked up. The building I was looking for was totally destroyed. I have documents for you to examine. I know the German language fluently. I can also type, but I was never a secretary. I am also fluent in Polish and I would be able to translate from one language to the other." With that said, she handed the documents to Mr. Van Klaus. He took a fast look and told her to put them away. He also told her he would provide more clothes for her.

Mr. Van Klaus's office was very bright with a large window facing the forest. The window was open and the fresh air streamed into the room. Robert dictated a letter for Liliana, now Helena, to type and he was pleased with her performance. He showed her his filing system and explained her office duties. There was a knock at the door. The housekeeper, Ingrid, came into the office with a tray of food: toast, coffee, cheese, eggs and grapes. She left the tray of food on the table and left the room. Robert invited Helena to the table and poured coffee for her and him. He told her to help herself to the food. He took a plate and filled it and she did the same, but she took very little.

There were a lot of letters that needed to be answered and some filing. Robert gave Helena some tasks to finish and before leaving, told her that he would explain more about office procedures the next day.

Helena returned to her room and asked Robert's permission if she could open her small window. He looked at her, and with a smile responded, "Yes, of course you can." Looking at him, she felt a strange pang in her stomach. She wondered what that feeling was, perhaps she was getting sick.

The housekeeper returned and told her to stay in the room, it would be locked, and she would return in the morning to wake her up. Ingrid said, "Don't despair; it is better for you this way. There are some books you could take from his office to read. Try to have a good night." and she left. Helena sat at a little table in her room with the food in front of her. Good, hot soup with small pieces of meat and vegetables, bread and an apple. She finished everything. She tried to read, but she could not. All she saw in front of her was her baby. Helena hoped the Witkowskis had left Warsaw. She knew there was no way to find out for sure, but she could only hope. The thought of the unknown was unbearable. She cried, not knowing for how long and finally fell asleep.

Helena was awakened by a knock at the door. It was Ingrid. "Please be ready and in Van Klaus's office in half of an hour. I would unlock the door for you." Helena was looking forward to working, and also to see Robert. She made herself as presentable as she could. She wished she had a lipstick and some rouge. This was the first time in her life that she cared to have any cosmetics. Before, it took someone else to remind her to "put on some lipstick, fix your hair!" etc.

Helena entered the office without knocking. It was a surprise. She found Robert seated at this desk. She said, "Sorry," and he politely gestured for her to come in and join him for breakfast. They ate in silence.

After their coffee, Robert told Helena he would explain the purpose of the camp and show her the immediate surroundings. He took her to a small balcony where she could see two other buildings similar to the one they were in. "The building to the right," said Robert, "is for the soldiers who are guarding the camp. They eat and sleep there. They have recreational facilities where they see movies, read and exercise. The building to the left is for food storage and some of the guards, who are not German, live there." The building they were in was for the officers of the camp. They had offices there and apartments to sleep. Mr. Hans Kraus, the commander of this camp, has his own office and his secretary was also housed next to his office.

Robert then assigned her a letter to translate from German to Polish. "Sorry, but for now, the door to your room must be locked. It is for your own good."

Helena turned to him, "Can I ask you some questions? What would all the other people who were on the train with me be doing here?"

Robert answered, "This is a working camp. We do all sorts of things," he said with not too much conviction, and she saw sadness on his face. She thought it would be better not to question him further. He showed her what other work to do and told her he had many meetings that day so most likely he would not see her anymore that day. "Please dial zero on the phone to reach the housekeeper. She would return you to your room. I have provided a radio for you. Have a good day," and Robert left.

Helena went back to the window. She heard women's voices, but she could not see them. From the window, she viewed the beautiful forest again. She tried to ignore the barbed wires. The air was crisp.

Helena wanted to do a good job for Robert. She knew that staying there would provide a certain amount of safety. She had to stay safe in order to survive this war and reunite with her family. She hoped Henry was safe and that all the upheaval would be just a nightmare that passed. She told herself, "I would not be like the spoiled, young woman I was. I have to do a good job for Robert, and not be replaced."

Helena found a German dictionary on the shelf, which would surely come in handy. Typing the letters was not hard. She put them neatly in a folder and placed them on Robert's desk. She took in the features of his office. It was very meticulous, and she thought, "I wonder who worked here before me, and where is she now?" On a small table she noticed a photo of an elderly couple. The man looked just like Robert. "They must be his parents," she thought.

Helena rang for Ingrid and within minutes she came in. Ingrid was very polite, but very distant and cold. Helena decided she had better be very nice to this woman. Ingrid said she would bring her some supper within the hour. Helena thanked her politely. Upon entering, Helena sensed immediately that someone else had been in the room. She ran to the place where she hid her documents. They were there, but someone had definitely looked through them. Then she noticed some clothes were put in the closet for her. The dresses were clean and very conservative in style. She found nightgowns, underwear in the drawers, all the right size. Some were new, some were used, but all were of the best quality. Ingrid probably did this, but Helena could not figure out where such quality clothes came from. She started to read one of the books and, before long, Ingrid came with the dinner. It was a long evening, filled with all kinds of thoughts for Helena.

She tried to concentrate on the book and knew she must do what was right to stay safe.

Helena started the next day very early. She was anxious to see Robert. She surprised herself that she felt that way. "Maybe it's because I am a prisoner and maybe because he has been gentle to me, unlike Ingrid. Maybe that's why I am feeling this way." Helena was ready for Ingrid to open the door so she could go into the office. As the door opened, she saw Mr. Kraus with a dog. Next to him was Ingrid, and Robert stood behind them.

"Good morning," said Helena, "What a handsome dog. Is he friendly?" She put out her hand and the dog came to her. "Can I give him a piece of toast leftover from last night?"

"Yes, yes of course," said Kraus, looking at her in a strange way. She took the toast and let the dog eat it from her hand. "Okay Robert, you can keep her as your secretary. She's definitely not Jewish, or my dog would have a feast of her," he said. Kraus and Ingrid had a good laugh.

The one who did not laugh was Robert. Kraus and Ingrid left the office. Robert apologized for the rudeness of Mr. Kraus.

All Helena answered was, "It doesn't matter. I love animals." She thought, at least she was still safe. And so the days passed in Robert's office, typing and translating. And she could not say she was very unhappy.

From time to time, she could hear rowdy noises, music and singing from the building next door. "Wow," she thought, "they must have a good time in there." The leaves in the forest were changing colors and dropping from the trees. It rained a lot and the winds howled at night. Helena was afraid to question Robert about what was going on in the world.

Robert said he was going home for three weeks. He would leave her work for that time. Ingrid was to oversee her. Helena was very scared to be without Robert. He must have sensed her uneasiness and promised that she would be safe in his absence. She asked if he could bring her back some newspapers or magazines, and he nodded. Helena could not sleep well; she worried about how things would be without him.

Robert was leaving in two days. The work he left for her could have been completed in three to four days. But he said he would be gone for weeks. She told him there was not enough work and he answered, "I know, but you must stretch it out, and you have to be in the office every day. Do you understand?" She did. "Do whatever you have to do to look busy and stay occupied. I would try to fill in the time with some more work."

The first day without Robert, Helena went through all the printed material in Robert's office just to appear busy and make the time pass. Everything was the same on a daily basis. Ingrid came in the morning, unlocked the door, brought her meals and escorted her into the office. It was a week before Helena started on the work left to her by Robert. Ingrid provided a small electric heater for her room. The nights had become cold. It felt like snow and within a few days the snow in fact started. The snow continued for many days. As she peered out the window in Robert's office, Helena saw the trees drooping with the weight of the snow. It looked so beautiful. She stared outside for hours.

Robert was about an hour from home. The streets and houses appeared so pristine. He could not wait to see his parents, but he left the camp with a heavy heart. He was worried about Helena. How innocent she was. She had no clue where she was or what was going on in the camp. He never felt this way with any other girl. He would not have gone home if he did not already have an "arrangement" with Hans Kraus. Perhaps he would be more generous with Kraus to insure Helena's safety. The driver announced they were at his home. Robert removed his duffel bag and thanked the driver.

His parents were at the door to greet him. At first sight, they appeared pale and thin. It was good to be home in his familiar surroundings. The warmth of the house and the wonderful smells from the kitchen made him sleepy.

Father wanted to know everything that was going on in the camp. Robert could not tell them everything. His parents were doing well. All his friends were somewhere around the world, serving in the army. There was no one left at home to visit. Father reported which of his son's friends had been killed, who was missing and who was wounded and recouping in some far away hospital. On the outside, the town looked the same. But inside, every home had a son who was away doing battle somewhere.

Robert went to the neighborhood bar for some beer. Everybody gave him a warm greeting. Of course the talk was about the war. Some sat quiet though their worried faces showed how they felt. But some were robust saying, "We would rule the world. We are meant to do it. Nothing would stop us!" Robert finished his cold beer and told himself he would never come back to this bar.

He left the bar to do some holiday shopping for his mother. He also bought some magazines and newspapers for Helena.

Sitting in the living room after dinner, Robert asked his father for a little more money to give to Hans Kraus. He explained he needed a favor from the Commander. His father asked no further questions and gave him the money. For this, Robert was grateful. His mother sat next to him, snuggling closely to her son, and she was happy. She quietly said, "I wish this war was over so you could be with us again. I hope it would be soon." Robert was happy to be home, but he also missed and worried about Helena. He was surprised how much he missed her. The time flew by quickly, and after a few days he would be return to the camp. He went shopping for some warm clothes. He bought a sweater for himself and some warm things for Helena as well.

The winter weather was in full swing, although Christmas was still a month away. The news from the front was not promising. The Germans were having a hard time with the Russians. More people were rebelling in the capital cities, and the German army was spread too thin. Robert wondered what the outcome of this war would be.

How could one nation hold hostage the whole of Europe and beyond? What would his future be?

The day came for Robert to return to camp. The hardest thing was to look into his parents' sad faces. He promised to take care of himself and asked the same from them.

The car picked him up and once they were under way, Robert was anxious to get back to the camp. He napped, his head drooping, for the long trip back. He thought he would arrive late, too late to see Helena. But the next morning he would greet her in his office.

Finally he arrived. The gate opened noisily. He went inside the building. Ingrid heard the noise of the gate. She waited for him in. All Robert wanted to know how Helena was and if anything unexpected happened.

He found a note on his nightstand from Commander Hans Kraus that said Robert was to come see him first thing the morning. Robert tossed around for a while, and finally fell asleep. First thing the following morning he was in the office of Hans Kraus. He was received in a friendly manner. They sat on the couch with a cup of coffee. Hans started to tell him how the times had changed. The trains brought more and more people into the camp and the "Final Solution" was upon them. Kraus needed Robert to be "more involved." Robert reminded him that he was not well. His heart condition would not allow him to do more than he was already doing. Robert also reminded the Commander that this was why he was not on the frontline. Hans scratched his big, shaven head, not knowing what to say. Robert suggested that he talk to the other officers in the camp and explain his situation. Then he got up and handed Hans the envelope. Hans saw there was more than his usual pay that Robert gave him to keep from being ''more involved'' in the dirty aspects of the war. He made a questioning gesture. Robert just replied, "Just remember our agreement. The additional money is to keep Helena where she is now." He wished Hans a good day and left the office. How Robert despised this big, rude man.

Robert entered his own office. Helena was there. She looked at Robert with disbelief. She jumped up, came close to Robert and said, "I missed you so much. I'm so happy you're here." His heart just melted. He lifted her face with his finger under her chin, looked into her beautiful blue eyes and kissed her. She did not withdraw. She trembled and she turned around.

"Helena, I am sorry," said Robert. He gave her a wrapped package and said, "This is for you. Open it. Let's see if you like it." Helena opened the package to find a beautiful warm robe, woolen socks and a very pretty light blue blouse. "The robe and socks would come in handy for the coming cold days. You can even sleep in them. All your work was so neatly done. Thank you Helena."

Ingrid came in with their breakfast. Robert told Helena about the visit with his parents. He gave her the newspapers and magazines that he bought for her. They had a short work day.

Helena was very distraught and could not wait to be alone to examine her feelings. Finally, Ingrid locked Helena's door. She sat on her bed and all she could think about was her baby and Henry and how she felt right then. Nothing made sense. She loved Robert's kiss. She never felt like that with Henry. Her sex life with Henry was bearable and she learned to tolerate it. Henry never demanded much from her, and after, he would always apologize. Just remembering Robert's kiss made her shiver. "I know I should not allow anything to happen between us." But that was her mind speaking. Her heart had different ideas. Helena tossed and turned all night.

She tried reading one of the newspapers Robert brought her. "Incredible," she thought to herself, "the Germans are taking over the whole world!"

But she also thought of what Robert said to her at breakfast. "Do not believe everything you read."

The next morning Helena was afraid to face Robert. She wished she knew how Robert felt about what had happened the previous day. Helena was sitting at her desk when she heard loud voices coming from outside of her window. "Stop! Stop!" a soldier was screaming. Helena ran to the window and saw a young woman running towards the fence. The soldier ran after her with his gun drawn. As the woman touched the fence, it sizzled, and she dropped to the ground. The soldier poked her with the gun, but she did not move.

Helena questioned herself, "What just happened?" Robert stood next to her. She hadn't even heard him come into the office. She turned and buried her face into his body.

Robert started to explain that the woman was a runaway. "The fence is electrified and kills on impact. It looks like one of the women that lived in the officers' building. It was most likely a lovers quarrel..." The way Helena looked at him, Robert knew she did not buy his explanation.

"Please tell me the truth," Helena urged.

"Do you remember the selected group of women that you were with when you first arrived in the camp? They, along with you, looked similar: tall, slim, blonde and fair skinned. They were assigned to the officers' building to make the officers *happy*. If any of the girls get pregnant, the baby is taken from them and raised by the German government in special facilities to grow up as *Perfect Germans*."

Helena asked, "Do you mean if I didn't speak or write in German, I would be one of them?"

"Most likely," answered Robert.

Helena didn't know how to react to this. She didn't know what Robert's opinion of this was and she definitely was afraid to ask him. Since she had been so sheltered, she could then only imagine how other prisoners were treated.

Helena just had coffee, but could not eat anything. Robert ate very little as well. His eyes were on her all the time. They heard some commotion outside. Helena wanted to go to the window again, but Robert would not allow her. He said, "Most likely the soldiers are showing the other women what would happen to them if they tried to run away."

"So everyone would stay here forever?" she asked.

"I don't think so," said Robert. "The war can't last that long."

The days passed by. Each time Robert passed Helena as he is dictated, her heart stopped. Each time he touched her as he looked over her work, she shivered. She wanted him and she realized she was falling in love. At the same time, she remembered her baby, her husband and who she really was. She was not Helena. She was Liliana. She was not a Polish heiress. She was a Jewish prisoner. She reasoned with herself, "What if there was no war and I met Robert and fell in love? I would probably take him as a lover, just like in the novels I read. I am so mixed up! If anything happens I would know God is a fake and a fraud. Although this is probably not the best way to win favor from Him. I hope the war would be over soon, I cannot take much more."

The cold woke up Helena the next morning. The electric heater was not working. The lights did not go on. There was no electricity. Helena walked into the office.

Robert came in and said, "It must be the partisans in the woods who did this. It would probably be repaired by tomorrow." Meanwhile, he advised her, "Wear the warm robe and socks over your clothes and you should be ok. Don't be concerned if you hear dogs barking. They are loose in the camp, to discourage any escapes." They worked the rest of the day. Dinner was sandwiches. They managed to have hot water for tea and Robert left.

Helena returned to her room and curled up in her bed. She couldn't read. It was too dark. Looking out the window, the moon generated enough light to see beyond the fence. She never saw a view like this. All was white and still. The branches were covered in snow. She stayed at the window for a long time. When she returned to her cold bed, she covered up to her nose and fell asleep.

In the dark, Helena heard the door open. She sat up in bed, and with a trembling voice, asked, "Who is there?" It was Robert. He sat on the edge of her bed and said, "Helena, I love you with all my heart. If you want me to leave, I would, right now." But Helena did not want him to leave. She wanted him. She hugged him and gave him a long kiss. She didn't even know she could kiss this way. They curled up in the small bed and made love. She had never felt pleasure like this before.

Robert left before dawn. Helena didn't know whether she should cry or be happy. But she soon knew she could not deny that she was happy.

Helena decided to live one day at a time without wondering what would happen in the future. Who knew how it would all end? She could not wait until morning to see Robert. She was not cold anymore. Her body was satisfied. In the morning, Robert gave her a kiss on her forehead, and whispered, "I love you."

The lights came back on. Helena could not concentrate on her work. Robert saw this, and just smiled. "Tonight we'll stay together in my room," said Robert. His apartment had a living room, bedroom and a small kitchen. It felt so good there. Helena could almost forget she was in a concentration camp. The anticipation of them being together again was great. Afterward, they laid in peace, their bodies entangled. That was how she wanted to stay the rest of her life.

But Helena knew that there was much to worry about. She thought, "What would Robert think if he knew the truth about me?" Was it possible for her to just live in the moment? She did ask Robert what would happen if anybody found out about them. He just said not to worry. He didn't really know the answer himself. In the morning he took Helena to her room. Ingrid opened the door, as usual, to let Helena out. Helena tried to see if Ingrid knew anything, but she did not think so, not yet anyway. The following few weeks were the same, except, Ingrid figured it out. She did not say anything though.

One night they heard the roar of planes. Robert said he thought the war was coming to an end. Helena did not know how she felt about this. She did not say anything to Robert, but she had missed her monthly period. "What would happen if my period does not come? What would he do? How much does he love me?" Helena worried. She did not speak to anyone. She only saw Ingrid and no one else.

Robert asked her if everything was ok. He said she seemed to be nervous and on edge. Helena thought, "Whatever happens, I'll keep my secret for a while." She was so naïve, she never even thought to protect herself. Another month had passed, and nothing happened. Then, she was sure she was pregnant. And all the while, she was falling more in love with Robert. In love with his caring, his gentleness, always assuring her that he loved her. They spent their nights with great passion, never having enough of each other. Helena knew she would have to tell Robert soon, but she was so afraid.

Robert suspected something wasn't right. He saw that some food made her nauseous. Finally Robert just asked, "Are you with child?" Instead of answering, Helena just burst into hysterical tears. Robert had a hard time to calming her down. When he finally did, he told her he would not abandon her. He had to think of a solution, but he was happy to become a father. Robert kept saying, "I have to get you out of this camp."

Robert fell asleep, but Helena couldn't stop thinking about if whether or not she could tell him the truth. She finally decided that one shock was enough for the time being.

The following day she saw very little of Robert. He told her that he had to see Commander Hans Kraus. Robert promised to pay Hans a high reward for allowing him to take Helena out of the camp. Of course, Ingrid had to be taken care of as well.

In the following week or so, Helena was to get sick, and for the record, die. She would be "just another prisoner" who did not survive the camp. Robert would take her to his parents' home. There, they would get married. He already sent word to his parents. "My God!" thought Helena, "I'm already married, and I already am a mother!" She felt very lonely, and her secret weighed heavy on her. "What should I do? What should I do?"

The day came for her to "get sick". When Ingrid came to open the door, Helena told her she had a fever and little red sores all over her body. Hannah smiled. She knew the whole thing was a set-up. Ingrid said, "I would report it." She brought food to Helena's room. Helena's "condition" was supposed to get worse and worse each day until the day that Robert took her to his apartment.

Robert told Helena to take only her documents. "How can I just disappear?" questioned Helena.

Robert explained to her, "They would take a girl from the camp that has died, place her in your room and a doctor would pronounce you dead." He said all of this without any emotion. He was just so matter of fact.

Helena looked at him with shock and said, "Everyday, there's more than one girl that dies in the camp?"

He answered, "Please, don't ask so many questions." Robert was very agitated.

Robert drove. Helena was concealed in the back seat among boxes and blankets, as they passed through the checkpoints. He told Helena that his parents knew about them and that he would have to return to the camp, but not for a while. Robert would have some doctor write a document saying that he was not well, and that was what allowed him to be able to remain at home for a month or so. Helena asked him if he was happy. He answered, "Yes, but I just wish this war would be over."

CHAPTER 3

S pring was coming. Everything smelled fresh. Helena was so happy to be out of confinement, and to see people and life after all the time in the camp. After many hours of driving, Robert said, "We are coming close to home." Helena panicked! How was this all going to be? But the truth was, she was a lucky woman. She decided she would keep her secret for a while longer, at least until the end of the war.

They entered the small, picturesque town of Regensburg, which was in the province of Bavaria. The city was registered as the first capital of Bavaria since the eleventh century. It was a very colorful town.

The sun was shining, people were strolling, kids were running, and yet war was raging all over the world, but not in Regensburg! Helena wondered how many places in Europe remained untouched by the war. She did not think too many. "What a beautiful town," she thought, "everyone looked so happy." Her face was glued to the window of the car. She knew Robert was looking at her. He saw her joy and appreciation of this town. He held her hand.

The road led from the center of town through a lush forest. In a short while they turned onto a small road and Helena saw a house. Well it was more like a small palace than a house, and she heard Robert say, "We are home." She clenched his hand. He said, "Do not worry, they would like you." He beeped the horn and two elderly people came out of the house.

Helena was paralyzed with fear. Robert opened the door on her side, to let her out of the car. She heard his mother say, "Oh my dear, you must be exhausted." His father extended his hand to help her out of the car. They introduced themselves, "Kurt and Helga Van Klaus."

Helena responded, "My name is Helena Michalowski."

"Come in, I'll prepare tea. Let the men unload the car," said Helga.

The house was beautiful and smelled of freshly baked cookies. Helga said she gave the housekeeper the day off so they could be alone and get acquainted with each other.

Helena asked if she could take a bath and borrow a robe, since she had to leave all her belongings behind. Robert's mother responded, "Everything is ready for you. Down this hall would lead to a guest apartment." She took Helena's hand, as one would take a child's hand. It felt so good to Helena.

The apartment had a small sitting room, a bedroom with a four poster bed covered in all white linen and a fluffy cover. Lots of pretty little things were scattered around and beautiful paintings hung on the walls. There was a great chair to read in next to a big picture window. The bedroom had wallpaper with tiny roses. Everything was spotless. A pink robe was on the bed, with more clothes in the closet.

The bath felt so good. Helena washed and braided her hair, dressed and was ready to meet everyone in the dining room. They were already seated. Robert was quick to rise and helped her into her chair, saying, "The chairs are very heavy." They ate in silence.

When tea was served with those aromatic cookies, Robert's father, Kurt, said, "We are welcoming you as our daughter. We honor our son's choice for a wife, and I understand that the wedding has to take place soon. We are happy to meet you, and we would talk soon about your parents and your family."

All Helena could utter was, "Thank you for your welcome." They spoke a little more, mostly about the war and how everybody was anxious for it to end. Robert's mother asked Helena what kind of a dress she wanted for the wedding, and she answered, "Very simple, please."

Robert took Helena to her room, and said, for the sake of his parents, they would stay in separate rooms until the following Sunday. He kissed her goodnight, and said, "I hope you like my parents, because you would have to live with them for a while, at least. They are very decent people, and so are you, so we should not have any problems." And he smiled.

The Van Klauses made arrangements for the wedding for that coming Sunday in a small church. Because of the war, they did not invite many guests. Everybody in their town was suffering losses and it was not a good time to celebrate a marriage.

Sunday morning was the start of a bright, sunny day. Helena wore a simple, off white dress, down to her ankles, with narrow, long sleeves, and Helga gave her a double string of pearls and told her, "They belonged to my mother. She gave them to me. And now I'm giving them to you." They were beautiful.

Local parishioners were in the church. They all knew the Van Klaus family. The service was short and not too complicated. Everyone congratulated the family. Somehow, Helena managed.

When the family returned home, the housekeeper had prepared a very nice lunch. She was a jolly, overweight woman in her fifties. She kept on kissing Robert, every chance she had, and kept repeating, "So good to see you happy." She also said her father was Polish, she loved him dearly, but he passed away a while ago. She spoke a little Polish, not too much. Her name was Gertrude. Helena told her she wanted to help with the house chores. It didn't matter. She would help with whatever had to be done. Gertrude smiled and said, "Oh, that's good, because this mistress has slowed down now, and it's a big house."

Robert and Helena's bedroom was prepared for them. It was big and comfortable, and above all, it was very bright. Adjacent to their room was a smaller room, and Robert whispered, "It's for our baby. Soon we'll start furnishing it." Everything was so normal, so nice. For Helena it felt like walking into someone else's life! Her soul was heavy. She wanted to burst out and tell the truth, but she felt she could not.

The days passed by. Helena saw a doctor and everything was normal. The baby was due sometime in November. Helena helped a lot around the house. Helga and Gertrude were teaching her the art of German cooking. Robert tried not to go back to camp. He tried to work with a doctor to let him have a Certificate of Dismissal, due to his alleged heart condition.

The couple would take long walks in the forest or go to town, which was very charming. Robert introduced Helena to all the people he knew since childhood. Helena felt so at home there. She got along with Robert's parents. However from time to time, she saw Kurt Van Klaus staring at her with what seemed to her to be a look of disbelief on his face. Maybe, deep in his heart, there was a big question mark.

Helena tried to imagine how her daughter must look. Rebecca was five years old then. Helena wondered if she would ever see her again. And what happened to Henry and to her parents?

She felt like screaming as she listened to the news. Everybody knew the war was nearing an end. Robert's father said one day, "Soon we would be able to get in touch with your parents in London. I would like very much to meet them." Helena knew now that she would have to tell Robert the truth, but when was good time to do it? Her head was preoccupied with those worries. She could not sleep or eat or rest in peace.

"Sometimes there are no good choices. We can only do what is least bad," she justified to herself. What sort of a person was she? Who could conceal sadness and excuse oneself with such stone cold practicality?

Robert was refurbishing his old cradle. He was happy after receiving the news that he could stay home for at least six months. Helena loved him very much and never wanted to be without him. She knew she was facing a situation without a solution. She questioned, "What would Robert do after he learns the truth. He would probably hate me." She could not bear those thoughts. But Helena must felt that she must think happy thoughts for the sake of the baby. "God help me."

Helena's cooking skills were improving, and she liked it. Helga said, "Soon you would replace me in the kitchen."

The housekeeper shook her head and said, "You would soon take over my job!"

Kurt took care of the garden. Robert took care of all sorts of repairs needed in the house. They all kept very busy.

Just as well, since that helped Helena from thinking too much. The more she thought, the less she knew what to do. Everybody knew the war would be over very soon. Helena knew the German people would be sad to lose the war, especially with the effort that they put into it. She thought the Germans were realizing what a huge mistake the war was. Of course she thought all this without realizing just how much horror and death it had cost.

It was the end of September 1945. Finally the war was over.

Robert was so happy, and so were his parents. They were happy mostly because they wouldn't have to send their son back into harm's way.

Robert's father said he tried to find out how to get in touch and locate some people in England. He asked for Helena's documents which she of course gave to him. He then mentioned it was way too early to get in touch with anyone and he would have to wait for a while. Helena gave a sigh of relief!

Slowly, they had been receiving information about the terrible things that happened during the war. Most of the people in the little town didn't believe such things had actually happened. They all said it was propaganda. It could not have happened. But Helena believed that it did happen.

Helena worried, "What about Henry, what about my parents, my baby, my brother..." and yet, she chose to smile.

Helena looked to see the expression on Robert's face, to understand how he felt, but he showed no emotion. Helena thought he did know of all the atrocities that Germany brought to the world.

It was the end of October, and it was getting colder. The trees were changing colors and almost looked unreal. It looked as though one was walking into a painting.

The baby was due in a month. Helena felt secure that Robert would not abandon her, even if he found out the truth. He loved her. That was her only comfort.

One day, in the middle of November, a police car stopped in front of their house. Helena saw Kurt run out and greet them. She knew it had to do with her!

"God, what are they telling him?" Helena worried. They handed him a folder and left. Kurt looked upset.

Kurt looked up to Helena's window. He knew she went to her bedroom for a little rest. Helena stood to the side of the window, hidden by the curtain. Her heart was racing, she was so scared. What did he find out? Robert came to take her down to dinner. She had become so big; she couldn't even see the stairs. He was very tender and looked at her sympathetically.

The family was all seated at the table. Helga was very pale, wrenching her hands in her knees. Gertrude had red eyes, as if she had been crying. Kurt was sitting with his head down. Helena took in this sight and asked "Is anything wrong?"

Kurt responded, "Let's eat." But no one had much of an appetite. Gertrude brought tea into the living room. Helena saw a folder on the desk. Gertrude remained in the entrance to the living room, as if she were waiting for something. Kurt cleared his throat and said to Helena, "Dear, I am afraid I have bad news for you. We did find out about your parents, as I had promised. The news is not good. We found out that the building your parents lived in was bombarded by the German air force, and was totally destroyed. Everyone in the vicinity perished. There is no sign of them since that bombing. The English authorities published that they were among the deceased."

Helena sat there in disbelief that this could be happening. All of the sudden she burst out in a spasmodic cry. Gertrude was wiping Helena's face with a wet napkin, Robert was holding her tight, his parents stood there holding hands and crying. Helena slowly calmed down. Her mind was racing. The cry was the relief of all the tension she held within her for months. She knew, for now, she would be safe, and did not have to tell anybody anything of her past. She could now await the birth of her baby calmly. Everybody was so sympathetic to Helena, especially Kurt. He always harbored doubts about Helena though. "If he only knew," she thought.

Robert never left Helena's side. It was decided that she would deliver the baby at home since the hospitals were overloaded with returning soldiers and there were not enough doctors or nurses. They were hopeful that the midwife would be available when the time came. Gertrude would be helpful too. They all had told Helena, "This is your first baby, and it would take time." But, it was not her first, not her first at all.

In the late afternoon, on November 21, Helena felt a sharp pain in her abdomen, just as it happened with Rebecca, she thought. She knew she was having the baby that day. She waited for a while before telling anybody.

She wanted the birth to have some urgency. She hoped the midwife would be too busy to notice that this was not her first delivery. The pain had gotten very strong, and Helena urged Robert to get the midwife. Gertrude took her to bed, and busied herself with preparations. She knew it wouldn't take too long now. Helga was holding her hand and crying. She said to Helena, "Don't worry, these are happy tears!"

By the time Robert returned with the midwife, the labor was rapid. In just a few minutes, the baby was born and uttered its first cry. "It's a boy, a healthy boy!" Robert brought his father into the room and placed the boy into his arms. They both cried.

The midwife cared for Helena, and watched her face for any signs of distress, but did not find any. She kept repeating, "You did really well, congratulations!" Robert brought the baby to Helena. He was a beautiful baby. Blonde-haired, with a handsome face. Just like his father.

The nurse recommended a nanny, Sabina, who came to the house the next day. She was a middle-aged woman, very gentle and spoke very little.

Helena gave Robert permission to choose the baby's name as he saw fit. She breast-fed the baby. He ate well and didn't like to be taken away from Helena. She loved holding him. He was a cuddly mama's boy. Helena could not help but to think of her daughter, Rebecca, all the time. "Where is she? How am I going to find her?"

The news was that Poland had fallen to the Russians and would become a Communist country. Czechoslovakia and Hungary would have the same fate. Kurt said the world was in terrible turmoil and he was happy not to be a young man anymore. He adored his grandson, singing to him and watching him for hours in the indoor garden, rocking him in his cradle. Robert and his parents decided on the date to baptize the baby who still had no name. It would take place the next week. Helena did not participate in the plans. Her heart was so heavy, one lie after another. The household thought it was normal to be a little depressed after delivery.

A lot of people came to the christening. Everybody admired the little boy, Maximilian, Max for short. This was Robert's grandfather's name. Helena could not help but smile at the irony of it all; a little Jewish boy being baptized in a church full of admiring Germans. Unreal!

CHAPTER 4

The big truck was full of people and bounced on the uneven road towards their home, or whatever was left of it. Among them was Henry. He did survive! He was thin, unshaven, dirty and in shabby clothes. He was holding the bench with his hands to try and break the bouncing of the truck. He had a plan: to try to find anybody in Warsaw, go to the little town of his parents, Gąbin, and find out what happened to his family. But mostly, he prayed he would find Liliana and his baby, Rebecca. His heart was full of hope. He lived through a horrible ordeal in the concentration camp of Treblinka. Even through the worst of times, he made himself survive, for his wife and child.

Finally the truck stopped. They all came off the truck and cried. Warsaw was no more! All they could see was ruins. You could not recognize the streets. Henry knew his friends, the Witkowskis, were not there. He figured and hoped they were all in Gdynia. First, Henry went to the Red Cross office to enter his name as a survivor and to check the list of those who did not survive, hoping not to find anyone. He wanted to find a place to stay, buy some clothes and above all, get a bath. He was walking aimlessly when he saw a little store with a long line of people. Everyone looked as shabby as he did. Henry felt hunger. He hoped he could buy something to eat. He waited in the line. Not much was in the store, but the storekeeper seemed nice and friendly. Henry quietly said to the storekeeper, "I need help. I need a place to stay for a little while, and I can pay." The shopkeeper told him to wait outside until closing time.

Henry was able to hide some of his small gold coins by sewing them into his clothes. When the shopkeeper came out of the store, he offered his hand and introduced himself. "My name is Wladek, and yours?"

"Henry." He offered Henry a room at his mother's place. There was a bed, but it had to be shared with other families. The price was reasonable, and Henry agreed. They walked for a while. Henry could not recognize the neighborhoods. Wladek was silent, did not ask anything, and Henry was glad. In the midst of the ruins stood a half destroyed house, and that was the place offered to Henry.

Wladek's mother was a pleasant woman. She showed him a tiny room, clean and warm. Henry asked Wladek where he could buy some clothes. Wladek said he would take him the next day. Henry ate, washed up a little, and all he wanted was to go to sleep. He locked the door and put a chair against it. The little window was big enough to escape in case he had to. Henry was never so paranoid, but the war taught him different. Bright and early the following morning, Wladek took him to a tailor who lived in another hole in the wall. Henry chose the fabric, and all would be ready in the next few days.

Henry started to recognize some parts of the city. He finally came to the place that was the Warsaw ghetto. There was almost nothing there. He saw other lost souls wandering about, probably looking for the same as he was....family.

The agencies that helped locate displaced families were not set up yet. Henry had little hope of finding anybody in Warsaw. Maybe just his wife and daughter were in Gdynia. Oh how he hoped for that.

After a few days of wandering and not finding a familiar face, Henry picked up his clothes. Wladek found a leather suitcase for him, and other necessities, and Henry was on a train to Gdynia. He knew to be extremely careful. There were all kinds of people, all desperate. He wore a shabby overcoat, on purpose, to hide his new clothes. After three days he reached Gdynia. The city had some damage, but most of the city looked like nothing ever happened. Henry was relieved.

At a local store, Henry asked for directions to the address he knew by heart. He was advised to take a carriage. There he was, in front of a charming little house. He was afraid to approach the door. Maybe it would be better to wait for someone to exit from the house. He waited to no avail, no one was coming out. Finally, he reached for the doorbell. He heard a little girl's voice, "Mommy, mommy, the doorbell." His heart almost stopped.

The door opened and he saw Sofia. She stood there with disbelief, and then he saw his little Rebecca. Sofia said, "Eva, this is your uncle. Say hello." Henry stooped down and asked for a hug.

Rebecca looked puzzled, "Can I mommy?" she asked.

"Yes, you can." At that moment Henry held his child in his arms. He felt a renewed appetite for life, for a good life. She was adorable, with the face of an angel. He looked into the hallway, hoping to see Liliana, but no one else was coming.

"Come in, Henry," said Sofia. The housekeeper was asked to take Eva for a walk. Sofia and Henry sat on the couch. She told him that a day after his disappearance, Liliana went to look for him and did not come back. They waited for a few days and then it became too dangerous so they left for Gdynia. Sophia told him that Rebecca thought she and Philip were her parents. She saw Henry's grave face, and asked him not to lose hope. People were still in different places, and she said Liliana just might show up one day. "Meanwhile, you stay with us," said Sofia. They waited for Philip to come back from the hospital. He was now the chief of the hospital, and they did not plan on going back to Warsaw.

Henry sat and watched his little girl play with her dolls. She would throw him a glance and a little smile from time to time. Sofia told Henry how much they both loved Rebecca, and she was truly like their own daughter. Philip finally walked in. The men both hugged in a very friendly embrace. Philip was genuinely glad to see Henry. After dinner, and putting Rebecca to sleep, Philip told Henry how they saved all his treasures.

The Witkowskis told Henry of how they decided to leave the city. Philip knew of the danger, but there was no choice. They left at night and packed the car to the brim. All the larger antique pieces were stored in the hidden room in the basement and they took all the smaller pieces of jewelry and coins. All was going well until early one morning they found themselves following a convoy of German military trucks. They decided to continue on until they heard an explosion. Philip saw a man running into the forest. He knew there were bands of Polacks forming a resistance. They were called partisans. Philip stopped the car and waited. He heard someone yelling, "The general is wounded!" Philip also saw that his car had been spotted.

He decided to get out of his car, and took his doctor's satchel with him. He proceeded to go towards the screaming soldier, shouting. "I am a doctor, I am a doctor. I can help!" A soldier took him to the general, who was bleeding profusely.

Philip stopped the bleeding as the general was pleading, "Please help me. I have to get back to my family."

Philip answered in a whisper, "I would save your life, if you help me. Get yourself into a comfortable car and have a convoy protect us, and I would take you to a good hospital in Gdynia. That's where I'm headed." The general agreed. Philip drove in the car with the general and a soldier drove his car with Sofia and Rebecca. They got to Gdynia and drove to the hospital first. Philip took the general into surgery and then took Sofia and Rebecca to their house. The general survived, and after three weeks, he was sent back to Germany. This shooting incident is what enabled the Witkowskis to get to Gdynia safely.

All of Henry's belongings were secure in their house. They also told Henry he could stay with them, and wait for Liliana to show up. They were so sure she was safe, that Henry started to believe so himself.

The days passed. Henry spent most of his time with Rebecca. She was amazing for her age. Sofia was teaching her reading and a little mathematics. She was like a sponge, taking in all her studies and she was not yet six.

Henry was doing a little research on his antiques and coins. It was still easy to cross to Germany, but slowly the communist regime was taking over. Henry did not know what to do. He knew a decision had to be made. He could cross to Germany and try to settle somewhere in Europe or the U.S., but if Liliana would eventually return, she might not be able to leave Poland.

The Witkowskis were urging Henry to stay with them, and make a life right there in Gdynia. That way Rebecca could stay and be with all of them. Philip's friends knew Henry as his cousin. And Rebecca, now called Eva, thought she was Catholic. She loved the church and all the holidays, and that was a problem for Henry.

He wanted to be with his own people. He was not going to give up his Jewishness. He wanted to be the person he was born. He wanted his daughter to know who she was. But Henry felt he could not take Rebecca with him yet. He would first have to find a place to live. He wanted to be in a town where his people lived. Henry heard that Wroclaw, formerly a German town, Breslau, in the lower Śląsk, was not terribly destroyed by the war and a lot of Jewish people were settling there.

Henry had a long conversation with his friends. He told them his plans. He promised to visit them often, and for now he was leaving Rebecca with them. The goodbye was very emotional. Rebecca hugged him, and in a quiet voice said, "Please come back soon." The train took him to Wroclaw.

It was hard to believe that four months had passed. Liliana had not come back. Henry was doubtful that she ever would. He was thrilled to find his daughter, and so grateful to his friends.

Wroclaw was chaotic. The synagogue was already functioning. It was more a gathering place than a place of prayers. No one had much to be thankful for. Henry was looking for a decent place to live. It was not easy. He knew he had to bribe somebody to get what he wanted.

His heart was broken. He could not accept that Liliana was gone. Every tall, blond woman on the street made his heart race, "Maybe it's her?" He went to the Red Cross office and spoke to a representative. Henry had very little information and he did not know what happened to Liliana. "Which concentration camp was she taken to? Maybe she perished in the ghetto." He could not stop thinking of her.

Henry solicited a man who was sort of like today's version of a real estate agent. Of course nothing like that existed in postwar Poland. This man seemed to know of available apartments. All of the apartments belonged to the state, but bribery raged in all aspects of communist Poland. Finally, there was success. A good looking apartment with two bedrooms, two baths, a large kitchen, living room and dining room that was tastefully furnished and included everything Henry would need. A German family lived there and returned to Germany, leaving everything behind. Henry paid the "agent" in gold for finding the apartment. He registered with the local government to take occupancy and he moved in.

The first night alone in the apartment was pretty hard. He was physically comfortable but mentally, he felt terrible. Henry could not picture his future without Liliana.

Henry was looking for a woman to care for his household; someone to wash, to cook and to clean. He had another appointment with the Red Cross. He would give them Liliana's assumed name. Maybe that was the name she was registered under. He met with the same clerk as before. She told him she would look up the list of survivors and the list of deceased from all the camps, and told him to return in two weeks. He offered her a little gold chain in gratitude. She promised to do the best she could. He also needed and official job. He could not only deal with coins and antiques since this was illegal in communist Poland. Everyone had to have a job sponsored by the government.

Henry heard in the synagogue that Saturday that there were plans to reopen the museum that was there before the war started. Most of the art work was found in the basement of the former museum. He got the name of the man in charge of this project. Henry would see him the next day, but in the meantime he decided to take a look at the building and its location. It was not too far from his apartment and not too far from a school for Rebecca. He felt strongly that he must keep her close to him, although he sometimes admitted to himself that the best thing for Rebecca would be to remain with the Witkowskis.

The interview with the manager of the museum was successful. Mr. Blum was an elderly man. They talked about art, the war and his lost family. He survived the war in Russia. Henry would find out if he got the job as the curator in the next few days.

He spent those days walking around the town to familiarize himself with his new surroundings. He met some new people. He knew he could make a new life for himself but he was still not sure if he should go ahead and leave Poland altogether. But wherever he might go abroad meant learning a new language and a new way of life. Henry was tired just thinking about this. He needed rest. He also needed to earn the love of his daughter. Maybe one day, but not then.

Henry met with Mr. Blum and got good news. The job was his. He would start in the next month. That was great. He would go and have a long visit in Gdynia, but not before he saw the woman in the Red Cross office.

Walking into the office and seeing the sad face of the woman at the Red Cross, he knew the news was not good. The clerk said that the new name made it easy for her to locate the camp and identify her. Henry was told that Helena was working in the office of the camp and that she died of pneumonia. She was listed as deceased on the camp's registry of Majdanek.

Henry felt tears on his cheeks and a total emptiness. He could not get up from his chair. The clerk gave him some water. "Drink it. It would make you feel better," she said. It did not make him feel better. He finally got up from the chair and ran out in to the street. It was much better not knowing. It was better to have a little hope. It was all so unfair.

It took Henry several days to collect himself. He did not leave his bed and he lost all interest in life. He only survived the war so he could find his family and take care of them. After all the terrible things he lived through in the concentration camp, and all the horrible dreams which still haunt him every night, how could he resume his life?

Thanks to Zosia, Henry's new housekeeper, he was able to survive those next few days. Zosia was a peasant girl, well mannered, simple, a great cook and very clean. She always heard "chicken soup is the best medicine," so this is all she served Henry for several days. She sat by his bed and urged him to drink the soup. Henry knew he had to live for his young daughter.

He could not recognize himself in the mirror. He washed himself, shaved and got dressed. He packed a small suitcase and bought some toys for Rebecca to take with him. He gave some money to Zosia and said, "I am going away for two weeks. When I come back I would start my new job. I'm bringing back a little girl about six years old. She is my daughter. I hope you would stay with us."

Henry could not wait to see his little daughter again. He made the decision to bring her to Wroclaw where she would start first grade at the local school. He would have to talk to his friends. It would not be easy. They loved her as if she was their own child.

Henry was so surprised by the welcome he received from Rebecca. She hugged him and clung to him, not leaving him for a second. He had to remember to call her Eva.

Philip and Sofia were very happy to see Henry. He felt so good to be with them. He took long walks with Eva on the beach. It was soothing. She was much smarter than her six years. She knew when to be silent and when to chatter on with no end. She was able to read and do simple math. She drew beautifully. She was truly a treasure. He watched her playing in the sand; her blond curls blew in the wind. Her blue eyes of her mother tore Henry's heart. Henry would talk to his friends that night. He put Eva to bed, read her a book about animals and kissed her goodnight. She did not ask for her mother, Sofia. How surprising.

The Witkowskis and Henry finally sat in the living room with a good glass of wine. Philip was sitting next to Sofia and held her hand. They must have known that sooner or later this conversation would take place. Henry told them about the apartment, about Zosia, about his job and what he found out about Liliana. Sofia cried and Philip, with a lump in his throat, said "You have my condolences."

Henry told them about his plans and asked them to remain in Rebecca's life. They were the only family he had now, and he truly loved and appreciated what they did for him and his daughter. Up until that September, she would stay with them, but somehow, she had to be told the truth. It would be difficult for a child to comprehend the situation. She did not remember her mother. This fact would actually make it easier.

Henry made plans to return to Wroclaw. The last few days he tried to spend as much time as he could with Rebecca. He knew life with this child would be wonderful. He already made plans to decorate her room and enroll her in school. He felt life again and had a renewed purpose to exist.

Back in town, his new job was wonderful, interesting, engaging. It required some travel, but not much. Henry signed Rebecca up for school under her birth name, Rebecca Kopel and presented her true documents which he took back from the Witkowskis.

Zosia turned out to be wonderful. She cleaned the whole apartment, everything shimmered. Henry told her about his daughter and she could not wait to meet her. Henry visited the synagogue from time to time, made some new friends, and did not feel so terrible anymore. Right then, all he wanted was for time to pass quickly so he could bring his little girl home. As a worker for the museum, he had access to a telephone and could speak to Rebecca every day. Because Philip was a doctor, he was permitted a phone as well.

Sofia started telling Eva about the war and what happened to people, especially the Jewish people. She was slowly teaching Eva about her life. Somehow she had to learn that Henry was her father and he wanted her with him. She had to learn that her mother was dead. Everyone wondered how much a six year old could absorb.

Henry sat in the newly decorated room for Rebecca. It was a very bright and happy room, full of toys and books. He had a very sad conversation with his daughter yesterday. She cried and begged him to let her stay where she was. She loved Sofia and Philip as her "Mommy and Daddy" and loved him as the best "Uncle".

Even though Henry expected this reaction, it hurt anyway. He tried his best to convince her that they would visit Gdynia often and the Witkowskis would also come to visit Wroclaw, and he promised to get her the nicest Christmas tree for the holiday. "We would be a family forever," he said. He would pick her up in the following three weeks and if she wanted to go back to Gdynia, after staying for six months with him, he would allow her to go back.

"Okay, Father," Rebecca quietly answered. Henry had a big task ahead to make his daughter love him unconditionally.

He would shortly have to travel abroad for the museum. That was a good opportunity to get to a bank and acquire a safety deposit box to store his extremely valuable gold coin collection. This was very important for Henry. It meant security for him and his daughter. He somehow had the feeling that Poland would not be the last place he would live in.

Leaving the country on official government business meant being searched. Henry had sewn hidden pockets on the inside of his jacket and since he had regained all his weight he had before, it was easy to hide the bulge.

As soon as he returned from this trip, Henry would pick up his daughter. Zosia spoke to Sofia to find out what kind of food to prepare for Rebecca. She was very excited to have a child in the home.

The train took Henry to Warsaw, the only city you could get an international flight from. Henry sat quietly, full of excitement. The Warsaw airport was lifeless. Not many people could get out of the country. Everything went smoothly and after three hours they landed in Zurich, Switzerland. Somebody from the Polish government escorted them. Somehow, Henry would have to escape out on his own to get to a bank. The Swiss bank was his destination.

After breakfast, they went on their official business, to examine some paintings to be exchanged for other artifacts. The next day Henry told his group he wasn't feeling well and would stay in bed until their afternoon appointment. He found a back door in the hotel and took a taxi to the bank. Everything went smoothly. He gave the banker the name of his daughter and the Witkowskis. They took his photo and fingerprints and gave Henry a secret vault number. Henry returned to his hotel relieved and happy. He ordered room service and relaxed in an easy chair. "Someone must be watching over me," he thought.

Thanks to Henry's smart negotiations at the meeting, the deal was done. Mr. Blum was thrilled with him. They even got a city tour. It was beautiful and strange. All Henry wanted to do was to get his little girl home with him.

Henry got ready to go to Gdynia with a beating heart. He would stay there for a few days to make it easier on everybody. Rebecca received him warmly, with a loving hug. She told him she was almost packed and asked him what her room was like. Henry was pleased with her "surrender". He thought it was hardest for Sofia. She was pale and distant, her eyes red from crying. He felt so sorry for her. The last time Henry spoke with Philip, he mentioned that they would adopt a baby, but the baby had to be an orphan so no one would take the child away. Henry sincerely hoped Philip would get his wish.

The journey to Wroclaw was in silence. Rebecca had her nose glued to the window of the train. They passed little towns, some almost destroyed. She questioned how they were destroyed. When Henry answered her, she asked, "Could it happen again?" Henry assured her it would never, ever happen again, but he was actually not so sure.

Finally they were home. Zosia was waiting anxiously with flowers in hand for Rebecca. She told Rebecca, "I would take care of you and love you and try to make you happy."

Rebecca ran into her new room. She loved it, going from one thing to another, and saying, "It's beautiful, it's beautiful!" Zosia unpacked her suitcase and watched

Rebecca wonder about the things that were prepared for her. Henry stood in the doorway observing the scene. He knew then that everything would be okay. He knew his new life had just begun.

CHAPTER 5

The days passed peacefully. Max was unbelievable, the most beautiful boy you could imagine. Robert was happy and Helena loved him more and more each day. With all that, there was still a dark cloud in her blue sky. How could she find out what happened to her daughter and Henry. She did not consider him as her husband anymore. Robert was much more her husband then. There was a small synagogue in town, and Helena saw people going in on Friday nights. She knew they would be able to find out information on her family. If she went she would jeopardize her identity and let Henry know where she was. That she could not do. She only wanted to know her family was safe and well. Either way she looked at it, she would lose a child. How could she choose? She could not.

Poland was a communist country at that point. You could not enter or leave the country. Helena saw more and more photos of how Poland was devastated by the war, and then learned of the concentration camps and how many Jews perished. It was all nerve wracking news. Helena's most difficult task was trying to maintain an appearance of calm and comfort and feel like everyone else. She felt a little afraid all the time. Helena did not mind being German, but she felt guilty and very uncomfortable making friends. Robert urged her to be a little more social with his friends and their wives. She was most happy with Robert and Max. She liked to garden and read, take care of the baby and be in the kitchen with Helga and Gertrude. That's when she felt most comfortable.

Robert's father, Kurt, totally lost his suspicion of her and was at ease with her. His grandson gave him a lot of happiness. Kurt spent most of his time with the baby and Max loved him in return.

Helena wanted to take some literature classes in the newly opened college. She had a need for something more. Max had a nanny, a grandma, a grandpa and, of course, his daddy. Robert kept busy with the administration of their land and real estate holdings. Constant calls and a lot of mail kept him occupied. Once a month there was a meeting in the house with all the managers. Kurt had left Robert with all the responsibilities of the business.

Robert was not happy about letting Helena out of the house to attend school. He said that she would get hurt. Not physically, but for sure emotionally. Helena felt that she couldn't be in a cocoon for the rest of her life and insisted on attending school. She also wanted to volunteer in the hospital, read to the sick and wounded and write letters to their families. Robert said he would inquire if a person like this was desired. He did not want to talk about it any further.

Those next few days Robert seemed unhappy. Helena finally asked him what the matter was. Robert complained that he could see that the baby and he were not enough for Helena and that she seemed to always look for excitement outside their home. Helena told him that she was very happy and content, but she needed to be an individual and to do something more with her life than just be a housewife. She thought Robert would have understood, but he still insisted she would get hurt and that he was just trying to spare her unnecessary pain. He may have been right, but she still wanted to try.

The next day Robert took her to the hospital to have an interview with the head nurse. The nurse was surprised by Helena's accent. Helena explained the origin of her accent. The nurse left the room. A few minutes later she returned and told Helena she could start the following day. Helena was very excited.

The next morning Helena said her goodbyes to everyone, kissed Max, and Robert drove her to the hospital. She was to work for five hours. This was the first job Helena ever really had. The head nurse showed her around and told her to feel free to ask any questions.

At the corner of the room, darkened by a shade on the window, Helena saw a boy around eighteen years old, pale, obviously in pain and moaning. She sat on a chair next to his bed and introduced herself and then she asked his name. "Rudolf," he said. He told her how he was injured on the last day of the war, and how he would never be the same. He had one leg amputated. He cried bitter tears. Helena asked him if he had family and he answered, "Only grandparents in a nearby village." That was why he was moved to that hospital to get a prosthesis and physical therapy. His parents were killed in one of the bombings in Berlin. He was drafted near the end of the war as were so many other young boys. They were still children. Helena held his hand and told him that things would get better and the prosthesis, with time, would feel like his own leg. He said his grandparents were coming to visit him the next day and asked if she would come also. She promised she would. She was so touched by this young boy. She left his bedside and walked around to recover from the sadness and spotted a young girl lying in another bed.

Helena approached and asked if she could help her with anything. The girl answered, "Yes, you can bring my parents and my little sister back."

39

Reality hit Helena. "All this pain," she thought, "It must be like this in Poland as well." Maybe her Henry was lying in some hospital. And there she was consoling Germans who may have hurt her family. She then understood what Robert meant when he said she would get hurt.

After a sleepless night, Helena decided she would go back to the hospital. The war hurt winners and losers alike. However, wars are started just by some and the rest have to defend themselves as best they could. She knew what she had to do. She would write a journal about all of the individuals she would meet at the hospital and tell their story. "Maybe this would discourage people from trying to rule the world," Helena thought. She packed a notebook and pen and prepared to return to the hospital.

Helena went back to Rudolf's bed, his grandparents were already there. She asked if she could bring him anything. He answered, "Yes, maybe some books."

Rudolf's grandparents were surprised by Helena's accent, but did not comment. That was when Helena made a conscious decision to get rid of her accent. She wanted to speak like everyone else. She did not tell Robert about this decision. Somehow, she thought, he would not be happy about it.

Helena kept very busy with her work at the hospital. The nuns ran the hospital and they were very grateful for her. One of them gave her a silver cross with a chain and asked her to wear it. They wrote a long note to her in-laws praising her and thanking them for sparing her. Her in-laws were very proud of her. But Robert was still sulking.

Helena's journal was filling quickly. The stories were amazing. She thought maybe one day she could write stories about people from other countries like Poland or stories about Jewish people. The busier she was, the less time she had to think of her own situation. She knew it was an escape, but so be it for now. She also signed up for literature courses at the local college. Classes were only two days a week for a few hours.

Baby Max was growing beautifully. He was spoiled by everyone. Max was a happy child. He learned how to give kisses.

Helena had a problem with the cross she received from the nun. She did not want to wear it and she did not know what to do. One Sunday, she and Robert stayed in bed a little longer than usual. Helena loved Sundays, and Robert's parents did not insist they go to church. Robert did not like going to church, "Thank God!" Helena thought. Although his parents went, it was not that often.

Helena told Robert about the cross necklace she received. Robert replied, "Oh, how nice."

But Helena explained, "Yes, but I cannot wear it. I am allergic to silver and my neck breaks out in red blotches."

"Then you would have to tell the nuns," said Robert. On that Monday she told the nuns, and assured them she would keep it on her nightstand and pray with it all the time.

Life was settled now. Helena was busy. Her thoughts of her family were always with her. From time to time, she checked on the little synagogue on Fridays, but always from far away. Having it nearby was like a little security blanket for her. She wondered if she would ever tell the truth. She thought, "Probably not until Robert's parents die." She knew if Rebecca had survived she must be with her friends, the Witkowskis. "They most likely love her as their own daughter," Helena thought. She also knew she would never return to Henry. She loved Robert too much. And she also had her son, Maximilian. She knew that there were situations which have no good solutions.

CHAPTER 6

Time passed so quickly. Maximilian was almost three years old. He spoke beautifully and he was so smart. His father adored him. The little discipline he got was from Helena. The parents discussed whether Max should be sent to a nursery school. Helena thought he should be with other children, not just adults. But Robert wanted to keep him sheltered.

At dinner one evening, Helena was not feeling well, maybe the flu. The next morning, she thought she knew what the matter was. She went to the hospital and was examined by a female gynecologist, who confirmed she was pregnant. She would tell the family the news over that upcoming weekend. She was not sure she was happy about this. Helena tried to be careful and Robert did not oppose this. He would say, "Whenever you are ready, and if not, I am content."

It was a beautiful, fall weekend. They were all relaxing on the veranda. Max was playing with his trucks. Gertrude brought out some tea and biscuits. Helena announced, "I have some important news for you." Everybody looked at her and she said, "We would have a new member of our family in about eight months." Everybody stood up, rushed to her with hugs, and announced how happy they were. Robert was the last one. He seemed happy, but something was not okay.

That night, in bed, she did ask him if he was happy. "Of course," he said, "it would be great for Max to have a new brother or sister." He urged Helena to give up her work at the hospital. He thought it would not be safe for her to be in a place with so much sickness. He was right, she had also thought about this. She told him she would give up her job, and give notice that Monday. The sisters at the hospital gave Helena a nice goodbye party and hoped to see her in the future.

Helena's German was then impeccable. There was almost no trace of an accent. She was very proud of this. Whenever she was alone, she spoke to herself in Polish or Yiddish; she did not want to forget, Helena's journal was filled with four hundred pages of stories about patients she met at the hospital. Each one was special. The hospitalized people changed. There were no more wounded soldiers. It was a normal hospital with the usual problems. Nothing to add to her journal. Since she was no longer working Helena wanted to put her notes in order and try to put them in the form of a book. Robert still had not seen it.

Finally everyone agreed that Max should attend nursery school. It was in the private home of a nursery teacher who had two of her own children and never had more than ten students, with two additional women to help. Max loved being there. Kurt took him to school every morning and picked him up at noon. Helena also spent more time with her son, teaching him the alphabet and numbers. Max was so willing to learn.

Helena was content. Her other life seemed like a dream from another lifetime. She felt much better during her pregnancy compared to when she was pregnant with Rebecca and Max. Robert and she agreed that the baby would be born at home, just like Max was. They would try to hire the gynecologist from the hospital to come and deliver the baby.

The doctor lived close by. Her name was Betty, and Helena and she had become friends. Betty was not married. She was sturdy, tall and not too pretty, but she had a heart of gold. She was an excellent physician and helped a lot of woman in the hospital. Helena had total trust in her.

Gertrude also had everything under control. All was prepared, but the baby was taking time, not in any hurry to enter the world! Helena became very uncomfortable. Betty said it would take time.

Finally labor started, of course in the middle of the night. Robert went to fetch Betty. Gertrude prepared the birthing room and Helga came to hold Helena's hand. Kurt was outside the door and Max was asleep. Betty arrived and assessed the labor. Helena's pain was excruciating. Helga assured Helena' "It would all be over soon." In the meantime Helena was wishing it was her own mother by her side. Finally, one last push and Betty held up a bloody little screaming baby. It was a boy, a perfect little boy! "What would you name him," asked Betty, but like the last time, Helena had not given thought to a name yet.

Betty handed the baby to Kurt. Robert came close to Helena and said, "I love you. You have given us a new life and the most precious gift of all, these two boys." He had tears in his eyes. Robert hardly looked at the baby. He was only concerned about Helena. He asked her, "Are you okay, are you in pain," and so on. But Helena was very tired and wanted to sleep. Betty placed the baby to his mother's breast, and he is started trying to suckle right away. It was very good to hold him. Helena didn't even realize she fell asleep.

When she awoke, the sun was high in the sky. She looked around and saw the baby sleeping in his cradle. Gertrude brought her tea and toast. Helena was sore all over, but remembered what Betty had instructed, "Get off the bed and try to walk a few steps at least." It was not easy, but she managed. Robert was right next to her. Helena wondered if Robert loved her more than his sons. At least this was how it appeared.

Max was very confused. From time to time he would look into the cradle and shake his head. Every morning he asked his mother if she still loved him, and every morning Helena reassured him with a hug and a kiss, though Max was not convinced. Max said, "I do not understand all the fuss over this baby. All he does is cry, sleep and eat. And he does not even have a name!"

In a week there would be a christening where the baby would be named. Helena and Robert did not want to make a big party, but instead only have their closest relatives there. Helga and Kurt immediately agreed. Robert asked Helena if the name Albert would be okay. Albert had been his closest friend who lost his life on Russian soil during the war. He was a scholar and a very good man. Helena had no problem with this. So there it was. His name would be Albert. The christening passed in a nice, quiet way. Nanny Sabina was great. The boys were the luckiest children to have so many people love and care for them.

Helena was finishing up the arrangement of her journal and then she would allow Robert to read it. She was anxious to hear what he would have to say about it. Robert was very busy. His father has given him full responsibility of the business. Kurt spent all his new-found time with his grandsons. Sabina was not so happy about this, but there was nothing she could do. So the time passed. Sometimes it seemed quick and sometimes it seemed slow, painfully slow.

CHAPTER 7

hree years had passed. Max was six and Albert was three. Max started school that September and Albert went to nursery school. Robert let Helena help him with some paper work. It took two to three hours daily and Helena was grateful for it. It gave her a steady chore. Her journal was read by Robert a while ago. His reasoning convinced her to wait before she tried to publish it. Robert thought that it was too soon after the war for that kind of a book. The nation was still healing. The wounds were too deep. Robert felt that it would take be quite a few years before people would be ready to read about the wounded soldiers and their experiences. But he did think it was a good journal.

One day Helena went to Robert to ask him to teach her how to drive. She knew he would not be thrilled about it, and she was right. "Why do you need to drive, I can always take you wherever you need to go," Robert said. But with a little bit of begging and conviction, he finally agreed. They were to start the next day. This would give her a lot of freedom. She didn't know why she needed it, but it felt good. Slowly, she did learn.

Helena could then do all of the food shopping. It was very rewarding. She also passed the little synagogue, just to see if it was still there. She didn't want it to go away. She felt comfort by its being there. Her father told her a long time ago, "Remember, if you ever need help go to a synagogue."

Helena volunteered to drive older people to their doctor visits and other necessities. "Only once a week," she begged Robert. He finally agreed. She still did his office work, and he trusted her more and more with his business. Helena did homework with Max, and kept busy in the kitchen. She became quite a good cook. In short, she was busy. It felt good. Kurt said she was the least lazy woman he had ever met.

Helena accepted an appointment to take an elderly woman from a downtown tenement to get x-rays in the hospital. Mrs. Stoval was her name. It sounded very Polish which was interesting to Helena. Mrs. Stoval met her at the front gate. She was a small woman in her fifties. She spoke German with a very heavy Polish accent. Helena was shaken up, and did not ask her about her accent. After the x-rays, Helena picked Mrs. Stoval up and drove her home. She did ask if all was okay, and the woman answered, "It's better than I thought." In the weeks to follow, Mrs. Stoval would still need some treatments in the hospital. She asked Helena if she would be able to drive her. Mrs. Stoval, with a smile, asked Helena, "Why haven't you asked me about my accent, and how I came to be in this picturesque little town?"

Helena answered, "I thought it was a private matter and I had no right to question you."

"You do not understand," Mrs. Stoval said. "You are German." Helena realized Mrs. Stoval did not detect even the slightest accent in her German. When they exited the hospital, Mrs. Stoval invited Helena for lunch. Helena could not refuse. It was a very typical Jewish meal. Helena could not believe it. Mrs. Stoval said, "Today is a Jewish holiday, and I prepared a special meal." She asked Helena if she minded. Helena was flabbergasted. During lunch, Mrs. Stoval told her she had survived the war on false documents as a Polish maid. She worked for an elderly couple, the parents of a German officer who did not survive the war. The elderly couple eventually died, but they did make sure to secure her future. They did not know she was Jewish.

Before the war, Mrs. Stoval had been married and was the mother of two sons. She did not know what happened to them. She was afraid to find out. Now that she was not well and did not know what the outcome of her sickness would be, she wanted to try to find out if her family survived. She asked Helena if she would contact the rabbi in the small synagogue to see if he could help her.

Driving home, Helena decided she would tell Robert Mrs. Stovel's story. Robert remained silent for a while, and then asked what she wanted to do. With a straight face, she answered, "I do not see why I should not help her."

"Then do it," Robert said. "The only thing is, someone may spot our car in front of the synagogue. Park the car someplace else, or better yet, take a taxi from Mrs. Stovall's house."

When Mrs. Stoval contacted Helena again, Helena had already spoken with the Rabbi. He wanted Helena to bring Mrs. Stoval in on that Friday, before sundown. Mrs. Stoval was ready. On Friday, late afternoon, Helena took Mrs. Stoval to the synagogue in a taxi. She was grateful that Helena came with her inside the synagogue. Helena's feelings were indescribable.

The rabbi was a pleasant man with a short white beard. He spoke perfect German and did not look anything like the rabbi Helena remembered from her childhood.

Helena said very little. Mrs. Stoval told the rabbi the story in broken German. The Rabbi said he would help her and contact her directly. He also suggested that she say goodbye to Helena because she would not remain in Germany too long. Helena gave Mrs. Stoval her address and telephone number, gave her a hug and a kiss and wished her good luck. Helena told Mrs. Stoval she was very brave. The Rabbi promised Helena he would keep her informed about Mrs. Stoval.

Driving back home, Helena was truly shaken up. She drove to a farm to get some vegetables and fresh eggs. She could not go home in that state. Robert would know there was something wrong with her. Finally, when she did get home, Robert met her outside. He asked how the meeting with the Rabbi was. She told him everything. Robert was apprehensive about the Rabbi calling them and of Mrs. Stoval sending them mail. He said, "I hope my father does not see this mail?"

Helena responded, "Remember, your father does not pick up the mail anymore!"

Helena did not sleep that night. Every night she tried to forget her past, there was something that shook her up. How strange.

The next few days, Robert observed her. Helena felt it but said nothing and made sure she behaved normal. Helena did not understand Robert's behavior. Did he know something? If he did, would he not tell her? Helena almost felt angry with him, but did not show it. Thereafter, every night Robert would tell her how much he loved her. She was secure in his love, but would it ever be a good time to tell him the truth about her past?

CHAPTER 8

I t was 1951. Henry was thinking how best to celebrate Rebecca's twelfth birthday. She had grown to become quite a remarkable young lady. She was pretty, not too tall, very smart, and a good student. The Witkowskis were coming from Gdynia. They come at least four times a year and always for Rebecca's birthday. Henry and Rebecca went to Gdynia every Christmas and for summer vacations. Their friendship was very strong. Rebecca loved the Witkowskis.

Two years earlier the Witkowskis adopted a boy. His name was Christopher. He was two years old and an orphan. They had been very happy with him. They were all coming for a visit in the following two weeks.

The next summer, Rebecca would go to a summer camp for one month, and then together, Henry and she would go to Gdynia. Henry's life was pretty much in order. Zosia was still with them all that time, and she was irreplaceable. Rebecca had lots of friends. Henry and her went to the opera, theater and saw all the current movies.

Life in communist Poland was not easy. You could not show your wealth or show any thoughts that you were not in agreement with the communist party. Henry maneuvered his life well. He had traveled abroad several times for the museum. He also conducted his own business at the same time. In 1948, some of the Jewish people were allowed to leave Poland. Henry tried to leave, but he was refused.

When the Witkowskis came, Henry had something very important to discuss with them. A year earlier he met a woman at the Jewish Club. Her name was Rose Goldberg. She was a widow as she had lost her husband during the war. Rose survived with her daughter, who was the same age as Rebecca. Rose worked in a factory as an engineer. She was attractive and smart. Henry's love towards her was nothing like the love he felt for Liliana, but he also did not want to remain alone. When the Witkowskis arrived, he would introduce Rose to them, but not to Rebecca yet. Henry purchased tickets to the opera for everyone, and then they would go to a nightclub, just for adults. The next day there was to be a birthday party for Rebecca.

Rebecca invited half of her school, but Henry did not mind. Everything she wanted is fine with him. He knew that he spoiled her. That was why is it was so difficult for him to make a decision about Rose. How would Rebecca accept her? Sometimes, on quiet evenings, Rebecca would still bring out her little treasure box where she stored photos of her mother. She took out one photo after another and saying how beautiful she was and how terrible it was that she was not with them then. Henry's heart ached when he watched this. The Witkowskis would bring more photos of Liliana with Rebecca. Rebecca had never seen photos of herself with her mother.

Zosia had cooked up a storm! She prepared all kinds of goodies. The Witkowskis loved her cooking. The Witkowskis arrived. Rebecca ran to greet them. She took little Christopher to her room. The boy adored her, and Rebecca called him her little brother. Henry took Rebecca aside and informed her they would have more company for dinner. He told her a nice lady with a daughter the same age as her would join them and that the girl's name was Fela and maybe they would become friends. Rebecca looked at him with suspicion. She did not love this situation and responded, "Okay, if I must." They all sat at the big dining room table, filled with the best of everything. Rebecca was observed Rose and her daughter. She was so intent, she forgot to eat. Henry was sorry he made the introduction at that time.

Rose looked around and could not believe her eyes. She never saw so much luxury, not even before the war. She came from a poor family and got her education after the war. She lost her husband in a concentration camp. She and her daughter were hidden by a peasant family and survived. Her daughter, Fela, was a smart girl, but very moody and unpleasant. The two young girls hardly exchanged any words. Nothing had worked as Henry imagined.

After Rose and her daughter left, and the children were asleep, Henry sat with Philip and Sofia to hear what they thought about Rose. Sofia said, "Well she is smart, well read, and quite pretty." But Sofia thought Rose may have a mean streak about her. Philip did not say much except that if Henry had to have a companion, then Rose was not a bad one to have.

Rebecca had hidden in the dining room and heard the whole conversation. She did not like what she heard. She did not want that lady to be her stepmother or Fela to be her stepsister. She would most likely not have been happy with anyone in those roles. Rebecca was happy the way things were then. She went to bed feeling very upset.

The next day, Rebecca had some of her friends over and Henry asked if she would like to invite Fela. Rebecca gave him a strong, short no! She seemed not to be happy and Christopher did not leave her side. Rebecca held his hand and also did not let go. Henry prepared little gifts for everyone and everyone had a good time.

The Witkowskis stayed another few days, and this made Rebecca very happy. They went to a concert and a famous restaurant. Poor little Christopher had to stay home with Zosia but Rebecca made sure he had a surprise toy every time they went out.

Sofia gave Rebecca new photos of her as a baby with her mother. Rebecca cherished those photos. She was missing a mother, but Henry then wondered if Rose could fill this role.

Henry wasn't sure what to do. Rose insisted they legitimize their relationship. She wanted to know where she stood. Henry knew Rose was right. He needed to make a decision. He wished Rose would not push to get married when Rebecca would be away at summer camp. He did not know if he should ask Rebecca or just tell her what would happen. Henry decided to wait a little longer. The following month he would have to tell Rebecca he was marrying Rose because if he merely asked Rebecca, her answer would be no.

Zosia prepared a list of things for Rebecca to take to camp. Rebecca was excited to go. Afterwards, during the last month of her vacation, would be spent in Gdynia. Rebecca loved going there. She felt very secure and loved. Her father told her about his plans to marry Rose. She was not happy, but he told her this marriage would be better for everyone, and she felt she had no choice.

Finally it was time to go to camp. This was the first time Rebecca was going away alone. It felt strange but at the same time she was happy. They were in the train station with lots of kids and their parents. Very few kids from her school were there, but it did not matter. Rebecca was ready to make new friends. Last kisses and hugs, and all the kids, counselors and their helpers were on the train. There was a lot of commotion. Rebecca did not know where to go or where to sit. She stood there helpless. She finally started to look for a place to sit. Every time she saw an empty seat, a kid would say, "It's taken", and pushed her away. She just stood there, ready to cry.

A boy approached her. He was older than she was, and he asked "What is your name?" She replied, and asked him what his name was. "Alex," he said. He took her hand to lead her to a seat near him. They exchanged a few words. Everyone in the compartment looked at her. A counselor came in and asked Alex to come with him. Before Alex left, he said to the rest of the kids, "take care of her until I come back," and everyone nodded. Rebecca thought he must be important in this camp. She did not know when he returned since she had fallen asleep. When she woke up, he was next to her. The first thing he said was, "Do not worry; I would take care of you, Rebecca." He had a beautiful smile and she trusted him.

The camp was fun, the food was bad, but the most wonderful thing was Alex! Everyone knew Alex. He had been coming to the camp since almost the beginning; about five years. He was a great sportsman and everyone told Rebecca he was a great student. She hoped she would continue to see him when they went back to the city.

Back at home, Rebecca had a huge surprise waiting for her. Henry had decided to get married when she was away, hoping it would be easier that way. Rebecca's room was divided in half and was redone nicely and Fela was very polite to her. But all

Rebecca wanted to do was cry. At dinner she just sat there not eating. She did not say a thing. Zosia patted her each time she passed as she served dinner. After dinner, Rebecca asked to be excused. She laid down and felt numb from all the change.

The following day, they were all to leave for Gdynia. Rebecca knew it was not going to be the same. To make herself feel better, she thought of Alex. She was growing up. Her body was changing and she was becoming a little woman.

They were one the train. Rebecca looked out the window. She missed her father sitting next to her. Fela was sitting next to her instead. Rose and her father sat across from them. Rebecca closed her eyes not wanting to look at them. Finally they arrived at Philip and Sofia's home. Christopher was jumping up and down. He was so happy to see Rebecca. He whispered into her ear, "You would sleep in my room, please?" And Rebecca thought what a good idea that was so she would not have to sleep in the same room as Fela. The first thing she asked Sofia was if she could, and Sofia agreed.

The weather was perfect, the sun was shining, the beach was soft and the water was not too cold. Rebecca tried to have a good time. On one occasion, Fela asked Rebecca, "We would have to ask our father's permission."

Rebecca replied to Fela in a chilling voice, "He is not your father and your mother is not my mother. Just remember that!" From then on, Fela stayed away from Rebecca. That was perfectly okay with Rebecca.

Soon they would return back home. Rose watched how Rebecca was so close with Sofia and she wondered why Rebecca did not like her. Rose would try harder when they returned home. Fela liked Henry but not Rebecca.

CHAPTER 9

This day had started a little scary. Kurt did not feel so good. After he took Albert around the garden for a walk, he came into the house with chest pains and shortness of breath. Helena called the hospital and the ambulance was on its way. Kurt was sitting in an easy chair, very pale. Finally the paramedics arrived and attended to him. Helga was holding the boys against her. The paramedics decided to take Kurt to the hospital for observation. Robert and Helga went with him. There was nothing else to do but wait. The hospital was pretty well equipped and they had very good doctors. Helena did not know how she felt. Was she sorry for Kurt, worried about him? She did want him to get better and be the wonderful grandpa he was for the boys. It took a week for Kurt to return home. He did have a mild heart attack. He would have to take it easy and change his diet a little, and no more beer! The boys were so happy to have him back and so was Helena.

Helena's life was very ordinary. She was busy with Robert's business. She worked for four to five hours a day. Robert let her help him with some decision making and she had little time to do anything else outside of the house. She had a suspicion that Robert arranged this on purpose. Helga was slowing down and Helena, with the help of the housekeeper, slowly took over the cooking. Sabina, the nanny, was also taking on other chores in the house. Robert was much more involved with his sons' homework, sports, reading of the classics, etc. Helena really did not have much time to do much more. The boys were growing up. Albert was starting school and Max was in the fourth grade. They were doing well in school, had many friends and were happy boys. They both looked very much like Robert except for Albert's smile. It was just like Helena's father's smile. Every time he smiled it was a reminder to Helena of her previous life. It was as if God did so on purpose as a reminder to never forget.

Helena suggested to Robert to take a vacation, but Robert did not show much enthusiasm. She thought that maybe they could go to Paris. She yearned for some excitement. There was too much sameness in her life. She would talk to him again, soon, the next day! And the next day Helena would go to the only travel agency in town.

Robert was thinking of purchasing a television set. That was amazing. It was like having a small movie theater at home. The boys wanted it so badly.

That day was a big surprise! Together with the business mail came a letter from an unlikely place, Israel. Helena knew right away whom it was from. Mrs. Stoval finally wrote. It was a long letter written in Polish. Robert was also surprised, and not too happy. He said something that surprised Helena. "I can only imagine what they must be thinking in our post office." Helena ignored his comment and opened her letter.

Mrs. Stoval apologized for the long delay, but so many things had happened and she was overwhelmed. The Jewish agency located some of her family. She lost her husband in the ghetto and one of her sons has become crippled after a long illness. One son was married and had two small children. She was so happy! Life in Israel was not easy, but they managed. She felt like she has been reborn. Israel was home for all Jews. She was grateful to Helena for her help. She was now happy to be of help to her ailing son and care for him. She was asking for a reply. Robert asked if Mrs. Stoval was okay, but he did not ask Helena to translate the letter, and Helena was happy and decided to reply.

The next day Helena received a call from the Rabbi. It was good that Robert was not home. She did not have to tell him about it. The Rabbi told Helena that he also received a letter from Mrs. Stoval and that he was very happy that her life had turned around. The Rabbi invited Helena's whole family to join in one of the Shabbat services, if they would like. She thanked him politely.

After so many years, Helena sat down to write a letter in Polish. She wondered if she remembered, but she did. She thanked Mrs. Stoval for her letter and asked for a reply. She wanted to know how her life was progressing and how things were progressing in Israel. Helena wanted to ask her to maybe try to find one of her own, but as usual, she was too afraid, and left it for another time. She mailed this letter without Robert's knowledge.

Kurt was ailing again. There was a brand new surgery. It was called open heart surgery, where they changed the veins to the heart, but it was in an experimental stage and it had to be done in Vienna, Austria. The doctor told them that Kurt was too weak and too old for this surgery. He was seventy five years old. Robert was worried. He did not think that his father had much longer. Kurt spent his days in his beloved garden and when the kids came home from school he was with them all the time, even if he just sat and watched them do their homework.

Helga did not take Kurt's illness well. Her eyes were red most of the time from crying. She tried to be brave but she was not doing a good job. The boys were aware of the situation and Helena felt sorry they had to live through this slow process of unhappiness. Kurt had problems breathing and the doctors had suggested using an oxygen supplement. Kurt did not want it, but eventually he would have no choice. All this took a terrible toll on Helga. She did not eat well. She did not sleep and it showed. She had lost weight. She was pale and not very stable. Helena talked to her and tried to make her understand how bad Kurt felt seeing her in that condition, knowing it was all because of him. Helga seemed to understand when Helena spoke to her, but it was short lived, and after a day or two, it was the same. She kept on saying, "He has so much to live for." Helena knew nobody could live forever. It all made the household very unhappy.

And so a few months had passed. Kurt was deteriorating fast. He wanted to go to the hospital. He knew his end was near. Robert made arrangements for Kurt to have a private room, large enough for one of them to stay every night. It was not easy. The boys came to visit every day after school and were very somber. But at home, they were normal, mischievous boys, as if they were rid of a heavy stone attached to them. Helena was surprised by their attitude. They adored their grandfather, but life always wins. Robert had a little talk with Helena and they decided that the boys would continue to visit at the hospital until Kurt was no longer aware. But when Kurt was unconscious they must stop the visits. They did not want the kids to be exposed to the horrors of death.

That next night was Helena's turn to stay with Kurt. He did not feel well. In the middle of the night Kurt called her name. Helena came close to his bed. He said, "I am glad you are here this night. I want you to know I did not trust you in the beginning but slowly my mistrust turned to appreciation of who you are. I still do not know for sure who you are, but it does not matter, because I love you for what's in your heart and what you gave me and my son." And just like that, he collapsed. Helena called the nurse and the doctor, but there was nothing they could do. His heart just stopped.

On the way home, Helena was thinking. She always knew Kurt did not believe her story, but she always knew he loved her.

Robert heard the noise of her coming home, and he knew! That night Helena held him close to her, and he cried like a little boy. In the morning, Robert went to his mother's room. Helena heard loud crying. Helena had to tell the boys. They cried, and Albert asked, "Is he in heaven now?"

And Helena said, "Of course he is." Max just shook his head. Robert came into the room to console the boys before he went to do the funeral arrangements. The priest came to their home and first sat with the boys. Helga did not come out of her room. She wanted to be alone. Sabina and Gertrude were distraught. The gardener, with his hat in hand, gave his condolences. Helena wished she knew what to do, but she did not know about Christian funerals. The funeral was scheduled for two days from then. The news spread fast in town and people came to place flowers in front of the gate.

Helena answered a phone call. It was the Rabbi. He asked if he could attend the funeral, saying "Kurt was a good man."

She answered, "It is better if you don't," and hung up. "What was this?" she thought.

Robert sat with the boys that evening. Helena stayed on the couch. Robert told the boys about the different beliefs people had and everyone's feelings and beliefs had to be respected as long as nobody hurt anybody because of their belief. Maximilian interrupted, "You mean do not do what Hitler did?"

Helena felt that Robert was speaking to her! Robert also said, "Grandfather had a long, happy life, and no one lives forever, and we have to celebrate his life. He did not suffer much and he is now in peace. Of course, we would all miss him and remember him."

The boys went to sleep and Robert went to his mother's room. Helena went to her own bedroom. She did not sleep and waited for Robert to come. She held him close. "I would never stop loving you," said Robert.

The day of the funeral was cold and cloudy. So many people came to the church service to say their goodbyes. Everybody praised Kurt for the help he gave to all who asked him during the war. He provided education for many of the injured soldiers that returned from war. The boys listened and felt very proud.

They had a family plot with many generations buried there. Helena had never been there. It was all walled in with different monuments dating back to the seventeenth century. After the burial, Robert took Helena's hand and walked her by each of the monuments explaining who each one was and what they had done. Helena knew she would never belong here! They all returned home. Robert prepared a gift for the boys. A new television was set up in the library. They were so excited. They all watched an old movie, and life went on without Kurt Van Klaus.

The boys wanted to know about Robert's childhood. They wanted to see photos and to know about their ancestors. They were growing up and showed interest in their family's history. Max asked Helena to help him start a journal about the family.

Christmas was coming soon and Helga, with Gertrude' help, set up the decorations. The children helped too. The gardener hung up the decorations on the outside of the house. The town was already decorated, and it looked like a fairy-tale town. All the trees were lit up. The light snow that was falling added to the atmosphere. Helena shopped for extra gifts to make their first holiday without Kurt a little bit more special. People in town were anticipating the holiday. They were smiling and very merry. It felt so happy. What a beautiful world it was right there in this small town of Regensburg. Helena did not forget her other family, but the pain was not so severe any longer. Helena's world was in Regensburg right then. The people she loved were there. Her sons gave her an enormous amount of pride and because of them she kept her secret.

CHAPTER 10

Henry was distraught. A year had passed and Rebecca was still very rebellious, ever since Rose and Fela had moved in. Rebecca did not want to have anything to do with Fela. She also did not respond to Rose. It was a good thing that Rose was busy working. The only one Rebecca had shown any affection to was Zosia and, of course, the Witkowskis. And she adored their little son Christopher. Rebecca never told Henry anything and she did not blame him but she was very unhappy. Henry felt very guilty and he missed the closeness they had before. If he could go back in time and undo his decision, he would.

One night at dinner Rebecca asked if she could go to the Witkowskis, alone, for Christmas break. Henry allowed her. Henry and Rose had a big argument. Rose was looking forward to going to Gdynia. Fela cried and said, "Rebecca makes all our lives miserable." Rebecca heard this and had a smug little smile on her face. Rebecca was hoping that maybe Rose and Fela would go away and things could be as they were before. She had been receiving letters from Alex and, for the first time, he asked if he could see her. She wanted this, but how?

Alex suggested they go and see a movie. He would come to pick her up. She did not want this. She was afraid her father would not allow it. Instead, they met at the movies and she told her father she was going to a girlfriend's. Rebecca had a great time with Alex and hoped to see him more often.

That next day she was on the train to Gdynia. She wanted to be with the Witkowskis very much. It would give her a break from acting mean all the time. The Witkowskis waited for her at the station. Christopher was jumping up and down, he was so excited. Rebecca had gifts for him which, for sure, he would like. Sofia hugged her all the time. Rebecca loved being there. Sofia tried to talk to her about the situation, but Rebecca was not responsive.

Rebecca thought to ask Sofia and Philip if she could stay with them. But she knew how unhappy this would make her father and she loved him so much. She also did not want to be away from Alex. After a lot of soul searching, she made the decision to be nicer to her father. But she still was not going to be friendly with Rose. She believed Rose did not love her father. She only wanted to have a good life and security. But for then, she had three more weeks of vacation and she would enjoy them. Christopher liked his gifts. He clung to her and told her all about his little life. He was like her little brother.

Back home everything was the same. Rebecca was kinder to her father, and he noticed. Rose and Fela did not care about Rebecca at all. It was one household with two separate lives. It was a very unusual situation and very unpleasant for all.

Henry got used to this. He was very busy at work. The museum gave him a lot of satisfaction. He was friendly with a lot of people in high positions. It was a different life in Poland than before the war, but it was what it was.

He knew he could not leave the country, but he also knew that one day there would be a way, and then, he would not think twice. He definitely would go. Henry was tired of feeling afraid all the time. So many of his friends were being interrogated repeatedly. Some were arrested and some were never heard from again. Henry was very careful.

His relationship with his wife was friendly but not exactly as it should have been. Henry was sorry that he married this woman, but he could not do anything about it right then. He did not share all his secrets with her. Henry's relationship with Rebecca improved significantly and he swore he would never endanger their closeness. She would always be first in his life. Rose urged him to officially adopt Fela but he did not want to do so. Somehow he knew he would not be with this woman all his remaining life.

Mr. Blum and Henry became very good friends. He was a good director and cared very much about the museum. He also totally trusted Henry. They prepared for a trip to Russia, not that they wanted to go, but they were invited, which meant they must go. They exchanged some artifacts, and it was clear they would receive some junk art and they would have to give up some very good pieces. But this was all part of dealing with communist Poland, and Russia was king. You could not oppose this. They sat and tried to figure out how to lose the least.

Henry felt pressured. He did not want to go. He was a little fearful. How could Rebecca survive without him if anything were to happen to him? But nothing could be changed, he had to go. He spoke to the Witkowskis, just in case. Zosia would take care of her at home so her school would not be interrupted. It was almost the end of the school year.

Rebecca would go again to the summer camp and then to Gdynia. But Rose and Fela would not join them. They would go to a spa in the Karpaty Mountains. Rebecca asked Henry not to share the Witkowskis with them, and so it was. Rebecca and her father went alone to Gdynia.

Right after summer, Henry and Mr. Blum were going to Russia. In a way, they were excited to go to this legendary country that had so much history and to witness the new regime of communism. The other communist bloc in Europe was forced upon them, but Russia initiated communism.

The artwork had already shipped and would be in Russia, ready to make a deal. It was up to Henry to convince the Russians what a good exchange it would be. The train ride was not too bad. It was first class, and in a way, very restful. Upon their arrival, they were greeted by the Russian representative of the Moscow museum. They were taken to their hotel. The next morning they were meeting at the museum.

There were four men who introduced themselves, all well dressed, and obviously with an art education. Henry talked about every single piece of art they brought from Poland. Their eyes lit up! They told Henry they were trying to create a museum in Moscow that would be a little like the Hermitage in Leningrad. They had a long way to go to compete with the Hermitage! They liked what Henry brought them. What a relief this was.

The next day Henry and Mr. Blum saw the art that they traded for. Let's see! That night they were going to a typical Russian restaurant and then to a concert. Mr. Blum and Henry were happy so far. The art they brought from Poland was not very significant, it just looked good. Henry had an idea to bring back some religious icons from Russia. They were unique to Russia. No one else did them in their way. Henry knew Russia had a lot of these religious icons and did not display them in museums. Religion was not in favor in Russia.

The dinner was superb and the concert was even better. Henry was surprised. They were promised a three day tour after finishing their business. The next morning they met again. The art presented to them was atrocious! Some modern paintings, some statues with no life in them, but Henry knew this was all he could expect. Henry asked if it was possible to get some of their religious icons. The Russians were surprised by this request and asked for a few minutes to talk amongst themselves. When they returned with a smile on their faces, Henry knew it would be okay. They agreed.

That night they were going to a French restaurant and the opera. Henry was shocked to see the people in the restaurant. Some were European, but a lot of them were Russians, well dressed and well groomed, and Henry knew that life here was not "equal" for everyone, as it was supposed to be.

The three days of their trip was well organized. Henry and Mr. Blum were not alone for one minute. What they saw was pretty and nice and well-orchestrated. The only time they were alone was at breakfast in the hotel, if you could call it alone. A small man with a big hat came over to their table and asked them in Yiddish if he could sit with them. They were shocked, and nodded yes. He talked fast, all in Yiddish. He was making them a proposition to smuggle gold into Poland, for an excellent price.

Mr. Blum and Henry looked at each and said, "We would have to think about it," and told him that he should come back the next morning. He did return, but Henry and Mr. Blum decided against it. They responded, again in Yiddish, and told the man, "We are not smugglers. We are here on official business." And then they explained that had he not spoken to them in Yiddish, they would have reported him to the Russian authorities. The man quickly got up and disappeared. Henry was convinced that this was a set-up. Mr. Blum was scared. They were going home the next day. They could not wait.

Rebecca and Zosia were waited for Henry at the train station. He was so happy to see her. She was changing almost every day. A taxi took them home and Henry was relieved to be in a safe place, he would sleep well tonight.

CHAPTER 11

The year was 1952. Rebecca was thirteen and Henry was forty-eight. His hair was half gray. He was not too wrinkled. He felt energetic and had no problems with his health. He thought, "I am getting older, but if this is how older feels, it is not too bad!"

Rebecca wanted to tell him a secret, so she asked that they go to dinner, without the others. Well, he could not wait, "Is it good news" he was asking himself. She proceeded to tell him about Alex. How much she liked him, what a genius he was. How he was finishing high school a year early and wanted to be an engineer, and how good looking he was, and, and, and...

Henry was not prepared for this kind of news. He sat quietly and he knew he must be very smart. "Okay, Rebecca, when do I meet this young man?"

Rebecca was surprised and answered, "Really, father, you do not mind?" They agreed to meet the following Sunday and would spend the day together. Rose and Fela would have dinner with them but then leave for the theater so that Rebecca and Henry would be alone with Alex. Henry was so hopeful that Alex would be a nice boy and was also hopeful that he would go to study in a town far away! After all, Alex was three years older than Rebecca was.

Henry knew that agreeing to meet Alex was the right decision. Sunday came fast enough. Alex was polite, smart and gave Henry his promise to respect his daughter. By the next September, Alex would be going to Warsaw to study engineering. That was good news for Henry. He did agree they could see each other on Sundays for a movie and return home for dinner. Henry started to like this young man, but he thought, "This is Rebecca's first boyfriend, she is only thirteen. We would see what would happen next."

Alex started college at age seventeen. He was a genius and Rebecca's and his young was lasting. Henry was glad, in a way, for Rebecca to have someone like Alex in .

The atmosphere in Poland was peculiar. The Jews still felt anti- Semitic behavior on the part of the Polacks. No one had any freedom. It was impossible to purchase anything. You had to bribe someone to get anything. So far, nothing was changing and Henry kept wondering how he would ever be able to get out of Poland. You could not get permission to visit any other country except another communist bloc country. Poland would never progress under this regime. The funny thing was no one wanted to be under the communist government bur for then, it was what it was. People had to make the best of it and try to live as normal a life as they could. It was easier for younger people. They did not know any other life. They only heard bad things about life in the west and they all believed it.

The Jewish community emphasized education for their children as the most important thing to accomplish. Children were encouraged to study hard so they could get accepted in the best universities. Nothing was too much to achieve this purpose. Rebecca was a happy young woman. Studies came easy for her, she had many friends and Alex was a big part of her life. She was pretty, with her mother's coloring but more of Henry's features. She was not too tall. Henry was sorry she did not look more like her mother. It would be easier for her to live in Poland and look Polish.

Time was passing. Henry listened to a radio program from Western Europe called "Free Europe". This was illegal and a lot of people were arrested for doing so. This radio program was the only way for people to find out what was happening in the rest of the world. The local news and Russian news was all communist propaganda.

Henry's work at the museum was progressing nicely. They did assemble a pretty nice, artistic place for the people to enjoy. Mr. Blum was very happy with Henry but lately, he was becoming very agitated. Finally, he told Henry that some people from Warsaw were coming to visit them and their museum. They were in charge of the Warsaw National Museum and would probably offer Henry a job. Henry was grateful that Mr. Blum warned him, so that he could be prepared with an answer. It was a great privilege and Warsaw was growing rapidly. Everyone wanted to live in Warsaw. But, of course, you could not. You had to have permission.

Henry thought that it might be nice to be back in Warsaw. After all, it was his home, but he would have to start all over again. Housing was a big problem and he would have to uproot Rebecca and she would have to make new friends. He truly did not want to do this. He was comfortable right here in Wroclaw in his nice apartment and he had just recently made new friends. They probably would make him join the communist party and he would be a very visible person, which he did not think was good for him. He definitely did not want to go. They might force him and then he would have no choice. Henry thought it would be best for him if he told the men from Warsaw that he was not well enough to undertake the new position. Just in case they would check, Henry went to his good friend, a doctor, and received some medication and had it on record that he had an enlarged heart. He also called his friend Philip in Gdynia and told him about this. Philip also put this illness on record for Henry.

The men from Warsaw arrived. Henry took them around to show them all the newly acquired art pieces. He prepared to show them a quality painting which he bought from an elderly woman who desperately needed money. He handed the painting to the men wrapped in paper and said, "This is for the great National Museum in Warsaw, for people to enjoy." They were very pleased. They all left for dinner and the theater and that's when they proposed the new job to Henry. Henry played his part very well. He made believe it was a big surprise. "I am so honored, and I wish I could do it but I cannot." Then he told them about his alleged illness. They were surprised and thanked him for his honesty. Henry promised he would help anytime they would think it was necessary.

Mr. Blum was very happy that Henry was to remain with him. Maybe there would be some additional trips to Warsaw, which should be fun.

CHAPTER 12

Helena was sipping a cup of tea on the veranda, watching her boys play soccer on the lawn. How fast they were growing up. Maximilian was twelve and Albert was nine. Handsome young boys, very loving, smart and accomplished. Both were good students, they adored their grandmother and were near her much of the time. She was almost always in a wheelchair then. She had been ailing ever since Kurt's death and her grandsons were giving her the incentive to live. She adored them. Even Robert was jealous of the attention she gave to her grandsons, saying "I don't ever remember being loved like this."

The year was 1957. Robert said at the dinner table, that it would be nice to take a family vacation to some exotic place, and all of them should apply for passports. Helena looked at him, but did not say anything. That night she asked Robert if she would have any problems getting her passport. He said, abruptly, "Don't worry. I would take care of it." They all went for their passport photos the next day. Helena wanted to know what explanation he would give to the authorities. After all, she never asked for German citizenship. How could she have a German passport? Robert answered that he had three witnesses to vouch for how long she lived in Germany. Her sons were born there and he had their marriage certificate that attested to the marriage of Helena Michalowski to Robert Van Klaus. This was enough documentation for all of them to get their passports. Now the question was where they would go. The boys had all kinds of ideas and were arguing over their destination. Helena did not take part in this. She did not want to go anywhere. The previous year Robert took the boys to Berlin. They went without her. She claimed she could not leave Helga alone. The Berlin trip was a success and the boys loved it.

They agreed on a destination, Israel. "Oh no," said Helena. "That is too far and too dangerous. You must pick some European country." Finally they agreed on Italy. The family was going for three weeks.

Helena was so relieved. She could not see how she could have gone to Israel without looking for Rebecca and Henry. She was hoping they were happy and alive, but she did not want to find them. Rebecca was now almost eighteen years old and in a few years would be independent. Helena argued with herself, as she always did since the end of the war, but nothing made sense.

Gertrude was moving to a retirement home and Sabina was to remain home with Helga. Everybody cried and Helena tried to console them. Gertrude promised to visit often, and then the taxi arrived to take her to the airport.

The family left for their vacation. They arrived in Italy and it was like a Garden of Eden! Lush, green, the people were very nice. Rome was incredible. All the antiquities and the Vatican were indescribable. They all had a wonderful time. They traveled to Florence and to Venice, went on a gondola, saw impressive museums, and ate unfamiliar foods which they loved.

Helena went to a little store in Rome, near the Vatican, where they were staying. The owner was an old, Hasidic Jew. Helena almost withdrew, but did not. She asked for a cookbook of Italian recipes in German. He answered, in Yiddish, that he could not help her since he did not speak German. Helena replied, "It's okay, you can speak Yiddish, I understand." He looked at her in disbelief, but still did not help her to select a cookbook. He asked, "Can it be that you are Jewish?" "Yes, I am," answered Helena, and she left the store. Walking back to the hotel, she realized that she admitted being Jewish for the first time since the middle of the war. It felt good. It was time to return home.

The boys were happy with their vacation, and so was Robert. Helena brought lots of gifts for everyone. Helga was hugging her grandsons and did not want to let them go. She was so happy they were home. But, the happiest of all was Helena. Her home was in Germany. It was her slice of heaven. The routine of her everyday life, her garden, her family, her magnificent estate was her cocoon. She no longer minded the periods of boredom. She read a lot, looked up news from all over the world, cooked the family meals and kept engaged. She was not helpful with the boy's homework but Robert helped with this.

Helga's health was deteriorating and she could hardly walk. She needed two people to help her. Only then, Helena convinced her to use the wheelchair at all times. Robert and the gardener built a ramp from the back entrance so she could spend time in the garden and on the patio. She was not unhappy. Helga realized that life had been good to her. She was grateful for her son's happy marriage and for her most wonderful grandsons.

Helena liked Helga very much. Helga did not have a mean bone in her body. Helga liked finding the good things in people. Helena became a little busier with Helga. Helga could not read anymore, so Helena read to her. They watched the news together, but Helga had a hard time to comprehend. The doctors said she had dementia. She would not get better, only worse. It was sad to watch a vibrant person become as helpless as a child. But Helga did not complain. Helena only hoped that Helga would not suffer. The boys complained, "Grandma did not recognize us today." They were very sad about this and did not understand why it was happening. They were getting a lesson in life, but Helena did not want them to learn.

Robert was spending a lot of time sitting with his mother just holding her hand. They did not talk and just sat there to be close together. He was very gentle and loving. Helena thought there was no other man like him on the planet.

Robert informed the family that the town leaders had proposed that he run for mayor of the town. But Robert refused, explaining that he had to stay close to home and his ailing mother and his business required all his attention. Helena was surprised that he refused such a prestigious offer. When she questioned him, Robert was abrupt and said, "I do not need prestige. I like to stay as private as I can for the sake of my family."

Helga was taken to the hospital one day. She had trouble breathing and did not recognize anybody, not even Robert. She looked at Robert and thought he was Kurt and begged him not to leave her. Robert spent most of his days with his mother in the hospital. They all visited her every day, but she did not know who they were. They got a call in the middle of one night. Helga was not doing too well. She had an oxygen mask on but needed to be on a respirator. This made no sense to Robert, so he decided against it. He was right. She died peacefully in the early morning.

The family was all beside themselves. They did expect her death, but it made no difference in their sorrow. The funeral was to take place two days later. Like at Kurt's funeral, a lot of people came to pay their respects. Helga was laid to rest next to her husband in the family plot.

The house was empty without Helga. Robert was truly mourning her death. The boys were sad. Sabina cried all the time. And to Helena's surprise, she was sad too, a lot more than she was when Kurt died. Helena knew that now was a perfect time to reveal the truth about herself. She would wait a month or so, until Robert finished grieving. Helena did not want the boys to know her secret. She wanted them stay happy and be proud of who they were. Helena was very stressed, now that she decided to tell Robert. She repeated, in her mind, how she would do it, and what she would say. But most of all, she feared how Robert would take it.

Would he be very upset, would he forgive her for all the lies, would things ever be the same? She decided she would tell him when they were home alone. The boys were going on a ski vacation with their school. At the same time, Sabina was going to visit her niece who just gave birth to a daughter. It would be a good time to be truthful to her husband.

Helena could not sleep or eat. She could not concentrate on her book. She was a mess. Robert saw it and kept telling her to see a doctor. Helena did not need a doctor. She knew exactly why she was acting the way she was. The boys and Sabina were leaving in two days. Helena made a reservation at a fine restaurant in town, and requested a secluded table, thinking he would not have a fit in public. She went to the beauty parlor to make herself beautiful and she would wear a nice dress that night and hope for the best. She would tell him after dinner but before dessert. Helena had it all planned out in her mind. The decision made her feel calmer.

Robert was surprised at her fancy look but was also delighted. They were seated in a quiet corner of the restaurant. The dinner was delightful. She asked the waiter to wait with the dessert for a little while. And she said, "Robert, we have been together for many years and we have been very happy, but I am holding a great secret from you and feel very guilty for it." She took his hand in hers. Robert sat still, with his eyes down. His hand felt cold in hers. But Helena had to continue, "I am not who you think I am."

And Robert interrupted and said, "Stop, I would tell you who you are! You are Jewish. Those papers you showed were fake documents. At the beginning I believed them, but later, when we slept together, you had terrible nightmares and you talked in your sleep in Yiddish. I was able to understand what you were saying as it was very similar to German. I know about Henry and Rebecca, your parents and your brother Daniel. You talked to all of them. I knew you were afraid to reveal the truth, but I loved you every day we were together. I watched you with our children and how good you were with my parents, and decided that it did not matter whether you would ever come out with the truth."

Helena sat in disbelief. She could not even open her fingers to let Robert's hand go. She was frozen. Finally, Helena said that she did not want to say anything until his parents had passed. She knew his father did not have trust in her until he learned of the death of the Michalowskis in London. When Helena cried out upon this news, it was a pressure relief for her. From that moment on she knew she had Kurt's confidence. She told Robert she wanted to keep her secret from the boys and that she had not attempted to find out anything about her lost family. She knew she must give up one family for the other. She chose this family, and above all, Robert. Helena told Robert he was the love of her life, and the boys she could never live without.

Helena also told Robert how she struggled, all these years, with the unknown about her daughter Rebecca. She said, "Time did calm down my urgency to know. Maybe she was happy with her father or with our friends, the Witkowskis. Maybe one day I would find out, but right now I would like to raise my sons to adulthood, and then we would see what would happen." She looked at Robert.

He listened intently, not even blinking his eyes. He told her how he fell in love with her the first time he saw her. How before the war he dated a lot of girls, but was never in love with any of them. The minute he saw Helena, he knew, "This was love!" The only thing he did not know was how this was going to play out. He also told her, "Our love is not the usual story." They sat at the table for a while without speaking. Finally, Robert said to Helena, "You must tell me everything about yourself that I do not know." She nodded. They agreed not to say anything to the boys. They were way too young to understand. They finally ordered dessert.

Helena felt reborn. On the way home she turned to Robert and said, "By the way, my name is Liliana."

"What a beautiful name," Robert said.

For the next few days, they sat under the big oak tree, holding hands while Helena would share her past life with him. She often cried and he tried to comfort her. She felt so close to him. She knew that from then on her life would be so much easier. It was as if her soul was released from bondage.

The boys came home from their ski vacation. Sabina returned as well. Helena kept busy keeping up with the house chores. The house was huge, and it was hard to clean every corner. Robert hired a cleaning company to come one day a week. Sabina was very watchful that the work was done properly and that nothing was missing. Helena and Robert's love grew so much stronger. Robert smiled more often and Helena lost her anxiety. It was a good time for everyone at home.

It was time for Maximilian to choose his courses that would prepare him for University in the following two years. More and more, he thought law would be his preference. For law, he would have to go to a big city, like Berlin or Dusseldorf or Colon. Helena did not like the thought of him leaving. Robert thought it would be the best choice for him to take over their estate one day.

Life flowed in peace and happiness for them. Helena remembered what her father used to say, "If you are happy, cherish the moment and remember it forever because being happy does not come too often." Yes, she would remember this time forever.

One morning, while watching her husband sleep, she noticed his first grey hair. "We must all grow up," she thought to herself. She ran to the mirror to look for her own grey hair. "Not yet!" Helena was not ready to be so grown up.

Sex was more important to her then than it had ever been before. She wanted to please her husband. She knew she would be one of those women who maintained elegance. She watched her diet, walked a lot, kept herself busy and so far, so good. Her body had not changed. Her face was still smooth with no wrinkles, but she did have a more grown up look. She wanted to go to the big city to shop for more fashionable clothes. She was planning to go and hoped that maybe Robert would come with her. Helena decided she would go to Munich for a few days and Robert agreed to go with her. Sabina and her brother would stay at home with the boys. Helena and Robert would go for only three to four days. Robert decided he needed some new clothes also. Max and Albert gave them a shopping list for themselves as well. Helena looked forward to maybe visiting a museum and some antique shops. They would travel by train. Meanwhile, Helena researched everything about Munich, its history and places to visit.

Helena was very excited as they boarded the train. She had never been to a large German city. Actually, she had not been anywhere except for their trip to Italy. She still did remember beautiful Warsaw from before the war.

Helena had an urgency to see the world! Upon their arrival in Munich, you could feel the pulse of the city. The hustle and bustle was felt by both Helena and Robert. The noise of the cars, the people walking at a fast pace, the blinking neon lights in the stores were all very exciting. The taxi took them to their hotel. It was late afternoon. They unpacked and went to the restaurant in the hotel. They planned to visit a museum and some stores the next day. In the evening they would to see a play.

Helena felt wonderful. From fashion magazines, she knew, more or less, what she wanted to shop for. She felt it would be easy to find clothes that would look good on her. The first store they went to was a men's fashion salon that was in business for one hundred years. They had everything Robert wanted and a few things for the boys too. The rest of the things for the boys would have to be purchased at a specialized sports store. Robert told Helena he had visited this store with his father and grandfather several times but it was all before the war.

The fashion shop for women was overflowing with beautiful things. Helena had a hard time to choosing but Robert was helpful. It was the first time Helena had shopped with him. Until then she had always shopped with Helga. She was surprised at what he was choosing for her. They could not carry all their purchases back to the hotel, so it was delivered for them.

After they shopped, they took a long walk through the city until they heard loud shouting and singing. They went to see what commotion was. It was groups of protesters. One group was on one side of the street and the other group was on the other side of the street. Helena's eyes gravitated to the side with the big Israeli flags. They were singing in Hebrew. All were young, fit and had lot of enthusiasm. Robert found out that both sides were disputing some kind of political issue. They were young students who came to Germany to get their education. Some were from Israel and some were from Egypt.

Helena was mesmerized watching the Israeli students. They had no fear, they were confidant, and not at all how she remembered young Jews from before the war. A wave of pride went through her. "So these are my people," she thought. The police came to disperse them and Robert pulled her away from the commotion.

But this incident lingered with her all through the night. It was a good experience. Again it was a reminder that God was saying, "Do not forget!"

The museum was impressive, but Helena could not forget that a lot of this art was stolen from all over Europe and brought to Germany by Hitler's regime. Some of the art was returned after the war, but most of it stayed in Germany; especially art that belonged to private collectors who were not alive to reclaim it.

Helena and Robert stayed in Munich a day longer than planned. The visits to antique galleries were not a great pleasure to Helena. She could not concentrate on what she was seeing. The rear door in each shop was covered by a heavy curtain, as it was in Henry's shop. In every store she expected to see Henry come out and politely introduce himself to her. It was a nightmare for her. They went to a few galleries, and she told Robert she could not do anymore. She thought Robert forgot about Henry and his profession and his gallery. Or maybe, Robert wanted to see how she reacted? They left Munich shortly thereafter.

As the taxi approached their home, Helena was happy. She would hug her boys shortly, give them their gifts, and above all feel at home again. How strange it was that she felt so good in this home. She felt safe, loved and appreciated. Tranquility surrounded her. She thought if she never left this place, she would never be unhappy.

Upon entering the house, the boys ran to hug their father first. Helena was jealous but not for long. Soon she had them in her arms and there was no better feeling!

In the distance, in the garden, she saw a little girl in the mist. She had a very sad face. "Rebecca," thought Helena.

She tried to fall asleep that night but Helena knew she would never have complete peace. She knew then that she would always be reminded of who she was and what she left behind. It was easier since Robert knew the truth, but he always knew. How generous of him to keep the secret to himself for so many years and wait until she was ready to tell him. He was her best friend.

The next morning at breakfast Robert said, "You know the minute you leave this house there would always be a thousand reminders for you, and you have to be prepared. Or else, we can tell our sons, and you can pursue finding your family or find out what happened to them." Helena nodded in agreement. But she wanted her sons to be grown before she told them. She wanted her sons to understand the circumstances of the times and the love she and Robert had for each other.

CHAPTER 13

The year was 1955. Rebecca was sixteen years old. She was beautiful.

Henry has a hard time with their relationship. It was four years since Henry had married Rose. Rose had never made an effort to get close to Rebecca and Rebecca, in turn, had a terrible dislike of Rose. It was almost impossible to have any pleasure at home. The atmosphere was so tense, Henry didn't know what to do.

Rose was a very vengeful person. Henry never told her about his hidden treasures. But she knew they lived a good life and it could not be from his salary.

Alex was studying in Warsaw and received an offer to continue his studies in Russia. It was a great privilege and very few students achieved such an honor. Rebecca was not happy. She would only be able to see Alex once a year during summer vacation. Alex, however, decided he had to take the opportunity to better his life and to better his family's life. He had a younger brother and his parents were having a hard time financially. Alex knew the offer to finish his last two years of college in Russia was his ticket to success. He would know the Russian language perfectly and a good job would be waiting for him. In the summer he would be at camp with Rebecca. In September he would leave for Russia.

Henry heard Rebecca crying some nights, but she did not confide in him. He finally decided to approach her like a grown up. He explained he could not change the situation at home just yet. He asked her to be patient and things would get better.

For a while, Rebecca tried her best to be understanding. She would tell herself, "Only until summer and you'll go to summer camp with Alex and all would be good."

Henry could see Rebecca was making more of an effort to be tolerant. But the more she tried, the more insensitive Rose became. Henry could not understand why Rose behaved this way.

Summer came fast and Rebecca was off for two months of fun and rest. Henry was worried about Rebecca being with Alex. "How responsible would they be?" he questioned himself. Henry visited them every two weeks. He felt it was time to meet Alex's parents.

Henry took the train to visit Rebecca. It was a slow trip. The weather was bad as it had been raining since morning. It was cold and very unpleasant. "Maybe the weather would improve when I get there," Henry hoped. He knew that Alex's parents were on the same train. Rebecca adored them, but Henry was in no hurry to meet them. It was probably a little jealousy on his part. It was hard for Henry to accept that sooner than later Rebecca would have her own life, separate from his.

The rain stopped. It was late afternoon when the train dragged into the small station. Some of the parents got off the train looking for transportation to take them to the camp. A farmer's wagon with benches showed up and they all climbed in it. Everybody sat quietly. Henry closed his eyes and put his hat low on his forehead. The trip to camp was about twenty minutes.

Rebecca jumped up and down with excitement. He ran to her and hugged her tight. She took him by the hand and led him to the camp's dining room where all the counselors and visitors gathered for dinner. Henry saw Alex with his parents and brother. He nodded and they nodded back. Rebecca was chattering and telling him all that was happening in camp. She also told him that Alex, his parents, she and he would get together.

Alex's parents were very nice people; polite and sincere, but not too sophisticated. They really didn't have much to say to each other. Henry was surprised as to why Rebecca was so much in love with them. He would have to ask her.

Henry was glad that Alex was going to Russia for two years. Their relationship was too serious for the both of them. They were too young. Henry wanted to see Rebecca as a free teenage girl for a change; not entangled in a serious relationship.

At home there was a much quieter coexistence when Rebecca was away. Rose was much more polite and pleasant. They did not fight and spent more time together. Henry knew that as soon as Rebecca would be back, everything would change. Henry could not understand the great dislike that Rebecca felt toward Rose. Well, he would enjoy the time he had while Rebecca was still in camp.

Henry had a very pleasant surprise. His cousin, who left Poland at the beginning of the war to go to Russia, showed up with some other Jews who left at the same time. They were called The Reparations. The cousin had already settled in a nearby little town called Dzierioniow. He found Henry in the Office of the Lost Relatives. Henry and his cousin met and talked a long time. His wife and children survived the war as well and all came back together. He was arrested in Russia as a spy and was sent for hard labor in the mines of Siberia for many years. He was not well and was in need of help. Of course Henry would help get them settled and as soon as Rebecca returned from camp they would go visit them.

The stories Henry heard from his cousin were incredible. They all went through hell. Henry was glad they were back in Poland. He just hoped that life for the younger generation would be better and safer.

At the museum things were going well except for Mr. Blum. Recently, he was ailing. He looked pale and had no energy. Henry worried about him. The doctors did not really know what was wrong with him. Maybe a good rest would help. Mr. Blum was going to a sanatorium in the mountains. Henry would take his place for a while. This meant he would be very busy. Henry would do anything to save Mr. Blum's job. He did not want any major changes.

The day came for Rebecca to return home. Henry missed her. She was about to start her last year of high school. Rebecca had to do well in school to be able to get admitted to a good university. She was tending towards medicine, or rather medical science or research. Her studies in this field would have to take place in Warsaw.

"She has arrived!" Henry was excited. He told her about his cousins. She was so surprised and glad. The next weekend they would go for a visit. Good that Rose would be busy. Henry and Rebecca would go without her. Maybe that would be a good time for Rebecca to explain why she had such deep love for Alex's parents.

Being at home, they had returned to their routine. Alex was leaving for Russia, which meant Rebecca would be spending more time at home. This meant the old conflict between Rose and Rebecca would flare up again. Henry was so tired of this. It was just impossible for him to grasp the situation. On their way to the cousins' home they spoke a little. Rebecca explained the feelings she had towards Alex's parents.

"They are so genuine, loving, fair and so warm. When I get a hug from Alex's mother it goes through my bones, muscles and nerves. It is like a shot of love that lasts for a while." Henry did understand literally, but not emotionally. Mr. and Mrs. Silber were older parents. They were poor and uneducated. Their apartment had only the essentials. They had a minimal amount of clothes. Their Polish was poor and they spoke with a heavy Jewish accent. Most of the time the Silber's spoke Yiddish. Yet they produced two perfect sons of high intelligence. The sons behaved like elitists and they were the best students at school. Henry's daughter loved the whole family, but Henry was still puzzled. There were many Jewish families, after the war, that were poor, uneducated and spoke poor Polish. Yet they produced a new generation of unbelievable intelligent and capable young people. Henry sees the young people make fun of their parents but it is done with love, respect and caring.

The visit with the cousins was a success. The stories they told about their life in Russia was a shock to Rebecca. On their way back home she asked her father again and again if it was possible that the stories were true, and Henry repeated, "Yes, yes, it is all true." That was probably the first time that Rebecca was disillusioned with the communist regime.

Rebecca was more open about her feelings toward Rose and she told her father, "Rose is cold, calculating and hostile to me. She has many faces and changes them accordingly. It is very difficult for me to be under the same roof with her." Henry decided that something must be done. He must create a situation so that Rose would want a divorce, even if it would cost him a fortune. Henry spoke with Mr. Blum and sought his advice. He also spoke with his friends, the Witkowskis. They had a very close friend who was an attorney. There had to be something he could do without having to suffer from her vindictiveness.

The next day Mr. Blum arrived at the museum very excited. "Henry, I must talk to you in private, I have very good news." Henry said they should go to the coffee shop. They sat at a very small table, ordered coffee and crumb cake. Mr. Blum quietly said that he heard rumors from good sources that Mr. Gomulka, the president of Poland, might let Jews immigrate to Israel. Henry looked up in disbelief. Mr. Blum said he would immigrate in a minute, and Henry felt the same. "But a lot of Jews would not go. They would remain in Poland." It was said that Prime Minister Gomulka had a Jewish wife. Maybe she influenced him. Henry's mind raced. He hoped this news to be true. He already had an idea how to incorporate this possibility with a divorce from Rose.

That night Henry would be busy entertaining an upcoming artist. He was so see the artwork and meet with the artist, and he was already late. After he passed through the gate of his building he found Rebecca at the bottom of the stairs sobbing. He hugged her and asked, "What happened?" Well Rose and Rebecca had a huge fight and Rebecca left the apartment. Henry could not understand how Rose did not run after her and allowed her to be out alone on the staircase. This was intolerable. Henry knew he had to get rid of this woman. He had to do it smartly though. The next day Rebecca begged her father to allow her to move in with the Silber's, even though Alex was not there. Henry agreed. He knew having Rebecca out of the house would make it easier for him to implement his plan.

CHAPTER 14

Within weeks the Jewish community heard the news about the possibility of immigration to Israel, but there was still was no official announcement from the government.

Rebecca was happy at Alex's parents' house. Henry made an agreement with the Silber's. He would send a delivery of food twice a week to ease the burden. He had a talk with Rose and suggested a divorce, explaining it would be purely for the intention of being able to transfer things to Israel as two separate families. They would have to act fast though. Henry would transfer furniture, artifacts and money to her name. He would find another apartment for her and her daughter and he told Rose that as soon as they got to Israel they would get together again. Henry knew this was not actually going to happen.

It was time to visit the Witkowskis in Gdynia. This time he went alone. Henry made an excuse to Rose and Rebecca that it was a business trip.

He had to retrieve the rest of the coins that the Witkowskis held for him. Some of his valuable paintings were still in frames. Henry had to remove them from their frames and pack them in a special way. He would return home when Rose was at work and carefully hide them from her. The Witkowskis questioned his decision to immigrate to Israel just before Rebecca was starting university. All they heard about Israel was that it was a desolate small country, mostly a desert, surrounded by enemies. But Henry knew that from Israel, he could then go anywhere he wanted in the world.

Still no official statement. Rose agreed to the arrangement and Henry got busy looking for an apartment. This was no easy task. With Mr. Blum's help and a substantial bribe, they found an apartment which was not so close to Henry's, which was fine. Zosia, the housekeeper, was so happy with this whole arrangement. All she wanted was to get Rebecca back home. Rose got busy packing and Henry found a good lawyer to speed up the process for divorce. He was promised it would take no longer than two months. It would cost Henry, but he did not care. Rose would take some of the paintings and some antiques. She took Fela's bedroom furniture and their bedroom furniture. Henry knew he would not be able to take the furniture out of the country anyway. He helped her get settled and decorate the new place. It looked pretty good! Henry wanted Rose to be happy so she would not suspect anything. He gave her some jewelry and she loved it.

Finally, Henry was alone. He could not believe how good it felt. He replaced the furniture, took the wall down and made Rebecca's room as it was before. At last the announcement was made by the Polish government that Jewish people would be allowed to immigrate only to Israel. Information about the details would be available soon. Henry could not apply until his divorce finalized.

Henry went to see Rebecca. Mrs. Silber cooked a great dinner. They talked. Alex would be done with his studies at the end of May. Rebecca was to finish high school also at the end of May. The Silber's thought they should not apply to immigrate until Alex returned from Russia. Henry agreed that they were right. They would all wait until the children finished school and received their diplomas.

The Jewish community was in turmoil. Some definitely wanted to leave, but some were afraid to go to Israel. All they knew about Israel was the official news from the Polish press or radio, and some from Free Europe radio. The little information from Free Europe usually came from England and it did not do justice to the young struggling country of Israel.

Henry was decisive. He was definitely immigrating and so were Alex's family upon the graduation of their children.

The divorce was granted and Henry was free. He played the game well and visited Rose from time to time. She was not sure she wanted to go to Israel and Henry would say, "There is no hurry, we would wait for a while." Rebecca was very excited about her father's decision to leave Poland. She promised to receive the best graduating certificate ever! Henry and Mr. Blum decided they would not apply for immigration together. They were afraid the government would hold one of them back. Mr. Blum would apply first. They also asked the new curator, a woman in her early forties who was very talented, intelligent and Polish, to work closely with them to learn everything. Henry got busy locating buyers for his furniture. They were unusual pieces. They were old, exceptionally crafted and had the signature of the Biedermeier brand. He needed buyers who understood the quality and the rarity of this furniture. Henry ordered some light wool suits for the warmer weather in Israel and some custom made shirts. Somebody was selling an English trench coat and Henry bought it.

Henry woke up every morning full of energy and hope. Mr. Blum received a bunch of documents to sign. Henry helped look them over and also got an idea of what he would be receiving in the near future. The spring was coming. It was felt in the air. Rebecca would graduate in two months and Alex sent a letter that he too would graduate in May and return home. He definitely wanted to receive the engineering degree before he left.

From what Henry had been hearing from others, no one had received a refusal to leave Poland. It took about six months from application to departure. Alex would get home a few days before Rebecca's graduation. He received his diploma.

The day came for Rebecca to graduate high school. The Silber's, Zosia and the Witkowskis came from Gdynia. Alex was there too, all proud of himself. Henry did not invite Rose or her daughter. He did not want to spoil it for Rebecca. Henry had tears in his eyes when her name was called. "Rebecca Kopel," and she was presented with her graduation diploma. Henry could not believe that his little girl had just graduated high school. She was now a young woman, no longer a child. He could not help himself. His thoughts went to Liliana and how happy she would have been that day.

The Witkowskis stayed a few more days and they all had a good time. When they left, Henry applied for their passports and permission to leave for Israel. Thank god all were in agreement. Henry made copies of Alex's degree and Rebecca's diploma and had them notarized so the originals could be hidden. Henry had heard that these kinds of documents were taken from the Jews on the train when they were crossing borders. Henry would give the officials the copies and say that he had to send the originals directly to Israel in order to pursue a job. Henry was determined not to let the Polish government take away something that Rebecca and Alex earned. After the applied everyone went to celebrate at the best restaurant in Wroclaw. Starting that moment, all they could do was wait.

Mr. Blum was leaving the next week. His ailing wife was full of hope that she would find help in Israel. They ordered two big wooden containers which held all their possessions and had them sent to Israel two days before they left. Mr. Blum waited in line for days to purchase suitcases to pack for his departure. Henry also bought some leather suitcases. He would order the shipping containers later, when he gets the permits to leave. Henry was still in disbelief. His furniture was already sold but he would hold on to them until the last day before he leaves.

Rebecca and Alex went to Gdynia to stay with the Witkowskis for a while. Henry assisted the Silber's with getting everything together. They were so helpless. Henry could not sleep at night. He was thinking of what to do first. He knew the government of Israel would provide housing but it would be in developing towns. This was not for him. He would rather rent a small apartment in Tel Aviv and see how things would follow. He needed a safe place for his valuables, most likely a bank vault. He would have to obtain an Israeli passport that would allow him to travel to Switzerland to the bank that currently held his wealth. He had to change the will that the bank currently had and change his address. Henry had to make sure that he got a tutor to teach Rebecca Hebrew as soon as possible so that she could enroll in the university.

He also wanted to help Alex as much as possible. Henry thought that Rebecca would most likely end up marrying Alex. It was obvious they loved each other and were so good together. They finished each other's sentences, liked the same things and always said "we". Henry thought, "Well, Alex is not a bad catch. He's very intelligent, he's well educated and ambitious. He is okay." Henry would help them build a life.

In the meantime, Henry continued teaching the young woman to grasp the management of the museum. She was very capable. She would do well. Henry never thought he would ever work at a museum or have an elegant apartment like he had then, but he did not mind. Something was chasing him out of Poland. At 54, no longer a young man, he needed to build a new future for his daughter and him. He felt happy and unhappy at the same time.

Finally permission and all the documents came. The Silber's received theirs at the same time. The two families had two months to leave. Henry ordered three containers for himself and one for the Silber's. Zosia walked around the apartment crying all the time. Henry promised her that she would never have to work again. He would provide for her. She knew he was always very generous. "It's not the money," she thought. She genuinely loved them. Henry and Rebecca were her life for the past twelve years and now she would never see them again. This was very hard for her to accept. Every time she had the chance, Rebecca would hug her. She understood her feelings of loss. Rebecca would miss Zosia terribly and never forget her.

Rose still had not applied for her permission to leave Poland, and said to Henry that she wanted to wait for a while. This was good news for Henry! He did not want to deal with her in Israel and he definitely knew he would never remarry her. He pretended that he was sad but gave her the freedom to determine her own future. He had a feeling he would never see her again.

The containers would leave in the following two weeks. Henry received the address of the port that would arrive at. Henry had to devise a secret hiding place within the containers to hold his treasures. He would take a lot of things himself. He would have to bribe a lot of people to assure that everything would get to Israel.

The containers had been shipped and the next week the Silber's, Rebecca and Henry would travel by train to Vienna, and after that, to Napoli. There they would depart on a ship to Haifa, a port city in Israel. The group was on edge, very nervous and a little afraid.

CHAPTER 15

"Goodbye Poland!" A place where Jews lived for a thousand years and, as hard as it was to believe, they were not sad to leave.

The big commotion in the Warsaw train station was unbelievable. Henry finally was able to secure a cabin for all of them. It was a little tight, but they were all together. The train was leaving shortly and they would get to the border that night. Henry was prepared to offer a large bribe as long as they did not touch his suitcases or him. Some people on the train were crying, some were singing, but they all felt the same, hopeful...

The inspection at the border went smoothly and they were on their way to Vienna. The train from Vienna would take them to Napoli. It was a long ride. Being together was very assuring. Henry didn't feel so alone. In Vienna they were not allowed to leave the station and transferred to another train immediately. They left within an hour. The authorities made sure the trains left as soon as possible. Some people escaped to Vienna. On the train to Napoli there were representatives from Israel who were to escort them all the way to Israel.

They arrived in Napoli exhausted. Buses took them to a hotel. It was a decent place. Henry and Rebecca had one room and the Silber's had another. Both rooms had private bathrooms and it was great to be able to take a shower. They were fed decent food although it was different compared to what they were used to in Poland. They stayed in Napoli for a few days and took advantage of this stopover and toured the city. Henry observed Rebecca and Alex. They were both wide eyed. All was new to them. It's no wonder. They had never seen anything except communist Poland.

Embarking on the ship to Haifa was chaotic. People purchased things in Italy, silly things like apples and dried salamis, etc. Supposedly, they did not have these in Israel. Henry got a good cabin on the upper lever, but the Silber's were placed down below. Henry made arrangements to have them moved next to him. They were so grateful. The voyage was expected to take a week.

"Now it was time to relax," thought Henry. He took in the sun on the deck, reading and strolling around the ship. Rebecca was busy with Alex the whole time. They had a lot of company. There were young people from all over Poland. They sat on the deck until late at night, singing Polish songs. Henry wondered what they would sing ten years from now. Everybody knew it was not going to be easy to adjust to a new life in Israel, but they all would. It was not the first time that the Jewish people had to build a new life in a new land. But this time they were coming home to the land from which they came.

The Israeli representatives paid a lot of attention to the young passengers. They taught them the Israeli songs they would sing upon their entry to Haifa. There were three days left until they get to their destination. One of the representatives, older than others, approached Henry while he was resting on the deck. He politely asked if Henry spoke Yiddish. "Yes, of course," answered Henry. He asked Henry why he remained alone while others gathered in groups, trying to guess what their future would be. "Well," answered Henry, "the key word is guessing. I would rather wait until I get there." They continued to talk about many things and decided to meet after dinner.

His name was Moshe. He was fifty two years old and was born in Israel. Henry was surprised. He never knew that some Jewish people never left Israel and lived there since the beginning. Moshe learned Yiddish from Jews who came to Israel from Europe before the Second World War. The Yiddish language existed for about four hundred and fifty years, since the beginning of the Hasidic movement. It was very similar to the German language, but written in Hebrew letters. It became the language for Jews all over Europe. The Jews from Arabic countries did not speak Yiddish.

Moshe met Henry in the evening. He wanted to know how Henry survived the war. Henry showed him the numbers on his arm and told him, in detail, his life story. Moshe told Henry how to contact him in Israel and promised to help him as much as he could. Henry told Moshe he didn't need financial help, only informational help. He wanted to get to Tel Aviv and get rooms in a small hotel where they would stay for two months. Henry wanted to find out how to get tutors for his daughter to learn Hebrew as soon as possible so she could attend University. He also asked if it would be possible to place the Silber's somewhere close to Tel Aviv so that he would be able to help them. All this was promised. Henry thanked Moshe by giving him an antique; a small silver menorah. Moshe loved it.

The next day Moshe brought Henry a list of information and said, "Everything is being prepared for the Silber's. They would go to Bat-Yam, a small town next to Tel Aviv, where the government has built a temporary settlement for the newcomers." Moshe promised they would be happy and gave Henry a document for them. Henry asked Moshe if they could get together from time to time. They shook hands in agreement. The following day was very busy for everybody. They were packing up their belongings and were very agitated. It would be a new life for everyone.

The ship arrived in Haifa in the late afternoon and it was decided they would leave the ship in the morning. Henry stood on the deck with his arm around his daughter's shoulder. Rebecca was crying, "Look father, how beautiful, we would be happy here." Henry had a lump in his throat which he could not get rid of. The men working at the port were loud, speaking Hebrew, which Henry understood a little from his studies as a child. The city was all in lights. It was almost like a dream. He could not believe he was in Israel. He was happy. The next morning he told the Silber's where they were going and where he was going. He asked them to keep Rebecca with them for a few days and then he would look them up. Of course they agreed. But Rebecca was uneasy. She did not want to leave her father alone. He promised he would be okay.

The number which was assigned to the Silber's was announced and they were off to the bus that would take them to their destination in Bat-Yam. Moshe told Henry that he called a taxi to take him to the hotel in Tel Aviv. He wanted to give some Israeli money to Henry, but Henry said he had American dollars to pay for the cab. As they parted, Moshe was smiling and said, "Do not worry. Almost everyone in Tel Aviv speaks Yiddish. You would be fine."

The drive to Tel Aviv took a little bit more than an hour and on his way, Henry saw smiling people, farms of fruit, everything was so green. The sun was shining much stronger than he ever saw in Poland. There was happiness in Henry's heart. He was thrilled to be in Israel.

Henry entered the city. There were lots of cars, restaurants and stores. People in a hurry about their business were everywhere, like any other big city, and yet different. The buildings were light in color. People were friendly to each other. Construction was everywhere. It was quite warm, but Henry never saw a sky more blue with no trace of a cloud.

The hotel where they arrived was right in the middle of town. It was not a big hotel, but was very clean and friendly. His luggage was taken to his rooms. It was more like a little apartment. It had a living room with a sleeper sofa, table and chairs in a small kitchen and a bedroom with a bath. It was pleasantly furnished with modern décor and it had a large balcony. Henry loved it. The owners of the hotel were from Hungary and spoke a fluent Yiddish. Henry paid for a week in advance and said he would stay for a while. He was able to eat in the hotel's small restaurant.

Henry unpacked his clothes and tried to find a secure hiding place for his treasures. Henry was tired but could not lay down to rest. He ate dinner and walked out to see a little bit of the city. He took the hotel's card, just in case he got lost. Already it was evening and the coffee shops were full of people. He went towards the ocean and took off his shoes to feel the almost white, soft sand. He walked up and down, but not too far. He saw a pinkish, art deco building. It had a sign, "Opera." How wonderful, right on the shore. He returned to the hotel since the next day he had to find a bank to deposit his valuables. He also needed to exchange his dollars for local currency and to secure a large safety deposit box. First thing in the morning, Henry would ask the hotel owner to direct him to a bank. Henry's apartment was on the second floor. The windows were open and there was a breeze. The bedding smelled fresh and Henry fell into a deep sleep on his first night. He dreamed of Liliana and almost felt her presence next to him. He awoke rested, refreshed and ready to go.

He was directed to the largest bank in Tel Aviv, not too far from the hotel. He went to interview the bank and hoped it would suit his needs. He entered a busy, modern facility and hoped to find someone who could speak Yiddish. They directed him to one of the managers. Henry discussed his needs and he was accommodated. He would return later in the day to finalize his business. The hotel clerk called for a taxi, and Henry took his suitcase to the bank. Henry secured a safety deposit box, opened an account to be kept in American dollars, and took some pocket money in Israeli currency. When he left the bank, he felt so much better.

That evening, just before Henry went to bed, the telephone rang. He was surprised, "Who could be calling me?" It was Moshe. Henry was happy to hear his voice. Moshe gave Henry some information about a Kibbutz that had an intensive Hebrew course, the best in Israel. Moshe could arrange to enroll Rebecca, Alex and his brother. They all could start the following week and Moshe could arrange transportation for them. It was a forty five minute trip from Tel Aviv. Henry would be able to visit there often. Henry would go to Bat-Yam the next day to see the Silber's and see how they were all doing .He would propose the courses in the Kibbutz called Ulpian. To master the language fully, the course would take one year. It was very intensive and they have to do well, but Henry was sure they would.

It took twenty minutes to get to Bat-Yam. The settlement was close to the beach and they were building new, little houses everywhere. They called them barracks. Henry found the Silber's' place and they were happy to see him. The house was small and sparsely furnished. Actually it just had beds, a table and some chairs. Henry asked, "Where are the kids?" Of course, they were at the beach. In the evening they all sat down for dinner, a poor dinner, but they were happy. Henry told them about the Hebrew courses in the Kibbutz. Alex immediately agreed and Rebecca followed suit. This was good, it would be easier on the Silber's too. Henry would stay for the night. The next day he would go food shopping for at least a week's supply for the Silber's. Alex slept on the floor and gave Henry his bed. They all became Henry's family now. They were decent people and Henry felt good to help them. Mrs. Silber tried to save money for Henry, and purchased as little as possible. It was very sweet of her. Henry returned to his hotel that evening.

Henry wandered around Tel Aviv for days and found a brand new neighborhood under construction. It was called Cafon, which meant North Tel Aviv. It had wide streets, beautiful houses with surrounding gardens and was, supposedly, the most expensive address in Tel Aviv. Dizengeft Street was close to this new neighborhood and offered everything that any European capital city had. Good restaurants, beautiful stores with items from all over the world. There was nothing to be missed here. Henry liked what he saw. He was not expecting to see such a place.

Henry decided he would take the kids to the Kibbutz so he could see exactly where they would be. He also wanted to visit a Kibbutz. He knew the theory of their existence. A Kibbutz was a collective small village where everything belonged to everybody. Usually it was a big farm. They grew apples, oranges, grapes, olives and flowers. They raised cattle and chickens and they also had a big egg production. People that belonged to the Kibbutz had small, comfortable houses, but all ate together in a large dining room. All the members of the kibbutz had kitchen duty. When they all left for the Kibbutz, they packed some clothes and personal items, said their goodbyes and the Silber's cried. Henry promised that he would take them there also, in the near future.

As they traveled in the taxi, Henry watched the kids in the back seat. They were wide eyed, observing everything that they passed. Everywhere green things were growing, buildings were being constructed as this was truly an expanding country. But most amazing to Henry was that all of this was being accomplished by Jews.

They entered the office of the Kibbutz. The woman that received them explained about the school that they would be attending for six hours each day. They would also work three hours each day and would have a lot of homework each evening. They would eat in the dining room and each would have a small single room, but showers were communal. She took them on a tour, showed them the rooms and introduced them to other students. Henry was satisfied with what he saw. They all ate dinner in the dining room. A lot of good, fresh food was served, people were smiling and friendly, they all looked happy and worry free. Henry was very sorry he was not eighteen!

On the return trip to Tel Aviv, Henry dozed off and was soon back to the city. The next day Henry sourced a few addresses of antique shops in Tel Aviv and also in Haifa, Jerusalem and Jaffa. Henry was determined to visit all of them. The first shop he stopped at was a small place in the town of Jaffa, right on the shore of the ocean. There was a small Arabic population in Jaffa. They dressed in their traditional garb which surprised Henry. Inside the store it was very dark and Henry had to adjust his eyes. He was greeted by an old man who said, "Shalom, what can I do for you?" Henry asked if he spoke Yiddish, and he did. Henry took a quick look through the shop and saw a few good pieces, but most of it was junk. Henry knew that this was not the shop to display his pieces. They talked further and the owner advised Henry that valuable pieces are never put on display. "They are offered to buyers by private showings," the man said. Henry promised he would come back.

That next shop was right in the heart of Tel Aviv on an elegant street called Allenby. It was a large gallery and Henry saw a lot of American tourists shopping there. Their clothing looked funny to Henry. They wore checkered shorts, a strong colored shirt and a camera hung from their neck. The women wore very colorful dresses and they all carried a huge tote. Henry looked through the store. There were some good paintings and original statues. Henry waited for the tourist to leave to speak to the owner. He knew he would have no problem selling off some of his treasures. The owner was very interested in acquiring some of Henry's antiques.

Henry was also surprised at the current price of gold. It was so much higher than he expected. It had been a good day for Henry. At dinner he sat with a Polish paper which was published daily in Tel Aviv. It was printed for the newcomers from Poland. The newspaper was interesting. It offered some politics and information on Aliyah, which is what they called immigration to Israel from all over the world. There was some advertising as well, but what peaked Henry's interest was the real estate ads. It got him thinking that maybe he should buy a nice place.

While Henry was waiting for the containers to arrive, he thought Tel Aviv would be the best place for Rebecca to start her university studies. So it looked like he would be staying there for a while. The decision to stay made Henry happy. He really liked everything he had seen so far. However he was disappointed he had not established any friends yet.

The majority of newcomers, like the Silber's, settled together in a place called Mabara. They were all similar financially and emotionally. They were waiting for permanent housing promised to them by the government and were all trying to find a job and start a new life. They gathered in the evenings in front of their little houses and shared their experiences and established friendships. Henry had not had this experience and realized he had to have a permanent address and get to know some people.

Henry contacted Moshe to meet up some evening to get some advice. Moshe was glad to come. They greeted each other like old friends. They engaged in small talk for a while. Henry thanked Moshe for arranging the placement for the kids at the Kibbutz. He told Moshe that he needed to speed up the citizenship process in order to purchase an apartment, but he was unsure whether he should buy an apartment just yet. He needed Moshe's advice.

Moshe said, "If you could afford it, an apartment is the best investment. I would help you to speed up the citizenship process." They continued to talk all evening long about everything. There was a natural camaraderie between them. They agreed they would meet weekly for good dinner and conversation.

Henry knew that he could easily afford to purchase an apartment. And he would feel good being in his own place. He would decorate it to his finer taste and Rebecca would have a home. He felt then that he did not want to live in any other country. So he decided he would search for a permanent residence and remain right there in sunny Tel Aviv. He contacted a real estate agent and had appointments throughout the following day. Henry selected the neighborhood he liked the most. It was North Tel Aviv. He liked its proximity to the beach and to the most beautiful street, Dizengeft. There, the neighborhoods were all new, had large apartments and were very elegant. They were not cheap, but affordable for Henry.

Henry selected a building that was eighty percent pre-sold. It was to be completed in approximately two months. The apartment had two bedrooms, two and a half baths, a large living room with a library nook, a modern kitchen and two balconies. It was a short walk to the beach and was on a very quiet street. Henry was already visualizing how he would decorate the rooms. He was happy. He thought he must write to Rebecca to let her know that she had a home once again!

CHAPTER 16

Henry needed to sell some of his possessions to raise the money for the purchase of his new apartment. He would start the next day. He stopped at some of the shops to look at furniture. He felt renewed and just had a brilliant idea. He would make his apartment a true showcase. All those who had purchased apartments were wealthy. They were Jews from Europe, United States and Canada. By decorating his apartment as a showcase, he would show it to those wealthy Jews and they would employ him to decorate their apartments. For a fee, he could advise them on their purchases of antiques and rugs. He had to go to the best stores to see what was in fashion. He felt he then had a purpose. He had to master Hebrew, and more importantly, English. He would soon be reaching fifty-five years of age and it was too early to retire.

For the next few years Rebecca would be very busy with school. Henry had no other family and no activities. But he did like dealing in antiques, coins and decorating. So he would set himself up to do just that. He found a night school to learn Hebrew and English. The school was just a few blocks away from his new apartment and the classes started just a few days after the closing of his new apartment. He also got information on the arrival of his containers. They were to arrive in the following two weeks, which would be just after he was to take possession of his new apartment. He kept busy selling some of the small items he carried with him from Poland. He thought selling those items would be much harder than it was. He met with the attorney that represented him for the closing of his apartment. Henry was ready start school.

Henry wrote to Rebecca and informed her that he was going to school and that he had made a decision regarding his future. He gave her all the small details of how he would accomplish his plans. Rebecca answered his letters promptly and gave him a good picture of what she was doing. The work was hard, but her studies were going well and she was having a lot of fun. Right now they were harvesting grapes. She told him she was suntanned and she thought she grew a little. She also said that Alex was happy as well and that they were in a "very good time and place together."

Henry was meeting Moshe for their weekly dinner together. Henry asked him for to recommend a moving company. Soon Henry would have to transfer the containers from Haifa to Tel Aviv. The containers would have to be unpacked before the contents could be taken up into the apartment and some of the things were very delicate. The movers had to be from a truly competent company. Moshe answered, "I have the right people to do this. The owner of the company is my friend. On special jobs, he would come along with his crew. His name is Joseph and I would contact him for you." Moshe also gave Henry the telephone number so that he could reach Joseph when he had the dates for the pickup.

School was easy for Henry. He remembered some Hebrew from his childhood. He had some problems with English, but he was overcoming it. He was totally busy and full of hope, but he still remained lonely. He missed the Witkowskis, he missed Rebecca. He feared that this loneliness would remain with him forever.

The real estate closing went smoothly. Henry paid for the apartment in cash and received the keys. He went to the apartment immediately and his hand was trembling as he unlocked the door. This was his home in his new country! The apartment was impressive and ready for occupancy. Mattresses were delivered but the bed frame was still on the container. His sleep was uneasy that night. The big, empty apartment felt like a cloud in the sky floating to nowhere.

Henry sat on the stone bench built on his balcony waiting for the trucks to arrive with his containers. He felt excited to finally see his belongings. He worried about whether they would all arrive undamaged and whether anything would be missing. Finally, he heard the roar of the trucks. It was late morning, and they had the whole day to unpack. A husky man in his late thirties jumped from the driver's side of the truck and looked to see if anyone was waiting to meet him. Henry rushed downstairs. As he came closer to the driver, the driver stopped in his tracks. He looked like he had just seen a ghost! Without any recognition, Henry asked, "Are you Joseph the mover?"

Joseph merely nodded, but could not utter a response. The whole crew was looking at Joseph with surprise. Finally Joseph found his voice and asked, "Is that you Henry, Henry Kopel, husband of Liliana? Is it you?" Henry looked puzzled. He did not recognize the man in front of him. "It is me, Joseph. I was the apprentice to your wife's father! Remember?" Henry almost lost his balance and ran to Joseph to embrace him. They both cried, looked at each other, and hugged again.

The men all around them watched in silence. They all knew of such meetings. It was a common sight. But each time it happened, it was a very emotional moment. Finally, after embracing, they proceeded to take care of the unloading. Joseph and Henry speak afterwards. Joseph did not ask about Liliana or Rebecca.

All the belongings were there. Nothing was lost or destroyed and the hiding places were still intact. Henry was relieved. Now he could not wait to sit and talk with Joseph. Once the truck and the workers left, Joseph suggested they go to a quiet little restaurant to have a bite and to talk. They found a rear table apart from other tables. Joseph ordered Israeli dishes and started to tell Henry, in short, his story.

Joseph survived the concentration camp, and in 1948 he left Poland for Israel and had a wife and three children. He owned a trucking business. Joseph's whole family was lost in the war, just like the majority of survivors. Joseph did not know how to begin to tell Henry of what he knew of Liliana, but it had to be said.

"Well," he said, "you probably do not know that I was in the concentration camp together with Liliana." Henry's fork fell on the floor and he turned as white as his napkin. Joseph told Henry about the selection and how Liliana was placed to the side with other attractive young women. "You know what that meant." Joseph continued to tell Henry that he later found out that because of her knowledge, Liliana became the secretary to the second in command of the camp. After a while, he was called to take away the body of a dead woman from Van Klaus's office. "My heart stopped," said Joseph. He and some other men went with the gurney to take the body to be burned. But Joseph moved the sheet from over the face of the woman and saw that it was not Liliana. "The tag on the woman's toe said Helena. I did not recognize the last name. Liliana disappeared from the camp the same time that the second in command disappeared who was seen again at the camp."

Henry felt as if he was glued to the chair, unable to talk. He did know that "Helena Michalowski" was registered as deceased in the camp. "So Joseph," asked Henry, "What do you think happened to her?"

They both decided they would meet with Moshe the next evening. If anyone knew what to do, it would be Moshe. They parted and Henry returned to his new apartment. It was supposed to be a happy moment, but Henry went to his balcony, cried and asked again and again, "Where are you, Liliana? What has happened to you?"

All thoughts crossed his mind. "Maybe she was lingering in a hospital or an institution somewhere, sick and unable to help herself." Henry tasted bitter bile in his mouth. "God help me to find her," he prayed.

Moshe, Joseph and Henry met the next day. Joseph re-explained everything to Moshe who took notes. He wrote the name that Liliana assumed, dates, etc. Moshe said that his search would take time. He asked for some photos of Liliana, if available. He wanted to make sure they would find the right person.

Henry sat wringing his hands. His first thought was that she could not be alive. "Otherwise she would have come back for her baby," he reasoned. But then Henry started rationalizing that Liliana had a good chance of surviving the war. "But she would have returned to the Witkowskis. She knew they had her daughter." He decided not to tell Rebecca any of this news until he had more information. All of this research would take months. Henry advised Moshe that he would pay all expenses for a private investigator. Moshe promised to do his best. He also asked Henry to provide an item that only Liliana would recognize. He gave Moshe the ring that he had given to Liliana upon the birth of Rebecca. He also gave Moshe a photo of Rebecca as a baby.

Henry was in total conflict. He could not believe she was alive. "Why wouldn't she try to find us?"

CHAPTER 17

The year was 1959. Maximilian was fourteen. He just entered high school. Albert was eleven. The boys are growing so fast. Life was flowing smoothly. Helena got another letter from Mrs. Stoval telling her some details of her life in Israel, about her son and grandchildren. She was happy. "I must answer the letter," thought Helena.

Robert was busy with his business. Helena was missing something. She was uneasy and bored. She felt she must find something meaningful with her life. She still thought about putting together the book about the life of the soldiers. The notes she took so long ago were still haunting her. She would talk to Robert about it. Her sons were very close to their father. She knew she was loved, but she longed for the closeness they had with Robert. Something was missing. Helena thought that it must be her, not able to achieve the relationship with her children the way she wanted.

Robert thought that the book should be written in an anonymous name. Helena did not mind. She knew it did not matter as long as the stories would be told. She got busy typing and editing the notes she took so long ago. By doing so, she remembered the people she had interviewed. Helena wondered if and how their lives progressed. So many tragic stories, she felt sorry for them. But then she thought about her own story. Wasn't it tragic? Who was feeling sorry for her? She knew that she would never have peace of mind until she found out what happened to her family and specifically, Rebecca.

It was not too hard to put the book together. She was almost done and it was time to look for a publishing company. For this, she needed Robert to help her. She did not know how to start looking for one. Robert promised to help her. The boys were excited about the book, but did not understand why it had to be under a strange name. Neither did Helena. Robert made several appointments with publishers; one in Berlin and one in Colon. They planned a trip a trip to Berlin first, and they were to take the boys with them. It would have to be the week between Christmas and New Year's since that was when the boys were off from school. They would fly so that they would have more time to explore the cities.

Helena prepared two copies of her book. She spoke with the editors and they seemed interested. Within two weeks Helena received an offer from a big publishing house. They did not like the insistence for anonymity, but Robert was very stubborn about this, and so it stayed.

Berlin was an upcoming town with new buildings coming up like mushrooms. Everything was brand new. Berlin was totally destroyed during the war and now the city was divided by a tall, thick wall. Robert did not like this wall at all. After they completed their business with the publisher, they decided to leave immediately for Colon.

It was a totally different feeling in Colon, what with the old cathedral and warm atmosphere and with Christmas decorations on the streets. One could really feel the holidays. The stores were filled with sweets and other holiday goodies. People were shopping for gifts. The boys had a good time. They saw a play and a concert and the time went by very fast. They were on their way home.

Helena loved returning home. There was not a better place anywhere in the world. She was waiting, with anticipation, to see her book printed, but that would take a few months. She had to be patient. The editors would call her with changes if any had to be made.

Helena thought of signing up for some classes, but she was not sure for what. She decided to take history classes two days a week for three hours. She got her material, books, etc. As she skimmed through the books, she was happy she chose history. It was the history of the nineteenth and twentieth century. Attending classes was strange for Helena. There were very few people her age. It was almost all young kids. She did not see a true interest in history on those young faces. Helena felt they were just there to get the college credits. She loved the lectures and sometimes there were guest speakers from other countries. It was very interesting to her.

Robert started to take interest in the universities around Germany for Maximilian. He did not want him to go abroad. Maximilian did ask to go to France or England, but Robert knew the wounds of war did not heal yet, and the Germans were not exactly loved in other parts of the world. But his son did not understand this. He was innocent about the war, almost as much as Helena was. However she did not know much because she chose not to know and Robert let that be. "What good would it do me to know all the truths," Helena thought.

Slowly, Robert was preparing his boys for the family business. They helped him as much as they could. He consulted with them about decision making. He wanted them to get familiarized with the business that one day they would run. Albert was showing a lot of interest in the business and Maximilian was leaning more towards law. That's a nice combination, thought Robert. He was very close with his boys, he took interest in their studies, in their private life and in their friends. They did ask him for his opinions. He had a good time with them. They were truly well raised, smart young men.

Finally, the book was released, with mostly great reviews. But some did complain that old wounds should not be disturbed. There was a lot of speculation about who authored the book. Helena had to admit that Robert was right when he insisted on the anonymity. Helena was very proud of herself. She spoke to the publishers, hoping that the book would be translated to many different languages. But she got no reply. No one wanted to know about the suffering of the German soldiers. The book was doing very well and royalties were pouring in. Robert opened a separate account for Helena. For the first time in her life, she owned something for herself. It made her feel good. Her classes were coming to the end. There would be a surprise lecturer for two days and after the summer she would sign up for more classes.

The surprise lecture was all about the history of the concentration camps. How it was decided to create them, the plans to eliminate all the Jews, the creation of a master race and eventually, the loss of the war. Helena wanted to leave those classes, but she knew she had to stay and learn. The professor warned the class it would be difficult to watch the documentaries and anyone who wanted to leave could do so. Helena could not stop crying. "How could this be? Was this how her family perished, with the other six million Jews?" she questioned herself.

Helena came home in a terrible state. She told Robert what she saw and asked him if it was true. Robert nodded yes, yes it was. Helena did not want to return the second day for the lecture, but Robert insisted that she must know what happened to her people. She owed it to them. She cannot remain blindfolded for the rest of her life. Helena went back the next day and it was torture for her. Only then she understood what Robert had done for her and how different he was from most Germans. Everything changed for Helena. She looked at everyone with suspicion. She understood why her book was not welcomed abroad. Helena questioned how many innocent people were killed.

She could not find peace. She could not sleep without nightmares. Her boys wanted to know what changed her. Finally, Robert explained to the boys about the lectures and that Helena knew very little about the truth of the war. He told them of how the lectures took a toll on her. "It would pass," Robert told his sons, "but it would take some time."

Helena became quite withdrawn. She sat in the quiet of the garden and was not interested in anything. She knew she was sick and hoped it was not a deep depression. All she needed, right then, was to be alone.

One evening while Robert was sitting on the veranda with Helena, he needed to talk to her. Some strange things were happening. Some people were asking about them in town. Robert felt he was being followed. That day somebody was trying to take his photograph in the super market. Robert was puzzled. "Are they looking for Helena, and who might it be?" he pondered anxiously. Helena said that she also sensed that she was being followed, but thought it was all in her head after her ordeal at the university. So they discussed what should they do. Let it be or hire a private investigator? They had to think hard. The boys were warned not to speak with any strangers and stay at home. The household was secure. It was all fenced in with a gate that was always closed. Robert knew, in his heart, that someone was looking for Helena. He just hoped that they were not looking for vengeance. Robert and Helena decided they would hire an investigator, but he was not told about Helena's past. They just told him that someone was following them and taking photos. Helena did not leave the household. Robert did. And suddenly, it stopped. But Robert knew that it was not the end, but rather only the beginning. They would face whatever would come. They did not have a choice. He was worried about Helena. She was so fragile now and so depressed. Whatever was to come, Robert hoped it would not be too soon. Time was the best healer of all.

CHAPTER 18

Henry was leaving for Rebecca's graduation from the Hebrew courses. He was picking up Alex's parents. Henry's feeling toward them had grown stronger. He almost had a good time with them. They were uncomplicated people and they loved his daughter. Rebecca was starting her university studies in the next two months and Alex would go to earn his master's degree. They both would go to Jerusalem. It was all very pleasant. The kids were packed and ready to come home. Some of the other kids liked life on the kibbutz and signed up to stay. All of them would have to go through the military system, men and women. Alex and Rebecca were spared for now until they finished their studies. Rebecca came home with Henry and Alex went home with his parents. Rebecca loved what Henry did with his apartment. She kept saying it looked like a grand European place.

Henry developed a small clientele. He decorated and sold items to a large part of his clients. They were mostly from the United States and they bought luxury apartments all over Israel.

Henry prepared all the foods that Rebecca loved for their first dinner at home. They sat on the balcony and sipped tea. Rebecca said she had something important to tell him. He kind of knew what she wanted to tell him.

"Father," she said. "Alex and I are thinking of getting married. There is no point in prolonging the inevitable." Henry said yes. In fact, he was happy. He offered them whatever help they may need. All they needed was to pick a date and finalize some details. The kids did not want anything special, just a few friends and a simple ceremony.

Rebecca wore a simple off-white short dress. Alex wore a brand new suit. Henry took them shopping for clothes. He rented an apartment for them near the university in Jerusalem. He set them up comfortably. All they had to do was study and enjoy their young lives.

Henry knew that in the next few months there would be some turmoil in his life. The kids were set up for at least the next three years, and he would deal with whatever would come his way. Henry prepared himself emotionally. All those sleepless nights, when he imagined all kinds of scenarios, would eventually help him to cope. Henry almost wished that she, Liliana, was not alive.

Finally, a call came from Moshe. "We have to meet," he said. "Would you like Joseph to be present?" The three had been meeting regularly.

Henry replied, "Yes, let all of us meet." They got together at Henry's apartment. His housekeeper prepared dinner for them and left them alone. They drank their tea on the balcony.

Moshe brought a folder filled with documents and said, "Okay, Henry, are you man enough to take what I have to report? It won't be easy, I promise you." Moshe started to explain that the search was done by professionals and there were no mistakes in the information. He told Henry Liliana was alive and well. She was never sick and not able to return. This was the start, and slowly all was explained to Henry, followed by photos of Liliana, her two sons and Robert.

With shaking hands, Henry took the photos. "Yes, it is Liliana, as beautiful as ever," he said. She looked happy to him. He did not feel when his tears started to flow. He was not angry at that moment, just so terribly sad. For the past fifteen years Henry went through life half dead. He was successful in business and always had a good material life, but the uncertainty of Liliana never let him have peace or happiness. He questioned, "And what should I do now?" Henry knew that he needed an explanation directly from Liliana, no matter how it would disturb her life. She did owe this to him.

Now, what about Rebecca? Should he tell her? The three of them decided that this was not a good time for Rebecca to find out about her mother. She should finish her studies and be happy in her new marriage. After all, it would be a great shock for her to find out that her mother abandoned her. The next few years would mature her for the shock, or maybe she should never find out. Henry agreed with this decision. It made the most sense.

Henry was told about the details of the investigation. It was done very delicately so as not to disturb Liliana's life. The investigators had help from the local rabbi who told them how Helena helped the Jewish woman, Mrs. Stoval. Helena knew way more than any Christian woman would know how to help Mrs. Stoval and the rabbi was suspicious from then on. The rabbi promised not to say or do anything.

Henry kept the folder with all the information, including the rabbi's telephone number, Liliana's address, etc. Henry's friends left the apartment and Henry remained on the balcony all through the night, examining the contents of the folder. He finally went to bed to straighten his bones from sitting for so many hours. He awoke with a huge headache. His housekeeper came in and looked at him with concern. He looked bad.

His decision was made. Henry would do nothing for a while. There was no point to hurry. Obviously Liliana was not held captive and she looked happy in the photos with her husband and two sons. Henry would adjust to this situation and think of the best way to approach Liliana.

A few months passed. Henry visited Rebecca often. She was happy. She liked the school and Jerusalem. Alex and she had a lot of new friends. Henry was glad for her.

Henry did get in touch with the rabbi in Regensburg and spoke to him at length. He found out everything about Robert and his ancestors, about his life and reputation. The rabbi sent him the book that Liliana wrote. He knew that she was the one that wrote it. The sisters in the hospital remembered that she had taken notes from the wounded soldiers. The book was in German and Henry had to give it to someone to translate.

Henry slowly prepared himself to meet Liliana. He would need the help of the rabbi. He decided it would not be a secret meeting. Henry wanted Robert to know about it. After all, they were together for almost twenty years. From what Henry learned, Robert was a decent man. The only thing that was an unknown was if Robert knew who Helena was. But Henry did not care at this point if Liliana or Robert were going to get hurt.

He decided to go to Germany. Henry prepared all that was necessary just in case something happened to him. He told Rebecca he was traveling for business. He handed copies of documents to the Silber's. The originals were being held by his attorney. They also were told that it was a business trip. Henry spoke to the rabbi and it was decided that he would wait to inform Liliana and Robert until after he arrived in Germany. Henry was very anxious about what would happen, but he knew he had to do this.

The taxi drove him to the airport. Henry first arrived in Berlin and then his final destination. The rabbi was to meet him. Henry made a reservation in a small hotel in town. The flight was short and all went according to plan. The rabbi waited for Henry and took him to his house for dinner. The rabbi wanted to know everything about Henry. They arrived at the hotel late in the evening and agreed to meet the next morning. Henry was tired but sleep would not come. How strange that he was now so close to Liliana, but so, so far away.

The next morning they sat in the rabbi's office planning on how to make the first approach. They agreed to do it after dinner hours, when most likely Robert and Helena would be home. But, for now, the rabbi took him for a ride around town and passed by the Van Klaus property. Henry had such mixed feelings. He was angry, sad and hopeful. He said to himself, "Take it easy, and be cool." They ate a small evening meal and the rabbi called the Van Klauses. One ring, two rings, by the third ring Albert picked up the phone. The rabbi asked to speak to Robert.

"Yes, this is Robert Van Klaus." The rabbi introduced himself and told Robert that he had some strange news for him and that this conversation would stay just between the parties involved. The rabbi said that he was just a man of God and that Robert should think of him just as he would a priest. There was silence on Robert's end of the line. "Are you there, Mr. Klaus?"

"Hello, yes, I am here," answered Robert.

The rabbi proceeded to tell Robert about Henry and finally told him that Henry wanted to meet his wife. It could be with him, or her alone, whatever pleased them. Again there was a long silence.

Finally Robert answered, "Could you give me a day or so, so that I can prepare Helena?"

"Of course. Please return my call when you are ready," said the rabbi.

Henry sat and listened perspired and pale. The rabbi gave him a glass of wine and patted his shoulder. "God would choose the right path."

Sarcastically, Henry responded, "Really?"

"Who was it?" asked Helena as she looked at a very pale Robert.

"We would talk in our bedroom after the boys go to sleep."

Helena's heart sank. She just knew her life as she knew it was about to change. Finally, in their room, by themselves, Robert told her of the phone call he received from the rabbi. Helena just sat at the edge of the bed, not speaking. Then she said, "I do not want to see him, I do not want to change anything in my life. Please, Robert, do not make me."

Robert responded that no one would make her do anything she did not want to do. He said he loved her and would be at her side, but she had to go and face Henry and finally find out all she had always wanted to know.

The next day Robert called the rabbi and agreed to meet them in a secluded little bar at the edge of town. Helena felt like she was going to her execution. She wondered how all of this would turn out.

Robert and Helena walked into the bar and Helena looked towards the rear of the bar. She saw Henry. Her heart was beating so fast and she felt as though she was going to faint. But she did not. Instead, she walked up to Henry and the rabbi and said her greetings in Yiddish.

Henry stood up and gave her a hug and asked them to sit down. Henry and Robert shook hands, but said nothing. The first question Liliana asked was about Rebecca and asked if Henry had a photo. Henry had photos from their wedding. She took them with trembling hands and looked at them with disbelief.

"How pretty she is, and so grown up." Liliana asked Henry if their daughter knew about her.

"No," said Henry. A short, strong, "No." Now that Henry was sitting next to Liliana, it did not feel as he imagined. Although there was no doubt about it, is was her, she was almost like a stranger to him. Henry's mind raced, "But how could this be? After all, this is my Liliana."

Liliana matured but was still very beautiful. Her slim, delicate body had not changed at all. Robert was speaking, but Henry did not hear anything. He just looked at Liliana. The rabbi suggested that Henry and Liliana meet alone. It was agreed and they would meet the following day.

Liliana asked if she could keep the photos. "Of course," said Henry. "After all, it is your daughter." He said this with a hint of sarcasm.

The drive home was in total silence. In the privacy of their bedroom, Helena sat close to Robert and showed him the photos and said, "This is my daughter. Isn't she beautiful?"

"She most definitely is," said Robert.

They laid in silence next to each other. Finally, Robert said, "Remember how much I love you and the boys love you!"

Liliana felt complete relief. She now knew Rebecca and Henry were alive and well. Surprisingly, she slept and had no nightmares that night.

The next day Robert drove her to the meeting. As she was leaving the car, Robert assured her, "I would be here the whole time, waiting for you."

Henry was waiting for her. They looked at each other and Helena asked Henry to tell it all. She wanted to hear about the family, about Rebecca. They talked a long time telling each other about their lives. Finally, they agreed to meet yet again the next day.

For Helena, it felt as if she was seeing a long, lost, good friend. But, she did not think that Henry felt the same. She saw how he looked at her. He even touched her hands. Helena planned on asking Henry if she could meet Rebecca.

As soon as they sat at the coffee shop that next day, Helena asked Henry her most important question, "Can I see Rebecca?"

"Well," answered Henry, "I don't think so. It is different for you and me to meet. Rebecca is a strong willed girl, very emotional, and I don't see how she would understand that her mother never returned for her. Rebecca has to finish her studies in peace, and enjoy her new married life." said Henry.

Helena did not understand this and her heart ached. She asked, "Would I ever be able to see her?"

Henry felt the meeting was over. He must return home to gather his feelings. It was becoming too much for him. There were too many feelings closing in on him. Love, hate, disappointment, revenge, and most of all, uncertainty of what the outcome would be.

Henry told Helena he was going back home and that he hoped they would stay in touch. Helena asked if he would like to meet her sons. Henry told her he did not, but that he might some other time. Helena took down all his contact information and noticed that Henry seemed very sad. She thought maybe he expected a different outcome. They said their cold goodbyes, and the next day Henry was on his way home.

Helena's feelings were so mixed. She mourned her deceased family, and the fact that she could not see her daughter. Yet, she still felt relief from her guilt. Robert was very understanding. He did not comment on anything, he just stood by her. But she did notice his uneasiness.

Helena never truly understood just how much she hurt both Robert and Henry. She only looked to relieve her own guilty feelings.

Henry journeyed back home in a daze. He arrived home late in the evening. He put himself at his favorite spot on the balcony and just sat there. He could not gather his thoughts. He could not figure out how he felt, but it was definitely not what he thought. All his emotions were crushing him. Yes, he loved her. Yes, he hated her. Yes, he liked to see her suffer. His father once told him, "The true feelings that people express are the nature of mankind."

Henry's thoughts reeled, "How could Liliana do it? How could she not come back? Did she not care at all? She didn't even try to find us, not knowing if we were dead or alive. I understand that during the war, she couldn't seek us out. But after? Why did she not try?" No matter how hard he tried to understand, Henry could not.

The next morning, the housekeeper found Henry still on the balcony. He never went to bed. She prepared breakfast for him. He took a long shower and made the decision to accept his life the best he could without Liliana. It would never be what it should have been.

Henry reached out to Rebecca. Hearing her voice was the best medicine for him. Henry definitely would not tell Rebecca about her mother. He would keep busy with his business and would visit the kids on the weekends.

That day he met with his two friends, Moshe and Joseph. They couldn't wait to hear the news of what happened in Germany. The trio sat at their favorite little restaurant. Henry started to tell them about his visit to Germany, but in the middle of it all, he burst into tears. He cried like a little boy. His friends hugged him, gave him some vodka and tried to calm him down.

Seeing Rebecca always put Henry in a good mood. She was doing well at the university, and so was Alex. They were both happy and so glad to see him. They went to a concert and to dinner at the King David Hotel, one of the best restaurants in the country.

CHAPTER 19

Time passed fast and soon Rebecca and Alex would be finished with their studies. Henry could not wait. He wanted a grandchild and to see Rebecca settled. One thing they did not have to worry over was money. This was one thing that always came easy to Henry. No matter what he touched, it turned to success. But the old saying was true, "Money does not buy happiness."

Henry still studied Hebrew and English. He was quite good at them both and very proud of himself. He did not buy Polish newspapers any longer. He read the Hebrew newspaper every morning. He also switched to reading books in English, and he became fluent in both languages.

Henry tried to forget Liliana and their meeting. He did not write to her. About six months later a letter came from Liliana. She expressed disappointment that he did not write to her and asked for more photos of Rebecca. Henry was angry. "What is she thinking?" He decided not to answer her letter.

A few more months passed and there was another letter from Liliana. This time she wrote in a little stronger tone. Henry knew he had to answer. He feared she might come to Israel to look for Rebecca.

He wrote back in a *matter of fact* style and said he was busy, Rebecca was fine, he does not have any new photos, but he would take some and send them to her. He did ask if she told her sons about their meeting and if she told them they have a half-sister in Israel. Henry also asked Liliana if she explained to her sons that, according to Jewish laws, they were Jews. He knew she knew what he was talking about. Henry would not accede to a one sided compromise. If she insisted on meeting Rebecca, she would have to involve her sons and the truth about herself.

Henry wondered how she would react to this letter and how she would answer. But he would not dwell on it. He took a *wait and see* approach. He wondered how long it would take to get an answer to his letter. He suspected that it would be quite a while.

Henry had a little relief from his business and thought about taking a vacation. He thought he should visit Switzerland and his bank there. He wanted to take some more of his treasures to the vault and he had to translate some of the Polish documents that were in the vault into English. He would go in the winter because he missed the snow and the crisp cold air. He had a few months to prepare.

Henry also wanted to see the United States, Brazil and Argentina. So he decided he would travel the world, and whenever possible, he would take the kids with him. He especially wanted them to go to Switzerland. Rebecca should know about the bank. The next time he saw the kids, they set a date that was good for all of them. They would have a winter vacation. For some reason Henry could never remember the exact dates.

The trip was planned and they were ready to leave. Rebecca was sitting on the plane in the middle seat between Henry and Alex. She was so excited. All she kept saying was, "I hope it's snowing when we get there."

Upon landing they put on their winter coats and boots, all of which Henry prepared for them. Rebecca's wish came true. It was snowing. It was cold and they were all loving it. They arrived at the hotel just in time for dinner. They enjoyed it and went to their rooms.

In the morning, they went with Henry to do their business at the bank. The bank took Rebecca's photo and fingerprints. Rebecca and Henry provided all the signatures necessary so that one day she could claim the account and the contents of the vault. Henry felt relieved that all of this was behind them. Now they could concentrate on having a good time.

The plan was to ski for three days outside of Zurich, then to see the opera in the city, to shop a little, visit museums and eat in great restaurants. Henry was very happy those ten days of vacation. He had great conversations with Alex. Rebecca, as always, was very loving and caring. The trip could not have been better, but all good things must come to an end, and they were on their way back home. Alex and Rebecca stayed with Henry for a few days and then returned to Jerusalem.

Henry was home alone again. Another letter came from Liliana. She complained about the harsh way Henry answered in his last letter. He decided he would not answer this letter. He would only send photos of Rebecca with no reply. She would know that they traveled because he would send photos from the slopes of Switzerland.

Henry resumed his usual days of work. He liked being busy. It made him think less of reality. He was meeting with his buddies that night. They were going to a movie and dinner. Then they would return to Henry's balcony and talk about everything in their lives. All this was very therapeutic. Henry trusted them and they trusted him. This was so much better than seeing a psychiatrist. They talked about their children, wives, work and everything in between.

Henry had an appointment in Jerusalem with a woman from London. She bought a house in there. She needed to refurbish and decorate it. Henry was recommended to her by another client whose house he decorated in Haifa. He never decorated anything in Jerusalem before and he hoped that the woman's taste was not too modern. He did some research of some very old pieces of furniture and tapestries. This was how he envisioned an old house in Jerusalem. They met in the King David Hotel and sat in the lobby and talked. She was a petite woman, very delicate, well educated. She had recently lost her husband. She had two children. She told him she would like to spend part of the year in Jerusalem. Henry was surprised with his English. It was not bad! She agreed with the vision that Henry had for her house. The next day they visited the property. It was built of the famous Jerusalem stone. Henry prepared some drawings to show to her. Henry liked this woman.

Henry saw the Jerusalem project as a warm, inviting and exciting place. It had a feel of a Moroccan environment. He was excited. He had never done a project like this before. The woman had a love for Jerusalem from her mother who was born in Jerusalem before she married an English man. The clients name was Eva.

Henry and Eva got along splendidly. She gave her approval for Henry's vision of the house and they began to shop. They had a very good time together. Henry told her about his life. She was generous with the tales of her life as well. Henry liked her more than just a client or a friend.

Henry desired her, but was a little timid with his approach. But one thing was different. He did no longer felt guilty about his feelings. Liliana did not impact him anymore. Henry invited Eva to stay with him in his apartment for a few days before her return to England. He thought they could shop a little more in the old town of Jaffa, go to the famous Habima Theater and see My Fair Lady. Eva agreed, and they were on their way to the train station.

In the taxi, on their return to Tel Aviv, Eva rested her head on Henry's shoulder. When they arrived he opened the door to his apartment, she was so surprised. She thought this was the best decorated apartment in Israel and beyond!

Henry gave Eva the guest bedroom. They rested a little, had some refreshments and went out for dinner. They had an amazing time. He even forgot to call Rebecca.

After Henry showered for the night and entered his bedroom, he found Eva in his bed. It had been a long time since Henry had been intimate with a woman. They enjoyed a very satisfying night, more than Henry thought he would ever have.

Eva and Henry stayed together for another two days. They were really a good match. They had the same interests, they liked the same things but, again, all good things come to an end. It was time for Eva to return home. She promised to be back as soon as she could. Eva's son was in the university. He was the same age as Rebecca. She also had a daughter. She was sixteen years old, and Eva had to be home for her. It was a sad goodbye. Henry was very upset to see her go. She promised again to call often. Eva had tears in her eyes, and so did Henry.

Henry returned to his apartment feeling very sorry for himself. Maybe it was good to cool off a little and think rationally. Eva lived in England. She would be coming to

Jerusalem only for a month or two each year. Henry must do her house so great that she would love to stay there and they would be together at least part of the year. For now he had a job to do.

The next morning Henry received a call from Eva. She arrived home and found her family safe and sound. Henry returned to Jerusalem and started his work on her house. He saw Rebecca and Alex for dinner every night. Henry was happy to have the kids so close. He called Eva very often to tell her about his progress. But really, he called to hear her voice.

After two weeks, Henry returned to Tel Aviv to do more shopping. At home, his housekeeper was waiting for him. His apartment smelled of good food and cleanliness. He loved being home. He would call his friends to meet, he had so much to tell them.

It's hard to believe almost three months had passed since Eva left. The house was almost done except for some small details. The look was unbelievable, it was like a place out of a fantasy. Henry could not wait until Eva returned to see it. He took the kids to see it, and they were overwhelmed.

Rebecca walked through the house and asked, "Father, how do you know how to do this, it is fabulous!" Henry smiled happily.

When Henry spoke to Eva, she told him she would be back in about two weeks and planned to stay for a month. Henry could not wait. He lost some weight, got a good, healthy suntan, and tried hard to improve his English.

The time came for Henry to pick Eva up from the airport. Henry paced in the waiting room of the airport, like a young boy. Finally, there she was, petite and pretty as always, wearing a huge black straw hat, oversized sunglasses and a white linen dress. She spotted him and ran toward him. Henry hugged her and gave her a kiss on the cheek. He hired a limo to take them to Jerusalem. It would take them a little over an hour to get to Jerusalem. She told him about her kids and some arrangements she had to make regarding her late husband's estate. She asked if Henry would like to stay with her. "What a silly question," he thought. He was dreaming this would happen. He hugged her again, and said yes.

They arrived at the front door of the house. Eva was hesitant to open the door. "And what if I don't like it?" she asked.

"Then I would redo it," replied Henry. "Open the door," he said.

The house was prepared as if someone had been living there forever. There was a housekeeper waiting for them with dinner prepared. There were flowers everywhere.

As Eva entered and ran through the house she was shouting, "It's unbelievable. It's beautiful. It feels like I am in the Maharaja's home. This is like a dream!"

"Does that mean you like it?" asked Henry.

She just said, "I have the most original and beautiful house in Israel." Henry was pleased.

They had dinner and went out onto the patio to have a drink. Eva asked if she could meet his daughter and her husband. Henry hesitated, and Eva said, "Only as a client," and she smiled.

"We would do it tomorrow," said Henry.

The next day they met Rebecca and Alex for dinner. Everybody was talkative. They had good wine and good food. When Henry took Rebecca and Alex back to their apartment, Rebecca asked, "Where are you staying Father?" Henry thought of how he should answer, and that's when Rebecca said, "You like this lady, right?"

"Yes, I do," answered Henry.

"That's good, I like her too," replied Rebecca.

Henry stayed with Eva in her house for a few days. They had a good time with each other. Every day Eva discovered something new in the house. Together, they went to Tel Aviv for a few days to do some shopping and stay on the beach. Henry took time off from work to spend the time with Eva. She invited him to London, and he promised he would come. Henry was as happy as he ever could remember, and worried that it would not last. But he would enjoy it as long as it was there.

CHAPTER 20

Helena received only a few cold letters from Henry and more photos of Rebecca. The year was 1962. Rebecca was graduating with a master's degree in biology and she wanted to work in research. Her husband also graduated with a master's degree in engineering. Both of them had received a great education.

All Henry wrote about himself was that he was doing very well in business. He still believed it was not a very good time for Helena to meet Rebecca. Helena did not understand. Rebecca was twenty three, not a child anymore. When would be a right time to meet?

Helena believed Henry would never tell Rebecca about her. Maybe that was his revenge. Her sons were also grown. Maximilian was seventeen and Albert was fourteen. Max was starting college in the fall. He decided to attend the school in their home town and take business administration. He also planned to work with his father in the family business. Helena was glad he was not going away. Otherwise, life was very uneventful.

Helena, with the help of a housekeeper, took care of the household. A gardener took care of the outside. Meals were prepared by Helena, she really loved to cook. It was a serene, quiet life.

But something was missing, at least for Helena. She did not know what. They really did not have any close friends, only acquaintances. Helena missed having some kind of a social life, but Robert did not. He was very pleased the way things were. After all, this was how he grew up. His parents also did not have any social life. But it was different for Helena. Her parents' house was always full of people, family, good food and laughter. And in her short time with Henry, they also had friends. Helena wanted to dress up, go to restaurants, a show or concerts, but Robert preferred to stay home. He provided her with tapes of all sorts of concerts, but it was not the same. Robert always said, "Why would you want to go to a restaurant if you have the best right here at home." It was a compliment to her, even if it wasn't appreciated as one.

Slowly, Helena was changing. She did not realize it, but she was no longer afraid. Now she knew her daughter was alive and well. In a letter, she did ask Henry for the address of the Witkowskis, but Henry ignored her request. Helena remembered a passage in the bible, "The truth would set you free." How accurate, but she had not been truthful.

She had two grown sons and they did not know anything true about her. Helena never wanted them to know and she was sure that Robert did not want them to know the truth either. "Well," she thought, "I can never be free, because I cannot tell the whole truth. And at least for now, it would have to stay this way."

Helena was hesitant to admit it, but she was growing bored. There must be something she could do with herself. Robert saw her uneasiness and asked her to help him a little with the office work, although he already had two girls working for him as well as Max.

Helena was sitting on the porch, her favorite place, sipping a cup of coffee, when the housekeeper came to tell her she had a phone call. It was the rabbi. Helena asked, in a cold voice, how she could help him.

"Well, I do not need any help," said the rabbi, "But I believe you do." She listened. He asked if she had any plans to see her daughter. She answered that she was still waiting for her daughter's father to decide when the best time to do it was. The rabbi responded, "You know you can decide on your own to see your daughter, without anyone's permission."

Helena asked, "Why are you interfering in my life?"

He answered, "I am a rabbi and your situation is very unique. You are a young woman, and I would like to see you happy. As long as you are living a lie, you would never be happy. Your daughter needs to know she has a mother. And your sons need to know who they are as well. After all, they are Jewish according to the Jewish laws."

This was too much for Helena. She was shaking, and in a loud voice, she asked the rabbi not to call her anymore and not to worry about her happiness. She hung up.

When Robert returned home that night, he knew that something was not right with Helena. She told him they would talk in their bedroom later. Finally she told him about the phone call from the rabbi. Robert was very upset, and said, "He had no right to do this. I would call him in the morning and make sure that he does not interfere any longer." Robert was very disturbed. How could the rabbi say his sons were Jewish? But most of all, Robert feared that the rabbi would not keep their secret.

The next morning Robert called the rabbi. In a very authoritative voice he told him never to call his wife again, and not to divulge any information to the townspeople. Knowing Helena's true identity, Robert had been supporting the synagogue financially. He reminded the rabbi of those contributions and what would become of the synagogue without them.

The rabbi said, in a quiet voice, "I understand. I would never bother you again. And your secrets are safe with me. I am a man of God."

A few days later, as Helena was passing the little synagogue, she saw a commotion. There was a moving truck. There were some young women shouting at children in Yiddish.

That evening she asked Robert if he knew what was happening in the, but didn't tell her two days ago. She did not question him though.

The next day she drove to the small Jewish cemetery that existed there for hundreds of years. There must have been more Jews buried here than there were living in the town.

She found the fresh grave of the rabbi. From home, she had brought some seashells to put on the grave. She said a prayer in Hebrew, and told the rabbi in Yiddish that one day the truth would be known to all of her children. She swore it. "Rest in peace, my friend," said Helena.

Henry was preparing for his trip to England. He was excited. He always wanted to go to England. His English was not too bad. He definitely could communicate and more. Before he left he wanted to see his kids. They were graduating soon and they said that when he returns, they would tell him something good and no, it was not a baby!

The four hour flight passed quickly and comfortably. He did wonder what he would find in London. "How does Eva live, how are her kids?" Henry pondered. He would not be able to stay in her house because of her young daughter. Eva made a reservation for him at a most elegant hotel. Henry was to meet her kids.

Eva was waiting for him at the airport. They went to the hotel and, in the evening, they would have dinner at her house with her children. Eva unpacked his clothes. He changed, took a shower and was ready.

Her house was more like an estate. The interior was very formal, good pieces of art, rugs and furniture. But something was missing, a warmth and comfort.

Her son and daughter came to the dinner table. They examined him. Henry felt awkward. But they were just children protecting their mother. They said they would see him in Jerusalem and that they were happy to have a home in Israel. Eva took him back to the hotel and whispered in his ear, "I would be with you tomorrow. We would tour the city and I would stay with you in the hotel." Henry was tired, and quickly fell asleep.

The next thing he knew, there was a knock on the door. Henry opened the door. It was Eva, all smiling and happy. "I ordered breakfast for us, it would be here shortly. Go take your shower now," she said.

Henry loved this! He wanted to be ordered by a woman, and not always be the one in charge. He heard the rattling of the dishes. He was hungry and ready for the day.

He had a robe on. They ate breakfast and laughed together. Eva came over to his chair and slowly loosened the belt of his robe, while whispering to him just how much she missed him and couldn't wait to have him.

Well, the whole day in the city turned out to be a half day in the city. They went to a museum and to the section of the city where the antique shops were. Henry held Eva's hand and he felt like a young boy.

In the evening they ate dinner in a typical English pub. The food they did not like, but the beer was good! They returned to the hotel. When Eva left for home they planned to meet again the next day. Henry could not fall asleep remembering every moment of the day. He was wondering if their relationship was leading anywhere. He figured he was most likely going to be a *part timer*. But Henry thought that that wouldn't be such a bad way to live.

The next day, bright and early, Eva returned to the hotel. "Today we would go to Buckingham Palace, a beautiful park and have tea in a special place," so on, and on she went. Henry agreed to everything, as long as he could hold her hand.

Good times always pass fast. It was time for Henry to go back home. Eva promised to come to Israel soon. For Henry, it was a roller coaster ride. "How could a relationship like this survive?" he asked himself worryingly. "Maybe if we were both younger, we could survive. But at my age?" Henry needed stability. He was sad as he boarded the plane.

Back home again and back to business. Thankfully for Henry he was busy and did not have too much time to think about his personal life. Over the weekend, Henry was going to see his kids. There was some news they wanted to discuss with him.

Rebecca hugged him and told him how much she loved him. Something was telling Henry that the news they had for him was not so good. Alex told him that a large, Canadian company had offered him a very well paying, three year contract. They would have to move to Munich. Rebecca would be able to get a job at a large hospital in their research department.

"To Germany!" This was all Henry could hear. God must be playing a joke on him. "And this would be so close to Liliana," he thought. Henry was devastated. He sat there not knowing what to say.

Alex continued to tell him how sad his parents were about their move. His mother said that he would be breaking up the family. But Alex insisted that this would only be for three years and it was an unbelievable opportunity for him.

Finally Henry found his voice. "Although I am not happy about this, and you are all that I have, I also know that I cannot stop you. You would do as you see it fit."

Henry asked about the details. The kids told him they were leaving in a month. Henry was extremely upset. How could all this be happening to him? How could he live so far away from Rebecca? How could he remain all alone in Israel? Henry could not concentrate on anything. Eva was coming soon and he would seek her advice. But what good would it do, the kids would leave anyway. He could not run after them. Who knows where life would take them. Henry did not expect this news at all. He had hoped they would live near him the rest of his life.

Henry helped them pack and put their things in storage. Rebecca kept saying, "It is only for three years. You would come and visit for a lengthy time, or, if you like, you can stay with us the whole time. Alex wouldn't mind at all." They drove, in silence, to Alex's parents' house. The Silber's just received a permanent place to live in the city of Hulon. Mrs. Silber had prepared dinner for all of them. Alex's brother came for the day. He was on leave from the military. He was the only happy one in the group. He was young. What did he know? Henry said that he would not take them to the airport. He just could not do it. He gave them a generous gift, kissed them and wished them all the best as his heart was breaking. Henry openly wept like a child all the way home.

Henry's apartment felt lonely. This was so not fair to him. He felt sorry for himself and felt strongly that he did not deserve this. It was a good thing that Eva moved up her visit to Israel. He thought she was doing it for him. He must have sounded really bad when he told her about his children's departure.

When he met her at the airport they went straight to Jerusalem. Her house would feel like an oasis. All they wanted to do was be with each other, and so they did. They shopped for food each morning, cooked together, sat in the small garden and read books and talked. Henry thought, "If only I could keep Eva here." But she had to go back. The two weeks passed so fast. He knew her home was not in Israel, but in England, with her children and family. Jerusalem was only her vacation place, just a whimsy.

Henry wondered what he was to Eva. He did not want to ask. He was afraid to. Henry told her that he loved her, but Eva did not reciprocate with a response. Henry told himself he must stop looking for a crutch. His destiny was probably to be alone until the end. This was a bad thing for Henry to accept.

It was three months since Rebecca left. Alex was thrilled with his job and so was Rebecca. They made new friends and wanted Henry to visit. They would have some time off the next month and wished that he would come. Henry decided he would go. Henry thought it was a little strange that they would all be so close to Liliana, but he still did not want to tell Rebecca.

The kids looked wonderful. They seemed happy. The company that Alex worked for provided them with a large, comfortable apartment. All the furnishings and household necessities were in place for them. Henry would stay with them in their apartment so they could really be together. Henry was so surprised to see Rebecca cooking and cleaning. Alex helped with all the chores to keep up the household. His daughter was happy and this meant a lot to Henry. They had ten days off from work and this was truly a great vacation for Henry.

They toured in the city, which was clean and orderly. There were great cultural events and the kids were learning a new language. Henry was realizing that it was not such a big tragedy that the kids were living in Munich for a while. What did concern him though, was that they were tasting the flavor of worldliness. This may trigger the taste for more of this kind of life. Henry would not be surprised if this was what would happen to his kids. But he has learned not to think ahead but to just take things day by day.

One thing Henry was grateful for was the freedom he had to do as he pleased. His financial situation was good. He did not have to work. He definitely had enough for himself and his daughter for the rest of their lives. He actually could follow his daughter wherever she chose to live. He did not have any other family. She was his only family. He was hoping for good health and maybe, in the near future, a couple of grandchildren. This visit was an eye opener for Henry. He could live wherever he wanted to or wherever his daughter was. The world was getting smaller. Within a few hours of flight, you could be anywhere.

Just for his curiosity, Henry inquired about temporary luxury rental properties. There was no problem. Money could buy him anything. He knew he would never sell his property in Israel and he would always return there for at least part of the year. He loved Israel. He believed Israel was his country, but he could be flexible. "For now, let's see if Rebecca returns home," he told himself. He would visit Munich often. The kids would come home for a month vacation and stay with him. Henry would visit with Eva before he returned to Israel and within two hours, he was in London.

Eva met him and apologized again that he had to stay in a hotel. She promised she would have a frank talk with her kids so they would understand their relationship. Her house was big and not a problem for him to have his own bedroom. "The next time," she promised.

As always, they had a wonderful time together. Henry returned home and had a million messages. Business was booming! He did not want to be so busy. He would have to be very selective with whom he took as a client.

Henry loved the hustle and bustle of Tel Aviv. He loved the people. All the people he passed on the street were *his people* in *his country*. He belonged here. His work kept him busy. Henry met Moshe and Joseph often. It was very soothing for him to be with them. They talked about everything. They had a natural bond. After a meeting with them, he always felt better. At least for a while. Henry would visit the Silber's and let them know the kids were doing well.

But his most important task was to prepare for early retirement. He would still trade in antiques, but decorating lost its appeal to him. But he had to finish what he started although he would no longer take on new clients. He wanted to be free to travel and stay as long as he wanted to at any given place.

One day he took a folding chair and went to the shore, just to enjoy a beautiful day. He gloried in the white sand and the noise of the waves. It was true that the best things in life were free. For lunch he had a falafel and it tasted great.

Henry received a letter from Liliana. She was begging for new photos. She has no clue that Rebecca was in Germany and he had no intention of letting her know. He chose some photos he had taken in the park and sent them to Liliana without including any letter. He could not bring himself to write to her.

CHAPTER 21

The year was 1962. Rebecca was twenty three and Henry would be turning sixty. He has a hard time believing it. He felt really good but he did realize he was no longer a youngster. He chose not to think about it. The kids would soon be coming for a one month vacation. He asked the housekeeper to come every day. He wanted Rebecca to truly have a real vacation. He would also make time to be with them as much as they wanted him to. Henry had to share them with the Silber's, but all would turn out just right. He was very excited about this visit. Henry refused to go on vacation with Eva until after the kids visit. This surprised her.

From time to time Helena received photos, but no letters. She did not know how Rebecca was doing or how her life was progressing. Henry never provided any information. She finally decided she would go to Israel to meet her daughter.

That evening, Robert and Helena had a heated discussion. Robert did not want her to go to Israel. Helena was a little surprised. She was questioning him, but was not getting a straight answer. Finally, quite upset, she asked him what his exact reason was.

"Well, here it is," said Robert. "They hate Germans in Israel, not that I blame them. Just now, they hanged Eichmann."

But Helena interrupted him. "He was a murderer. He killed thousands of people. He was the one who gave the orders to kill."

Robert answered, "Yes, and others followed those orders and did nothing about it. Does that make them better?" Quietly he mumbled, "And I was one of them, and I have to live with that for the rest of my life. I cannot go to Israel." But then Robert yelled, "And what would we say to our sons?" Helena never saw him this angry. She was glad no one was home.

They were home alone. Robert, in a more calm voice told her that he could not understand her. He thought that she made a decision many years ago that this her new life. He was sure that going to Israel and letting her daughter know the truth would definitely come back to haunt them. He questioned how Rebecca would behave and what she would do? There was no way to hide all this from their sons. Robert was adamant that the boys were never to learn the truth.

Helena said quietly, "This is not all up to us. Is it? If our boys have to know the truth, wouldn't it be better if they heard it from us? For now I would do whatever you say, but I do not promise this forever." And she walked out of the garden.

Helena cried bitterly but she could not justify why. She never thought of her Robert as one of the Nazis; one of the killers. She thought, "Maybe he didn't kill with his own hands, but he did know about it, and he definitely was one of those people that did not do anything about it." Helena knew this all these years, but she never let this information get to her heart, because it was Robert, her husband and she loved him and she still did.

She went back to the house and found Robert in the library, standing by the window holding his head in his hands. She put her hands on his shoulder and said, "Sorry. I would never do this to you again. I love you and would do whatever you say." He hugged her and together they sat at the window looking out on their beautiful garden.

How peaceful it seemed as they looked out on the garden. But how turbulent their hearts were. Helena knew that, above anything else, she loved Robert. She decided that she would no longer beg for photos from Henry or write to him anymore. She would let it all be as it was. Helena reasoned that she could no longer consider herself a mother to a twenty three year old girl although she knew that would probably make Rebecca very angry and unhappy. Helena had to let it go. She had to.

The decision was very liberating for Helena. She would live by it. That night, at the dinner table she had a renewed appreciation for her family. She looked upon her two boys, smart, handsome and accomplished. She loved them with all her heart and did not want to hurt them. They would have a happy life and she would do nothing to disturb that.

Robert looked at her and smiled. He knew what she was thinking. Helena smiled back. Robert announced, "It is time to think about our next family vacation, a good one. Something exotic would be nice. All of us should suggest where to go so all of us would be pleased." The boys started to argue right away. Robert gave them three days to decide. "And then mother and I have to approve," he finished.

The boys were excited. They prepared a folder with information on where they wanted to go and when. They spread out a map of Africa and announced that they wanted to go on a safari. Robert and Helena looked at each other, and Robert responded, "Why not, it's a great idea!"

Helena suggested that they go to Munich to a larger tourist bureau to make final arrangements. The family went together for a few days. Munich was full of life with crowded streets, traffic everywhere and no place to park. They found the tourist office and it took over an hour to make all the arrangements. They stayed in a hotel in the middle of the city. After they freshened up, they went out on the town. Munich was not really far from their home, about a two hour drive, but they rarely visited. There was something very appealing about the big city. They did a little bit of shopping and sightseeing. By the time the evening rolled in, they were starving. They went to a famous restaurant not too far from the airport. It was full of customers, locals and tourists, but Robert managed to get a table. They made themselves comfortable.

Not far from their table sat a young couple having dinner just before their departure to Israel. As Robert passed them on his way to the buffet, he turned back. He had to take a second look at this young woman. She seemed so familiar. Her smile was so very much like Helena's. He stopped in his tracks, turned back around and returned to his table and said, "The selection on the buffet is not what we want. Let's order from the menu instead."

The sight of that girl made him so upset. He was convinced she could be Helena's daughter, "But what was she doing in Munich?" he thought to himself. Robert said nothing to Helena, but he continued to watch the young couple. He made an excuse to get up again and passed close to their table. He heard the young woman talking. She had the same husky voice as Helena and she spoke with the same accent. Now he was convinced she was Helena's daughter. He thought, "God makes all the decisions, and we are but the puppets pulled by his hand." Robert no longer felt that the world was so big.

The family ordered their dinner but Robert could not eat. He just continued to stare at the couple. He also looked at Helena thinking, "If she saw the couple, would she recognize the girl?" But, obviously, Helena did not notice them. The young couple finished their dinner and left.

The family had only two weeks to prepare for their trip. Robert took care of his business. The housekeeper and gardener would stay at the house and all should be okay. Helena was reviewing the list provided by the travel agency for the clothes they should take. Helena was so excited and happy and the boys could not wait for their departure.

A representative from the tour was waiting for them at the airport. Their group consisted of twelve tourists. The representative would stay with them until the end of the tour. The group would stay in Johannesburg for two days and tour the city to see the modern life of South Africa. Then they would continue by train to the wilderness. Johannesburg was a big and bustling city. The hotel was very luxurious but it was not what they wanted to experience. They were anxious to move on.

As they traveled on the train they were able to see the change in the scenery. The land was like nothing they had ever seen before. It was dry and yellow. From time to time they passed a small village and saw a few huts, a cow or goats, and this was all. They finally reached their destination. A few jeeps were waiting to take them to their camp. From their camp they would take day trips out into the wild to see villages and lions and elephants in their natural habitat.

When they entered their tents they were totally surprised. They were huge with every amenity you could imagine. There were beds, bathrooms, closets, fresh linens. The boys had their own tent next to Helena and Roberts. The whole group dined together. At night they lit tall torches. The tent had electric lights powered by a generator. Warm showers were available. It was hard to believe all of this was available to them so far from civilization.

In the morning, the group had breakfast in the main tent. The tour guides and all the help spoke English. They were going out to see elephant herds. The road into the jungle was rough. The jeep was bumpy, and this did not please Helena.

Finally, they heard the roar of elephants. It was exciting to see them close up. The elephants were curious too, as they gazed back at them. They stayed for a while. The tour group also saw a small village of local people. It looked just like the movies one would see on National Geographic. The villagers did not pay any attention to the group. The guide explained that the tribe's people were used to seeing tourists.

The trip was very exciting for Max and Albert. They saw a completely different way of life, and animals that they had only ever seen in zoos. There, they were so close they could almost touch them. The lives of the local people were so selfless, so different from the tour group's *civilized* world.

It was a thrilling trip, especially for the boys. For weeks after, they only spoke of their experiences on the trip, citing all the details. But for Helena, it took her over a week to recuperate. It was a grueling trip meant for the young and adventurous.

School started for Helena's sons and everything returned to its usual routine. That was a problem for Helena. More than ever, she needed to find something meaningful to take up her time.

Robert became involved in the politics of their town. Most of the people in their town did not want to allow immigrants to settle there any longer. In Germany, the big cities allowed immigrants from all over the world to settle there. Shortly thereafter, however, they were sorry. The immigrants stayed amongst each other. They had their own neighborhoods, their own restaurants and their own life. Robert discussed the issue with Helena. He also did not want *strange* people in his beloved town. He wanted to preserve life in his town just as it was. Helena thought of her sons. She hoped they would find nice German girls to make their lives complete. She hoped this mostly because she knew Robert would never truly accept any girl other than a German. Robert liked making decisions for the town, renewing roads, addressing the sewer systems. Robert cared very much about the condition of his town. He would say his involvement was all for the benefit of his sons. It never entered his mind that his sons might one day relocate to any other location.

CHAPTER 22

Time passed quickly. It was almost a year after the safari trip. Helena never wrote to Henry again, and he never sent any more photos or letters. Helena expected that he would continue to send photos. Now she knew that if she did not beg for a photo or a little information none, would be forthcoming. She did not know what to do. She knew going to Robert for advice was not a good idea. She knew what he would say.

Lately, Helena was not feeling so good. She had a mild pain in her stomach, but with time, the pain was getting worse. She was hoping it would go away, but she knew she must go to a doctor. She had hoped it was just nerves. She asked Robert to go with her to a doctor, and he was surprised.

The doctor took many tests and strongly suggested a specific stomach test provided in a hospital in Munich. There, they had the latest equipment and very good specialists. The doctor scheduled an appointment at the hospital for her. Helena overheard him saying on the phone, "No, no, this cannot wait so long. It has to be done soon." Helena felt her knees buckling. She knew she must be very sick.

Two days later they went to the hospital in Munich. Robert tried not to show his anxiety. But Helena knew him too well. She knew he was afraid. After the test was given, they had to wait two days to receive the results. They decided to go home and then come back.

All Helena wanted was to be with her sons in her beautiful home, the place she had lived for the past twenty years. It was truly her haven. The following two days were torture for them all.

Going back to the hospital became a family trip. The boys insisted on going with them. They were all in the office when the doctor entered. The news was not good. The doctor started to say that the tests showed there was cancer. The good news was that it was isolated to one part of the stomach and it was operable. He told them that with surgery and some chemotherapy, it all should be okay. Helena could not breathe, but she did not cry. She heard herself say, "I want the surgery right away." The doctor

nodded and said that was a very wise decision. He picked up the phone and started to make arrangements for her procedure. Helena remained in the hospital.

Robert took the boys home and made arrangements for the house and his business. He would come back to stay with Helena in Munich for as long as she would have to be in the hospital. Robert made a reservation for a week in a nearby hotel. Helena made herself as comfortable as she could be in a hospital room. Robert insisted that she had a private room.

Somehow, Helena knew she would be okay, but it would take some suffering. She was resigned to go along with whatever treatment was necessary. She put on the nightgown that Robert brought for her from home. It was two sizes too big, but it was soft and it hugged her. She could not sleep. For the first time in her life, she was grateful for the television. The nurse brought some mint tea and crackers. She informed Helena that at 8:00AM they would come for Helena to have some more tests done in preparation for her surgery. Helena finally fell asleep with the television on.

In the morning the nurse woke her up. Helena could not believe she slept through the night. Robert phoned and told her he would be there in the late afternoon and bring her anything she needed. He sounded tired. He probably did not sleep. Helena knew she had to lift his spirits and make him hopeful. She was worried about him.

Still, Helena did not process her whole situation. But she knew she would not die. She thought that maybe it was her time to suffer. She almost welcomed it. All that was important to her now was to go to surgery as fast as possible. Different tests were done on her all day and when she returned to her room she was very tired. Robert was there waiting for her. Being with him made her feel much better. He told her what he had done that day and said that he was staying in Munich until they both went home together.

The doctor came in and said they were all ready for her surgery to be the following day. Helena was glad. She wanted this to be over. She told Robert to go back to the hotel, have dinner and a good night's sleep. She also put him at ease by telling him she knew she would be all right and not to worry. The nurse gave Helena a sleeping pill. She kissed Robert and went to bed. When she woke up the next morning she was very drowsy and sleepy. It was from the medicine they gave her the night before. Robert was back already. They gave Helena an injection and she was asleep again.

And then a miracle happened...

Helena's mother, father and her brother Daniel also, were standing at her bedside telling her she would be all right. And her little girl Rebecca was hugging her. Henry was there also, but he stood far away and had a very sad face. They were all surrounding her, touching her and smiling. She felt so comforted and so happy to see them. Then she heard a voice, "Mrs. Van Klaus, wake up. It's all over now, open your eyes." Helena did not want to open her eyes. She wanted to stay with her family.

She looked around, and they were gone. When she did open her eyes, Robert was standing there with a smile and caring eyes. She felt some pain, but it was not too bad. The doctor came in and told them that the operation was a success. They cut out a small portion of her stomach and the rest of her stomach was clean. Just as a precaution she would have a mild chemotherapy treatment.

Helena welcomed all her treatments. She wanted to get well. She asked Robert to bring the boys as soon as possible. Helena did not forget her dream. This was the first time she had such vivid visions of her family. She could swear they were right there. She could feel their touch. It was so real to her. Helena did not share her dream with Robert. She would never forget the dream.

Helena had a private nurse for the night. Robert went home in order to bring the boys to the hospital the next day. In the morning, Helena's pain was almost unbearable. She agreed to take painkillers which made her very sleepy. In the evening Robert and the boys came. They sat on each side of the bed holding her hands, and looked very worried. Helena assured them that everything would be all right. When they all left, she was glad. She needed a painkiller again. The boys would stay with Robert in the hotel and come to visit again the next day. Helena was hoping for another dream, but it never came.

By the next morning she felt much better. The nurse sat her up in a chair for a while. They gave her some clear broth which was very painful for her to keep in her stomach. Helena realized that it would not be easy to recuperate, but she would do her best. As a result of her dream, she was now determined to meet her daughter, even if Robert would not agree.

Helena made up her mind that as soon as she returned home she would write to Henry and beg!

The next day Helena walked a few steps, and everyday thereafter she felt stronger. Robert stayed with her the whole time. They read, watched television and talked about little nothings. Every day he brought her fresh flowers and was very attentive. In short, he was perfect. In the next few days she would go home. It was decided that she would return in a month for the chemotherapy. Robert slowly became more relieved. Now he did believe that Helena would be herself again. At night he slept better.

In the morning when he came into Helena's room it was empty. She was taken for some additional tests before she could be released from the hospital.

Robert decided to meet her where the test was being administered. The nurse showed him which elevator to take. He was alone in the elevator when it stopped. A young woman came on and said good morning to him in a deep husky voice. She smiled at him. Robert could not believe his eyes. It was the same girl he saw in the airport restaurant. The smile and the voice was just like Helena's. She even had the same accent as Helena had had years ago. This could not be. He managed to find his voice and said, "I think I am on the wrong elevator. I am meeting my wife. She had some test done."

The girl said, "I work in the research department of this hospital. It is on the same floor where your wife's tests are being done." When the elevator door opened, they both walked out. She said, "Good luck to your wife." Robert was convinced more than ever, it was her. It had to be Rebecca. But Robert knew she was in Israel. He was confused. Robert decided he would write to Henry. He had to find out.

The prognosis for Helena was excellent. Robert felt the grip around his heart loosening. She would be okay. He could not imagine his life without her.

Robert wrote a letter to Henry, telling about Helena's illness. And he did ask, if by any chance, was his daughter Rebecca in Munich. He told Henry about the two incidences he had. He also wrote that he agreed with Henry that a meeting would not be good for anyone. Robert politely asked if Henry would send a letter to Helena and maybe include a photo or two. Robert said that she would appreciate it very much. He told Henry that Helena missed any information about Rebecca. Robert provided his business address for Henry to reply back to.

With flowers in hand, a smiling Helena was returning home. Gertrude, the housekeeper greeted them at the entrance. The boys were running alongside the car from the main gate. Helena was glad to be home. Her goal was to get well. Robert explained to Gertrude the special diet Helena had to be on. He gave a very detailed description of how to prepare her meals and how everything needed to be blended. The boys sat on each side of Helena on her beloved veranda.

Helena felt so loved and happy. The following month she took it easy. She ate well and gained some weight. Books became her best friends. In the next few days she was returning to the hospital for some follow up tests and she would start the chemotherapy. She felt a little anxious, but it was very important for her to get well.

Robert, Max and Albert all went with her. The test results were great. Helena was cancer free but she would still have to start chemotherapy as an insurance policy. Helena received a mild dose and by the evening, they returned home. The nausea lasted only a few days, and thereafter, she felt fine. Helena would be rechecked in a few months. Her scars had healed nicely.

One day Helena's spirits were lifted. She received a letter and photos from Henry. He asked how was she was recuperating and Helena was surprised. "How did he know?" she wondered. Helena found out that Robert had written to Henry. How wonderful was he. The photos were great. Her daughter looked beautiful and all grown up. One of the photos showed Rebecca wearing a white doctor's coat. She worked in medical research. Henry wrote a little about her and her husband and asked Helena to reply and provide the status of her health. Helena was moved.

Robert did not receive a reply to his letter. Helena showed Robert the photos of her daughter. Robert was upset upon seeing the photos. It definitely was the young woman he met twice, but he did not say anything to Helena. She thanked Robert for his thoughtfulness. She was happy.

Robert knew then for sure that Rebecca was right there in Munich, and that was why Henry never responded to his letter.

Helena hid the photos in a special place only she knew about.

Helena took walks around the property. They went to the movies often. Slowly her health was returning to normal.

Robert avoided Munich as much as he could.

Maximilian graduated the university and would start his master's degree in the fall. Albert attended the same university. Max just told his parents he had a girlfriend. She went to school with him. He claimed their relationship was not serious.

* * *

Henry had just received another letter from Robert and was very saddened by the news. He forgot that we all could be mortal. After all, he cared much more than he let himself believe. He answered right away, but not to Robert. He did not want to acknowledge to Robert that Rebecca was in Munich. He hoped that Liliana would write to him soon.

The three year plan to stay in Munich had become longer, but Henry did not mind anymore. He often traveled to Germany and to England. The kids came back to visit also. They took trips all over Europe. Henry's health was okay, and so was his life. Henry went to Munich to visit the kids. As usual, the kids met him at the airport, but they seemed very anxious. Henry asked, "Did something happen?"

And they replied, "We have to talk."

CHAPTER 23

The year was 1967. A war was inevitable. Israel was prepared but how could a country defend itself with enemies on all sides? In the midst of those times, Henry was visiting in Munich.

That evening the kids sat with him and said the company Alex worked for wanted to send him to the United States on a work visa. "We do not know for how long, but the pay is unbelievable and the opportunity to learn is great." Rebecca also added, "I can get a job in my field anywhere." There was silence, interrupted by Alex.

He said, "I really want to take this opportunity. This is a once in a lifetime chance."

All Henry was able to say was, "It is so far away." But in his mind he thought, "America. Everybody's dream. They would live right in New York, the heart of the world." He asked them, "What would you do if I said no?"

"We would still go," answered Rebecca and Alex in unison.

This made them all laugh, but Henry's heart was breaking. He was glad they would be leaving Munich, and thought of how the next time he visited them would be in New York. Henry also told himself he had to make sure that his English improved!

The reports from Israel were not good. Everyone believed a war was imminent.

Henry cut his visit short. He felt he should return to Israel. Rebecca begged him to stay and move with them. She promised they would make sure he could get a visa to enter the United States with them. But Henry wanted to be in Israel during its time of trouble. He almost felt as if it was his obligation.

The next day he left for Israel and promised that within the next two to three months he would visit with them in the United States.

He did tell Alex to write a long letter to his parents with an explanation of why he was not returning to Israel. Henry did not want to see the disappointment on the Silber's' faces when they heard about the departure of the kids.

Henry was glad to return to Israel and immediately called his friends Moshe and Joseph to meet the next day. His friends were very sad. Their kids were in the military as was Alex's brother. Henry would have to go to see the Silber's. From his friends, Henry found out how serious the situation in Israel really was.

"We need God to help us, and we need to be brave," said Moshe.

"We are at war!" the newscaster said. Henry installed black shades on the windows and he prepared an adequate supply of water and food in his apartment.

The Silber's asked Henry to stay with them, rather than be alone, but he could not look at Mrs. Silber's shaking hands. She was so afraid for her son. They were almost thankful that Alex was abroad, and Henry agreed.

Within six days, the Israelis were victorious. A true miracle! There were a lot of tragedies. Too many soldiers lost their lives. These were the children of the survivors of the holocaust. It was too much to ask of them. The stories of heroism were reported in the news daily. One story was of a young nineteen year old soldier. His name was Leon-Arie Rotmensz. He gave his life in order to save the life of his commander. He was the son of holocaust survivors.

Slowly the country returned to normalcy, but the Six Day War would never be forgotten.

Henry received the visa he needed for his trip to the United States. "Well, I've never been in the United States" he thought to himself. He was having a hard time imagine himself being there, especially in New York.

The kids settled in Manhattan. They were happy and excited in their new place. They loved New York. Rebecca got a job in New York University Hospital and Alex could not believe his luck. He loved his job. Henry thought, "How can I possibly argue against a situation like this?" He knew he had to resign himself to whatever the kids decided.

The trip from Israel was long, but Henry flew first class, which made it easier. Henry was emotional upon landing. He had not seen the kids for almost four months and had missed them, but he was also very excited to be in the United States. From the plane he could see all of Manhattan. The sight of the city was amazing. There was no other place anywhere in the world like New York.

The kids greeted him. They picked him up in their new, huge American car. They looked so happy. Their apartment was very roomy. Henry helped them purchase furniture and other things. Rebecca prepared a special dinner all by herself. Henry, as always, was so happy to be with them.

At dinner Rebecca said, "I have some good news to give you." Henry was all ears. "Well, Mr. Henry Kopel, in six months you will be a grandfather!"

Henry almost fainted from joy. He questioned her about everything. "Maybe you should not work, maybe you should have help in the apartment, maybe you should have a nanny," Henry continued on. But Rebecca just laughed out loud. "Just like Liliana," he thought to himself.

Henry reminded himself that he eventually would have to tell Rebecca about her mother, but it was certainly not a good time. It would have to wait until after the birth.

Henry decided that he must be in New York for the birth of the baby. Alex and Rebecca scheduled a visit with the doctor. Everything was normal. Rebecca looked and felt good. After the doctor visit, the threesome went furniture shopping for themselves and the baby. He was beside himself. "A Grandfather," he was dreaming about it!

New York was exciting. Henry visited the museums, antique shops and, of course, Sotheby's and Christies. Henry was in heaven. He was thinking of opening a bank account in New York. He also was seriously considering purchasing a good apartment in New York. Somehow, he had a feeling that the kids would be staying in America.

Henry planned on coming to the states often and for long visits. He wanted to be a part of his grandchild's life. The newspapers were full of advertisements for apartments. But first Henry wanted to see an attorney. He made an appointment with an attorney who had a familiar Polish, Jewish name. He wanted to feel comfortable to talk about many things he had in mind. The attorney was a polite man in his forties. He had come to the States just before the war, as a young boy. He spoke some Polish, but not too much. Henry was communicating quite well in English.

Henry made sure that he could buy an apartment legally in New York and open a bank account that he could forward some money to. And of course, Henry would have the attorney represent him here in the USA. All was possible. Then Henry needed a good realtor and his lawyer introduced him to a very reputable real estate office. In a couple days he would go to view some apartments. But first, he had to talk to the kids. In the evening he would tell him what he was arranging. They were thrilled with his decisions.

Henry walked around the city for hours. He could not get enough of it. He already met the realtor and explained what he was looking for. He opened the account at the bank, visited Sotheby's and familiarized himself with antique prices. On his next visit, Henry would bring some of his silver and paintings to sell. He phoned Eva in London. He told her about his good news and spoke about the amazing New York City. He promised he would visit her on his way back to Israel. He told her it would be great if sometimes they could meet in the States. She agreed.

The apartments he saw were okay, but Henry wanted something better. He wanted a really elegant building in the best location, and it must be spacious. The realtor made some more appointments over the next few days.

Henry felt full of life and excited for the future. Only one thing was still nagging him. When should he tell Rebecca about her mother? Liliana did not know her daughter's married name nor where she was. Henry was still not ready to tell Rebecca. His daughter would definitely be very hurt. She would be upset with him also for not telling her right away. He did not want to upset her before the baby was born. Now was not a good time.

Rebecca prepared a lunch basket and they all went for a picnic in Central Park. It was within walking distance from Rebecca's apartment. Henry took some photos of Rebecca but made sure the New York skyline was never captured in the pictures. They ate, told jokes among themselves, and then Rebecca became very quiet and said, "Father, tell me. How was my mother when she was pregnant with me?"

Henry was surprised by this question. He told her all that he remembered, but his voice was trembling. Rebecca said she was sorry for opening old wounds, but she wanted to know a little more about her mother. Henry didn't know if he was doing the right thing by not telling Rebecca about her mother right then.

Henry found a beautiful apartment on Park Ave., close to Central Park and to Rebecca. It was a convenient location for Henry. The building was elegant with all the expected amenities and it did not have to be renovated. The moldings in the apartment were exquisite. The parquet floors were beautiful and the large windows let in a lot of light. The apartment was on the seventh floor which eliminated the noise of the street. The building had two elevators and an impressive lobby with a concierge and doorman. This was exactly what Henry was looking for. He would decorate it with love, just as he did with the apartment in Israel. For now, Henry needed some furniture so that he could stay in the apartment when he returned the next time. He began furniture shopping and decorating.

Rebecca and Alex left their apartment early in the mornings and returned late in the evenings. They worked so very hard. Henry tried to explain to them that they did not have to work so hard, but they still felt they had to. Before leaving New York, Henry wanted to update his will. He made an appointment with his attorney and the kids. The apartment was willed to Rebecca.

The furniture was scheduled to arrive at Henry's New York apartment in days. Henry shopped for bedding and some other necessities. He ordered window treatments and Rebecca would let the installers into the apartment in her father's absence.

Henry was ready to leave for London. He was satisfied with all that he had accomplished. They all agreed that Henry would return two months before the birth of the baby so that he could finish his apartment and help Rebecca with all she might need.

Alex spoke to his parents and told them their good news. They were so happy. Alex invited his parents to come to the states and visit with them. But all the Silber's wanted was for the kids to return home to Israel. Henry would see them when he returns to Tel Aviv.

CHAPTER 24

enry landed in London on a very dark and rainy day. Henry hated days like this. Every bone in his body ached. Eva was waiting for him. He had so much to tell her and wanted to seek her advice. Henry always felt so welcomed by Eva. She said that he would stay at her house. She told him her children asked why he didn't always stay at her house. The children said they liked him a lot. Henry was surprised and pleased to hear this. Henry brought a nice gift for Eva which he got in Sotheby's. It was an elegant, antique necklace. It was very unique. She loved it. The room she prepared for him had a balcony and an en suite bath. It was on the opposite side of the house from the kids. He bathed, took a short nap and was refreshed for dinner. Her kids greeted him with smiles. Henry had gifts for them also; a sport watch for the boy and a ring for the girl. The children noticed the new necklace Eva was wearing. They loved it. Their father never bought their mother any gifts. She always had to buy everything for herself. Eva was able to purchase whatever she wanted, but to receive a gift from someone else was something special to her.

Henry and Eva talked late into the night. Eva was smart and Henry valued her opinion. She loved the idea of him purchasing the apartment in New York, but she had doubts about holding on to the secret of Rebecca's mother. Eva agreed to wait for the birth of the baby before telling Rebecca because it definitely would be very emotional. Eva also agreed that the meeting with Rebecca and her mother should also include the husband and sons. Henry said he would discuss this with Liliana in his next letter.

Eva prepared a small party for her closest friends and family to meet Henry. And as always, they lusted for each other. Henry desired Eva more than any other woman in his life, even more than Liliana. He had been enamored by his young wife, but there was never any passion.

Henry had already communicated with his kids. Rebecca was well and this was what was most important to him. Henry dreamt for her to have a little boy, but whatever comes would be just fine with him, as long as everybody was in good health.

After ten days in London, Henry was going home to Israel. *Home*. This is how Henry felt about Israel, it was his *home*!

Henry flew back on the Israeli airline El Al and as always, it felt so emotional. Upon landing they play Hatikva and everybody sang. The comradeship was amazing. Joseph met Henry at the airport. They told each other their latest news. Joseph had some bad news. Moshe fell ill. He was diagnosed with a cancer of the skin and was in a hospital in Jerusalem where they had the latest methods and medicine to fight his illness. Joseph explained it was serious, but they hoped Moshe would be victorious. Joseph and Henry planned to visit Moshe together.

When they arrived at Henry's apartment, his housekeeper had dinner prepared and they ate in silence. This was very bad news for Henry. He told himself, "These are the surprises that life brings. You're never ready for sickness, never ready for the end of life." Henry decided he would help Moshe in every way possible.

The next day, Joseph and Henry arrived in Jerusalem. The city had a very distinctive smell and look, different from any other place on earth. You could almost feel the holiness of the city. Not only for Jews, but Christians and Muslims felt this too; yet the three religions could not live together in peace.

Henry and Joseph got to the hospital in time to meet with the doctors. Henry spoke with the chief of the department. He asked if there was any new medicine, not yet approved or available, that could help Moshe. The doctor thought, and said, "There is a medicine that is in its final stage of research, not yet tried on humans." But the doctor continued to say that for then, Moshe should start with conventional medications, "And then we can talk again."

Henry said, "It does not matter how much the new medicine costs, I will pay for any treatment for Moshe."

They went to Moshe's room. He was sleeping. Henry and Joseph sat and waited for him to wake up. Moshe did not look good. He was pale, had lost some weight and had very dark circles under his eyes.

Moshe woke up with a shallow scream. It must have been a bad dream. He saw his two friends and gave them a smile. "Don't look so worried, I will fight this and win, you will see." They agreed with him. They stayed for a while and promised to visit often. On their way out Henry asked for the doctor's business card.

When Henry returned to Tel Aviv, he called Moshe's wife to ask if she needed anything. She was grateful and told him she was okay. Henry also called Rebecca and asked her to find out if there was anything new in the United States that could help Moshe. He sent Rebecca his friend's medical report. Henry promised himself he would move heaven and earth to help his friend Moshe.

Henry returned to visit Moshe again. He did not look any better although he said he felt better. The doctor said Moshe was responding well to the treatments. "Let's wait and see if he continues to improve before we try the new treatment still in trials," said the doctor. Henry sat with Moshe for a while. Mostly they spoke about politics. Henry brought some sweets and fruits.

Henry was in touch with Rebecca almost daily. He worried about her. She wanted to continue working until about six weeks before her due date. He remembered how her mother was pampered during her pregnancy with Rebecca. But his daughter was different. She had no fear of anything. She was full of life and hope. Rebecca was not afraid of hard work even though she knew she didn't have to work at all.

Henry was preparing for a long stay in America. He sent some things ahead. His apartment in Israel would be taken care of by his housekeeper. In an emergency, Joseph was there to help. Henry made some banking arrangements and was ready to leave. Moshe was doing much better. He was released from the hospital and was with his family. Henry would stay in touch with everybody. He would see Eva in London on his way to the States. He hoped to relax there, he felt tired. He never felt this way before. Maybe age was catching up with him.

Henry arrived in London. As usual, Eva was very pretty, very kind and very amorous. He stayed with her for two weeks. He rested but was anxious to go see his daughter.

Henry did not let his kids know his exact arrival date. He wanted to get to is apartment first. It was midmorning when he arrived at his building. The doorman recognized him and helped him with his luggage. The apartment was in great shape. It needed some more decorating. He would do it during his stay. Towards evening, after he had a rest and did some food shopping, Henry called Rebecca. He told her he would be at her apartment within an hour. He walked there. It took him about ten minutes. He rang the bell and there she was.

Her belly was large. She stopped working now. Her due date was about three weeks. She took her father's hand and placed it on her belly. Henry felt the baby's movement. He remembered he did the same when Liliana was pregnant. Alex came home after work and was happy to see Henry. "Thank God you are here," he said. "I am so worried about leaving Rebecca home alone." Rebecca was laughing, a happy laughter.

The next morning Henry came early to make breakfast for Rebecca. Alex left for work. Henry was finished with his decorating. He took long walks and spent time with his very pregnant daughter. He would remember these pleasant times waiting for the birth.

The artwork which Henry sent from Israel arrived. He used some of the pieces but planned to sell most of the rest.

A call came in the middle of the night. Henry knew who it was. Alex said they were on their way to the hospital. Henry called a cab and left soon after. Alex was with Rebecca, but Henry had to sit in the waiting room. Alex came often to report what was going on. Rebecca was in labor for quite a while. Finally Alex came and said, "Come and see a miracle!"

Rebecca was in bed, all smiles, holding a tiny new baby and said, "Father, here is your new grandson. His name is Samuel, after your father." Henry stood staring at the baby and felt the tears run down his face. He was so moved by the moment.

He came to the hospital every morning and stayed all day. Alex was busy picking up all the things to prepare the nursery. They had already been purchased, but stayed in the store until the baby was born. It is a Jewish tradition not to bring home anything for the baby until after the birth.

After three days, mother and baby were coming home. Henry ordered a limo to take them in comfort and style. Henry was holding Sam in the car. He did not trust anyone else to do it. Everything had been prepared for their arrival. The cleaning company scrubbed the apartment, shopping was done, the linens changed and the nursery was outfitted for a prince. Rebecca decided she would breast feed the baby, at least for a few months, until she returned to work. Henry thought she should give up her research job and stay home with the baby, but he didn't say anything yet. There was time to convince her to change her mind later. The circumcision was done in private, they had no one to invite. They hired a housekeeper to help with the apartment and with the baby also. Henry was there every day and stayed for most of the day. He changed the baby's diapers, walked the baby in his carriage and let Rebecca sleep as much as she needed. Central Park was right next to them, so Henry took the baby out daily to get fresh air. As Henry strolled in the park, he saw a lot of nannies walking the babies. He thought, maybe Rebecca was right in wanting to return to work. Times are changing, and he sees woman were no longer attached only to their home.

Sam's first smile was for Henry. His first gurgle was for Henry. There was an absolute love affair between them. Sam had beautiful blue eyes, light brown hair and a very fair complexion. He was becoming a chubby baby as he loved to eat. He was always sucking on something, his mother, a toy or a pacifier. He showed interest in everything he saw. Henry thought there was no more perfect baby than this in the whole world. Henry could not imagine parting from him. "How am I going to do it" he asked himself. Henry feared the baby would forget him. Henry knew he was in trouble, and as much as he tried pushed the thought out of his mind, he knew he had to eventually return to Israel.

Eva was coming to New York. The apartment was finished and Henry was ready to be a host. He wanted to show Eva New York, the city that Henry had fallen in love with. They also planned a trip to Washington D.C. where they would take guided tours and stay a few days.

Rebecca was interviewing nannies, but promised Henry she would not go back to work until Eva returned to London. Sam was trying to crawl and when he saw Henry, his face would light up. It was so obvious that Grandpa was his favorite person.

On the coffee table in Henry's apartment, he only had baby books, how-to books, and spoke only about the baby. Eva patiently listened. He would complain if he did not see the baby for one whole day. It was becoming overbearing.

Rebecca made dinner for all. She wanted to please Eva and show off for her father. As they walked into the hallway of the apartment, Henry heard Sam laughing. He ran to him and Sam was beside himself. He put his head on his shoulder and held himself tight to Henry's body. Eva could not believe it. The baby was gorgeous and the bond between them was so obvious. They all spent a lovely evening together. Of course, Henry gave Sam his bath and put him to sleep. "Well, Sam is Henry's life and nothing else is as important to him, not even me," thought Eva.

Eva and Henry left for Washington the next day. They took the train and stayed in the Washington Hotel, right next to the White House. They arrived late afternoon and decided to have dinner and some dancing right in the hotel. The next morning they would start their tour of the city. The museums in Washington were unbelievable. The Congress building, the White House, the monuments; it was nothing like Europe. The whole country was so unlike Europe.

"The next trip in America should be California," said Henry. Eva agreed.

The few days passed fast and Henry could not wait to see Sam again. They returned late in the evening, too late to go see Sam. Henry was inconsolable. "Maybe we can go and take and peek to see him sleeping. What do you say?" he pleaded with Eva. She just looked at him and shook her head.

They went for a late dinner at a local restaurant, had some good wine and that gave Eva more confidence to talk to Henry. She tried to explain to Henry, "You must let the baby love his parents as he loves you. It is not fair to them. Maybe it is time for you to go back to Israel for a while. You should only be a grandfather, not a mother, father and nanny all in one." Henry gazed at Eva from across the table and he could not understand the meaning of what she was saying. How could he love the baby less? But deep in his heart he knew she was right. Henry would have to plan on leaving for a while.

Henry asked Eva to mail a letter and photos to Liliana. He did not want the postmark to be from the USA. He was very careful not to leave a trace of Rebecca's whereabouts. This letter would most likely be a surprise for Liliana, and he wondered how she would react.

Eva left for London and Henry prepared to leave for Israel. When he told his kids he was going home, they were not too sad. Henry thought that Eva was right.

Rebecca hired a nanny; a pleasant woman in her forties. She came with many good recommendations and Sam seemed to like her. Alex was doing very well at his job.

He was very appreciated for his knowledge. Rebecca would return to the research department at the hospital part-time, only five hours a day. This made Henry very happy. It was time for Henry's departure. Hugs and kisses all around. Sam, Rebecca and Alex took him to the airport.

The long flight, even in first class, was excruciating to Henry. Finally, after eleven hours, he landed. He was home. Henry would relax for a few days and then meet up with Joseph and together they would visit Moshe. Henry had stayed in touch with his two friends but wanted to see for himself how Moshe was doing. He was also expecting a letter from Liliana.

It is good to be home, to sip coffee in his favorite place on the balcony, watch the sunset and hear the waves breaking on the Mediterranean Ocean. The Silber's just got a telephone line and Henry spoke to them. Every week Alex sent them new photos of the baby, but when Henry was telling them about the baby, he detected some jealousy. He offered the Silber's his apartment in Manhattan if they would like to go to the States for a visit, but stupidly, they resisted. They felt their son should come to them.

Joseph was very busy. He did visit with Moshe the prior week, so Henry went to see Moshe by himself. He traveled by taxi and it would return in four hours to take him back home. Moshe looked good and was in good spirits. He gained some weight and strength. The doctor's prognosis was good. Moshe was even back to work but could not travel abroad yet. Henry thought the worst was over. He had a very pleasant visit. Henry told Moshe about the letter he sent to Liliana. Moshe agreed with the contents. He thought it was fair. Moshe promised he would come to visit Henry soon.

Finally, the long awaited letter from Liliana arrived. Henry was afraid to open it. He sat on the balcony fingering the envelope. Upon reading the letter, Henry knew she was influenced by her husband Robert. But still, it was unbelievable to Henry. He thought irately, "Well, it will never happen this way!"

CHAPTER 25

Helena's sickness was in the past. She felt good and looked great. Maximilian had a steady girlfriend. She was a lovely girl. They met at the University. She was from Dusseldorf, an only child of a well-known heart surgeon. Her mother was a housewife. Helena liked the girl very much, and so did Robert.

Finally Helena received the photos of Sam, Rebecca's baby. Helena could not believe she was a grandmother. Shortly thereafter, another letter and new photos arrived. The second letter was a surprise to Helena and she wondered if she ever would meet her daughter. She showed the letter to Robert. First Robert admired the baby but as he read the letter you could see the anger he felt. He was saying, "He cannot do this to us, he just cannot do this." Henry was determined that their meeting should include everyone, meaning their sons would have to be told the truth. Henry did not want his daughter to come to see her mother in secret from her half-brothers, like an unwanted bastard. This would cause her a lot of pain. It would be very hard for Rebecca to understand that she was abandoned by her mother and for a long time not knowing that Rebecca was alive. Rebecca would never understand why her mother did not come looking for her. She also would be angry with her father for keeping the secret for more than ten years. Henry insisted that a meeting must be arranged with dignity and fairness to all involved. That was Henry's demand.

Robert was fuming. He wanted a secure life for his sons without drama, without having to wonder who they were. Robert felt his sons were too young for such news. If it was to happen it must be later, when they were more mature. Robert would not allow this meeting to happen for now. Helena was crying and Robert said to her, in anger, "You cannot make your three children miserable for your own selfish reasons!"

In a way, Helena was able to understand what Robert meant, but she wanted so much to meet her daughter and grandson. She started to believe a meeting would never take place. But she was determined that she would achieve this meeting, no matter how much it would disturb Robert or her sons. She would wait for a while and explain to Henry why the meeting could not happen very soon and begged him to stay in touch and keep sending letters and photos. Helena felt that Henry was right about his demands. Rebecca deserved to be treated with respect. She was raised without a mother, a mother that was not dead, just too comfortable to seek out her own daughter. Looking back, Helena knew she could have done much more to find her daughter, but she did not. Helena began to believe that the turmoil that she was going through must be God's punishment. That is what she thought. She also felt that she deserved it. Helena could not find peace of mind. It reflected on her relationship with Robert, not that she blamed him for his decisions to keep her sons happy and free of life's turbulences. Helena could not sleep. She asked her doctor to give her something for the night. She needed to sleep and not to think twenty four hours a day. The prescription helped and she was grateful for those little tiny white pills. If only she could take something for the day time, she would be alright. She became very friendly with the liquor cabinet. It dulled her feelings during the day and Helena was able to cope. The problem was that she needed more and more of the alcohol until Robert recognized there was a problem with her. He was angry that she could not cope with the situation and turned to alcohol for help. He felt she had no self-discipline and he locked all the wine and liquor in the basement.

It was lucky Robert recognized what was happening early enough. Robert did not know how to behave with Helena. He wanted to help her and he suffered to see her so unhappy. He was at a loss for a decision. He thought she should seek help from a psychiatrist, but it would have to be in a big city, where no one knew them and under an assumed name. Robert had to be in Berlin for business. That would be a good opportunity to find a doctor. But for then he would spend more time with Helena. He would take her out more often. The boys did not recognize anything unusual with their mother. They were involved in their own young lives. They had a very full social life. They traveled all over Europe. They worked with their father and enhanced the business. Maximilian was twenty four and Albert was twenty one. They were very close with each other; good friends and loving brothers. Robert was very proud of them. Whenever he looked at them it confirmed his decision to keep them from the truth. Robert really believed the boys should not know their mother's secret.

Max had a confidential talk with his father. He was very serious about the girl he was dating. The girls name was Katherine, Katy for short. Max told his father that he loved her and wanted her to be his wife. Robert felt Max was too young to make such an important decision. But Max was very insistent. It was decided that Max and Katy would become engaged and wait for at least two years before the wedding. Now they would tell Helena the plan. She would probably be very happy because she adored Katy.

As predicted, Helena was thrilled. Robert was very happy to see Helena respond this way. She took out the jewelry box that belonged to Robert's mother and the women in the family before her.

Helga Van Klaus, Robert's mother, loved her jewelry. She wore it as often as she could. It belonged to many generations of the Van Klaus family. Helena hardly ever touched the jewelry. She always had the feeling that it did not belong to her.

Max selected a beautiful ruby and diamond ring from the jewelry box to give to Katy. He placed the ring in a small, silver box. He would give Katy the ring after he asked her father for her hand.

Max was very excited with the thought of his engagement. That weekend, when they went to visit her parents, was when he would ask permission.

Max found Katy's father in the library and asked for a few minutes of his time. "Of course," responded her father, "what can I do for you?"

"I would like to ask for the hand of your daughter, sir," said Max. Katy's father was surprised, and said something about them being so young.

But Max responded, "We will wait to get married for at least two years. But for now, I want her to wear the family ring as an engagement commitment." He promised he would keep Katy protected and happy.

"We love you Max, and I would be honored to have you as a son-in-law," said Katy's father.

Max was thrilled. Now all he had to do was ask Katy to be his wife. They went out to their favorite little restaurant and there he proposed to Katy. She cried and right away answered yes. Max gave her the ring and explained its origin. She loved it.

* * *

Robert and Helena called Katy's parents and informed them of a party they were planning in honor of their children's engagement. They invited her parents and other members of their family to stay at their estate.

Now Helena became busy and was pleasantly distracted. She was planning a big bash. She hired caterers and a small band to play classical music. Helena wanted everything to be perfect. She ordered that her garden be perfectly groomed. The gardener would have to hire additional people to help him. Max really did not want such a big fuss but his parents insisted.

There were approximately twelve people from Katy's family to be housed. All the rooms were prepared and ready for their visit. The next day everyone would arrive and the party would follow the day after. Helena wanted all of her guests to be impressed and they were. Katy's family thought this kind of elegant life ended after the war. Obviously not!

The party was classy, with fine food, good music. The garden was lit by torches. Little tables and chairs were placed very purposefully on the lawn. The caterers took great care of all the guests. Helena looked beautiful, wearing a light pink chiffon dress and Robert's mother's necklace that was absolutely stunning. Katy wore her ring and was showing it off to everyone. Robert was watching Helena, and as always she surprised him with her grace. It was as if she was born to the role of a noble woman. Who would ever believe she was the daughter of a Jewish watchmaker? She looked the role and played it to perfection. She was a great hostess, smiling and making small talk. But, above all, she looked fabulous. Time did not damage her beauty. She remained tall, slim, smooth-faced, and those eyes were beautiful as ever. And her perfect golden hair fell softly on her shoulder. "Perfect," thought Robert.

The party was over. So much preparation, thought Helena. But everything went as planned. The party was a great success. The local papers wrote about it and inserted some photos. Helena was very proud. Robert thanked her for the great party and said how proud he was to have her as his wife.

Helena liked Katy's relatives. Maximilian was marrying into a nice family. Helena thought that she must convince Katy to make their residence right here in the family compound. Helena had time on her side to convince her. Helena would try hard to make Katy love this house in her frequent visits to them. She would try hard to earn Katy's love for Robert and her. All this made Helena forget about Rebecca for a while. Even though Henry did send photos and a few words from time to time.

Helena felt very satisfied and happy with herself. She knew how much she had changed from the young, frightened girl Robert met in the camp. But most surprising was how she felt about being who she was now. Helena achieved a comfort in her life, as if she had been born into it. It was so far from where she had come from.

Life had resumed normalcy back into the household. Helena rested from the commotion. Her thoughts were of the wedding. She had two years to make it perfect. But first they all had to decide where the wedding would take place; Max's home town or in Dusseldorf. But Helena knew there was no need to rush in making such decision just then.

Helena was helping Robert more and more with the office work. Robert spent more time in the office since Max had assumed the location work. Albert also helped as much as he could. He was working on his law degree and it was very time consuming for him.

Robert said that he had a project in mind to discuss with all of them one weekend. Helena wondered what it was but he did not want to tell her yet. She was waiting for some excitement. She was getting bored again. "It would be good to do something," thought Helena.

That Sunday, after dinner, the family sat in the living room. It was already too cold to sit outside. The weather was changing fast and winter would soon be upon them. They sipped tea and waited for Robert to start. Robert pulled out some drawings and placed them on the coffee table. They all looked puzzled.

"Well," he said. "I was thinking of building one or two houses on our property. I would like to hear if you think this is a good idea. First, I have to ask you, my sons, if you would like to live here? The decision does not have to be made immediately." They all stared at each other. It really was a surprise. But it all made sense. The property was big, twenty-some acres. It was enough to provide privacy and still keep the family together.

Helena was first to say, "It is great. It would be just wonderful!" The boys did not say anything other than to ask for a few days to decide. Helena could not be happier. When they went to bed that night she told Robert that he was a genius.

The next day Helena went out to look for architectural magazines. She felt certain the boys would say yes to the proposal. Robert asked that Helena not bother the boys. They must make the decision themselves. Helena could not wait for their answer, but she had to be patient. She kept the magazines in her room.

A few days later, after dinner, Albert said they made a decision. "Let's discuss it a little bit further," he said. The boys wanted to know who would live where, exactly where the houses would stand and all sorts of small detail questions. Robert explained that there were two small hills on the property with some distance between. It would not be hard to make a road there. The boys agreed.

"But what kind of a houses?" they asked. Robert said that they would make those decisions together though he already had a pretty good idea of what he wanted to see. He believed they should not be very modern and that they would match the main house. He also wanted them be built of stone and concrete. They would have to look for a good architect to help them decide. They all hugged and everyone was happy, but most of all Helena. She would never lose her sons.

They hired a young architect. He came to preview the existing mansion and access the land for the new houses. He would return with some recommendations and drawings.

Robert decided to subdivide the property into five acre lots. They all agreed that the deeds would have the restriction that the land would always stay with the family. The boys became busy making decisions for their houses. They all agreed on a traditional look for the buildings. The construction would start in the spring and it would take about a year to complete. Robert was very pleased with the situation. This would become a little heaven on earth for him. He was thinking of the future grandchildren and hoped there would be many of them. The only thing that worried him was his tiredness. He blamed it on his age, but knew he had better see a physician.

The plans for the two houses were completed. The architecture was similar to the main house. It was what the boys started to call their home.

The new houses would be very spacious, comfortable, outfitted with all the modern amenities. Helena knew it would be a great mess they would have to endure during the construction, but it definitely would be worth it. Some restoration would be done in the main house too. Helena would be very busy now. She liked being involved in all the plans.

Winter came early that year. There was a thin layer of snow in the garden that looked like a white blanket to Helena. She did not mind the winter at all. To her it had its own charm, like a fantasy place. It always gave her an urge to cozy up in the house by the fireplace with a warm blanket and a good book. She prepared hearty soups all through the winter. Helena though there was nothing better than a bowl of hot soup and a crisp roll. The whole family loved it.

A letter came from Henry mailed from London. "What was he doing in London?" thought Helena. Some photos were included. Rebecca looked radiant and Sam was adorable. In one of the photos Henry was holding the baby and you could see the happiness on his face. Helena was jealous. Henry wrote a little about Rebecca, but mostly about how wonderful the baby was. Helena put the letter away with the others in her secret place. She took them out, from time to time, to reread them. She often thought how she would talk to her daughter. The only language they had in common would be Polish and Helena was not sure she could communicate in Polish. Henry's letters were written in Polish but to speak the language was another matter. She decided she would start to think in Polish and talk to herself in the language. She did believe that one day she would meet her daughter.

CHAPTER 26

The construction had started. They fenced off the properties to be built on. The land was thawing and would be ready for excavation. Spring was in the air. The excitement was mounting and Helena was feeling full of hope. She never was witness to construction of a new building. It was a huge endeavor. After all, this would be the place where her sons would live, and after them, their children and so on.

After the completion of construction she would prepare for the wedding. A very exciting time awaited Helena. She was making her best effort to be close to Katy and Katy was very responsive. Helena invited her parents to come see the start of the construction. They would visit for a long week-end.

Helena thought of hiring a young girl to help the housekeeper. She was getting older and it was becoming too much work around the house for one person. There were some empty rooms in the attic with a functional bathroom. It needed a little fresh paint and some decorating and it would be ready for a new occupant. Helena contacted an agency to find someone who would be willing to be a live-in.

Young girls came for interviews but most only wanted a job for a year or two. This was not acceptable for Helena. Finally a girl came along, short and chubby and smiley. She lived on a nearby farm. She was perfect. Her name was Mary. Helena spoke with Gertrude and explained that her sons would have a household of their own and they would need a housekeeper. Helena needed Gertrude to teach her all she knew. Gertrude was proud and promised to do her best.

Katy's parents were to come the following weekend. Helena prepared their guest rooms and was doing the cooking. All of them would witness the breaking of the ground. Max and Albert would bury something in the ground and it was a secret. Katy's parents arrived in the early afternoon on Friday. They were very pleasant and friendly. Sarah, Katy's mother, offered to help with dinner and Helena accepted, not wanting to offend her. They stood in the kitchen, side by side, and made small talk. Sarah offered to make a chopped liver pate. Mary, the young housekeeper, was helping her. Helena was watching and was very surprised. It was not like the German pate at all. It was how Helena's mother prepared chopped liver every Friday for Shabbat. It also tasted like her mothers. Helena asked Sarah, "How did you learn to make it this way?"

Sarah answered, "That is how my mother and grandmother made it. Do you like it?"

"I love it," answered Helena.

They all sat for dinner and Helena asked Robert if he liked the pate that Sarah made. He loved it.

"I can prepare it this way from now on," said Helena with a mysterious smile. "Sarah, you must teach me some more of your mother's dishes," Helena asked politely.

The next day started with great tumult. All the trucks and machinery for digging out the basement were in place. The architect was there too. The houses that were being built slightly resembled the main house.

They all gathered to see the first shovel to break the ground. Robert was visibly moved. Helena saw it in his face. Both of them were happy. . Albert stood next to his parents. Maximilian had his arms around Katy and Mr. and Mrs. Rothman looked on as well. They were happy for their daughter. They loved Maximilian and his family and they knew Katy would become a noble woman. As far as Katy's father, Stephen, was concerned, Maximilian's mother came from Polish nobility and she behaved like a princess. He was very pleased.

They finally left the site. It was very dusty and noisy. The veranda of the main house was in the back of the construction site and it was quiet. The brunch was served there. They all enjoyed themselves and later they visited in the family library and made small talk and took a long walk around the property. The families were deciding where the wedding would take place.

Helena and Sarah went to the kitchen to see how Gertrude and Mary were doing preparing for dinner. Sarah asked if she could prepare the vegetables. "It's little on the sweet side," she said, "It has carrots and more." Helena watched in amazement again. As far as she remembered, that was how tzimmes was made - carrots, brown sugar, raisins. Helena asked Sarah if this was also her mother's recipe. "Oh yes," said Sarah.

At dinner, all enjoyed themselves and praised the carrots that Sarah prepared. Most of all, Helena enjoyed them. It was exactly how her mother did it.

At night, in their bedroom, Helena asked Robert if the carrots were a German delicacy. "No, I never ate them before, but it was good," answered Robert.

Helena did not know what to think. It was very strange. "I wonder what other Jewish delicacies she can cook. We will see," Helena thought to herself. "Maybe

Sarah's grandmother worked for a Jewish family and learned how to prepare Jewish dishes." All this occupied Helena's mind.

The Rothmans almost begged for the wedding to take place in Dusseldorf. All their friends and family were there. Robert and Helena agreed. They would make the wedding the following spring, in May. Katy's parents insisted that they pay for the whole wedding. As much as Helena wanted to be part of the preparations, she knew she had to let go. Sarah promised to stay in touch and to ask for Helena's opinions each step of the way. They parted with hugs and kisses and promised to visit again soon. Helena also promised to visit them. She wanted very much to see their lifestyle.

From then on the next few months were going to be noisy and dusty but also very exciting. Helena bought every book on decorating that she could find. But she also recognized that the best thing to do would be to hire a good decorator. So she shopped for one. She asked Katy what she would like. Katy answered, "Lots of light, high ceilings and open space." And Max left it all up to Katy to decide. Robert said that all he would do was to oversee the construction. Helena knew she would be responsible for all the rest. It was good for Helena to be busy again. She would make it a masterpiece, she thought.

CHAPTER 27

Henry stayed in Israel a few months, mainly for business. He missed Sam terribly. He spoke to Rebecca daily. Her family was doing well. Sam was trying to walk. Henry wondered if Sam would remember him. In another month, Henry would go to New York and stay for a while. But he knew he must not get as attached to Sam as he did on his last visit.

There was so much to do before he was ready to leave. Henry was very fortunate to have good neighbors. They kept an eye on his apartment. Joseph stopped in from time to time, and the housekeeper cleaned and aired out every room regularly.

Israel was growing rapidly. Construction was everywhere. Tel Aviv was becoming a metropolis. Henry was so torn between Israel and the United States. The people that he loved most were in the big USA, but the country he loved most was Israel. He also felt fortunate that he could afford to hop from one place to the other and to help the kids to live in luxury. He was able to secure their financial future and also maintain a good life for himself.

Henry planned on going with Joseph to visit Moshe and spend the day together. He was very happy that Joseph and Moshe were such close friends. They visited each other with their families, and spent holidays together. Henry joined them whenever he was in Israel.

Eva had not visited her Jerusalem home for a few months. She told Henry that they had to coordinate better. For Eva, being in Israel without Henry felt empty. Henry agreed to do better but for then he would visit Eva in London on his way to the United States.

Henry was finally on the plane and he knew it would take at least two days before he would recover from the flight. He blamed it on his age, but he knew he would have to get checked out by a doctor. He could not believe how his legs swelled up. He had another pair of shoes, two sizes larger, which he wore by the time he landed.

Eva was right there, as usual, all smiles and happy to see him. Henry could not wait to be indoors. He almost never saw real sunshine in

London. It was grey, cold and rained almost every day. But most of all, it made him feel swollen and sore.

Dinner was at home with Eva's kids. The fireplace was lit, the bright chandelier gave a warm glow, the food was good and Henry felt better. He told them about Israel and the United States. He invited them all to New York and they promised to come.

Later Eva came to his room with some good liquor. They spoke a little, and Eva said, "Have a good night's sleep. We will be together tomorrow." Henry was grateful for her understanding.

The bed was inviting, with fluffy warm blankets and crisp white linens. He slept like a baby. In the morning, Henry was awakened by a stream of sunshine that came through the window and the smell of good coffee. His spirits were high again. After a good shower he went downstairs to find everybody at the table. He was hungry and the biscuits, eggs and cold-cuts looked good. The coffee was phenomenal. Eva said she had bought tickets for a concert that night, and that they would dine in Henry's favorite restaurant. She said she had to go out for two to three hours on business and told Henry to enjoy the sunshine in the garden. She had some antique magazines for him. And that was exactly what he needed, a little peace and quiet.

He sat on the wicker chair and the sunshine penetrated his body. He looked at the magazines but his eyes were closing. He took a long nap. It must have been a long nap because the next thing he heard was Eva's voice. She came to the garden, sat next to him and told him that he must have brought the sunshine from Israel, because London had not had such a nice day for a long time. They ate a small lunch and looked at the calendar to make arrangements to be together in Jerusalem. Henry hoped that maybe Rebecca and her family could come as well as Eva's children. For him it would be grand if they could manage it.

The days passed quickly. They had a good time, as always. Henry thought of how great it would be to have Eva with him all the time, but he knew that was impossible. Henry was thinking of how many more goodbyes he would have to endure. It was never easy for him. It always tore his heart.

Henry found himself at the airport once again. He could not wait to hold Sam. He missed him so much. Alex, Rebecca and Sam were waiting for him. Henry stretched out his hands to Sam and a miracle of miracles happened. Sam ran to him and put his head on Henry's shoulder, as if Henry had never left. Henry was in seventh heaven. As they drove from Kennedy Airport to Manhattan, Sam held Henry's finger from his car seat the whole way. "I think he did not forget me," thought Henry relieved.

He gave Sam a bath before putting him to sleep. Sam grew so much. He was even more beautiful than before. He had almost mastered walking. He was smart. Henry's heart was full.

Rebecca took a week off from work. They would be together. The first night Henry stayed in Rebecca's home. When Sam woke up and saw Henry, he squealed with happiness. They sat and talked. All the while Sam sat on Henry's lap. They took a walk, with Sam in his carriage, to Henry's apartment. Rebecca had made arrangements for his place to be aired and cleaned and it was a pleasure to enter his apartment. Rebecca shopped for him and the refrigerator was full. Henry decided he would stay in New York for a long while. This was where his heart was.

Rebecca looked great. She had lost the weight from her pregnancy and she was slim and trim again. Henry knew he must establish a routine for himself. He could not be with the baby all the time.

Tomorrow he would find out where a Jewish Center might be, close to his apartment. He knew they would have great lectures, a gym and a pool. He would meet people. If he was to stay in New York for a better part of a year he must make some friends and have a social life.

His business in the states was limited. He thought maybe he should pay attention to it a bit more. But first he had to make sure that the kids would stay in the USA as a permanent place.

The closest JCC he found was on Lexington Ave., not too far from his apartment. He made an appointment with a representative to show him around. He enjoyed his day in the apartment, it was grand. The housekeeper would come every day to take care of him and the place. Henry invited the kids for dinner. They came without Sam and Henry was so disappointed. The nanny put him to sleep at 7:30pm. It was too late to take him out for dinner.

But Henry was happy to be a host again to his daughter and son-in-law. They talked about their work, politics, local and international events. They were knowledgeable and they cared. Alex had guilty feelings about his parents. They were stubborn and did not want to accept anything from them, not even tickets to journey to the states to see their grandson. His brother was studying at the University of Tel Aviv and they were a little short of money. Alex begged them to accept some help, but they were so proud and not willing to do so. It was a source of guilt and unhappiness for Alexander Silber.

Henry could sympathize with his son-in-law, and thought how happiness was never totally complete. Maybe if Alex's parents knew how much they hurt him, they would change their mind. Henry thought he must have a serious talk with them when he returned to Israel.

The JCC was amazing. Henry signed up for a membership immediately. He planned to go daily for a swim and sauna and visit the gym room. There was a lecture scheduled about the relationship between the USA and Israel. Henry thought it would be interesting.

He would see Sam that evening. If only Sam was a little less happy to see his grandfather, it would be easier to keep his promise to himself for their relationship to not be so overwhelming. But Henry so loved it when he held his grandson and the baby's little fat arms were around his neck.

Henry met some nice people at the JCC. He played chess game with a man he recently met. Henry went almost every day. There was always something interesting going on. But most amazing to Henry was the instant camaraderie he felt, no matter where the Jewish people came from or what language they spoke.

Henry mastered English pretty well, but of course his accent was pretty strong and most likely would stay that way. There was one man who made him not care so much. He would listen to Dr. Kissinger and his accent. This politician had a lot to say and important people listened to him.

Henry read the New York Times every morning, watched the news on television and read history books about the United States. It was amazing to Henry to think that this mighty country was only about two hundred years old. The United States was made up of people from all over the world. Those people born in the USA did not understand how lucky they were, he thought. Henry had become very interested in the politics of the USA.

Henry could have immigrated to the United States immediately after the war, but instead he waited for Liliana until it was too late to get out of Communist Poland. This fact always led him to a bitter taste in his mouth. He spoke to his attorney to find out if it would be possible to become a citizen of the United States. He was advised it wouldn't be easy, but it was possible. Alex and Rebecca applied already, and of course Sam was a born citizen.

New York was full of life always. Henry was at ease and never bored there. He fell in love with Broadway and saw most of the shows. The opera was splendid. There was so much to do. He also spent hours in the museums of New York. He learned so much about art.

Henry received a great offer from Sotheby's for some of the antiques he brought to them. He was not sure he wanted to sell them yet. He had to think hard to make a decision.

Joseph forwarded mail to Henry. Among it, was a letter from Liliana. She wrote about the upcoming wedding of her son, and thanked him for the photos. It was a warm letter, but Henry always felt bitter after reading her letters. He cared nothing about her son or her life. He could not understand why he was even keeping in touch with her. Each time he received a letter from her it was painful for him. He was distraught for days. He often thought that maybe he should just cut off all communication and not bother to tell Rebecca anything ever. It would probably be best for everyone.

A visit with Sam took all the blues away. He walked now and there was no stopping him. He walked all the time. Henry did not have the strength to run after him. The baby's energy had no bounds. The nanny surely had her hands full. Rebecca had spoiled Sam terribly and so did Henry. The only discipline he got was from his father. Sam loved cars, trucks and huggable stuffed animals. The apartment was full of them. Henry was on the floor playing with Sam. The problem was that after a while he could not get up from the floor. His bones ached and over all, Henry started to feel his age, but he chased those thoughts away.

One of his chess playing partners invited Henry to dinner. Henry brought a large bouquet of flowers and a good bottle of wine. The apartment was on Lexington Avenue in a magnificent pre-war building, but the décor was terrible. The food was equally bad.

The dinner guests there were inquisitive about Henry. They asked all kinds of questions, some of them private, which Henry did not answer. Henry was also curious about them. Some of them had lived in the United States for generations. Most had a good life, a good education, never went hungry or cold or heard bombs over their heads. He had a hard time to bond with these people. He did not believe he could find a true close friend among them. Now Henry understood why Alex and Rebecca had friends with the same background as they had. Well, this was a big problem for Henry. He would always feel a stranger. He started to appreciate Israel and the way he felt there even more.

Henry was truly trying to convince the kids to come and visit Israel, mainly for Alex's parents' sake. Also, he was trying to get Eva and her kids to come to Jerusalem. All of them would be invited to stay in Eva's house. They were trying to coordinate their vacations. Henry hoped it would all fall in to place.

But for then, his best friend was Sam. Henry spent time in the JCC. He was known as one of the best chess players. Everybody wanted to play with him. Henry was proud of his new fame. Henry was considering making a dinner party for a few of his new acquaintances, but he was not sure yet.

Finally Alex and Rebecca told him that they were coming to Israel with him for three weeks. "Hallelujah," thought Henry. They would leave together in a little over a month. They were taking the nanny with them. Afterwards, Henry would stay in Israel. He called Eva and told her the good news. She was happy. She would come a week before them with her kids. All the plans were made.

Henry had some business to finalize, so he would be busy until they left. He also urged his JCC friends to visit Israel. Most of them had never been there and Henry could not understand it.

That Friday, Henry was invited to go to the synagogue on Fifth Avenue. He could not remember the last time he had been in a synagogue. He wanted to see the new services that were conducted in the United States. Rebecca shook her head. She could not believe he was going. She knew he was not a religious man.

The temple was very impressive. It was big, and rich and there was not an empty seat in the place. Henry was truly surprised at the way he felt. There was a calmness that made him feel responsive to the prayers. It reminded him of being in the synagogue before the war. It felt good to be here. He knew he belonged here and promised himself to attend often. He never remembered what made him make the conscious decision not to go to synagogue. It probably was his anger with God for the Holocaust, he thought. Henry knew a lot of survivors had a hard time returning to the bosom of God, but it was not only God that Jews were seeking. Just as important was their feeling of belonging and being with their own people and sharing the same beliefs.

The day came for Henry to finalize the details of their trip to Israel. His housekeeper would take care of both apartments while they were gone. All was settled for their departure. Henry was excited that they were all going to be together. Rebecca would spend a week with the Silber's. That week Henry would take Eva and her kids sightseeing in Israel. Then all of them would enjoy being together in Eva's beautiful villa in Jerusalem.

Henry considered seeing a cardiologist in New York before the trip. He got tired much more often and now also short of breath. He did not say anything to Rebecca. At the JCC, he asked his friends for a recommendation of a good specialist and made an appointment.

Henry was apprehensive but he tried to keep his cool. Sitting in a chair opposite the doctor gave him a chill. After some tests, the doctor told him that he needed more accurate tests and that they should be done when he returned from Israel. He advised Henry to take it easy and definitely lose some weight. They would see each other in two months and the doctor left the room. Henry remained seated in his chair. "So, there is something wrong with me," he thought.

As Henry was walking the streets of New York, he made a decision and a promise to follow the doctor's advice. He was not ready to turn into an old, sick man and depart from this world. He wanted to see his grandchild grow and maybe have another grandchild. With all these thoughts, he reached his apartment.

That night Henry was invited to dinner by one of his colleagues from the JCC. He changed and was ready to go and have a good time.

The next day he met with Rebecca to and helped her start packing for the trip. Sam was adorable, he wanted to pack all of his toys. They played with him more than doing any packing. Rebecca and Alex are very excited to go and show off their son. Alex had not seen his parents or his brother for a long time. It was about time for them to make this journey.

CHAPTER 28

They were all ready. The car service picked them up. They departed from Newark Airport on El Al Airlines. It was a long flight and Henry bought first class tickets for more comfort. Sam was at the window and watched the planes around them, repeating, "Big plane, big plane!" Henry closed his eyes, and for the first time, asked God to keep them safe. He never prayed before. He surprised himself at the urgency to do so, but it did give him comfort. The plane took off without a hitch. Sam fell asleep and Henry felt tired too. Rebecca sat next to her father. Henry held her hand and fell asleep. He probably could have slept longer, but Sam's crying woke him. Henry looked at his watch and saw that three hours had passed.

He felt refreshed and offered to care for Sam so that Rebecca and Alex could take a nap. Henry took Sam on his lap and whispered sweet nothings in his ear. Sam loved it and soon fell asleep again in Henry's arms. Henry was listening to his steady breathing. All was very quiet and Henry thought this was a good moment to remember and cherish. It was amazing how such small things could give you happiness. It was as his father always told him, "The best things in life are free."

In an hour they would be landing. Rebecca was gathering their things and Sam was again at the window, repeating "Clouds, clouds!" Henry felt tired and achy, another reminder that there must be something wrong with him. He thought it might be wise to see a doctor in Israel. They had very good medical care and were known for their new ways of treating illnesses. Henry decided not say anything to Eva yet. He knew she would be unhappy about it. Henry did not want anyone to worry. He wanted everyone to have a good time.

Henry held the baby while Alex and Rebecca took care of the luggage. Henry spotted the Silber's soon after they exited. He whispered to Sam, "Please be nice to these people, do it for me." Sam looked at him as if he understood.

Henry handed Sam to the Silber's and said, "Here is your grandson, Samuel."

Mr. Silber had tears in his eyes and could only say, "Thank you, thank you." Henry stood aside and observed the greetings. They were all crying. Sam was so good. He let them kiss and hug him without shedding a tear, as if he understood how important this was.

Henry went to his apartment and Rebecca, Alex and Sam went to the Silber's' home. Eva and her kids were going straight to the villa. They would all meet in Jerusalem in a week.

The two taxis went in opposite directions. Henry always enjoyed returning to his apartment in Tel Aviv. It was like entering the safest place in the world. He slept well that night and was awoken by the ringing of the phone. The Silber's were calling to invite him for dinner tomorrow.

The first thing Henry did was to dress and go to the beach. The smell of the water was like nowhere else in the world. He took a big breath. The waves were quietly lapping the shore. All was peaceful. It was early in the morning and the beachgoers had not arrived yet. Henry went to a little coffee shop where the owner knew and greeted him by asking, "Where were you this time?" Henry just had coffee and a biscuit, knowing that his housekeeper would prepare a big breakfast.

Again, Henry saw changes in Israel. There was a growth of high tech, high rise buildings. Almost every technology company had representation in Israel. The higher standard for education in Israel pushed the students to achieve perfection to fill the jobs of various international companies. Henry was so proud of this little country.

After breakfast and a refreshing shower, Henry went about his business. He felt good. Later Henry would call Joseph and Moshe to meet with him. Eva and her kids were at the villa and Henry was planned on going there in two days. They had spoken on the phone. He missed her and could not wait to see her.

Dinner at the Silber's was a treat. It gave Henry pleasure to see the happiness on their faces. The family was all together. In a week Rebecca and Alex would come to Jerusalem. Henry was leaving tomorrow.

Henry took a car service to Jerusalem. The road was smooth and he was close to the villa. The hellos were warm and sincere. The villa looked amazing. They ate dinner together and later they sat in the garden. The air was fresh and crisp. Henry and Eva talked nonstop to catch up with their news. Eva finally took his hand and led him to the bedroom. Henry was afraid of his performance due to his poor health. Soon, this was forgotten. They were happy again just resting in each other's arms.

The next morning a driver arrived to take them sightseeing. They were going to Cesarea. Cesarea was a historic place to visit and had a great museum. The weather was perfect and each day thereafter they went to see another sight.

Henry's kids were arriving. He was hoping for a friendly co-existence. They had never all been together, but Eva's kids were eager to meet his family, especially Sam. Eva greeted them at the entry. Sam quickly jumped into Henry's arms. Rebecca was admiring the villa and Alex was unpacking. They all relaxed that week, enjoying each other's company and the beautiful setting. It was so good to be together. They were meant to live as a family. But fate had its own ways.

They all agreed they must reunite every year. Eva and her kids were leaving soon. Rebecca, Alex and Sam were going to the Silber's' for another few days before returning to New York. Henry would stay in Tel Aviv for a while. Next week he was meeting with his two friends again. His heart was full, he felt complete. It was a very successful visit, everyone was happy.

Henry was enjoying the freedom of being alone. He slept late and took leisurely walks on the sands of the shore. The kids had returned home safely. Eva and her family went back to London. He was having his friends come over for dinner. The housekeeper prepared a nice meal that she served to the three men.

They all talked and caught up with news of their families. Moshe looked well and his illness was forgotten. Henry told them about how he had been feeling and asked for a recommendation to see the best cardiologist. Moshe said he would need a few days to arrange an appointment for Henry.

The appointment was made in Jerusalem with a well-known cardiologist. Moshe picked Henry up and went with him for the check-up. They drove in silence. Henry was a little scared. All the tests were scheduled for that day. Henry appreciated Moshe being with him. It was not good to be alone at a time like this.

Blood work was taken and next came the stress test, actually two of them, and then an MRI. The doctor would see him in about two hours; the longest two hours for Henry. The doctor came into the examining room with a smile on his face. Maybe it was not as bad as Henry was thinking.

"You have an enlarged heart," said the doctor, "and you will have to learn to live with it. There is no surgery or medication necessary, but your lifestyle will have to change drastically. You need special exercises and you need to keep a good diet and lose weight. This is the only way to keep the condition from getting worse. It is all up to you, Mr. Kopel."

Henry expected worse, but this was not so great either. Okay, he thought, he would follow the advice. Henry's plans were to return to New York and to see another doctor. But diet starts today.

CHAPTER 29

The construction was almost completed. Another two weeks and it would all be done. Helena was so proud of herself. She oversaw the project from the start. Robert was there also, but mostly for technical advice. The houses were finished beautifully, more than they had hoped for.

Max and Katy would be there soon. Helena looked after dinner. The following day they were all leaving for Dusseldorf for a few days to finalize the wedding preparations. Helena could not wait to see how the Rothman family lived. Robert prepared the suitcases and reminded Helena not to butt in on anything. He kept saying, "Let them have the wedding. We will have them living near us all the time." Helena knew he was right.

They all arrived in Dusseldorf in the early afternoon, a little tired but happy. Sarah was a great hostess. All was prepared for them. She seemed to be glad they all came.

The dinner was fantastic. They enjoyed the delicious meal and the gracious table set by Sarah. They conversed about the wedding and they planned to go see the banquet hall the next day. They also planned on going to the church where the wedding would take place. Helena could not help but think how awkward this was for her. Nonetheless, they would meet the priest that would conduct the ceremony. Helena and Katy needed to shop for their dresses as well. There was a lot to do, but it was all great fun for Helena.

That evening, while lying in bed, Helena had a million thoughts. She had not heard from Henry in a long time. There was no way for her to know of any news regarding her daughter and grandson unless Henry decided to communicate. Helena had so many conflicting feelings, "What if anything happens to Henry. How would I ever be able to find my daughter?" She must get in touch with Henry soon.

Finally sleep came and in the morning she awoke refreshed and ready for a day of adventure. Sarah showed Helena the hall for the wedding reception. It was an elegant, classy place. The church was in the oldest section of the city. It was old, dark and dingy, a little scary for Helena. Afterwards, they had lunch and proceeded to a very famous dress salon that specialized in wedding gowns.

"So much to choose from," thought Helena. She wanted something classy and simple and light in color. But first they would see some wedding dresses for Katy. Whatever Katy put on looked beautiful on her. Helena decided she would not give any advice. She left this for Katy's mother. Sarah also did know which dress was best. They finally left it up to Katy to make the final choice of a dress.

Sarah and Helena tried on a few gowns as well. It was a lot of fun, but no decisions were made. Robert would need a new tuxedo too.

Sarah prepared a veal goulash for dinner that night. It was absolutely delicious. And again, Helena was reminded of the tastes of her family's meals. Helena liked Sarah more each day. Too bad they did not live closer to each other, thought Helena. Everyone had agreed on the wedding decisions and it was time to return home. Helena wanted to have time to decorate both villas.

Max and Albert had different tastes, and Helena liked to please both of them. Max liked more of a modern style with a few antiques around. But Albert preferred a darker, antique style. Not so much a German style, more of an English style.

There was a large room in the main house where there were a lot of antiques used by previous generations. Helena definitely planned on using them for the boys. She made an appointment with a decorator to help her, but Helena would make the final choices.

Helena sat at her desk and wrote a letter to Henry. She begged him, again, to provide some information. Her feelings were mixed. Helena was angry with him, but she could not blame him.

The next day was a good day. The decorator understood the wishes of Helena's sons, and soon the work would start. All would be completed in about three months. Max wanted to move in as soon as possible. He wanted to live in the house alone at least six months before the wedding.

Helena went with Robert to Munich to shop for her dress, get a tuxedo for Robert and to relax a little.

Robert relied more and more on Max and Albert with regards to his business. As a matter of fact, they introduced some new and smart ideas. Robert was relaxing more now that he knew his business was in good hands.

Helena was immersed in the preparations for the wedding and the decorating, and it did her good.

Robert and Helena did not discuss Rebecca anymore. Helena used to tell Robert whenever she heard from Henry, but she did not bother anymore. However, the awkward situation was on Robert's mind all the time. He knew that things would explode one day. But later was better than sooner. The boys were becoming men and their understanding would be more mature. Or maybe, the truth would never be told to them. This was what Robert was hoping for.

Robert was looking forward to the wedding. Katy was a fine young woman and Max was so happy with her. Helena liked her very much as well.

Albert had been very uptight lately. His final exams for his law degree were coming up. He studied all the time, biting his fingernails, and talking to himself. He did not have the self-confidence of his brother, Max.

Shopping with Helena was almost fun! She found a suitable gown in the lightest shade of lilac, made of silk chiffon. Helena looked sensational. Robert and she continued to shop for the right shoes and evening bag. It was all done in one day. Next they would shop for Robert's tuxedo. The one he had at home did not fit him anymore. They also planned on seeing a play and having dinner in the hotel. Robert loved being with Helena on these short excursions. They always had a good time.

Robert enjoyed seeing Helena happy because most of the time she was quiet and there was a sadness in her face. Her face only lit up when she saw her sons. With age, Helena was becoming more secretive with her feelings. Robert did not understand this change. "Why doesn't she share her soul with me?" He wanted to know, but he was not brave enough to ask. She was his life, his love. For him, his feelings never changed.

The next day it was Robert's turn. They shopped only for him. The tuxedo was ordered. Robert never cared for fashion and yet he was always immaculately dressed in the finest clothes, but this was only because Helena took care of it.

The houses were finally complete. The road was paved and the gardener was planted the last flower beds. The interiors were taking shape. All the old furniture from the main house had been placed in the new houses. Max was going to move in shortly. Helena was looking for a housekeeper for Max.

Helena was a reader. She read all kinds of books and novels, whether they be history, sociology, art, etc. The intense reading throughout her years taught her all aspects of life. History, life of the rich and famous, poverty, greed and love. Helena was never quite sure that all she read was really true in life. She had always been sheltered from reality. She knew very few people intimately and books became her real life. She wanted to be more involved with humanity.

Helena learned that a good housekeeper should be a plump, sturdy woman in her late forties with some experience. Helena read novels about the tragedies caused by young and ambitious help. She did not want to take a chance by hiring the wrong person. She would interview all the applicants herself. She saw some women already, but none were good enough for her son. Helena wanted to be involved in her sons' lives and maybe in the future with her grandchildren's lives.

Albert completed his studies. He needed to work in a law office for two years, and then, if he wanted, he could open his own law firm. He was now more relaxed and would take a short vacation with his girlfriend.

Robert felt as if a great burden left his soul. His two sons were educated, grown-up, young adults who could take care of their own lives.

Helena made reservations for the family to stay in Dusseldorf for a few days before and after the wedding. Albert came back from his mini vacation and announced that he would not be bringing his girlfriend to the wedding. He explained to his parents that he was not sure about his feelings for this girl. He imagined that love would feel different. Helena and Robert understood their son. They always had a feeling that something was missing in Albert's relationships.

Finally Helena hired a nice woman to be her son's housekeeper. Her name was Felicia. She would move in right away. She had her own car and would be self-sufficient. Maximilian approved and he could not wait to move in too. His room in the main house would remain the same. Only his clothes and personal things would be moved to the new house. Helena had a pang in her heart, even though her son would be so close by. She could not imagine her son not living with them in the main house.

Albert seemed to be alright. He was not suffering over the breakup of his relationship. He got a job in a good law firm specializing in business. He would be working long hours. When asked if he was ready to move into his new house, he answered with a short "No." Helena was glad.

Helena wanted to hear from Henry, but so far there was only silence. She wanted to know the whereabouts of Rebecca, where she lived, what her married name was. At times, Helena was so angry with Henry. Helena recognized that she would never be forgiven. The only way she would be able to see her daughter would be on Henry's terms. Robert did not want them to meet under Henry's terms. How could she change his mind? After the wedding, Helena must persuade Robert to understand the situation her way.

Helena went her first whole day without seeing her son Max. It felt strange. Before she went to sleep, Helena looked to see a light in her son's home. The wedding was in two months.

* * *

Before they returned to Dusseldorf to finalize the wedding preparations, Katy's family came to see and stay at the completed house. Robert hired a limo so that he would be free to talk with them on the way from the airport. Maximilian went too. Helena was looking forward to the visit. They would first come to her house for lunch before going to Maximilian's house. At the table they all talked and laughed. The food was excellent. Helena tried so hard to please them and it did not go unnoticed.

After lunch, Max took Katy's hand and said to all, "Come see where we will begin our life together." They all followed the couple to the new house.

Flowers were placed everywhere. Felicia was a good housekeeper. Everything was spotless. Helena was curious to see everyone's reaction to the house. Upon their arrival all Helena could hear was how beautiful and elegant the house was. Katy had tears in her eyes. She kissed Helena and told her that a thank you was not enough. She could not wait to move in. The house was truly amazing. Robert watched Helena and saw that she was beaming. For Robert and Helena both, this was a moment to remember.

When the Rothman family left it became quiet again. Helena was ready for the wedding. They would soon meet in Dusseldorf. Robert made reservations with the airlines. Helena decided she would take it easy and relax for a while to take her mind off the wedding and everything else.

The weather was beautiful and Helena took advantage of it. She sat on her veranda, listening to the birds and the shushing of the leaves. Whenever she took time to relax and took time with nature, she was always amazed by the beauty of her surroundings. It was truly heavenly. Helena never wanted to know about the troubles in the world, about politics or about the poverty in so many nations. She only saw and cared about her little world. Robert tried to engage her. He encouraged her to listen to the news, but she never wanted to. She did not even want to know about Israel or her own country. Her world consisted of her husband, her sons and the manicured twenty acres of their estate. Helena loved to read books which showed the beauty of other countries. She had a good mind and learned quickly. Whenever she did venture out, it was always to return to her roots somehow. Helena always sought this out.

Robert even surprised himself by his determination to keep their secret. He wanted to preserve his family from a scandal and he was not sure how his sons would receive it. Would they hate the truth or embrace it? The only people who knew the secret was Henry, Helena and himself. That was at least what Robert thought. He did not know about Joseph or Moshe or the Witkowskis, in Poland. The older Robert became, the more this issue was on his mind.

CHAPTER 30

The wedding day arrived. Everyone was getting ready. Maximilian was nervous but happy. He looked handsome. Helena could not stop looking at him. She could not believe that this was her son. Albert was teasing his brother. He looked just as good as Max. The limo waited to take them to the church. Helena hoped that the ceremony would not take too long. The church really looked scary to her. The church had a lot of history and the Rothman family insisted the ceremony be there. So be it. There was no changing it then.

The family was seated in the front row. Helena was surprised at the amount of people there. The guests all nodded at them as they passed to their seats. As Helena waited for the priest to come out, she examined the church. It had stain glass windows, a lot of "scary" statues of the devil and symbols from another world. The few old chandeliers that were there did not give off enough light. Helena hated darkness. The priest finally arrived.

The ceremony was short and sweet. Katy was a breathtaking bride. Sarah had an elegant long gown made of silk. Helena received a lot of compliments on her dress as well.

After the ceremony, the guests and family moved on to the reception. The banquet hall was elegant. They ate good food and danced. Helena was approached by almost everybody. First to congratulate her and then to ask all about their estate and the history of the family. And, just like that, the party was over. The newlyweds left. It was a secret as to where they were honeymooning.

The Van Klauses stayed for another few days with the Rothman family. They would go to the theater and concerts and meet the immediate family more intimately at Sarah's dinner parties. It was all great fun. Helena looked for more familiar dishes that Sarah prepared. One of them was dumplings filled with meat and onions served with chicken broth. This was exactly what Helena's mother prepared for the Jewish New Year. And that mysterious smile found its way on to Helena's face once again.

Every time something unfamiliar was served she asked Robert if it was a German dish. He always answered, "No it is not, but it is delicious. Maybe you ask for the recipes and serve it at home."

It was time to go home. Helena invited the immediate family for the Christmas holidays. When the plane left the ground, Helena was happy to be going home to her quiet existence which she had become so accustomed to. She took a long nap on the plane and dreamed of introducing her sons to her mother and father. In the dream her parents were so enchanted. They looked happy and did not hold anything against Helena. But she did dream that they said, "Do not forget your daughter."

Helena was awoken abruptly being shaken by Robert. "We are home, darling," he said. Helena asked if she had been talking during her nap. "No, you were not," said Robert. But she was not so sure. When they entered their home, Helena was so glad.

Maximilian and Katy returned from their honeymoon. They looked rested, happy and in love. Felicia prepared the house for their homecoming. Max would go back to work the following day. And so their new life began.

Helena knew she should not visit them until invited, but it was difficult to stay away. Katy had a few interviews scheduled. She wanted to start working as soon as was possible. After a few days, Katy called Helena and Robert and invited them for dinner. It felt awkward for Helena to be a guest in her son's home for dinner. Katy was a charming hostess and she prepared some of the dishes herself, with Felicia's help. The table was set impeccably with flowers and china. The home had a lovely scent. After dinner, they sat by the fireplace looking at photos from their honeymoon. "What a lovely evening," said Robert to Helena as they walked back to their home.

Helena decided she should write to Henry again. She had not received a response to her last two letters and by now she was very uneasy.

Sarah called Helena regularly. They spoke about little nothings and she always invited Helena to visit. Helena thought that maybe she should go, without Robert, and stay for a week. That night she asked Robert. Reluctantly, Robert agreed.

Sarah was delighted to hear the news. She promised Helena a good time. Stephen and Sarah waited for her at the airport. The room was prepared for Helena with the utmost care. It had fresh white linens, flowers everywhere and her own bathroom with lotions and soaps. At breakfast they had so much to talk about. Sarah had planned a luncheon for her cousins and good friends so Helena could get to know them better. She also promised to show Helena old family photos and some memorabilia from past generations. This was what Helena was anxious to see.

The luncheon was fun. All the ladies where chattering at the same time and showing off photos of their children and grandchildren. They were exchanging recipes and sharing the latest gossip. It was obvious that they did lunches like this very often. Helena felt out of her element. She could not decide if she liked it or not. She sat and looked upon the ladies with amazement. It was definitely a new experience for her. Helena was never a guest at such a gathering before.

In the evening, they sat in front of a table covered with old photos. Sarah started to identify the people in them, "My uncle, my great aunt, my cousins," and so on.

"Good looking people," thought Helena, until she took a photo in her hand of a little girl in a fancy velvety dress wearing a necklace. Helena looked at the necklace carefully. She was unsure of what she was seeing. She asked who the child was.

Sarah answered, "This is my grandmother." Helena asked for a magnifying glass to see the photo better. She looked at the other photos also, but soon returned to the photo of the little girl again. What she saw shocked her. The little girl's necklace was a Star of David on a chain made of little, tiny pearls. Helena did not comment and placed the photo down. She wanted to keep the photo but could not figure how she could manage this. For the moment, she looked intensely to see if there was anything else unusual about the other photos.

The photos of Sarah's family were plentiful. Helena asked Sarah how she was able to save them all during the war. "Well, they stayed in Dusseldorf during the war since the family did not relocate." Sarah talked of those people in the photos. She identified who they were and what they did. They left the photos on the table in the library and planned on returning to them the next day.

They all retired for the night. Helena could not sleep. All she could see in front of her eyes was that little girl wearing the Star of David necklace. She would ask Sarah her name tomorrow.

The next day was full of activities. They went shopping, sightseeing and caught a concert in the evening. They did not have time to return to the photos again that night.

Helena finally thought of a good reason for why she wanted to borrow the photo. She would make an enlargement to give to Katy for her new home. The next day when they sat to look at the photos again, Helena asked for the photo. Sarah was glad to give it to her. On the back of the photo it said, "Sarah, age 3, Dusseldorf." So, Katy's mother was named after her grandmother.

Helena would get the picture enlarged and somehow mask the Star of David. It was small and could resemble a heart. But Helena would have the photo enlarged at a store in another town where no one knew her. Robert was going on a business trip shortly. She would go with him and do it there. They were staying in Berlin for four days which would give her enough time to get this done.

But now Helena knew the origin of the family, at least from the mother's side. If Katy had a Jewish great-grandmother, grandmother and mother, then that would make Katy Jewish according to Jewish belief, even if there was no religious conversion. And according to the Jewish religion, Helena's sons were Jewish as well. "What are the odds of this happening," thought Helena. She was not sure how she felt about this revelation. She would keep this a secret and tell no one. She placed the photo in her underwear drawer, where no one would discover it.

Back home Helena resumed her normal routine. Katy came to visit and inquired about her parents. She missed them. She also complained about the lack of jobs available to her. They had a good talk and as they said goodbye, Katy kissed Helena on her cheek. Helena liked this girl even more now.

Helena asked Robert if she could join him on his business trip to Berlin. He agreed but wondered about it. She never wanted to go with him before. But he was glad. He hated to come back to an empty hotel room after an entire day of meetings.

Helena invited Max and Katy for dinner. Before they left the main house, Max said, "It's good to be home. I thought you forgot you had a son." The next day Helena and Robert left for Berlin.

The weather did not cooperate. It was raining and it was cold. At the front desk of the hotel, Helena found out about the best photo shop in town. She took a taxi and was on her way there.

A young man at the photo shop offered his help. He spoke German with a heavy accent. Reluctantly, she showed him the photo and explained what she wanted him to do. The man took a magnifying glass and took a closer look. "Yes, it is true. It is a Star of David. And yes, I can make an enlargement and change the Star of David to look more like a ball or a little heart." This is exactly what Helena wanted. She left him the photo and asked for a speedy job. She selected a frame for the picture and she would return in two days to pick it up. Helena felt a strong gaze from the clerk but he did not say anything.

A big rainstorm plagued Berlin the next day. Helena did venture out to a brand new department store close by. It was an elegant store full of foreign merchandise. She bought very little. She did not want to overcrowd her closet with clothes she did not need. She bought gifts for her sons and daughter in-law and a few trinkets for the help. When she returned to the hotel she found a comfortable spot in the beautiful lobby. She ordered coffee and watched the people go by. She liked watching people. She would imagine what secrets they held. Or maybe she was the only one with a secret.

Time was dragging on. Robert was not coming back until dinner time, hours from then. Helena went back to the room, laid down on the fluffy bed and fell asleep. She had a dream, though it was more like a memory, so real and so vivid. She saw Rebecca as a little girl. She felt her little hands around her neck and heard her first word, "Mommy." She saw Henry admiring them with so much love on his face, and then darkness. She heard only the voice of Rebecca crying, "Mommy, Mommy!" Helena awoke drenched in sweat and shaking. She turned on the television for a diversion and tried very hard to relax, but all she did was cry. She was glad she was alone at that moment.

After that episode she took a long shower, sat on the easy chair and looked out on the street through the window. She was afraid to go to bed again, afraid to dream again. She pulled herself together before Robert arrived. They went downstairs for dinner.

The time came to pick up the photos. Helena arrived at the shop. The young clerk was there again. He gave a sly smile and said, "It all came out perfect." The enlarged photo in the frame was an artistic masterpiece. It looked more like a painting. The Star of David looked more like a little heart. He also made two additional copies of the original photo. Helena would keep those for herself and return the original to the Rothmans. She would tell Robert about the copy but not about the necklace.

The day was pleasant. She returned to the hotel, left the framed photo and went out for a walk. The city was buzzing with life, noisy and dusty.

Helena thought she could never live in a big city again. She remembered Warsaw before the war. Then, she liked the city life that she disliked so much now. "Thank God we are going home tomorrow," thought Helena.

Back home, Helena called the kids and asked them to come dinner. After dinner, she presented a package to Katy and said, "Open it and see if you like it."

Katy opened the wrapping and looked at the little girl in amazement. "It's beautiful, who is this girl?" she asked.

And Helena answered, "It is your great-grandmother."

"It is?" asked Katy in surprise. "I never saw it before. I love it and will put it on the wall immediately! Thank you so much." Helena told them how Katy's mother showed her the old photos, and Helena picked that one to enlarge. Katy gave her a big hug and kiss.

Max said, looking at the photo carefully, "This girl looks a lot like Katy, don't you think so mother?" Helena nodded in agreement.

Robert gave Helena a great compliment that evening as they were undressing in their bedroom. He told her how special the gift was. "If only he knew just how special," thought Helena.

Everyone was getting used to their new living arrangements. Unable to find a suitable job, Katy went back to school. Maximilian worked with his father and Albert was doing very well at the law firm. Helena tried to convince Albert to move into his new home, but he did not want to. "Not until I get married," he answered. He spent a lot of time in his brother's home.

Albert just let them know that he met a nice girl, but it was too early to introduce her to the family. She was also an attorney and they met at the courthouse. She was a local girl and studied in Berlin. Her family lived in Regensburg where they had lived for many generations, just like the Van Klaus family, except they were not as privileged. Her family owned a large orchard farm which had been in the family for a long time. The farm was located on the outskirts of town and Albert was going there to meet her family on Sunday. Her name was Monica and Albert was in love.

Helena asked Robert to find out anything he could about her family. Robert did not care for such a request, only because he already knew, but told Helena he would.

Albert returned from his Sunday visit and Helena was all over him. He had to answer a lot of questions. Robert did not ask any. Albert told them that he was received nicely and politely. The farm was fabulous, well run. It had a lot of cows and sheep and a lot of small animals like chickens, ducks, dogs, pigs. There was great order within this commotion and it was run by Monica's father and older brother who lived on the premises. There were two houses close together. Monica's brother, Wolf, was married and had two daughters. One thing Albert did not like about his visit was how Monica's family questioned him about his mother. But Albert thought it best not to share this with his parents. He had a feeling that all was not well. His father had not said a word. Albert would have to talk to his father as soon as they could be alone.

That opportunity came the next day. Robert asked Albert if he loved Monica and told him that if the answer was yes, then nothing else mattered. But Robert also did tell him that Monica's family and the Van Klaus's were on opposite sides before the war. Before the war, some Germans followed Hitler and others did not. The Van Klauses did not. However, once the war started, a young German had three choices: flee, join the Nazi army or be killed. So Robert's family made sure that Robert would never see combat and would be in a position where he would never have anyone's blood on his hands. Monica's family were Nazis and followers of the Hitler regime to the fullest before the war, during the war and so much so after the war, that they were considered radicals. They probably did not like that Albert's mother was not born German. But they liked the fact that the Van Klaus family was a very noble family and also very rich. Albert told Monica's family that Helena was a countess from Poland, but they seemed to know that already. Albert truly loved Monica and decided not to think about her family's past.

Monica was coming to visit the Van Klauses that coming Sunday. They would have a family dinner with Max and Katy too.

Monica was a pretty girl and looked very German. She was tall, strong, blonde, blue-eyed and very outspoken. She was very intelligent and opinionated too. Helena never thought that Albert would pick a girl like this. Albert was delicate, quiet, slim and very tall. "Well, as they say, opposites attract," Helena thought.

Monica was very polite and not very talkative. But when you looked at her eyes, you could see that she was observing everything. Albert did not show her his house or his brother's house and asked his family not to either.

Helena was not sure how she felt about this girl. She only knew that she would have to learn to like her.

CHAPTER 31

enry picked up his mail. He had returned to New York earlier that week. It took him a few days to get over his jet lag, but he felt good. He lost some weight and he was very careful about his diet, no fat, no salt. He made an appointment with a well-known New York cardiologist.

Looking over the mail, he found a letter from Liliana. It was the third letter she had sent. He did not reply to the previous ones. He refused to open it until he returned from his doctor's appointment. Henry did not want to get upset right then. The letters were forwarded from Israel. Liliana had no clue that he and Rebecca were in the United States.

The tests that he took were exactly the same as the tests he took in Israel. He was waiting to hear the results from his doctor. The doctor told Henry the same report as the doctors in Israel had although his blood pressure was lower, if not almost normal. Henry had become more careful. He did not lift heavy objects, including his grandson. He would follow all the doctor's instructions and return in six months to see if there were any changes. Henry was relieved. He understood that he could not be perfectly healthy for the rest of his life.

Rebecca and Alex were coming for dinner, and of course Sam. His housekeeper, with Henry's help, prepared dinner. Henry changed his clothes and looked over the mail again. The last envelope in his hand was the letter from Liliana. After reading it, Henry felt a little sorry for Liliana. She was begging him for an answer. He decided this time he would write back.

It was a pleasure to be a host to his kids. Sam sat at the table on a bunch of pillows and ate with them using a fork and knife, like a little man. He was almost three years old. After dinner they watched television and then Rebecca said she had some good news. She was expecting another child, due in seven months. She was smiling. "It's a gift from Israel," she said. Henry was thrilled. He felt fortunate. Alex stood there looking very proud of himself.

After they left, Henry could not fall asleep. He started wondering if it would be a boy or a girl, but it really did not matter. "Just, please God, let it be healthy," he pleaded. He planned on talking to Rebecca to try and persuade her to work less hours. With that thought, he fell asleep.

The next day he sat down to write a letter to Liliana. He was very confused about his feelings. Each time he wrote to her, it made him angry, and it also made him feel sorry for himself. They could have had a nice life together. Back then he loved her very much. But he was not so sure of his feelings now. "Is it possible that I still love her?" he was questioned his feelings. If he did not care, than why was he having such strange feelings when he received these letters from her? He was sure he felt anger towards her, but could you be angry and in love with someone at the same time? Probably, yes. Henry had been chasing away thoughts of her for a long time. Sometimes it was memories and sometimes it was anger and disappointment. He could never get to the point of indifference.

The letter he wrote was dry and cold. He informed Liliana about Rebecca being pregnant again and about the progress Sam was making. But he did not answer the request for Rebecca's address or her married name. These were the only things he had in order to be vengeful. He did not write anything about himself.

Henry went to the JCC in the afternoon and met some of his buddies. They were happy to see him. He played some chess again. He was asked to join them for dinner, men only, to which he agreed. That evening they questioned Henry about Israel and his views on politics. There were heated discussions about how the men felt and behaved towards Israel. It was obvious they cared. They discussed what, if any, was their obligation or involvement.

American Jews had a happy life in the United States. They never felt danger. But it was as if they were oblivious to Israel's very existence; ignorant as to why Israel was so important and unaware of the impact Israel had on them. Henry wondered why Israel was not taking any steps to correct this. He would speak to Moshe about it.

Henry's exercise regime was to take long walks, which in New York, was very easy. That day he walked in the neighborhood of the antique galleries. It was always a great surprise to him to see how many fakes were introduced to him as originals. This could never have happened before the war in Warsaw. Antique galleries had good reputations. Antiques were never cheap and people did not negotiate price. Everything was different in the antique business now and none of it was for the better. Henry still had to search for a reputable place that specializes in old gold coins. He wanted to sell some and get more involved in the stock market. The stock market fascinated him very much.

Rebecca received notice that she and Alex would be able to become citizens of the USA within the next three months. This was happy news. It would happen before the new baby would be born. They received books to study in order to be prepared for the citizenship exam. Henry was happy. He informed his lawyer. This would make it faster for him to become a citizen as well.

The loss of weight made Henry feel so much better and walking made him feel light on his feet again.

The New York Public Library was full of people. It was a magnificent building well equipped with all that was needed to be called a "great library." Henry looked for publications on the largest American companies, their history and up to date performances. He wanted to learn all he could before he ventured out to be an investor. He was amazed at American ingenuity. It was very interesting and he wanted to know more and more. Henry was sorry he was not a young man anymore. He felt he could have done so much, but age plays a big role.

Finally, Henry was introduced to a reliable coin dealer. Henry liked him. He showed him a sample coin and wanted to hear what the he had to say. The dealer was very knowledgeable and Henry was surprised at the price he offered. It was much more than Henry anticipated. The value was not only in the weight of the gold but also in the rarity of the coin. The dealer thought it would only rise in price in time and Henry had to rethink whether he would sell it or not.

Henry wrote to his old friend, Philip Witkowski. He had not written to him for many years. Under the Communist regime, it was not good for Dr. Witkowski to receive correspondence from Israel or the United States. But Henry was anxious to know how he and his wife, Sofia, were doing. He also still had some of Henry's treasures that Henry was unable to take with him when he left Poland. Henry had to be very careful about how he worded this letter. Before Henry left Poland, they agreed on a code word. He wrote about Rebecca, about his life now and asked the doctor to reply. Henry sent the letter by registered mail in hopes that it would not disappear. He wanted to see the Witkowskis very much, but at the moment, it was not possible. The political atmosphere was changing a little, but freedom for Poland and Eastern Europe was still but a dream.

With his renewed energy and feeling so much better, Henry wanted to do something. He was bored and ready for a new adventure. He did decide to purchase some stocks but this did not keep him busy enough. Sam entered nursery school and told him about his new friends. His vocabulary was impressive for his age.

Rebecca was feeling very tired at the end of each day. Her current pregnancy was not as easy as her previous one. Henry urged her not to work. For now, she only listened, but did not do anything about it. Henry was frustrated. Most people worked because they needed money. She did not. Alex also urged her to stop, but to no avail. Why was she so driven? What was she trying to achieve? No one knew. Maybe she did not have an answer either.

In her fifth month of pregnancy, Rebecca started to feel worse. She was bigger than she was with Sam. Her ankles were swollen all the time. She was irritable and out of breath. She finally decided she had to stop working. Henry was happy. She became more relaxed, had patience with Sam, started to cook a little and visited her father more often.

Henry decided he would stay in New York until the baby was born. As the due date was coming closer, Henry became uneasy. He knew this was not good for his health and he tried to control his anxiety. He talked to himself, saying, "There is nothing wrong with Rebecca, she's fine. The doctors are happy with her progress."

Henry met a stock broker who was recommended to him by somebody at the JCC. The broker suggested an investment in a new company that started to develop computers. Henry knew nothing about computers but he would investigate and get back to the broker.

Henry spent hours in the library researching, and came to the realization that computers would be the industry of the future, but it would take some time. He had to think hard before making a decision. Ultimately he did invest because he recognized that computers would make an amazing change in the lives of people all over the world by a click of a button. Although this industry still felt like a fantasy to Henry, he had the feeling that it would be something special, and Henry went with this feeling. He made a large investment for the long term. He went to his attorney to assign the stocks to Sam.

Henry was excited. He would witness Rebecca and Alexander become citizens of this great country. The swearing in would take place in City Hall. Rebecca was uneasy, heavy with child and cranky. Henry felt sorry for her and wished it would be over soon. The ceremony was very emotional. They immediately applied for passports.

Henry attended the JCC religiously. He had a private trainer and his physique was changing. It was a slow process, but his belly was disappearing and his double chin was almost gone. The change was truly amazing.

When he returned home, the housekeeper met him at the door, wringing her hands. "What happened?" asked Henry.

"Rebecca and Alex left for the hospital. The nanny is with Sam. All is okay," said the nanny.

Henry quickly showered and dressed and went to the hospital. They allowed him in the waiting room and Alex was in the room with Rebecca. He came out for a minute to report that all was okay and normal, but no one knew how long this would take. Henry found a chair to sit down and prepared himself for many hours of waiting. He was napping when Alex tapped him on the shoulder.

"Dad, wake up, we have a little girl. A beautiful little girl! She is healthy and so is Rebecca," said Alex.

"Really," repeated Henry, "can I see them?"

"In a half hour," said Alex.

When Alex left the room, Henry wept. The cry helped him release the tension he had been feeling for months. "What would they name her?" questioned Henry. Finally he was able to see Rebecca and the baby. Rebecca looked good, all smiles. She was relieved. You could see it on her face. The baby looked like a little doll. Henry looked at her with awe. She opened her little eyes, looked at him, and he could swear she smiled.

When they left the hospital, Alex said that Henry should go home and get a good night's sleep. But Henry did not want to go home and be alone. He wanted to be with his family. Alex gave Henry a hug and together they went to the kids' apartment. Henry slept like a baby.

In the morning, Sam came into his bed. "Grandpa Henry, we have a new little girl. Do you think you will love her as much as you love me?"

Henry answered, "I have a lot of love, enough for both of you." Henry didn't think Sam liked that answer.

Rebecca was coming home in three days. The apartment was ready for her and the baby. They hired a nurse for two weeks. Henry was asked to do the food shopping. He loved to be needed and this certainly was a happy occasion.

As the baby slept in the bassinet, Henry sat and watched her. She looked so much like Rebecca, but also like Liliana. Rebecca and Alex named the baby. They named her after Rebecca's mother... Liliana. They would call her Lilly, for short.

Henry could not object, although he felt Liliana did not deserve this honor. He decided that he would only call the baby Lilly. Sam was good with the baby and called her "my little Lilly." Henry snapped a photo of Sam and baby Lilly to send to Liliana. He sent a note telling her it was a photo of her new grand-daughter. He told her that they named her Liliana, after her and that they would call her Lilly. That was all he wrote.

Henry spoke with Eva and told her the good news. She was happy for him but she did complain a little. She had not seen him for many months and she missed him. Henry understood that he did have some obligation towards her and their relationship. He was torn and decided that he would stop in London on his way to Israel. But this decision did not give him the same thrill that it did years before.

This feeling, or lack thereof, made him think. Was he no longer interested in women? But Eva was more than just a woman to him. He really loved being with her and trusted her. She was his good friend, but distance was the worst enemy of any relationship.

Rebecca and Alex got themselves pretty organized and Henry felt as though he could leave. "I will always be available for the kids. It's only a flight away," he thought.

Even in first class, these flights were getting progressively more difficult. But finally Henry saw Eva's smiling face and all was better. Henry gave her a big hug and kiss. He sat close to her in the taxi. At home the children gave him a warm greeting. He felt welcome.

The next morning, at breakfast, Eva looked distant. She smiled, she was polite, but she was not really there. There was something wrong, but Henry could not put his finger on it. Throughout the day, Henry continued to have this feeling. He encouraged her to tell him if anything was wrong. But she only smiled and gave no answer. The next ten days were pleasant. Henry enjoyed himself and thought that maybe he had made a mistake thinking her feelings for him had changed.

Henry was always glad to be back in Israel. He met with his friends and mentioned his concern about Israel not educating the American Jews to make them aware of how necessary they were for the successful progress of their country. Moshe promised to speak to the right people. He definitely agreed and Henry promised to help as much as he could to make changes.

Henry went about his business for the next few days. He visited his doctor in Jerusalem and went to check up on Eva's house. He was surprised to see changes in the house even though it was being maintained by a cleaning service. The garden was in need of more attention. The exterior needed some touching up. Henry would take care of the repairs. An empty house not lived in permanently deteriorates. He was able to see small changes, but he knew this was just the beginning. Henry would have to talk to Eva about it. Maybe it would be wise to rent it out.

Henry was giving a lot of thought to Eva. Did he want to marry her? Was he ready to spend a reasonable amount of time in London? It was a hassle for him to be in two places, could he add a third one? So many questions and so few answers. He was not sure what he wanted. Was he prepared to lose Eva?

He needed to answer all these questions soon. Eva did not say anything to him, but he had a feeling she would next time he saw her. He would be in London soon on his way to the United States.

Henry spoke to Rebecca every day. All was fine. He went to see the Silber's. He had a lot of photos to show them. He also met the girl that Alex's brother was engaged to. It would be great if they had a grandchild close to them. The girl that was marrying Alex's brother was very nice, educated and in love. Henry was happy with her. She would become a part of his family. He knew Rebecca was going to like her.

Henry was thinking ahead about whether everyone was going to be able to attend the wedding. Lilly was too young to travel. Of course they had not even confirmed a date yet. He asked the Silber's to let him know as soon as they made that decision. Henry took measurements for a wedding ring that he would send them from New York. He promised to see them again before he left for London. They had some gifts for the kids for Henry to deliver.

Henry went twice a day for his favorite walks on the shore. He never had enough of it. The repairs at Eva's house were taken care of. He visited the Silber's again, picked up the gifts and said goodbye to his friends. Moshe gave him a contact in the Israeli Embassy in New York and urged Henry to get in touch with him as soon as he got to New York. Henry was ready to leave Israel.

CHAPTER 32

Eva was so happy that Henry was planning on staying longer. She was very eager to see him. London was as usual, bleak and rainy. The only bright sight was Eva in her yellow raincoat with a smile. Henry just saw her recently, but it seemed as though she had lost some weight. He questioned her about it, but she smiled and said she had to keep up with him.

Henry observed her kids. They seemed to be kind of sad. They tried to smile and be merry, but he could tell they were hiding something. Henry decided to find out what was happening. He questioned Eva about her business, but she said everything was good. She did question him about preparing a will and how to structure it to make sure her children would be well provided for. He gave her advice and again asked if everything was okay.

She nervously said, "Of course it is," but Henry knew something was wrong. He let it go for the evening, but he would pursue it further. The next day they met with Eva's friends for dinner at home. Finally, in the late evening, they were alone. The kids were out, and they sat on the couch to watch TV. Eva curled up to him and they talked about little nothings. The moment was perfect and he did not want to spoil it by questioning her further.

That night Henry was awoken by a noise in the bathroom. He came close to the door and heard Eva vomiting. He knocked at the door and asked if he could help. But Eva said, "No, I'll be right out."

Henry turned on the lights and when she came out of the bathroom, Henry got scared. Eva was pale as a ghost. She could not keep her balance. He helped her into bed. She laid there without saying a word. Henry brought her some water and said to her, "You must tell me what is going on." She finally agreed. Eva had been keeping the truth from him. She was hoping to tell him in a few months. Eva was diagnosed with breast cancer and she was scheduled to undergo a double mastectomy soon. The medicine she was taking made her vomit and lose weight. She said she was in good spirits and believed the outcome would be positive. Henry was in shock. He was not prepared to hear this. But he told her he would be with her throughout. He would return to the states to see the kids briefly, but would return shortly to be with her. He thought he owed her that much.

Henry was going to the states tomorrow so he could be back as early as possible. He tried to nap on the plane, but could not. He was thinking of Eva. "What a bad break," he thought. "Can she win this battle?"

Alex waited for him at the airport. He was alone and Henry was glad. He told Alex what happened and what he must do. They went to the Rebecca's apartment. Henry could not wait to see the kids. Sam was held his grandpa's hand. Lilly was smiling and cooing. She was a very small delicate baby; dainty, but healthy. Nothing like Sam; a robust big boy.

All was okay with the kids. Rebecca adjusted to being home with the children and was glad. She had a routine. She took Sam to nursery school and then took long walks in the park with Lilly. Rebecca was trying hard to get back to her old weight. She was almost there. The housekeeper now lived with them.

Rebecca started to talk to Alex about a change. Alex would be staying with the company for the foreseeable future. Rebecca wanted to move to the suburbs. She wanted a large, comfortable home with a big garden and a good school nearby for Sam and Lilly; one with small classes and big parental involvement. Most of all, Rebecca wanted a little peace and quiet away from the bustling city.

The problem was that she was afraid of her father's reaction. He loved living close to her and she did not think he could live in the suburbs. Rebecca would wait to tell him about her wanting to move until Henry returned from London. Presently he was understandably very upset with Eva's situation.

First Rebecca had to convince Alex. Maybe they could start looking at homes while her father was in London. Some of their friends had already made the move to the suburbs and they loved it. Alex and Rebecca went to visit a few of their friends. Rebecca loved it but Alex had his doubts. He loved the city and all it had to offer.

Rebecca felt sorry for her father. He really liked this lady from London, and she did too. They seemed a perfect match, intellectually and otherwise. Rebecca hoped for a speedy recovery. It would truly be a devastating blow to her father if anything bad were to happen.

Alex started to teach Sam the alphabet and some easy math. He was like a sponge. It was so easy to teach him. It was also very encouraging. It was a good sign of his intellect.

Lately, Rebecca thought a lot about her mother. Being a mother herself brought out a lot of feelings. She wanted to question her father more but each time she did, it was extremely hard for her father. She knew he did not want to talk about it and Rebecca did not want to force him. But time passed by quickly and her father was not a youngster anymore and somehow Rebecca would have to get him to talk about her mother. She wanted to know as much as she could about the whole family.

Some of her friends lost their parents and there was no one left that could tell them about their past. Her friends were all very sorry that they lost their whole memory of their family. It was not fair for the perished not to be remembered. Being remembered meant one would live forever.

Henry was leaving in a few days. He put all his affairs in order. The only thing he had to put off was the meeting with the diplomat at the Israeli Embassy. He was able to get in touch with him on the phone. He did explain himself and promised to get in touch again as soon as he returned.

Henry was very uneasy about the situation in London. He wanted to help Eva. He just hoped he would be able to. He was afraid.

Henry took a few good books with him. He figured there would be a lot of waiting time in the hospital and later in Eva's home. He inquired about good convalescent homes in London. Eva had two sisters who could stay at home with her kids so that they could continue school and not be interrupted. The kids attended the university in London and lived at home.

Eva's son picked Henry up at the airport. Eva was in the hospital already. The surgery was scheduled for tomorrow and she wanted to be alone. Henry would see her after the procedure. He tried to rest, but sleep did not come. Henry opened the shades on the window in his room and watched the sky turn from darkness to light.

At six in the morning Henry took a long hot shower to loosen his muscles. He put on his most comfortable suit, no tie. He took a big umbrella and his book. He was ready. As he left his bedroom, he heard some commotion in the kitchen and took a look. Henry was surprised to see the housekeeper and the kids up and ready for breakfast. The kids were coming with him to the hospital. They thanked him for being there and told him how much it meant for their mother. Henry was very touched.

In the hospital, they were shown to a waiting room and told the doctor would see them before the surgery and shortly after. Eva's kids sat on each side of Henry and they began the long wait. After a while the nurse came in to report that everything was going along as scheduled and they were approximately half way through the surgery. Henry asked the kids to go out and stretch their legs a little. They shook their heads and just sat closer to him. They put on the television to see some news.

Finally the doctor came in with a big smile. He informed them that all looked clean, but Eva would have to undergo chemotherapy and check with him often. She was sleeping now but in about two hours they could see her.

"Well," said Henry. "The worst is over. Let's go have an early dinner and then return to visit with your mother." They gladly got up and left the hospital.

Upon their return, standing in front of Eva's room, they looked at each other and thought, who would be the first one to open the door. Henry opened the door. Eva was not sleeping. She gave them a faint smile and thanked them for being there with her. She said she was in a little bit of pain. She got some painkillers and went to sleep. Henry hired a private nurse to stay with Eva. "By tomorrow morning it all would be much better," she said. They left for home.

Eva's sister was waiting for them. She had already spoken to the doctor and had the full report. They all had a cup of hot tea and decided to go to bed. Tomorrow they would all return to visit Eva again.

Henry was very tired and was glad for some privacy. He took a relaxing bath and went to bed. He thought the worst was over, and he fell into a deep sleep.

After breakfast they all left to visit Eva. To everyone's surprise, she was sitting up in an easy chair having some tea. She looked good and gave them all a kiss. She told them not to worry and that everything was under control.

Henry watched Eva's sister. She was the only one not expressing a happy face. "Strange," thought Henry. They had a good visit and Henry promised to return before dinner.

When he returned Henry took Eva for a slow walk in the corridor. She was reassuring him that she was okay and in a few months she would have reconstructive surgery and would be as she was before. Henry said that this was not important. The only thing that mattered was her good health. They watched a little television, ate dinner together and then Henry left.

Eva was home within a few days. She did not want to go to a convalescent home. She claimed she would recuperate better at home. Henry was next to her the whole time. He prepared a few Israeli dishes. They watched old movies, spoke about their businesses and current events. One day, for the first time, they went out to the theater. Little by little, Eva was returning to her old self.

Eva would start chemotherapy soon. She wanted Henry to return to his home during that time. She had enough help and she did not want him to see her suffer.

Henry was surprised at how he felt. He was glad to go away. He had stayed in London for one month. He became very close to Eva's children but he missed his own children terribly. He could not wait to be back with them.

CHAPTER 33

Henry was back home with his children. Lilly had grown, Sam was a good big brother. He played with Lilly and watched over her. Rebecca looked well.

Henry returned to his apartment late in the evening. Everything was in order. There was a note on the table from the housekeeper that she would be back in the morning. Rebecca made sure that all was prepared for him the way he liked it. She was a perfectionist, just like her father.

The jet lag was always troublesome for a few days, but Henry was glad to be home next to his kids. In the morning, Henry could hear the noise of the city through the open window. He loved it. The sun was shining and fresh air was blowing in from Central Park. Henry called the park "the lungs" of the city.

On his way to the JCC, Henry saw people hurrying somewhere and there was life that you could see and feel. The JCC friends were glad to see him and asked how long he would be staying in New York.

Henry got in touch with the Israeli diplomat and they were to meet the next day in Henry's apartment for lunch.

The next day at noon a tall man in his late forties arrived. Henry looked at him with surprise. He looked more like an Englishman, but he was a Sabra, a name given to those who are born in Israel. Sabra was the name of a fruit that was prickly on the outside, but very sweet inside.

The diplomat spoke perfect English without an accent. He was also fluent in Arabic and French. He was a very smart man. Henry spoke to him about the void that exists all over the world. There was a need for awareness of Israel and what was happening there and how the Jews of the world should and could help. Henry spoke to him in Hebrew. The diplomat agreed and asked if Henry could put a plan together. The embassy would send a writer to help him prepare a speech and provide information. Maybe the first presentation could take place at the JCC in New York.

Henry was to ask for permission from the director of the JCC to have this gathering.

When the diplomat left, he promised to be in touch. Henry was happy to get an important task like this. He always wanted to do something for his people. He would start this project immediately.

The plan was to arrange small dinner parties, very exclusive, and each guest would pay for the privilege to attend. After a few of those dinner parties, Henry would host a large, elegant bash at the JCC and maybe one at the embassy as well. Someone from the embassy must come to each of the dinner parties and present a speech and a slide show. The reason the dinners needed to be expensive and elegant was so they could lure those who could afford to donate to Israel.

Henry had a lot of ideas which he was putting in writing. It was sort of a plan which he would give to the diplomat when he returned in a week.

Henry spoke with Eva every day. They had lengthy conversations. Eva's sister stayed with her. The chemotherapy was rough. Her kids were wonderful to her, but she said she was missing him. She hoped he would come as soon as she was finished with her treatments. Henry promised he would.

The most joyous thing for Henry was to be with his grandchildren. It was more than love. It was the satisfaction of the continuation of his family. It was his pride.

Rebecca invited her father for dinner and a talk. Henry wondered what about. He hoped she was not moving to some faraway place again. "Here we go," said Rebecca. "Dad, we would like to move to a suburb. We would like to buy a big house with a lot of land for the kids to run. We want good schools and clean air." She said this fast without taking a breath. Alex sat with his head lowered, and did not say anything.

Henry swallowed the last bite of his dessert trying to keep his cool. He answered, "It seems you have already made up your mind and there is nothing I can say. It is your life and you have to live it the way you want to." Henry said he would not move with her. He would stay in New York and visit as much as he could.

That night he could not sleep. This news was not good for him. He would not be able to see them as often as he had been and it would feel like they were far, far away. He was also disappointed in Rebecca. Why did they have to move from their large apartment right by Central Park, the best location in New York? He felt like crying to relieve his frustration.

Henry was determined not to show Rebecca his disappointment. It would not make a difference anyway. That Sunday they would drive an hour out of the city, to Westchester County, to see a house that Rebecca liked.

The house was beautiful, big with lots of bedrooms and bathrooms. It had a huge modern kitchen, and above all, a great garden. The streets were wide and all the surrounding houses were well manicured, like a fantasy land.

Actually, Henry had never seen a wealthy suburban town. "Not bad," thought Henry. He could not say that he did not like it. He thought about how he would need a lot of money for car services to get there to visit. He had no choice so he may as well like it. Henry offered to purchase the house for them, but they had to promise not to sell or rent their apartment in the city. This would allow them to come visit from time to time.

All agreed. The move would take place in two months. Henry would help Rebecca decorate. The housekeeper would move with them. Henry's housekeeper would care for their apartment in the city.

Rebecca was ecstatic and Alex kept saying, "Thank you," and "thank you," and "thank you again."

Henry and Rebecca sat together for a few evenings to decide what to do in the house. Henry hired a Manhattan renovating company that he knew and work would start soon. It would take Henry a little time to find the right furniture. Rebecca insisted that one of the master suites would be for him. No one would use this space and he was welcome anytime. Henry liked that.

Henry met with the diplomat and presented his plan. Henry was told that it had to be reviewed and presented to his superiors. He would get back in touch with him.

All of this kept Henry busy and it was getting very tiring. He was feeling like he had a little melon growing in his chest. It did not hurt, but it scared Henry very much. He saw his doctor and he was told not to ignore the doctor's advice. He would have to take better care of himself if he wanted to live.

Henry spoke with Eva. She completed the chemotherapy and was getting stronger day by day. She would come to New York to be with him for a while. Henry did not know if he felt happy about this. He was busy with his kids and the project for the Israeli Embassy was being finalized. And he, himself, did not feel so good.

Henry's goal was to complete Rebecca's house. The workers were starting any day now. Eva would not come for at least a month. This would give him time to finish this project.

Henry was making time to rest more during the day. He was eating better and learning not to rush.

Finally, Henry received a call from the embassy. All was a go! Henry knew he could not accomplish all this by himself. He requested a meeting to propose his plan on how to start, but he needed help. He needed a capable assistant to implement his plans and carry out his instructions. He explained that he was not well and would not be able to do this task on his own. They were not happy about it, but agreed. They would get someone capable to get in touch with him soon.

Rebecca was moving. All the renovations and decorating were completed. They were ready to start their new life in the suburbs. Henry went to see their apartment after she moved. It was cleaned and the furnishings were there, but there was no life. All was very quiet. Henry stood there with tears in his eyes. He thought maybe it would have been better if they remained in Israel, living in a small apartment, worrying about everyday life, but together. As they say, "Money does not buy happiness." How true.

Shortly after the move Henry's future assistant called. They would meet to discuss Henry's plan and Henry would give him directions on what to do and how to go about it. The assistant's name was David. He turned out to be perfect for the job. They sat together to write the first speech which Henry would deliver at a dinner party for $500 a plate.

Henry was a little nervous but his speech was good, right to the point. He practiced it all evening and he was ready for the next night. The crowd he encountered was not familiar to him. He had never met anyone there. After dinner and before dessert, Henry gave his speech and he received loud applause.

David got some other willing people to host another dinner party. They all requested that Henry give the speech. Henry would have to present different speeches, not repeat himself and keep it interesting. It became immensely satisfying to Henry.

Henry was on the train going to Rebecca's house for the week-end. This was his first visit. He packed a few things and some gifts for the kids. Rebecca picked him up at the station and it took a few minutes to get to the house. Door to door, the trip took less than one hour. "Not so bad," thought Henry. Sam was waiting on the lawn ready for hugs and Lilly gave him her shy, sweet smile and put her head on nanny's shoulder. The week-end was great. Henry watched the kids play in the grass. The air was fresh and the house was so comfortable. His room was away from the kids. He could not hear anything. He had a restful night.

The next day he met some of their friends who came to visit with their children. Henry took pride in his daughter. She was a mother, a wife, a hostess and friend. She did it all with ease. She was very confident, smart and beautiful. It was a good feeling to see she was capable of taking care of herself and her family. Henry never paid attention to her age. She was thirty three years old. It was hard for him to believe. Henry did not fault his daughter for choosing to move to the suburbs. It was close enough to the city and yet it was a young family's paradise. He knew they were safe there, better than any other place on Earth. Rebecca asked him to leave his clothes and things at the house so that eventually he would not have to bring anything with him. She promised to come to the city for a few days soon.

Henry felt a great burden removed from his shoulders. He was sitting on the train going back to the city at a late hour. The city was full of life. It was truly a city that never slept. Henry entered his apartment in a good mood. He liked where Rebecca relocated. Whatever may happen with him, they would be okay.

Henry wanted to concentrate on his mission for Israel. It was all going great and it gave him a great satisfaction.

Eva was coming soon and he was not feeling as excited as he should. He was busy and a little bit concerned that he would find himself in a mothering role. Henry questioned the way he felt. What did it mean? Did he love her or was it just a convenient relationship? But he did not have the answers to any of these questions. It did not matter. She would be here shortly.

As Henry waited for Eva to arrive, he bought a cup of coffee. With every sip he took, he knew it was bad for him, but he did it anyway. He spotted Eva in the crowd. She looked frail and thin. As she came closer, Henry could see her pale face with dark circles under her eyes. Henry was disturbed by her appearance. He gave her a huge hug and kiss.

At the apartment, all was ready for her. He brought in the food she requested, her toiletries, etc. She said she felt good, but it did not seem that way. They had dinner in the apartment and relaxed. Henry had designated a separate bedroom for her and told her that both bedrooms were for both of them and that she should do whatever felt better for her. They talked late into the night. She was sweet and always smart. She went to her bedroom and bid goodnight to Henry. But in the early morning Henry felt her in his bed.

The first day they went to the Metropolitan Museum, the place that Eva liked the most. Every time they went there they visited a different section. They ate lunch at the museum and Henry told her about his project in progress. Eva listened and said that he could do the same in London.

Henry scheduled a weekend at Rebecca's house. Rebecca had prepared a splendid weekend, but Eva was the most happy when she was with Sam and Lilly. Afterwards, on their way back to the city, Eva told Henry that Rebecca was right to move to the suburbs and that it was the best place to raise children.

Everyday Henry planned something to do with Eva. She went with him to one of his dinner presentations. She was so proud of him. That evening she told Henry that life was unfair that they could not be together always. She never felt so comfortable or protected or loved as she felt with him.

Henry read between the lines. Eva wanted them to be together, but Henry did not. He was set in his ways and he would not move to London, and mainly he was afraid of Eva's sickness. He felt very guilty about these feelings. He pretended he did not understand her small hints.

Eva was not feeling so good. She became fatigued very often and Henry could hear her moan at times. His heart was breaking for her. They toured different places. Henry proposed a trip to California but Eva declined. She had no strength for it. They made small trips close by, but Eva liked Manhattan most of all.

The time came for Eva to leave. Henry promised he would visit London soon. On his way back from the airport, relaxing in the back seat of the taxi, Henry felt an enormous relief. He was glad Eva left.

He went to stay with the kids for a few days. That always perked him up. He instructed the housekeeper to thoroughly clean his apartment and he left for Rebecca's house. His grandchildren were his greatest achievement. He never had enough of them. He carried little Lilly and whispered in her ear. She loved it. Henry taught Sam to play checkers and talked to him about all sorts of things. Henry was never bored with the kids.

At night, in his suite, he was free to think, "Did I ever love Eva?" He could not be sure. He appreciated her smarts, her elegance and her beauty. Henry wondered how he would have felt about Liliana after so many years, but that was easy to answer. There was not one day that he did not think of her. She was always in the back of his mind. The lovemaking with Eva was very sensual and satisfying, much better than with Liliana. But Henry would give anything for Liliana to be with him instead of Eva. As much as he did not forgive Liliana, he still loved her. He was angry with her and jealous. Henry had a small glass of cognac and fell asleep.

Henry stayed with Rebecca for a few days and did not feel like going home. But David insisted he return. There was so much to do. Henry must get back to work but it was becoming too much for him. It took many hours of preparation. Henry knew he had to talk to his contact at the embassy. He must ease off a little.

David turned out to be a very capable young man. He was knowledgeable and a fast learner but was afraid of public speaking. Henry was teaching him not to be afraid. Henry spoke to the diplomat at the embassy and convinced them of David's capabilities. From then on Henry would help, but the bulk of the presentations would fall on David. Rebecca was pleased with this. Maybe now her father would be able to spend more time with her family at the house. She noticed that her father was easily fatigued. Sometimes she saw him put his hand on his heart. He did not tell her anything about his health and she was afraid to ask.

Alex was advancing in his company. He was very accomplished. His brother in Israel was expecting his first child. Life could not be better for him. He was happy that they had moved to the suburbs and they still had kept their attachment to Manhattan. They visit the city and stay in their apartment often. Alex appreciated what Henry had done for them. They would never have had such a comfortable life without him.

Henry spoke with Eva. She was crying. She needed new tests to see what was happening in her lungs. She was having difficulty breathing and the doctor suspected cancer. Henry tried to console her and told her not to think of the worst but it did not help. All she wanted was for Henry to be with her. Henry spoke to Rebecca. She felt he should go London. He really did not want to go. He felt he could not handle the adversity. This whole circumstance was very upsetting to him. His chest felt full and sore. Henry was trying to relax but it was not easy. Rebecca was booking a ticket for him. He packed a few things and he would depart tonight.

CHAPTER 34

For the first time, no one met him at the airport. Henry took a taxi and soon stood in front of Eva's house. Her son opened the door. His eyes were red. He smiled and told Henry how wonderful it was that he came. In the living room Eva's daughter sat and was embracing her mother. When Eva saw Henry she started to cry. He was so surprised at her behavior. He thought Eva was so strong, but obviously she was not. He hugged her and asked why was she giving up; why was she thinking the worst? He promised they would fight together and all would be well. Eva calmed down. He took her to bed and then he went to speak with her children.

Both of them sat on the couch holding hands. Eva's sister was on a chair wringing her hands. Henry did not know what to do or what to say. Finally he told them they must be strong and life must go on. They could not sit and cry with their mother.

The next day Henry made an appointment with her doctors. He wanted to know from them the truth about Eva's future. He sat in the doctor's office waiting to be called in. The minutes felt like hours but finally the doctor entered. From his expression, Henry knew the news was not going to be good. It was not.

The doctor explained to Henry that Eva did not have a lot of time. The best thing would be to keep her comfortable and sedated. The doctor felt should be in a hospital under supervision that the children should see a psychologist to help them get through this difficult time. There was nothing else that he could do. The doctor concluded with, "I am very sorry," and with that, he was out the door.

Henry felt numb. He felt the tears on his face.

Back at Eva's house, Henry spoke with Eva's sister. She knew the gravity of the situation. She had already spoken to the doctors. Henry asked her to find the best psychologist for the kids and the best place in London to take Eva to. She agreed.

Henry spoke with Rebecca and explained everything to her. He said he would stay in London with Eva until the end.

The hardest part was going to be talking to Eva but she made it easy. She knew that there was no hope for her. She understood what had to be done. The only thing she wanted was for Henry to stay with her on this last journey, which he promised to do. She took strong medication for pain and it made her sleep most of the time.

When she was awake they talked. Henry told her about his years in the concentration camp. He never told anyone that part of his life. Eva told him about parts of her private life also. Sometimes they laughed and sometimes they cried. The kids were near her. Her two sisters came all the time. Eva did not want to go to a hospital. A nurse was hired to stay for twenty four hours a day. The kids began to get counseling. It helped them to get through a very difficult time. They continued to go to their classes and see their friends.

Eva had prepared her will much earlier. One of her sisters, with her family, would move into the house. This would allow the kids to stay at home and continue their life in the place where they were born.

Eva's son would soon become an attorney and her daughter an engineer. Henry had to promise Eva that he would come to their weddings and stand beside them in her place.

Eva did not suffer from pain. She slipped in and out of consciousness. When she was awake she was always looking for Henry. By now she had a hard time speaking so they just held hands. Henry continued to talk to her about all sorts of things. Some things he told her surprised even him. He told Eva, "You will wait there for me and we will be together forever." He thought, "Where did that come from?" She really liked hearing this from him, and it made her smile. She was losing weight, she hardly ate anything, but she still held on to life. Henry had a hard time watching her slip away. He never saw anybody die slowly. He saw death in the camp, but it was fast and impersonal.

Eva took a turn for the worse. She was unconscious and the doctor advised that she would not make it through the morning. The kids were at her bedside and talked to their mother. Henry could swear she heard them. They were calm as they waited for the end. Henry sat on the other side of the bed holding Eva's hand. He fell asleep and was awakened by the kids sobbing. Eva was gone.

Eva's family made arrangements for the funeral which took place the next day. Henry was in a daze. The Shiva was held in Eva's house. Henry stayed in his room most of the time. He needed to rest emotionally and physically. He was not sure what he felt but he knew he did the right thing by staying with Eva until the last minute.

Henry felt needed and loved. He also knew that this would be his last romantic encounter. It was time for Henry to leave. The kids thanked him for staying with them but mostly for being with their mother. Henry promised to stay in touch with them and invited them to New York or Israel anytime.

Henry had planned to go to Israel, but at the last minute, changed his mind and went to the States. He wanted to be with his family. Alex picked him up and they drove straight to his house. Rebecca gave him the longest hug and told him how sorry she was. The grandchildren where already asleep but Henry went to their rooms just to take a look at them. Henry slept well that night and was so glad to be with his family.

The next few days Henry did nothing but sleep and play with the kids. He was slowly recovering.

Henry left for New York and got in touch with David to see how he was doing. Henry's first speech, upon his return, was going to be in the largest synagogue in New York, on Fifth Avenue. David helped him with the text and Henry was prepared. He was happy to resume his work for Israel.

Henry saw the doctor and told him about his ordeal and that it was very emotional and stressful but he had no choice, he had to do it. After the new tests the doctor called and told Henry there were no significant changes but urged Henry to get some serious relaxation. Henry renewed his gym routine, ate healthy and rested a lot.

His big speech was coming up. Rebecca and Alex would be there. Some officials from the embassy, including the Ambassador from Israel, would be attending. Henry did not feel uneasy. He was confidant.

Henry was dressing for the event. His new suit fit him perfectly. The limo came to pick him up and David met him at the door. Henry saw Rebecca and Alex seated in the front row. The synagogue was full of elegantly dressed people. Henry was soon introduced and he started his speech.

CHAPTER 35

lbert's relationship with Monica progressed. He seemed to be happy. Monica stayed at their home for a week-end and Helena had a chance to observe her. She seemed to Helena to be in love with Albert. She was a straight forward girl with not too much class. She was smart with a good memory, but Helena could not warm up to her. Helena knew she had to try harder because it appeared that Albert was serious about this girl.

They talked about Monica. Robert felt the same as Helena about her. He did not like her family. He knew that they were still Nazi sympathizers. After World War II, most Germans did their best to disassociate themselves with anything that had to do with Hitler and/or Nazis, even those that fought in the war. However, there were those that carried on Hitler's belief system and were proud to continue being called Nazis. Robert already warned Albert about them, but it did not do any good. Albert was well aware of who her family was but was in love and felt that Monica was nothing like her family. He wanted to become engaged. Helena was overwhelmed. She sat on her bed and held her head. Robert said that they would have to accept her or they might lose their son.

The next day Helena gave a family ring to Albert. He hugged his mother and said that everything would be okay. Albert did not ask Monica's father for her hand. He proposed to Monica and she agreed.

Her parents were preparing an engagement party just for the immediate family. Monica knew better. She did not want the Van Klauses to see her parents' "friends."

Robert, Helena, Maximilian and Katy drove in silence to Monica's house. Mr. and Mrs. Shultz, Monica's brother Wolf and his wife and Monica waited for them at the gate. The house was full with aunts, uncles and cousins. The music was loud with old German songs. The food was typically German: pork, sauerkraut, potato salad and sausages. Robert and Helena shook everybody's hand and smiled. But their hearts were bleeding.

All Helena could think was, "This cannot be. This cannot be the family for my baby son!"

On the drive home, Katy held Helena's hand and said, "Do not worry. Monica will be with us, away from her family. She is already different from all of them. She has a higher education. She just needs a little chance."

Helena nodded her head and thought, "Thank God for Katy!"

The next day Albert said that he wanted to move into the new house with Monica. Robert and Helena were glad. They all had dinner at the main house. Helena gave Monica a kiss and welcomed her to the family.

Monica brought only her clothes and toiletries. Helena proceeded to search for a housekeeper for Albert. Luckily the housekeeper for Maximilian had a cousin that wanted job. Helena asked Monica to interview her and see if she was to her liking. She was a strong, heavy set woman. Her name was Adeline.

Monica's response was "No thank you, I don't need a housekeeper. That is how the upper class lives." Helena pretended she did not understand this innuendo. Helena was thinking, let's see how Monica would handle a rich comfortable life, would she embrace it or leave it.

After getting to know her for a while, Helena knew that Monica would embrace this rich comfortable life. Adeline asked Monica for instructions but Monica answered, "You do what has to be done. I have no clue how to instruct you. But if you need directions, ask my future mother-in-law."

Monica worked hard. She was a great attorney. She had ambitions of opening her own office. She did not see herself being home and nurturing kids. She also loved politics. Maybe in the future she would attempt to pursue a political office. She also knew that marrying into this family would help her realize all of her dreams. She loved Albert. He was all that she was not. He was reserved, quiet, smart and not very ambitious, and he loved her. And so they began their life together.

Monica slowly started to appreciate her new life. She observed Helena and Katy. She knew that she could not be like them but she wanted to try to be as close as possible. It was very comfortable to return to a magnificent home where everything was done for her, dinner was cooked, clothing arranged, the garden tended. All she had to do was to concentrate on her career. Yes, she did appreciate her new life!

Slowly, Helena was getting used to Monica. She wondered why Albert and she had not yet married. She would talk to Monica about this.

A letter came from Henry with photos. Actually, it was not a letter, just a note. Her grandson Sam looked amazing and Lilly was a beauty. She sat a long time looking at Rebecca with her kids. She longed for her. Helena did not know what to do, how to make it right. How would she ever see them? She did not show the photos to Robert and he did not ask if she got mail from Henry.

Helena decided to talk to Robert about Rebecca. She decided that she did not want to wait any longer. She wanted to meet her daughter. Her sons were grown. The world was different now and Robert must understand her. She approached him after dinner as they sat on the veranda to relax.

Robert was fuming again. "You cannot do this," he said. "Wait until I die." It was very dramatic. Helena was surprised again by his reaction. She was lost. What was she to do? She could not go against his wishes. She did not have the courage to just do it and be done with it. It must be done with his knowledge and with his approval.

In her next letter, Helena begged Henry to allow her to come and meet Rebecca. She found herself between two very stubborn men and each one was right in their own way. She pleaded with Robert, "When will be the right time?"

And he replied predictably with a strong, "NEVER!"

Time passed. Monica seemed happy. She had changed since she moved in with Albert. She became quieter, more patient. She changed the way she dressed and used much less makeup. Katy was a big influence. She had the patience to point things out to Monica. They actually became good friends.

At first Albert and Monica would visit her family often. But in time, those visits became less and less frequent and lately Monica would visit them alone. After her last visit, Monica returned with red eyes, but said nothing.

The next day Albert spoke to Helena. Monica's father did not approve that she was living with Albert without marrying him. He thought she was being taken advantage of. Her father gave her an ultimatum. Either they get married or she must come back home. Albert said that getting married was not a problem, but the wedding reception would be. Mostly because Monica's father wanted to have a wedding that everyone would remember. That meant a lot of guests, a lot of drinking and a lot of fights. Albert did not want that. Neither did Monica.

Helena suggested that they have a civil ceremony in the town hall or even a small wedding in the church with only one witness. Robert said that the type of wedding her father was planning, with all his so called "friends" would not be a good thing for the Van Klaus family.

So it was agreed. Monica chose Katy as her witness. The ceremony would be as soon as they choose between either the city hall or the church. They would make arrangements as soon as possible.

Helena stood at the front door to see the kids off to town hall. Monica wore a short beautiful dress and Albert wore a dark navy blue suit. They had a limo pick them up. Photos were taken. Helena was crying and Monica, in a whisper, told her, "I love you." Helena was shocked.

Robert, Maximilian and Helena waited for them to come back. Helena had prepared a very elegant dinner for all of them. Finally the car beeped at the gate. They came out, very happy. Monica was waving a piece of paper that was the marriage certificate. They came into the house and all hugged and kissed. And, just like that, it was done.

The next day they went to Monica's parents' house to show them their marriage certificate. Monica wanted to wait but Albert thought it best to get rid of the problem as soon as possible. They did not expect this visit to be a pleasant one, and they were right.

Monica's father was screaming and was beside himself. "Why did you do this? I wanted to give you the biggest wedding ever!" he raged.

Monica answered, "That is exactly why we did it."

Monica's mother hugged them and suggested they leave and come back in a few days. They gladly left.

Monica told Albert that her father would probably want to throw a big party anyway. Albert agreed and said, "It won't be a wedding so my family would not have to attend." He put his arm around Monica and said, "We will sail through this, don't worry."

As they thought, her father was preparing a huge party in three weeks.

Helena decided they should look for a great vacation destination for all of them. She brought home a lot of brochures. Helena wanted something extraordinary, money was no object. The vacation had to be fun, elegant and interesting. She did not want to go to Europe or North America. She finally decided on Argentina and Brazil. She would go to the travel agent and go over all the details. But first, she had to talk to her family and establish everyone's schedules. The logistics were not easy, but she was determined, saying to all of them, "Where there's a will there's a way."

They all agreed on the destination and now they had to coordinate the dates. Robert was very excited too. He needed a good rest.

Finally the dates were confirmed and Helena booked the flights, hotels and side trips. She arranged three different flights. She did not want all of them to fly together. They flew on the same day, but on different flights.

The vacation was wonderful. The family traveled together and away from outside influences. Helena knew that this kind of togetherness was the best way to preserve her family unity.

Helena saw how Monica changed every day but still kept her special spark. Helena knew that Katy was the biggest contributor to this change. Their experiences on the trip were unforgettable. The night before returning home, at dinner, Monica gave little speech thanking Helena for the wonderful vacation. She spoke about how much fun it was and ow it was a great bond for the family. In the far future, Monica would do the same for the family. Helena was surprised by Monica's total understanding of what Helena was aiming for. Yes, Monica was very smart.

After returning from vacation, Katy studied for exams. If successful, she would be earning her master's degree. She liked studying and was thinking of continuing school to get a doctorate degree. She had no ambition to earn money. There was plenty of money in her husband's family to last for generations. She thought of becoming a mother though. But Max still wanted to wait. Katy did not understand why. So she decided she would get pregnant without Maximilian's approval. She was very excited about this decision.

A few months passed and Katy was pregnant! She decided not to say anything. But her morning sickness was apparent to the whole family. Helena was the first to ask if she was pregnant. Katy, in an innocent voice said, "I don't know." A visit to the doctor made it official. Katy was pregnant. Everyone was happy except Max. Katy apologized to her husband and claimed it was an accident. He believed her. Max got used to the fact and looked forward to becoming a father. They were slowly preparing a nursery.

Helena was beside herself. She was so happy that she forgot about Rebecca until she received a letter from Henry refusing her request again. "It all has to be done in a completely open fashion," he said. "Do not come in secret."

Helena was furious. She thought of hiring a private investigator, but she knew she would be unable to hide it from Robert. So that idea would not work. She felt caught between the two men. She did not reply to Henry's letter.

Helena was in touch with Katy's mother. The Rothmans would soon visit and Helena looked forward to seeing Sarah and Stephen. She felt very close to them and now a child would bond them even more.

Katy asked that everybody stop spoiling her. She continued with school and did all her usual chores. Helena was looking for a good nanny to have for at least six months.

The Rothman family arrived and stayed in Katy's house. Helena would not disturb them. She wanted to be with them, but she would wait to be invited. After a while, Sarah knocked at the door. They hugged and cried with joy. "We will be grandmothers to the same child. Isn't it wonderful?"

Katy made lunch for everybody. Robert and Stephen discussed politics and current events. Monica was there also. She was helping Katy. But she was saddened knowing that her parents would never have the same relationship that Katy's parents had with the Van Klauses.

Katy's parents stayed for a few days. Helena and Sarah discussed the nursery for the baby. Sarah said, "My grandmother and mother never prepared anything in advance for the baby. They waited until the baby was born." When Helena asked why, Sarah answered, "Some old superstition thing." But Helena knew why. Jewish people do not prepare anything for the baby in advance. They wait until the baby is born.

Helena said they would do the same for this baby. Sarah said she would send the nanny that served everyone in her family. All the cousins' children were raised by her.

Helena prepared a family dinner. She asked Monica if she wanted to invite her parents. Helena offered to invite them personally if Monica preferred. But Monica did not want to, which was actually quite a relief to Helena. It's just that she could see that Monica was sad and jealous.

All was quiet again. The guests were gone and life resumed at familiar pace. Katy felt well. She saw her doctor regularly. It was business as usual. Robert was very excited to be a grandfather. He was hoping they would have a boy so the family name would live on. This was very important to him.

Helena knew that things with her daughter, Rebecca, needed to be resolved. She needed to take a stronger stand, but she was unsure about how or when she would do so. Maybe she should wait until the baby was born so Robert would be preoccupied and happy. Maybe then it would be easier to persuade him.

She also needed to write a letter to Henry and make him understand Robert's point of view and, of course, try and make him understand her pain. She postponed this last decision. She always seemed to find excuses for not taking action. Mostly because Helena realized there would be severe consequences once these secrets were let loose. She was understandably afraid. She feared for her family and what this would do to them.

CHAPTER 36

Towards the end of his speech, Henry saw Rebecca wiping her eyes. She was visibly moved. And then there was applause and a standing ovation. Henry was so surprised. He thanked everybody and left the podium. Rebecca hugged him and told him that he was wonderful. Her approval meant the most to him.

The Ambassador came to shake his hand and quietly said, "I have no doubt that we will collect a large amount of money tonight. Good job, very true and moving. It was a great help."

People gathered all around Henry with questions and suggestions. All wanted to know how to get in touch with him. David stayed by Henry's side the whole time and never moved more than two steps away. Finally things quieted down. Rebecca left for home and David and Henry sat for a cup of coffee.

David gave Henry quite the compliment by saying that he wanted to be just like him and would try his best to achieve that. Henry must teach him how he was able to touch everybody's heart and bring the audience to tears.

Henry was tired, a kind of emotional tiredness. He found his apartment to be a sanctuary. He needed to relax. The housekeeper prepared meals for him and Henry stayed in the apartment, in his pajamas, the entire weekend. The only phone calls he picked up were from his daughter. The others he let go straight to the answering machine. He watched television, read the New York Times and The Jerusalem Post and napped on the couch. It was seldom that Henry took the time to have a good rest. During one of his naps he dreamt of Liliana. This surprised him since he had not thought of her for quite some time. But she must have been on his mind. Why else would he dream about her? He tried to shake off any thoughts about her, but it was not easy.

One of the messages was from the Ambassador asking Henry to visit his office as soon as possible. Henry wants to take David with him. He decided he would just show up with him rather than asking. Henry wondered what the urgency was.

Henry and David went to the Embassy, but he was asked in to the ambassador's office without David. The ambassador had a serious face. Henry was asked to sit and the ambassador asked if Henry was aware of the current political situation. Henry was. The ambassador asked that Henry do more presentations to collect money. It was urgent. Henry agreed he would do whatever he could, but he requested a good and reliable secretary and, of course, David. All this was agreed. Henry did not mention that he was not feeling so well. He would take it as easy as he could.

Henry went to Rebecca's home for the Jewish New Year and Yom Kippur. They joined the reformed synagogue for the High Holy Days services. They were not all that religious but it was a gesture of belonging.

Henry went alone for the Yom Kippur prayers. That's when the worst news they could ever hear came. Israel was attacked by the Egyptian and Syrian forces. It was a complete surprise. Israel was outnumbered. It was the High Holidays and everyone was at home with their families. Things looked glum. The U.S. had demanded that Russia stop supplying Egypt and Syria with weapons. Russia ignored those demands, putting Egypt and Syria in a position to attack. Israel was not at all prepared for this war. The Arab states had the upper hand. Many Israeli soldiers were being killed. It was a disastrous situation. This was the first time Israel faced a surprise attack and it was very scary.

Immediately Henry was called upon to appeal to mass gatherings of Jews in the greater New York area. Money had to be raised immediately and sent to Israel to support the war. This effort was taking place throughout major cities in the U.S. Henry was most influential in raising vast sums of money and support for Israel.

The war ended on October 22, 1973 when the United Nations adopted a Resolution for a Ceasefire.

Henry felt guilty that he was not back in Israel. He spoke to Moshe and Joseph and heard firsthand how the people of Israel felt about the war. Alex's brother was called upon to fight in the war. He was back home now and was okay.

Henry was convinced that the Jews of the world were very scared too. Israel must exist for the Jews of the world. But how would peace ever take place? How could it be achieved? There was no clear answer.

Israel needed to achieve respect for bringing new and important innovations and technology to the world. They needed high tech companies from all over the world to move to, or at least be represented in, Israel. But above all they needed people to serve their small country. Education must me a primary plan for Israel. Henry met with the ambassador to discuss this. There was great pressure being put on Henry. He had to work much harder than he originally thought.

There was a great need for Henry's services. The ambassador wanted to send him abroad to England, Australia, South America and Europe to raise funds. He could take David and his secretary with him. All would be arranged by the embassy. Henry needed to write the speeches and deliver them. Henry could not refuse. He was hoping that physically he could do it.

Henry made an appointment with his cardiologist to see if he could get additional medication to keep him going. He wanted to prevail in this undertaking.

He was given one month to prepare to travel abroad. Henry would have to compose many speeches. The Jews of different countries all needed different incentives to respond and open their wallets.

Henry spoke with Rebecca and she was enormously proud of him, but she did not know about his failing health. They spent a nice weekend together before he left. Sam was now five years old and Lilly was two. Sam was in kindergarten and Lilly in nursery school. Rebecca had started a new job, just part-time, working from home. She translated medical documents from English to German.

Henry knew that once he departed, he would not be back for a long while.

David was with Henry all the time. He learned to recognize when Henry was not feeling so well and he knew when Henry needed to rest or nap. He was Henry's shadow. Henry did notice and was surprised and touched by his knowledge of his well-being. Henry asked David how he always knew exactly what he needed and when. David told him that the authorities knew everything about him and it was his job to keep Henry as comfortable as possible and learn as much as he could. David adored Henry and was in awe of him. Henry wondered if the authorities knew of Liliana. He thought they probably did. He did not care.

Henry's first stop was London. He visited Eva's children and invited them to the event. They both waited at the airport for him. It was so good to see them. Tomorrow he would take them to visit Eva's grave. Henry inquired about their school, their daily lives and how they were being taken care of. He contacted their lawyer just to make sure the estate was being handled properly. Eva's whole family would be coming to his presentation.

At the event, Henry observed the audience switch from their cool demeanors to their unavoidable tears. That was exactly what he wanted and needed to achieve. He aimed to find the hearts and sense of belonging from the audience.

After a day of rest they proceeded to the next location. Everywhere they went it was the same; an absolute success. The speeches may have been different from country to country but the core and intention was the same. Towards the end of the trip, which took almost a month, Henry was exhausted. He spoke to Rebecca and his grandkids almost every day. Rebecca was anxious for him to come home already. She knew he was tired.

David made an appointment with the ambassador a week after their return so Henry could have some time to rest.

He was finally home in his daughter's house. The kids knew not to disturb grandpa too much. The absolute quiet of the suburbs was soothing for him. He was so glad to be there.

After a week of good rest, Henry and David went to their meeting at the embassy. The ambassador greeted Henry with a handshake and a hug. He complimented Henry and thanked him for an excellent job and encouraged Henry to take care of himself because they had further plans for him. They wanted to send Henry to all the major cities in the USA. Henry asked for a little time. He also asked which cities so that he could prepare.

This visit to the doctor did not go well at all. He had a good and honest talk with his doctor. Henry was told that if he continues his life the way he had been, he would not have a long life to live. The doctor was aware of what Henry had been doing. He even went to hear him speak, so he knew how important it was for Henry to continue. It was up to Henry decide how he would live the rest of his life. But if it was solely up to the doctor, he would put Henry on permanent rest and have him do nothing at all. The doctor suggested that he speak to his daughter and let her know of his condition. That was one of the hardest things for him to do. Henry decided he would have the talk in a little while.

Henry's thoughts were clear. He would not relegate himself to a life on a couch only to die slowly. He would rather continue the important work he was doing and leave it to God to take him whenever he saw fit. Henry would have to make this clear to Rebecca.

While writing his speeches for various cities in the USA, Henry thought he would write a few words for his grandchildren. He had some good sayings and some life advice for them. He was happy with this idea.

David continued to be Henry's shadow. He even came with Henry to Rebecca's home.

Henry finally had *the talk* with his daughter. She carried on about how he could maybe have a heart transplant or that maybe he should consult with some other doctors. Finally, she calmed down. She spoke with Henry's doctor herself in order to better understand the nature of his illness. She knew that her father was making the right decision. She would do the same.

Henry familiarized Rebecca with all his business dealings. She went with him to meet his attorneys. Henry also reminded her of the Witkowskis in Poland. There were still some treasures there, but for the moment they couldn't do anything about that. They hoped that maybe one day things would change. Henry stopped writing to them when they explained how bad it was for them to receive mail from the USA or Israel. He wished so much that he could see them once again but he knew it was impossible. They were very true friends and when he needed them most they went well above and beyond the call of friendship to help Henry and Rebecca. He missed them.

Henry wrote down some of his favorite sayings in a small, leather bound book:

"It's not the load that breaks you down, it's the way you carry it." "If it a plant, eat it. If it was made in a plant, don't." "There is no magic to achievement. It is really about hard work and persistence." "Temptation is not a sin. Giving in to it is." "Being good is not good enough."

"Whatever you want to say, wait a moment before you do. Whatever you want to do, wait and think for a day or two."

These were just a few of the sayings, but he would find many more.

In a way, Henry liked the fact that he knew of his future. He kind of prepared himself and was at peace with it. But there was a nagging feeling in his heart. He must see Liliana one more time. He thought of her often. Maybe after the US tour, they could schedule a presentation in Munich. He would talk to David about this. By now there was a large Jewish population in Germany.

Henry was rested. He had done some studying about the cities he was going to visit and incorporated the information in his speeches.

Henry's tour of the big cities had begun. It was an amazing experience for Henry. The cities were all different and so were the people, but in all of them there was something in common. After all it was the "United States." You could feel the love for this country in every city and state. Henry was always in awe how this country was only two hundred years old and had achieved so much.

Henry got used to his success. He was no longer nervous before his speeches. He always received a standing ovation and the familiarity made him less tired. David did his job well. He made sure that Henry rested and ate properly. He took care of Henry's wardrobe and was a fast learner. Henry had no doubts that David would be able to take over his job.

David had no family to take care of. He was close to forty, handsome, educated and street smart. So what was wrong? One of these days, Henry would ask him. David became very dear to Henry. He was spending more time with David than with anyone else. He had a good heart, he was a patriot and thought that Henry was a genius.

The tour continued as scheduled. Everyplace they went they were welcomed. Henry received calls of appreciation from the embassy. It made him feel great that he was doing something significant with his life.

Towards the end of the trip Henry needed more rest. Arriving home to Rebecca's was a great relief. He hardly went to his apartment in Manhattan. He loved being with the kids and enjoyed the quiet environment of the house. He would have a good rest now.

Rebecca catered to Henry's every wish. David left for Manhattan, but returned a few days later with a new project. It was what Henry had requested, a trip to several cities in Germany. It would take a few months before they would go. Henry was asked if he could present his speeches in German. He was not sure if he still had enough knowledge of the language.

Henry wrote a warm and informative letter to Liliana. He told her about what he was doing, about his health and about Rebecca, in detail. New photos of everyone were included. He also asked if he could see her in a few months when he would be in Munich. He did not mind if she came with Robert. The letter was mailed from Manhattan.

Henry went to his Manhattan apartment for a few days. The housekeeper and David were there with him. Rebecca made sure that he was never alone. David took Henry to the Embassy and they all agreed that he would speak German in Germany. David would help Henry compose the speeches. He was fluent in the language. Henry never knew this. Up until now, Henry had memorized all his speeches.

David and Henry took long walks around the city and in Central Park. They talked about politics and the latest inventions. Henry's walks were becoming slower and slower. He had to rest a lot, but he wanted to walk. It made him feel better physically and definitely, mentally. Henry now appreciated every small detail - the green grass, the shining sun, the gentle breezes, the beauty of the trees, the color of the flowers. All had beauty to him.

The next day he visited the Metropolitan Museum. It was a favorite place for Henry. He looked at art differently also. He could stare at a painting for a long time and study each stroke of the brush. The smallest details became visible to him. He could even see the reason behind a particular painting.

As they walked out of the museum, Henry said to David, "You know the saying that youth is wasted on the young? It is so true."

They had lunch in a small restaurant on a side street. Henry ordered steak and David had to remind him that he could not have steak. Henry looked at him and asked, "Does it really matter? I still want to enjoy the food I like." David let him.

Henry looked closer at David and asked if one day he would tell his story, before it was too late. David nodded and said, "One day I will."

It was Friday and the build-up of traffic was just starting as it did every Friday. Henry and David were headed to the train station. They were going to Rebecca's house for a restful weekend. The welcome Henry received from his grandchildren always amazed David. This was pure love.

Helena received the long letter from Henry and fabulous photos. Helena thought Rebecca was so beautiful and that the children were extraordinary. Young Lilly looked a little like herself. The letter was sad. Henry was not well. He informed her that he left a letter with his attorney telling their whole story and included Liliana's address and phone number. Henry said he would still try to tell Rebecca himself. The letter at the lawyer's was just in case he never got the opportunity. The decision would be up to Rebecca if she chose to contact her mother.

Henry also wrote about what he was doing for Israel and how much satisfaction it gave him. Then he wrote something that she did not expect. He wrote that he missed her and that he had felt that way all his life.

As Helena read the letter alone on the veranda, she felt herself blushing. And then she felt a wave of guilt. Helena would tell Robert that Henry was coming to Munich and that she would meet him. She would invite Robert to accompany her, but in her heart, she hoped he would not. That night she showed Robert the photos. He admitted how beautiful the children were.

Henry promised to let her know when he was arriving. Helena was relieved to hear that eventually Rebecca would know about her. This was sort of good news, halfway good.

CHAPTER 37

K aty was expecting her baby any day. The Rothman family wanted to be near their daughter at the time of delivery. They arrived and stayed in Maximilian's and Katy's house.

Helena invited everyone for dinner at her house. They were all happy to be together.

Katy was uncomfortable. She could not find a comfortable place to sit and she was very fidgety. She could not eat much. Sarah was carefully watching her daughter and whispered to Helena that she thought the baby would be born that night.

After Helena went to bed, she could not fall asleep. Her phone rang and Max excitedly informed her that they were leaving for the hospital. Robert and Helena got dressed as fast as they could and drove to the hospital as well.

Katy was already in the birthing room. Max was with her but no one else was allowed. Helena, Sarah, Robert and Stephen sat in the waiting room. From time to time a nurse came in to report that all was okay. At 9:00am the next morning, Katy still had not delivered her baby. It took another three hours. At exactly noon the nurse came to the waiting room with a big smile on her face. A boy was born. He was healthy, big and beautiful and the mother was doing fine. The four of them jumped from their chairs, hugged, kissed and cried all at the same time. They left the waiting room to get a bite to eat and a much needed cup of coffee. Within an hour they were waiting outside Katy's room.

The nurse asked them in and instructed that they could look but not touch the baby. Katy was all smiles and looked a little tired and pale but very happy. The baby was perfect. He had a fair complexion, blonde hair and blue eyes.

Robert was visibly pleased. Now there was a boy to continue the family name. Helena looked at the baby and remembered when Maximilian was born. The baby looked very much like him.

Albert and Monica came to visit. Albert cried. Helena looked at him and thought of how sensitive he was.

Katy would be home in a few days. The nanny was coming tomorrow. The Rothman family would stay with Katy for a while. Katy would breast feed the baby. Helena was glad. So many young mothers did not want to then. The baby did not have a name yet. Robert was hoping they would name the baby after his father, Kurt.

The baby came home. The nanny and the bassinet were waiting for him. All the family gathered around and admired him. Robert put out his finger for the baby to hold. He held on so strongly and did not let go. Robert was in heaven. Helena watched and was happy to see his joy. Robert's eyes spotted her and he gave her a smile which she had not seen for a long time.

That night everyone came to Helena's house for a celebration dinner. At dinner, Max asked Robert if he could give his son his great grandfather's name, Kurt. Robert was very moved.

The baptism would take place on the seventh day of his birth. That was at the request of Katy's mother. She stated that this was a family tradition. Helena again could not believe her ears. The Jewish people have a circumcision ceremony on the seventh day of a boy's birth also. Helena wanted to know if Sarah knew there was a meaning to those traditions.

The children did not want a big celebration for the baptism, just a family dinner. Monica's parents along with her brother and his wife were invited. Monica's mother asked if she could also bring her two granddaughters. Helena responded, "Of course." They would all attend the church ceremony and then return to Helena's home for celebration. Monica was nervous again about bringing the families together, but Helena calmed her by assuring her that it would all be alright.

The day came for the christening and Kurt would wear the baptismal gown that his great grandfather, grandfather and father wore. Helena had washed and pressed the delicate garment. Age had turned it a little yellowish but it still was befitting a prince.

Monica's family met them at the church and then joined them at the house for the celebration. They admired the baby and congratulated all the grandparents. Helena looked at them and thought they must have decided to behave so that they could continue being in their daughter's life. Most of all, Monica was surprised at their good behavior, and very relieved. They all touched her belly and said it was time for her to have a fine boy, just like Kurt. Monica's niece's kneeled by the bassinet and just stared at the baby. It was a very happy time for all. Even Robert had warmed up to Monica's father. Monica's father had promised to deliver some good meat and fresh eggs from the farm. Helena was watching and thinking how all this would change if they ever found out the truth. She did not want this to happen. After she admitted this to herself, she felt guilty again. There would always be someone who would get hurt.

Baby Kurt was a delight. Sarah was already upset that she had to go home but she promised that she would be a frequent guest. The Rothman family left that afternoon.

Helena held the baby as often as she could. It felt so amazing. It was more pleasurable to her than holding her own sons when they were infants. Helena picked up her handsome grandson and raised him above her head. She could swear he smiled. Katy brought the baby to the main house daily to say hello or to let the grandparents walk around the property with the baby carriage.

Katy and Helena discussed whether or not she should find a job or just stay home with baby Kurt. Katy just received her master's degree and wanted to get a job. But the thought of leaving Kurt for a whole day, even with the best of help, just did not feel right. Katy did not have to work for the money and so she decided she would stay at home. Helena agreed and Sarah was happy too. This decision would make easier for Katy to visit her parents in the future and to have them as her guests for longer periods of time. She promised herself that she would always stay close with her family. Maximilian wanted her to be home also. He was very proud to be a father.

Not too long after, Sarah came again. She could not stay away. This time she came alone. Helena was happy to see her. They took care of the baby, went out shopping, had lunch and did the same the next day. They were never bored with each other.

Robert, on the way home from the office, would stop by Max's house first to see the baby, and only then would go to his house. He was obsessed with Kurt.

* * *

Helena answered the letter from Henry. She told him about the birth of her grandson, Kurt. And, of course, that she would meet him in Munich. She just asked that he tell her of his arrival a few days in advance. She told him she was sorry that he was not in the best of health and urged him to take care of himself. It was a warm and caring letter. She sealed the letter and was off to the post office. She did not want Robert to read it.

She stopped at a local bookstore to find a good book and hoped no one would recognize her. The bookstore was full of young people and Helena was glad. The younger generation did not really care who was who and if you were not on television, they did not know nor care who you were. She browsed and found two books. Then she went to the magazine section. One of the magazines featured a write up on Israel. It had photos and interviews. Helena bought the magazine.

Coming home, she stopped at Katy's to see the baby. Helena played with the baby and Katy offered a salad for lunch with her. She gladly agreed. They chatted and then Helena went home. She was anxious to look at the magazine. Robert would be home in a few hours so she had plenty of time to relax on the veranda and look through the magazine and see what was happening in the land where her daughter lived. At least that was where she thought her daughter lived.

Helena was proud of what this little country had achieved. It was filled with people from all over the world who had suffered through a horrible war. They lost most of their family, spoke different languages and the only thing they had in common was their religion. It was amazing to Helena. She thought it probably impressed people all over the world. Helena wanted to go to Israel and see it with her own eyes. She knew that Robert would never agree. Helena hid the magazine from him.

CHAPTER 38

Katy was pampered by everyone. Monica was a little jealous. "Maybe I should have a baby also," she thought. She worked very hard, long hours but for what? She already had a great house, a good car, clothes and a great husband. Most people work all their lives and never have what she already had. The only thing that made sense to her if she continued to work so hard was to achieve a life in political office. But she was not sure if she would like that. Maybe she should have a baby now. She would talk to Albert to see how he felt about this.

Monica had a talk with Albert and he agreed that there was no point in waiting. Albert, too, wanted to be a father. He watched his older brother and saw the great love between parents and child. Just like Monica, he did not see the benefit of waiting. They both were happy with their decision and after a short two months, Monica became pregnant. They wanted to wait a little longer before they told the family but Monica could not hide her pregnancy. She did not feel well most of the time and could not even look at food. Everyone was happy. Max talked about how their kids would be able to grow up together. This was good for everyone. Monica quit her job and did not regret it for a moment.

The family was growing, thought Helena. It was like living a dream. Nothing felt real. Maybe that was how life was.

Monica finally told her family the news of her pregnancy at a picnic gathering. She begged her father to keep it quiet for a while. He was very pleased. All he wanted was a big healthy boy whose name was going to be Van Klaus.

Monica was monitored by a doctor specializing in troubled pregnancies. After four months she still did not feel well, and then it all became clear. She was pregnant with twins. The babies were big and it was almost certain she would have to undergo a caesarian section. Everybody was very worried. Monica was never left alone. Helena and Robert took her for slow walks. Katy was there all the time. Finally Monica started to feel better. All they had to do was to be patient and hope for a full term pregnancy.

Monica's parents came to visit and they behaved. They knew not to upset their daughter. Helena was very nice to them. She offered lunch and made plans with them for the birth of the babies.

Sarah was in touch with Helena and was coming soon for a visit. Today Monica's brother with his family came to visit. They brought a big bouquet of flowers. Everyone was counting down the time with great anticipation. Robert became very close with Monica. He loved her intellect and her view of the world. Her interest in international politics impressed him. They were always immersed in conversation.

Albert was becoming restless. He worried about his wife and the wellbeing of the babies. Monica was getting bigger. She now had a hard time taking walks.

Katy's nanny was helping to find someone suitable for Monica. Monica was feeling some pain in her abdomen, but the doctor said this often happens with twins. It was also suspected that the babies were large. The doctor suggested that the last two to three weeks of the pregnancy she should be in the hospital. She would have a private room and her own nurse. The only visitors would be her immediate family. Albert stayed with her most of the day. Everybody's nerves were on edge.

They found a nanny. She had been taking care of twins until they were old enough to go to school. The nanny visited Monica in the hospital. Monica liked her. Robert came daily to watch the news on television with Monica. His dedication was true.

About one week before the due date, Monica developed high blood pressure which was dangerous for the mother and the babies. The doctors determined that the babies were big enough to be born. Monica would have a C-section tomorrow.

The next morning the whole family was in the hospital, including Monica's parents. The procedure was not long. In a short while, the doctor came in with good news. Two healthy boys! They all jumped for joy, hugging and crying together. Soon they would all see the babies.

One by one they went into the room. It was so amazing to see the two babies next to each other, sleeping peacefully. They were big for newborns, blonde and fair with button noses and fat cheeks. The doctors said they were perfectly healthy. Monica was well also. Her blood pressure was normal but she needed to rest. She would breast feed, but it was possible she would not have enough milk for both babies. Then she would have to supplement with formula.

In five days she would go home. The christening would take place in a month, when Monica would be feeling better. The babies' names were Sygmunt Van Klaus and Frederick Van Klaus. The names were chosen by Robert. They were named for past Van Klauses. The Shultz family was thrilled, especially Monica's father. He had two Van Klaus grandsons.

Robert would have a personal talk with Monica's father right after the christening.

The nanny they hired was very capable. Helena was also there to help. Everyone settled into a routine. Helena had to pinch herself every morning. She thought it was a dream... four grandsons and one granddaughter.

Robert had a permanent smile on his face. He was thrilled.

There was a small note in the local paper announcing the birth of the twins. The family received a lot of congratulations from the citizens of their small town of Regensburg. They were total strangers.

Robert started writing the family history of the Van Klaus family that went back hundreds of years. Included would be the three newest boys born into the family. This was a great satisfaction to him. He often forgot that Helena had a part in all this as well.

The christening was a big event. A lot of uninvited people from town came to the church. They all wanted to see the Van Klaus twins. Monica's father was bursting with pride. He was dressed properly and his behavior was superb. He was shaking hands with total strangers from town and he felt very important.

Robert spoke with Mr. Shultz in a friendly manner. He explained to him, in a simple way, that he had to choose his daughter and the Van Klaus family over his friends and their unacceptable beliefs. Robert further explained that these beliefs brought only hatred and unhappiness. Their drunkenness and rough behavior would not be accepted by most of the people in town. Robert suggested that it could be very pleasant if he made the right decision to be together with him and raise these wonderful two boys. After the short speech he hugged Mr. Shultz. Mr. Shultz was surprised and sad.

"Thank you for speaking to me so frankly." said Mr. Shultz.

Monica was feeling better every day. The boys were doing well. Monica had enough milk to feed them both. She read a lot and tended to the babies. Soon she would start exercising together with Katy. She wanted to look good for Albert.

Helena was waiting to receive the information letting her know when Henry was arriving in Munich. She told Robert that Henry was coming and he agreed to see him and listen to his speech also. "What a surprise," thought Helena.

Helena was hopping from one house to the other to see the babies and see if she was needed. All three boys looked the same. They had the same coloring. Baby Kurt already recognized his grandmother and he stretched out his hands to her as soon as he saw her. As soon as Robert returned from the office he ran to see the kids before he ate dinner. He would say it gave him a better appetite. He sat at the dinner table every night and described the boys. "This one did this, and the other one did that." Helena was always surprised at how he saw those small happenings.

One night, and for the first time, Robert discussed a business opportunity with Helena. It was a matter of making an investment in a high rise building in the United States. Robert explained that it was a very good location and a good opportunity.

Helena asked what would happen if the deal turned out to be bad. How would this change their lives?

"It would not at all," answered Robert.

"Then you should do it, "said Helena.

Robert would discuss this with his sons before he made a final decision. Helena was so glad that Robert had asked her opinion. It made her feel like she belonged in the family because sometimes she had her doubts.

Robert suggested they make a trip to the United States to finalize the investment. His sons believed it was a good business decision. Helena wanted to go with him on this trip, but something was holding her back. Finally she did agree to accompany him and the date for departure was chosen.

Quickly Helena wrote a letter to Henry letting him know about the dates of her trip. She did not want to miss him in Munich.

Robert and Helena would stay in a hotel in Manhattan and then tour the east coast of the United States. They would be away for three weeks. Helena was uneasy about leaving the kids and grandchildren for so long. She spoke with Sarah and she and her husband would come and stay for a week. Robert spoke with Mr. Schultz and asked him to keep an eye on the kids as well. He was thrilled to do it.

So all was set for a great adventure. They started to get ready. Helena could not believe that she was going to the United States. That was a dream that everyone in the world wished to achieve.

Henry responded quickly. He offered to meet them in Manhattan, saying that he would be there at the same time. Helena asked Robert if he would meet Henry with her. If he would be too busy, then she would see Henry alone.

Robert looked at her in surprise. He thought she was showing quite a bit of courage lately. Robert agreed that he would be with her for the meeting.

Helena again wrote to Henry to give the confirmed dates in Manhattan. They would be staying at the Waldorf Astoria Hotel. In the same letter she indicated that she would also like to meet up with him in Munich and attend the gathering and hear his speech.

Helena decided that she would pack very little. It was time to change her wardrobe anyway. She planned to shop in New York at Saks Fifth Avenue, Neiman Marcus and other famous stores. She was very excited about the trip, touring and the shopping spree. But she did wonder what Henry was doing in the United States. And her curiosity surprised her.

Katy came to help her pack and baby Kurt was right there pulling out everything they put in the suitcase. It was very funny. They did not accomplish much but they had a good laugh.

Mr. Schultz offered to take them to the airport and Robert accepted his offer.

Two days before they left, Sarah arrived. She took baby Kurt to see the twins and visit with Monica. She always knew to do the right thing. She asked Mr. Schultz to bring fresh eggs from his farm. He was more than happy to oblige. Sarah also requested that he bring his wife so they both could take care of the twins.

Helena was departing with an ease in her heart.

CHAPTER 39

As they approached the landing, Helena was awestruck by the New York skyline. No matter how much she had heard and read about it, seeing it with her own eyes was an experience without compare. It was impressive to take in the majesty of the tall buildings and the bridges. The roadways looped all through the city. The plane had an easy landing. They arrived early in the morning and took a taxi to Manhattan.

The energy from the crowds on the street was palpable even in the early morning. Once they reached their hotel they got settled and went out for breakfast in the city. They wanted to experience a taste of New York. They left their hotel and turned onto Fifth Avenue. They selected a small restaurant and sat by the window. The waitress was patient and helped them to order. As they gazed out the window the first thing they noticed was all the different kinds of people passing by. White, black, Asian, and everything in between. This was amazing, they thought. There was no place like this anywhere in the world.

After breakfast they took a long walk. The city was alive. Everybody was in a hurry to go somewhere. There was a lot of traffic on the streets. New York was just what they had heard it was. They got to witness first-hand the hustle and bustle of the city. It was fun to experience it but Helena knew she wouldn't want to live there.

Helena and Robert were meeting Henry the following evening in the hotel. Helena invited Henry for dinner. In the afternoon she would go to the beauty parlor. She wanted to look her best. Robert would be busy all day with his business appointment so she would have the day to herself.

That evening they went down to a very elegant restaurant in the hotel. Henry was already there waiting for them. Helena was nervous. She looked good but many years had passed since she saw him last. She could not understand why she cared so much about how she looked, but brushed it off as just a case of vanity.

Henry looked almost the same. He was totally gray by then and a little bit slimmer. Robert greeted him with a handshake and Henry gave Helena a kiss and said, "Liliana, you look well. The years have been kind to you." Helena could feel herself blush.

They sat at the table after dinner for a long time. They talked about their families, exchanged photos and all was good until the inevitable came about. Henry told them what he was doing. He did mention that he had an apartment in the city, but did not say where Rebecca was. He told them that he was not well and that he did not think he had many years left. He would like to put this *big meeting* behind him. He tried hard to explain to them why the meeting must be inclusive, and that it did not have to be at their home or even in Germany. But Henry impressed upon them that all involved, including their children, had to be present. Rebecca had two half-brothers and three nephews. Why should she not know them? Henry's speech was very convincing. Even Robert could not challenge this and Helena cried, of course. Robert said that they would discuss it and meet again.

Henry wanted to take them on a tour of the city. They all agreed and in two days they would meet again. They parted in agreement for the first time.

Helena did not sleep that night. The next day she was going shopping. She did not want to dwell on what would happen. Helena went shopping alone. She loved it but she could not fully enjoy the spree. Her head was preoccupied with thoughts of the previous night.

Helena met Robert for dinner and they were both very quiet. Robert told her a little about the business that he would be finalizing in a few days.

Tomorrow they would meet Henry again.

The next morning was beautiful. Henry was waiting in a limo with a chauffeur to take them around the city and then they would go to his apartment for dinner.

The driver took them uptown and downtown. Henry was giving instructions, in perfect English, to his driver. Helena was surprised and impressed by him. He knew the city well. They passed all the noteworthy museums and the Empire State building. They drove through Central Park, and then down to the tip of Manhattan where they could see the Statue of Liberty. Helena and Robert where pleased by Henry's generous gesture.

Henry and Robert got along splendidly. Early in the evening they went to Henry's apartment. The housekeeper was ready with dinner. Henry made sure that everything would be perfect, and it was. The Van Klauses were amazed. Robert recognized that Henry's apartment was extremely expensive and so were all the antiques and paintings in it. He figured that this man must be very wealthy. Helena stood in front of a large photograph. It was her daughter, with her husband and two gorgeous kids. Robert stood behind her and admired the photo also.

Robert said, "Beautiful, just beautiful. I wish that we lived in the states. Then all of this would be so much easier." Helena nodded in agreement.

They had tea after dinner and resumed their talk. Now Robert was speaking. He tried so hard to convince Henry that it was not necessary for his sons to be a part of the meeting. Robert explained that his sons had a legacy from his family that went back hundreds of years and that now there were also in-laws to consider.

Henry politely listened. At the end he said, "The children always pay for the parent's mistakes. It says so in the bible." Henry reminded them that there was a detailed letter with the whole family history in his attorney's office and Rebecca would get it upon his death. Henry said that he was not sure what she would do, but added that knowing her, she would act on it. Henry predicted that Rebecca would not take this information passively. "So it is up to you, what you choose to do now," Henry concluded.

In truth, Henry was afraid of the meeting too. Rebecca would definitely have anger knowing that he kept this secret from her for so many years. Henry turned to Helena and said, "If Rebecca decides not to meet you, you will never find her." With that said, they parted in a peaceful way.

As soon as Henry closed the door behind them and the driver took them to the hotel, Helena started to cry. Robert put his hand on her shoulder, but did not say anything.

They left the city for an organized trip of the east coast of the United States. But Helena could not make herself stay interested. All she kept thinking about was the meeting with Henry. An impossible situation, with no way out. Deep in her heart she agreed with Robert. She also did not want to disturb her sons' lives.

On the plane trip back home, Helena was still not herself. Robert said, "Sometimes there are situations that you cannot do anything about. And, sometimes, in your darkest hours, you find the strength."

But Helena thought, "But these are not my darkest hours." Her darkest hours were when she lost her whole family and herself.

Seeing her sons and grandsons eased Helena's depression. They were all grand. Everyday life took its course and slowly Helena was returning to herself.

Mr. and Mrs. Schultz had come by often during their absence. They played with the boys and brought fresh eggs and vegetables. Monica was very grateful and Katy just loved them. They were not well educated; they were simple people. It was apparent that they decided to keep a close knit family. Sarah had stayed for almost two weeks.

All was normal until a new letter came from Henry informing Helena that he would be in Munich in one month. He invited them to his event. He told them he would be staying in Munich for only two days and would then proceed to other major cities in Germany.

Robert did not want to go to Munich. He knew it would be Jewish gathering and he did not feel comfortable being there. Helena understood, but she did not want to go alone. She would still try to persuade Robert to come along.

It came time to make arrangements to go to Munich, but Robert refused to go. Helena decided that she would go alone. Robert was opposed to this.

He said, "You may meet people that you do not want to see, and hear things that you would rather not hear."

Helena knew that he was right. She wrote a letter to Henry that she was not feeling well and would not be able to attend. In a way this was a relief. She felt uneasy about being in a Jewish gathering and was hesitant to be so close to Henry. Not surprisingly, she was a bit of a coward. In the past, when she had the opportunities to assert herself or make her feelings known, she withdrew. She would be depressed for a while but she would rebound. She would resume her comfortable, rich suburban life as a German noble lady.

CHAPTER 40

The trip to Germany was fast approaching. Henry received a letter from Liliana that said she would not be attending his speech in Munich. He had a feeling she would not. "Oh well," he thought.

He was meeting with David. They would rehearse the speeches one more time. The speeches would be recited in German and, surprisingly, David was fluent in German. David and Henry had lunch together and Henry began his speeches. David did not correct anything Henry said. There was nothing to correct.

As David sat on an easy chair admiring the apartment, he said, "Now is a good time to tell you my story." David was born in 1930 in Germany to a Jewish family. His father was a professor and his mother was a dentist. They were very assimilated and seldom visited a synagogue. They had a comfortable life and a large family. When the war broke out, David was nine years old. He remembered the chaos and the fear. He did not understand why anyone would want them dead. His entire family was to be deported to Poland. His father wanted to hide David with a Christian family in Germany. It took a long time to find somebody to take in a nine year old boy. Finally they found a couple who were moving out of town to a small village. They were childless and they were too old to pass as his parents so it was decided that they would pose as his grandparents. David changed his name and went to the village with his "grandparents."

He kept his distance from other children, fearing that they may guess the truth. The couple that cared for him were nice, simple people. They did a lot of gardening, listened to the radio and paid little attention to David. A lot of the time David was by himself, worrying about his family. He did attend the local school, but most of the time he played sick. He read anything that he could find. The war was raging throughout the world, but in his little village, it was not felt. From time to time military trucks came to take food from the villagers. Even David's "grandparents" gave some fruit and vegetables to them.

Toward the end of the war they could hear the bombardment in Berlin. David heard that the main road was full of German citizens escaping from Berlin. But the village was too far away from the main road so those fleeing the city did not stop there.

When David was fourteen the war ended. The "grandparents" told him to be patient and wait for his family to come and get him. Every week felt like a year and no one came. A year after the war, his "grandparents" decided to take David to Berlin to see what they could find out about his family.

Berlin was unrecognizable. This vibrant big city lay in ruins. They went to an attorney to find out if he could help find David's family. Everyone who was looking for lost family registered with the Red Cross Agency. The office reviewed all the names that people gave them, but there were no names of David's family on their lists. The lawyer found out that the German Jews from Berlin were taken to concentration camps and they all perished. David did not believe it. He thought, "How could this be? My family will show up."

There was an orphanage for Jewish children in a suburb of Berlin. This was where his "grandparents" left him. David was glad. He started school, made friends and waited. From time to time a parent showed up to retrieve their child. But this was very rare.

Another year had passed. It was now 1948 and Israel became an independent country. For all those children still waiting, it became clear that no one was coming to pick them up. By then David was almost sixteen years old. It was decided that all the occupants of the orphanage would be transported to Israel and placed in a Kibbutz.

This was how David found himself in a Kibbutz. He was assigned to a family that was very nice to him. He immersed himself in studying Hebrew, Arabic and English at the same time. He was talented and in no time he mastered the languages. He loved his life on the Kibbutz. At the age of almost nineteen, he entered the military. Then his real education started.

At that time he had learned that his whole family was taken to Auschwitz and they all perished shortly upon arriving. David was the sole survivor of his whole family. He was not the only one; many young people shared this same experience.

David moved up in the ranks in the military. He never married or had children. The last few years he had been assigned to the Israeli Embassy in New York.

Henry just sat there and listened. Another sad story. Another shattered life. There were so many of them, he thought. Henry got up from his chair and went to David and gave him a big bear hug. He did not say a word; he just held him a long time in his arms.

When David and Henry left the apartment and walked to the embassy for the last visit before they would go to Germany, Henry said, "David, you know I love you. You are like a son to me."

That weekend they would stay at Rebecca's house. On Monday they had a flight to Frankfurt. That was their first stop on the speaking tour. The gathering would be on Thursday. That gave them enough time to rest and see some sights. They both spoke German. That made it easier. They were met by Israeli representatives who took them to their hotel.

Towards the end of the day, they both agreed they did not feel very comfortable in Germany. The city had grown a lot. There was new construction everywhere. People were so civilized and polite. Was it possible that these were the same people who waged such a horrible war only twenty years ago?

The large hall was filled with people. There were no more seats; standing room only. Henry was informed that the audience was not only Jewish and that there were many young people who wanted to know what was happening in Israel.

The evening was a success again. No one wanted to leave. There were so many questions about Israel. The predominant question was if Germans would be welcomed in Israel.

So they traveled all over Germany. The newspapers always had articles featuring their program. Everybody had an opinion. Some were happy, some were critical and some quite hostile.

Henry's health was deteriorating. David was very concerned and proposed that they return to the states, but Henry would not hear of it. He wanted to finish the tour. "Two more cities," David said. "The last stop will be Munich."

Henry had an urgent feeling to speak with Eva's children. He called them that evening. All was okay with them. They had adjusted and their family was all around them.

Henry spoke to Rebecca every day. He also knew that Rebecca spoke to David to find out how her father was doing with regard to his health.

They finally arrived in Munich, the last stop. The press was there and Henry was pleased because he knew that Liliana and her husband would read about this. It was going to be the largest gathering he had in Germany. Henry gave the best speech of his life. The audience was roaring. They just loved him. Back in the hotel, they re-watched the whole thing on television. Henry was pleased.

Henry did not feel well at all. He could not fall asleep. He had a pain in his chest and he could not breathe deeply. He was only able to manage shallow breaths. He knew he had to go to a hospital. He woke up David and they were off to the hospital. Henry was taken care of immediately, but the doctors were worried. They spoke with Henry's doctors in the United States. They told David that Henry would not make it back to New York. If there was family that he would like to see, they must hurry.

David knew that Henry was dying. Informing Rebecca was extremely difficult. Rebecca cried on the phone and told him they would all be there the next day.

Rebecca, Alex, Sam and Lilly came into Henry's room. He was so happy to see them. He could hardly speak but he could touch the kids. Rebecca had red eyes from crying and the saddest face Henry ever saw. He asked Alex if he could be with Rebecca alone for a little while. They all left and went to the waiting room.

Henry asked Rebecca to sit really close to him so that she could hear better. He told her not to interrupt him until he was finished with what he had to say. She promised. Rebecca held her father's hand ready to listen.

Henry spoke in a weak but clear voice. The story began when Rebecca was born and it continued. Henry spoke of his time in the concentration camp, life after the war, and finally how he ended up in Israel. And then, he told her the unbelievable story of her mother and how things progressed, and what he wanted for Rebecca. He told Rebecca of the correspondence and meetings between her mother and him and told her where she could find the letters. And Henry gave her the attorney in New York contact information and told her that had the address and all the necessary explanations for Rebecca.

Rebecca's eyes doubled in size. Henry said he did what he felt was best for her. He could not give her an explanation as to why it all happened the way it did.

Henry could not speak any longer. He asked that Rebecca bring in the children. She did. And Alex came in to the room with tears in his eyes. David came in with them. In a very quiet whisper, Henry told David that he wanted to be buried in Israel, in Jerusalem. David promised. They stayed for a while and David took Alex and the kids back to the hotel. Rebecca stayed with Henry.

Rebecca sat with her father, holding his hand. He received medication to ease his breathing and also an oxygen mask. Henry fell asleep and Rebecca sat on a chair and put her head next to her father's.

When Rebecca awoke, it was morning. She looked at her father and he was gone. He died quietly in his sleep, without a struggle. Rebecca cried bitter tears and promised that she would do exactly what her father wanted for her. She rang for the nurse and then left for the hotel.

Rebecca saw David first. She knew he would make all the arrangements. He did. The next day they all flew to Israel with Henry's body. The funeral was in Jerusalem. The only people at the gravesite were Alex, Rebecca, the kids, Moshe, Joseph and David.

The next day David ordered the monument and then they all got on a plane back to the states. Sam cried the whole time. He understood that his beloved grandfather was not coming back, and he could not make peace with it.

At home, the housekeeper was waiting for them and tried to make them as comfortable as she could. David came with them. Rebecca told him he must stay in her life, like a brother. They parted with a hug.

They rested for two days. Then Rebecca got in touch with her father's attorney to make sure everything was in order. Rebecca did not realize how rich she would become. But this was not that important to her.

Rebecca spoke with Alex and he felt she should let her mother go and not get in touch her. Rebecca disagreed. She would get in touch with her and do what her father had wanted to do for so many years. She was not doing it for the love of her mother, but for the love of her father.

CHAPTER 41

Rebecca's bitterness grew stronger by the day. She finally decided to place the call to Germany. She picked a morning hour in Germany. The phone rang twice and a woman answered. Rebecca spoke in German. She asked for Mrs. Helena Van Klaus. The woman who answered told her to wait. Then a voice, so much like her own, came on the line. "May I help you?", she said. Rebecca thought she was stronger, but hearing this woman took her breath away.

Finally Rebecca answered, "My name is Rebecca Kopel-Silber and I am your daughter."

There was silence on the other end of the line. Rebecca waited. Finally a broken voice, full of emotion, answered in Polish, "I do not know what to say, Rebecca. I have waited to see you for so long. Are you in Germany?"

"No," answered Rebecca. And then she proceeded to tell her about Henry's death, two weeks ago, in Munich.

Rebecca heard a gasp over the line, and then, "Oh, my God!" Rebecca said if Helena needed some time to process, she could call back in a few days. But Helena said, "Oh no, please don't hang up, please." Rebecca waited and Helena finally said, "I would like to come see you and your family."

Rebecca said she would rather come to Germany with her family so that she could meet her half-brothers and their families.

Again, silence. Finally Rebecca heard, in a broken voice, Helena's request for her phone number so that she could call her back. Helena said, "This is a total shock for me, and I need to compose myself." Rebecca gave her the phone number, they said their goodbyes and hung up.

Rebecca stood there not knowing how she felt. It was obvious that her mother was distraught. But her father said she wanted to keep Rebecca a secret and did not want to disturb her son's life with the truth.

Rebecca was more angry than happy. And she would insist on having a meeting her way, even if it would not be the nicest way. She waited for the return phone call which came in two days. Rebecca was home alone. The nanny had taken Lilly for a walk and Sam was in school.

Helena spoke softly and tried to explain her situation. She wanted to explain how everything happened. She said it was a long story and it could not be told over the phone. Rebecca listened and didn't say anything. Helena begged her for a meeting. Rebecca said she would call back soon. She needed to talk all this over with her husband. Before Helena hung up, she told Rebecca that not a day went by that she didn't think of her.

Rebecca called David and met with him. He knew the whole story and Rebecca wanted to know what he thought of this difficult situation. David said there were all kinds of stories from the war, but that this one was really unique. The only thing he could not understand was why having a Jewish wife or mother would be such a great tragedy for Helena's family. Even if the lives of her half-brothers would change, there was still no denying the truth. David agreed that Henry's decision to have all the family members meet was the right thing to do. He told Rebecca that she should either do as her father wanted or just let it be and have no reunion at all. Rebecca asked David to stay with them for the weekend so all three of them could decide what steps to take.

Alex came home from work and was happy to see David. He stayed, but was very sad. Every corner reminded him of Henry. He missed him very much. After dinner, they made themselves comfortable on the big sofas and decided to come to a decision.

Alex felt that they should just forget about the meeting and should not open a can of worms. He felt there would never be a meeting put together with love. At best, it would only be done out of revenge on Rebecca's part.

Rebecca said, "Even if it is only revenge, it would be worth it!" She continued to say that she would be doing it for her father.

David agreed with Rebecca. So he advised that Rebecca be straight forward and ask for an open meeting with all the parties and Rebecca would come to them with her family. If Helena would refuse, Rebecca had to inform her that she was coming anyway and not alone. Perhaps the press would also be included. The press would certainly be interested such an unusual war story.

Now it would be up to Rebecca as to when and if she placed the call to Helena and put this plan in motion. Rebecca knew that her mother's comfort and love for her sons was much more important than her love for her, and that fact hurt. Of course she wanted to be welcomed with open arms and love. Rebecca was sorry that her father did not sever the relationship from the start. It would have been easier to think that her mother had perished in the concentration camp, like so many others, then having to negotiate this meeting and force it upon her. Rebecca felt strongly that she had to do this. So she prepared for the difficult call. She knew the longer she waited, the more difficult it would become.

Rebecca woke up early in the morning. Everyone was still asleep. She went into the children's bedroom. She did so every morning and night. They slept so peacefully with no worry in the world. Rebecca wanted to keep them this way, but reality was different. Reality brought so many unexpected situations. Everyone had to deal with those situations the best way they could.

Rebecca was ready to make the call.

* * *

Helena was afraid to answer the phone, and often she didn't. She had lost weight and could not sleep. The daily fights with Robert had become unbearable. Ever since Rebecca called there was no peace at home. Both Helena and Robert had to pretend that all was normal in front of the kids and the help. It was not easy.

Somehow, Helena knew that her daughter would force their meeting, and she knew she would let her. Robert and her sons would have to deal with it. Helena had no more strength to fight. She was only sorry that Henry did not live to see it happen. Helena was shocked by Henry's passing and she was so surprised at how deeply she mourned him. Her guilt was enormous. If only she had a little courage, she would have gone to Munich.

The phone rang. Helena knew it was Rebecca.

For the first time, Rebecca said, "Hello mother."

Helena responded, "Hello daughter."

Rebecca just said that she and her family would be coming in a month and that she hoped to meet her brothers and their families. She said this very matter-of-factly.

Helena answered, "You will be welcomed with open arms."

Now Helena had to open the arms of her husband and her sons, but she still had a little time to prepare all of them. She would speak to Robert.

As they sat on the veranda, Helena sat close to Robert and he said, "You wouldn't be trying to persuade me again, would you?"

Helena said, "No, not to persuade you, just to inform you. Rebecca will be here in a month." Robert sprung from the couch and opened his mouth to scream, but Helena just said, "Hush. It is all done and now we just have to accept it. Oh, and one more thing. If it is so terrible for you to admit the truth, you should never have saved me. You should have left me in the concentration camp along with the rest of my kind. I will hear of it no longer and I will no longer endure your outrageous fits. It's done! I'm done!"

Robert was surprised. He sat back on the couch and quietly said, "You are right. Let's think of the best way to do this."

They decided that the next day, after dinner, they would talk more. They both did not sleep that night. The next evening they could not wait for dinner to be over. Sitting in the same spot, Robert was the first to speak about how this all should be taken care of. Before he told Helena his plan though, he told her that he loved her more at that moment than at any time before, and gave her a warm kiss.

Helena hugged him and said, "It will be okay, you will see."

Robert wanted to have a family meeting with just the sons and their wives; no in-laws. It had to be kept quiet. The help should not know anything. He felt Helena should speak first and then he would follow.

"We will tell them everything," said Robert. Helena totally agreed.

Robert called both of his sons to his house. The housekeeper had the day off. They would be home alone.

They gathered in the dining room at the large table. Maximilian and Albert guessed that this was going to be a serious meeting. Helena asked her sons not to interrupt. All would be explained.

Helena started by stating, "My real name is Liliana Wise and I am Jewish." With that profound statement she began to tell her story, emphasizing her love for Robert. She tried to control her emotions. The story was long and she had to tell it all.

Helena knew that everything would be all right when her sons sat next to her and put their arms around her. At the end of her story they told her they would be happy to meet their sister and her family.

It was easier for Robert to tell his story after seeing his sons' reactions. He also started from the very beginning, even from before the war and before he met Liliana. The young men sat mesmerized. After a long while, all was told. The sons hugged their parents in silence.

Robert asked his sons to tell their wives. They should share this story in private and not include their in-laws. The family secret should remain only within those living on the grounds and not beyond the gates. Their lives should not change in any way. They nodded in agreement and left for their houses. But not immediately. Helena saw the two boys sitting on a bench not far from her house. The boys talked for a long while and before they parted, they hugged each other. Helena was glad to see this.

The next day was Sunday. No one went to work. After lunch the three families gathered together. Maximilian asked his parents to retell their story to the wives adding that no one could tell it as well as they could. And so it was repeated.

Robert said that he must make sure they are all in agreement for the good of all of them. He stressed that this story could not leave the compound, explaining that keeping the story to themselves was important for them, for their sons and for future generations. He asked if they were all in agreement. They all were.

Katy asked, "What about the help? Who will they think these guests are?" Katy suggested that it would be the task of the women to keep the help away as much as they could.

So the preparations started. The guests would stay for three days. Rebecca was bringing her own nanny and they would have a driver.

Helena could not believe this was really happening. She would see and touch her daughter soon. Helena's daughter in-laws were amazed at the story. They thought this was the biggest love story they had ever heard and they were proud to be a part of it. No one ever mentioned the "Jewish" part of it. Helena wondered why.

Robert suggested that when the visit was over, they would all go for a long trip to Israel. Helena agreed. They let the help know that their guests were from abroad and they requested privacy. Plans were made on how to implement this.

All were hoping for a good first impression. Of all of them, Robert was the most nervous. Helena worried about him. He would not say why he was so upset. It seemed to Helena that Robert was almost scared to see Rebecca.

That night Rebecca and her family arrived in Munich and they would be at the house the next morning.

It was 10:00am. The time was here. The limo drove up to the gate which automatically opened. The whole family stood in front of Helena's house to greet them. The twins and Kurt were in their parent's arms. Kurt was two years old and Sygmunt and Frederick were one year old. Helena, being supported by Robert, felt as if she would faint. The car came up the drive.

The driver opened the door and first to come out were the kids. Samuel was seven years old and Lilly was four years old. They were shy, nicely dressed and very handsome children.

Katy was the first to greet them. She said, "Come, see the babies." They ran to them.

Then came Rebecca, looking elegant. She stood by the car with her husband next to her. She could not take a step. Helena walked to her with her arms stretched out. And so Rebecca was in her mother's embrace. They both cried as did the daughters-in-law. The kids were already together with Katy and Monica. The introductions began.

Maximilian and Albert came together to hug Rebecca and said, "Welcome to our lives, sister."

Robert shook Alexander's hand and said, "We are the least important people in this drama."

The weather was changing. It looked like it would rain any minute. They all went into the house. The mutual language they spoke was English. The brothers and their wives were hovering around Rebecca.

Helena stood by, just looking at her daughter. Her feelings were mixed. Her emotions didn't seem to befit the occasion. Helena wanted to feel something special. She expected so much more emotion, but she did not feel it. Her thoughts reeled, "What is wrong with me? Why are my feelings so shallow?"

Helena came to Rebecca, took her hand and said, "I just want to hold on to you so that I won't lose you again." She said this in Polish so that it was just between the two of them. Helena was just trying to experience the special feeling that she had expected to feel.

And so the visit proceeded. They ate, they laughed, they talked, and they asked a lot of questions.

In her bedroom that night, Rebecca said to Alex, "You know, my feelings are not as I expected."

The visit continued for the next three days. The men did not go to work. They were all trying to get to know each other. Helena tried to be as close to Rebecca as possible. But Rebecca was more interested in her brothers. Somehow she felt that the brothers were the most sincere and their wives were more curious about her.

Rebecca sensed that her mother was trying hard to get closer to her. But she could not forget the fact that her mother abandoned her for so many years and only by force was she there. Her hurt did not end with this short visit.

Towards the end of their visit, Rebecca invited all of them to come to the United States for a visit. To her mother she said it would be very nice if she came soon so that they could get to know each other better and so they could have some time with each other.

Helena promised that she would come soon.

On their flight back, Rebecca thought that her father made a big mistake by fighting so hard for this meeting. She was not so sure that it was all worth it.

Thinking back to the visit, Rebecca had a nagging sense that she had met Robert before.

* * *

Back in the compound they all relaxed. Robert said, "As they say in the United States... United We Stand!"

Their plan worked. Helena noticed her daughters-in-law guarded their secret very well. But Helena didn't feel good about that. How they all cared to hide her life, her Jewishness, and her daughter. It made her feel as if she was something less than they were.

Life was complicated for Helena. Her feelings were very hurt and she could not share that with anybody. She promised herself that she would make that visit with

Rebecca as soon as possible. She spoke with Robert and informed him that instead of going to Israel, she wanted to go to her daughter, by herself, for a lengthy visit. Robert agreed.

Helena spoke with Rebecca. Everything was arranged for her visit in two weeks. Helena was very excited to leave. All she thought about was how to improve her relationship with Rebecca. Helena wanted to develop a closeness as mother and daughter.

Most of all, Helena wanted to be Jewish, without hiding it or thinking of herself as a lesser person. This was what she thought of herself the moment she entered the concentration camp.

Even Helena's beloved sons had trouble making peace with the fact that they were half Jewish. They just chose to ignore it.

CHAPTER 42

Helena was greeted by Rebecca at Kennedy Airport and they drove to Rebecca's house. Rebecca told her that they would also spend some time in Manhattan and that she had an apartment in the city.

At the house, the nanny and the housekeeper along with the kids, met them at the door. Rebecca took her mother into Henry's room and said, "This was my father's designated wing of the house. I think he would be happy to know that you were here."

Helena rested for a while, looked around and felt at home. The décor reminded her of her apartment in Warsaw. There was definitely a touch of Henry there. It made her feel good, a little like being embraced by Henry.

Rebecca called her for dinner. There was a man at the table and Helena recognized him. It was the driver of the limo in Germany. She learned he was not really a driver. He was David. He had insisted on accompanying Rebecca on the trip to Germany. At the table he was introduced as Henry's protégé and a close family friend. Rebecca said. "He is like my brother. In the days to come, David will take us on our tour of New York."

Helena asked if they could make arrangements for her to attend a Shabbat service at a synagogue. Rebecca, Alex and David looked very surprised at this request. David said he would take her.

Her grand-daughter Lilly was peeking at them from behind the door. Helena gestured for her to come in. The little girl ran to her grandmother, sat on her lap and snuggled in. Helena loved this. The lack of a mutual language between Helena and her grandchildren was a problem. Helena vowed she would speak only English, even though she was not very fluent. That night she slept better than any night she could remember. She dreamed of Henry.

The next morning the kids left for school. Helena and Rebecca went out for a walk around the neighborhood. Helena was impressed by the surroundings. The homes did not have gates, fences or walls, like all over the world. Rebecca explained that the United States was not like the rest of the world. She explained that there was freedom there and that no one had to surround their homes with fences. There was also freedom of religion. No one had to be ashamed of what they believed in.

When they returned to the house, they sat on the patio and drank fresh orange juice prepared by the housekeeper. Helena asked if David would be with them today. Rebecca explained that he was very busy but he would come as soon as he could. The kids returned from school. Lilly came running up to Helena and asked if she could call her grandmother.

"Of course, I am your grandmother. And if you would like, I have a special name for you to use. You can call me Babcia."

Lilly loved this. She stayed near Helena all the time. Helena fed her, made hot chocolate for her and Sam. At bedtime Sam asked her to read to them. Helena was aware that Rebecca was observing her interaction with the children. She thought, "This must be my test."

Slowly Helena started to be aware of the beautiful things around the house. In a glass cabinet she noticed a Menorah. She cried out, "Oh my God." Rebecca came running into the living room and saw her mother crying. She explained, "This Menorah was in our apartment in Warsaw before the war."

Rebecca answered "I know, father told me." Helena wanted to know what else she had from before the war.

"I have photographs that the Witkowskis hid for us and all sorts of antiques," said Rebecca. She took her mother to the couch and brought out the photographs with a magnifying glass. Then she left the room.

Helena was afraid to look. She slowly opened the album. The first page took her breath away. Helena looked at a picture of a teenage girl. It was her. Then came the wedding photo and Rebecca's pictures as a baby. The Witkowski family was there too. There was a picture of Henry in his store. Helena stared at each photograph for a long time, as if she would never be able to see it again.

From time to time Rebecca checked in on her mother. She told her she could take the album into her room if she wanted.

Rebecca showed Helena all sorts of things that Helena remembered from before the war.

Rebecca's harsh feelings about her mother slowly softened. She saw how Helena cared about the accomplishments of her father, how she behaved with the children and how hard she tried to be liked.

That night David came for dinner and told Helena that she would take her to the synagogue on Friday. To his surprise, Rebecca said that she wanted to go also. Alex joined them. Before entering the synagogue, Helena had a funny feeling that someone or something would punish her for abandoning her roots. They all went in and sat on a bench. Helena picked up a prayer book, her hands were shaking and she was pale.

Rebecca looked at her in amazement. David put his arms around Helena's shoulders. He felt so sorry for her.

The services started and Helena could not help it; her tears were flowing. She wiped her eyes hoping no one would see. But Rebecca saw and so did Alex and David. Sitting there and listening to the familiar prayers long forgotten, brought memories of her previous life. Helena remembered her family, and the life she shared with Henry.

After the services were over, and when they got home, Helena asked to be excused. When she got to her room, she did not turn on the lights. She just sat on the chair, remembering the night. The prayers and the chanting were still in her head. But the confusion in her soul was inconsolable. She went back to the thought of her family in Germany, wondering why she was not missing them. To her it was as if they were from a long dream, not like real life.

Helena was mentally exhausted. She laid down on her bed, with her clothes still on, and this was how she fell asleep.

In the morning, Rebecca knocked on Helena's door. It was 10:00am and Helena still had not come out of her room. When Rebecca entered the room she saw her mother in bed, fully dressed. She came closer to her and Helena woke up and saw Rebecca standing in front of her. She stretched out her hands for a hug, and Rebecca hugged her. Helena whispered in her ear, "I love you daughter."

Rebecca helped her out of her clothes and drew a bath for her. She helped her mother into fresh clothes and took her into the dining room for breakfast.

The kids were at the table as were Alex and David. Sam looked at his grandmother and said, "You overslept today."

Helena answered, "It is because of a long dream I had."

The family ate in silence. After breakfast, Helena asked Rebecca if she could tell Sam about her dream. It was about Henry. Rebecca nodded a yes. Helena sat with her grandchildren in the garden and shared her dream.

Sam became very sad and said, "I miss my grandfather very much." Helena hugged him and he did not withdraw.

That day they were all going to New York to see Henry's apartment and Rebecca's apartment. Rebecca did not know that Helena had already been to Henry's apartment, and Helena did not tell her. She did not want Rebecca to be upset with her father.

Rebecca's apartment was as impressive as her father's was.

At dinner, Rebecca told her mother that if she wanted, she could stay with her forever. She could stay either in her house or in her father's apartment. She would always be welcomed. Helena was very touched.

The days of the visit were passing quickly. Helena was never bored. Little Lilly was in love with her. It was a mutual feeling.

Helena asked to go to the synagogue again. Rebecca asked if she was sure. Last time it seemed traumatic for her. But Helena promised that would not be the case again. They all went together. This time Helena was able to enjoy the services much more. She looked around the congregation to see the people. They looked different than the people from her synagogue before the war. They were not timid, they held their heads high, they looked like the people in Robert's church, sure of themselves.

The services were more relaxed and they were in Hebrew with an English translation, so everyone could understand as they followed the prayers.

The Jewish children also got educated in Hebrew school. They learned the language, history and religion. Sam would be starting Hebrew school the next school year. He would attend twice a week for a few hours.

The time was nearing for Helena's return home. But, for the first time in her life, she did not want to go back. She felt that she belonged there with her daughter more than in Germany. Rebecca was warm to her. Helena had not expected this. But, after a while, Rebecca began to feel sorry for her mother. She saw that she was lost and vulnerable. Rebecca felt a twitch in her heart, thinking that her mother would be leaving soon. But, in a way, this was a test. Rebecca wondered if she would ever return again.

Helena played with Lilly and her dolls. They pretended to dress and feed them. Rebecca was peeking in just to see how her mother was playing with her daughter. She could swear that she remembered how she played like this with her mother. Rebecca knew Lilly would miss her grandmother. That night, when the kids were sleeping, Rebecca repeated once more, and said to Helena that she was welcome to stay forever.

Alex took Helena's hands in his, looked in her eyes and said, "We love you and we really want you to stay."

Helena was moved to tears. She said she would return often, very often. She wanted to be with them, but she also had her other family. For then, she had to go back, but not for long, she promised.

CHAPTER 43

Helena arrived home early in the morning. Robert was waiting for her at the airport alone. He was nervous, stepping from one foot to the other. She saw him from afar, and slowed down to take a good look at him. She did love this tall, slim, grey-haired man. They drove in silence.

Finally Robert asked how her visit was, and Helena answered, "In short, wonderful."

At the house, everyone was waiting for her. Her sons, daughters-in law and the babies were there. She greeted them all, hugged her grandsons and looked intensely into their faces. Her grandsons were her blood. But it did not feel like they were.

Helena could not understand her feelings. She was worried about how she felt and she could not share so with anybody. Despite her tiredness, she could not sleep. In the morning she woke up with the worst headache. She could not pick her head up from the pillow. Robert brought her some medication and a cold wet towel for her forehead, and a big cup of coffee. After a while, she felt better. She took a long shower, got dressed and went to her grandsons. She wanted to find the love for them.

Helena went to see Katy and Kurt. Kurt was adorable, a loving and beautiful boy. She played with him and fed him. Katy made lunch and Kurt went for a nap. Katy looked at Helena and asked what was wrong? She noticed she was not herself. Helena said that she did not think it showed. But the truth was she did not know why she was not herself. "Maybe because my visit and the trip were just too much," she said to Katy. Helena kissed Katy on her head and left.

Helena went to see Monica and the twins. Monica made a cup of tea. The twins were playing with each other, touching their faces, putting their hands into each other's mouths. It was fun to watch. She came closer and took them on her lap. They were pulling on her blouse. "Robust boys," said Helena. She stayed for a while. Monica was very polite and told Helena that if she needed anything, she would was there for her.

Helena could not ask for more, but nothing made her happy.

Helena wanted to see a psychiatrist and tell her story but this was not possible. She was feeling depression surrounding her and getting tighter and tighter.

Helena placed a call to Rebecca and spoke to the kids. Lilly was asking when was she coming back. Rebecca was sweet and asked about her health. At the end of their conversation she said, "I love you, mama."

Helena cried bitter tears but no one witnessed it. Helena was on her own. She had to make a decision on her own. No one could help her. So she tried to spend long visits with her grandsons and make her relationship with her daughters-in-law as strong as possible.

Sarah came to visit again. Helena tried to see if Sarah sensed anything about her past. But she concluded that she did not.

Mrs. Schultz showed up from time to time, but she was very timid and never felt very comfortable in Helena's house. It did not matter to Helena how they felt, as long as they came.

The young generation was busy with their lives. Their offspring were their biggest priority, as it should be. The sons expanded the family business and were very busy.

Max and Albert were in touch with their sister. Max and his wife announced they were going to visit Rebecca. Helena was surprised. She shopped for gifts for the children for Max to take with him.

Robert was not feeling well. It was nothing specific, just an overall malaise. Helena went with him to the clinic. He underwent all sorts of tests. Robert was almost sixty-seven years old. He looked good but his energy was obviously diminishing. Helena and Robert spent a whole day taking tests. Helena was talked into taking tests as well. The results would be available in a week.

As soon as Max returned from his trip and provided that Robert was okay, Helena wanted to take a trip to Israel with Rebecca. She felt a strong need to do this.

Kurt was missing Mommy and Daddy a lot. Helena and Robert spent a lot of time with him while Max and Katy were away. Monica and Albert were available for him also, but it did not make any difference. He wanted his parents. They all agreed that he was too young to understand that his parents were coming back. Helena could not help but to think that Rebecca had felt the same way when her parents disappeared from her young life.

Finally Max and Katy came back all smiles and happy. Kurt did not leave his parents arms. Helena made dinner for all of them so Max could tell them about the trip.

Max told them how Rebecca was a perfect hostess. They stayed in her house in the suburbs and also alone in her apartment in Manhattan. They took trips and visited the museums in the city. Rebecca was with them most of the time. When she could not be, her friend David was with them. Max did not have enough words of praise for

Rebecca. They got to know each other better and Katy was in love with Rebecca. Helena was thrilled to hear this, but Robert was silent.

It was time to return to the doctor's office. The reports from their tests were in. The doctor started with Helena stating that over all, she was in good health. She had elevated blood pressure and high cholesterol, but this could be remedied with medication. But with Robert, it was another story. The reason for his fatigue was because he had a mass on his prostate which was most likely cancerous. More tests would have to be done and then it had to be removed. Helena held her hand to her mouth, not to let out a gasp. Robert sat quietly and listened. Finally he said that he would do whatever was necessary.

The next day Robert would undergo more tests and the surgery would be scheduled in a Munich hospital. They left the building and as they entered the parking lot, Helena felt she could not take another step. She was going to faint. Robert caught her at the last minute. "It is going to be alright, you'll see," urged Robert. He led her to their car. As they drove home, Robert asked Helena not to say anything to their kids yet. He would tell them himself at the necessary time. Helena nodded.

Unable to hide her feelings, Helena told the kids that she caught a virus and she would stay home for a few days.

Robert continued to work long hours in his office. He prepared himself for the worst and wanted to put everything in order. He would tell his sons.

Two days later they received a call from the doctor. The surgery was scheduled in five days.

Helena knew she could not hide in her bedroom any longer. She made a reservation in a hotel for herself. She packed comfortable clothes, took a two week supply of her medication and she was ready. She must be strong because now she was needed. She placed a call to Rebecca and told her what was happening. She would call her as soon as possible to follow up.

Robert and Helena left for Munich. First they stopped at the hotel and left the car there. They walked to the hospital, it was only two blocks away. The registration took only a few minutes and they were led to Robert's room. It was a private room with all the comforts. Robert changed into a hospital gown and they waited to see the doctor to discuss the procedure.

They gave Robert medication to have a good night's sleep. The surgery would take place in the morning. Helena waited for Robert to fall asleep. It took only a few minutes. She covered him tenderly, kissed his forehead and left the room.

Helena went to her hotel, ordered room service and placed a call to her sons. They talked for a while and Max would come in the morning. Albert would stay home to take care of the business and the family. Helena was tired, took a bath and went to bed. She turned on the television for a while and then fell asleep. She woke up at five in the morning. She was just thinking, "God, please restore his health."

The surgery started at 9:00 am. Helena and Max were in the waiting room. There was nothing to do but wait.

The television was on and other people were waiting too. After four hours, the nurse informed them that the surgery was over and the doctor would speak to them shortly. Max held his mother's hand. Helena felt she was shaking and she could not control it.

Max quietly said, "It will be okay, mama."

Finally the doctor showed up. He sat with Helena and Max and informed them the growth was malignant. He took out all he could but Robert would have to receive chemotherapy. The treatment would start in one month and it would be administered in the hospital. He said that they had some success and some fatality. It was a hard cancer to beat. With that said, he left.

Robert would spend the rest of the day and night in the recovery room. Max hired a private nurse to stay with his father. He took his mother for lunch.

They both could not eat. Max was worried about his mother. He sat across from her in the restaurant. He took her hands into his and said, "Mother, he will be okay. This is what we have to believe so father will believe it too. You have to hide your emotions and show a positive attitude. Most of all, you have to smile."

Max placed a call to his brother and they spoke for a while. Max would stay for two days and then Albert would come. They all would go home in about one week.

They went back to the hospital and were allowed to see Robert for a little while. He gave them a faint smile. He was in pain. They were told to return in about three hours so they went to the hotel to rest.

Max was on the phone and Helena went to bed. She ached all over. She felt every bone in her body and her headache was severe. She took two aspirins and hoped for the best. She did not remember when she fell asleep. When she woke up it was time to go back to the hospital.

Robert was up and he smiled. He said he would get through this surgery and treatment. He would be fine.

Max left and Albert came in his place. Robert was not alone for a minute. Helena was there all the time. Robert did not despair. He was hopeful and that was what made Helena believe that he would be okay.

After a week, Robert came home. In a month the chemotherapy would start in a local hospital. Helena had a list of the food he should eat to strengthen his immune system.

Maximilian and Albert took over the responsibility of the business and told their father to only take care of himself. But after two days at home, Robert asked that they take him to the office, just for a few hours.

Helena spoke to Rebecca. Rebecca wanted to take her mother to Israel and Helena wanted to go too before Robert started his chemotherapy. She would talk to Robert.

Robert wanted her to go. He had a lot of help at home. He knew that the treatment wouldn't be easy. For now it would be better for her to go. Helena agreed and she would be away for three weeks. She would be back home a few days before the treatment started.

CHAPTER 44

Rebecca and Helena would meet in Israel. She was not bringing the family. Rebecca arrived at the airport two hours before her mother. When Helena landed they hugged and kissed.

Helena was very excited. She asked Rebecca if it would be okay if she met Alex's family. Rebecca was surprised at this request. They would stay in Rebecca's apartment and visit Henry's apartment also. They would do sightseeing and other touristy things.

Helena was in awe of being in Israel. She said to her daughter, "Forgive me for this question. Is everyone I see Jewish? They do not look like the Jewish people I remember from before the war."

Rebecca smiled and hugged her mother. Helena forgot for a while that she left a gravely sick husband at home. When she remembered, she felt guilty. It seemed that quite often in her life she felt guilt.

The next day was very busy. They started their sightseeing and tasted Israeli food. They had dinner with Alex's family, the Silber's. Helena could sense their curiosity. They tried to hide it but could not. Rebecca could feel it too, therefore she made the evening as short as possible. They said their goodbyes and Rebecca told them there would be no time to visit again. She said this in a cool voice and Helena understood that her daughter was standing up for her. Even so, Helena was glad she met them. She wanted to know the people in her daughter's life.

The next stop was Jerusalem. It was very emotional for Helena. She remembered at the end of every Jewish prayer it was said, "Next year in Jerusalem." Helena touched every stone she saw. The visit to the Wailing Wall had a tremendous impact on her. She did not want to leave. She kept both her hands on the stone wall. She remembered and prayed in Hebrew. Rebecca stood there bewildered.

When they left, Helena took Rebecca's hand and asked her to promise that she would bury her in Jerusalem. If it was possible she asked to be buried next to Henry. Rebecca promised.

Next they went to the cemetery and Henry's grave. Helena just stood there. It was unreal to her that Henry was gone. She put a single yellow rose on his grave and kissed his monument. "Rest in peace," she said, as they were walking out of the cemetery.

Rebecca told her mother that Henry was the very best father and grandfather that one could have, and that she missed him terribly.

The trip continued. They stopped in Haifa, Caesarea, Acco and Jaffa. Helena wanted to see it all. She walked briskly and never tired. She was amazing.

They returned to Tel Aviv. Rebecca took Helena to Henry's apartment. Helena said that Henry definitely had superb taste.

Rebecca called Moshe and Joseph to ask if they would like to meet Helena. They did not.

And so as everything must come to an end their trip to Israel was over. Rebecca would return to New York and Helena was going back to her family in Germany.

CHAPTER 45

Helena had to remind herself that she was returning to a very ill husband. Upon arriving home, she was pleasantly surprised. Robert looked well. He got his energy back and looked happy to see her back home.

Everybody greeted her. The most fun was with her grandsons. They were changing so fast. Katy had prepared a festive dinner for all.

In two days Robert's treatments would begin. The doctors explained that Robert would not feel very well and that people reacted differently to the treatments.

Helena sat next to Robert and told him all about her trip. He did not ask but she told him anyway.

Robert responded to the treatments well but he felt drained. He would receive another dose in two months followed by a check-up with the doctor.

Robert was a very much a disciplined man. He committed to living his life to the fullest. Helena pampered him and did what she could to make him comfortable. His sons were at his side all the time and he knew he was in good hands.

Every few days Rebecca called. Helena spoke to Sam and Lilly often. She felt Rebecca wanted to maintain a certain closeness with her. Helena was surprised that her sons and daughters-in-law never asked about her trip. It was obvious that they would never truly accept who she was. It was a very painful realization. She did not know how to react. She wondered if she should let them know how she felt or if she should just ignore it.

Now Albert and Monica wanted to visit Rebecca. The twins would stay home. Rebecca was happy to host them. Within the week they were gone.

Albert and Monica loved America. When they got back Monica was almost sorry they were not poor. Because then they could just pick themselves up and immigrate to the big, wonderful USA. Of course, they could not do that.

CHAPTER 46

Rebecca received a call from Eva's children. They wanted her to help them find someone reliable to sell their mother's house in Jerusalem. Rebecca was surprised. She knew how their mother loved her oasis in Jerusalem. They explained that they were too busy with their studies and that afterwards they were taking over the responsibilities of the family business so they could not see themselves taking advantage of the house for some time.

Rebecca called Joseph and Moshe. They would take care of it. Moshe asked Rebecca how her trip to Israel with her mother was. Rebecca said she was sorry they did not want to meet her. Rebecca told him her mother was such a lost soul.

Rebecca was happy that her brothers came to visit her. It gave her confidence that she might go to visit them too.

Rebecca called Moshe again for a favor. She asked if he could secure the land around her father's grave. She explained why and Moshe was speechless. Finally he responded that he would get back to her as soon as he had accomplished this.

Alex's family was coming to the United States for a visit. Rebecca wanted to make them feel welcomed. She had never forgotten how they treated her so generously in Poland when she was a young girl. At that time it was a big sacrifice to have another mouth to feed.

Rebecca was hoping that the weather would not turn too cold. The fall was coming and it was very beautiful. The trees were turning all different colors and the air was crisp. Rebecca loved this time of year.

She heard back from Moshe. He advised her that he was able to secure the surrounding land around Henry's grave. Rebecca sent a check to pay for it. He also told her that he received an offer on Eva's house. The government was interested in purchasing the property to use as a guest house for people who wanted anonymity. Eva's son would come for the closing. Rebecca had a mixed feeling about that house. It was a piece of her father. She spoke to Eva's children. They were happy with the deal and thanked her very much. Rebecca asked that they stay in touch. She was glad to be of help to them.

Alex's family arrived. Rebecca was ready for their visit. Sam and Lilly were thrilled. They loved company and the commotion that came with it. Rebecca's mother in law was not that interested in touring. She wanted to stay in the kitchen and cook. She taught Rebecca all different kinds of dishes to cook and she talked a mile a minute. But when it came to talk about Rebecca's mother, Rebecca put a fast stop to it, saying that she did not want to talk about her. Rebecca remembered her mother-in-law's reaction to Helena when they were in Israel. She was not in the mood to answer a million questions.

CHAPTER 47

Rebecca placed a call to Germany. She spoke to Monica. It turned out that the news was not so good. Robert's cancer had now traveled to his liver. Monica told her that Helena was more distressed than Robert was. Max and Albert were not dealing with it so well either. They all did not know what to do next. Rebecca decided she would call her mother the next day.

Helena did not know how to accept this change in Robert's condition. The doctors told them that more or less, treatment was hopeless. Helena thought that maybe they should seek out treatment somewhere else, maybe even the United States. She would speak to her sons.

Robert was not in pain. But he was fatigued and slept most of the time. Helena met with her sons and proposed that they take Robert to the famous Mayo Clinic in the United States. But her sons said that the doctor explained that no one could do anything to save his life. They would keep him pain free and comfortable. This was all that could be done.

Helena could not make peace with that. There must be something she could do. People with cancer did get better. Some even were cured. Helena did not want to quit. The next day she called the hospital in Munich and spoke to Robert's doctor. She wanted Robert's medical report to be sent to her immediately.

It came the next day. She wanted to translate and mail it to Rebecca. Helena called and asked Rebecca to show the report to the best specialists in New York right away. After she sent the report Helena told her sons what she did. They just looked at each other and said nothing.

Robert was resigned to his fate. He rested a lot. The babies were around him all the time. The daughters-in-law made sure of it. Helena did not leave his side. Robert told her not to take the news so hard.

Rebecca took the medical report to New York's Sloane Kettering Hospital. David contacted a specialist who agreed to see them in two days. They gave him the report and waited for him to contact them. After a few days the specialist called. The news was not good. Robert was in Stage IV cancer. The cancer had spread throughout his liver. There was nothing that could be done for him.

It was a very unfortunate situation for Rebecca. She wanted to get closer to her mother but of course, now everything was put on hold.

Rebecca did not know who to give the report to, her mother or her brothers. She arranged for Max to be with Albert and their mother when she called. When Rebecca reached them she was surprised by her mother's calmness. Helena thanked Rebecca and said she would call back soon.

Helena spoke with her sons to determine how they thought their father should spend the time he had left. Maximilian spoke with his father to see what his preference was. They received the answer they expected. Robert wanted to be surrounded by his family and no one else. He did not want to go to the hospital. When the time came he wanted them to hire a nurse to give some relief to Helena. He wanted to be in the big, guest bedroom upstairs. It had a huge window that looked out to the gardens and he could see the flicker of the lights in his son's homes.

Robert said to his sons, "I'm sixty eight years old and I had a good life. I am not bitter and I would like to go in peace. You all have to help me with this. I need to see your smiling faces and you must carry on with your lives."

Helena felt so helpless. It was the worst feeling not being able to help someone you love. The sleepless nights made her weak and lifeless. She lost weight and now her sons worried about both their parents. The doctor prescribed a sleeping medication for Helena. It became more bearable. She understood that to do her best, she had to acknowledge the truth to herself and stay with Robert all the time. So she did just that. She read to him, they watched TV together, the grandchildren visited all the time. Her sons gave their father daily reports about the business. Robert gave his opinion about what they should do. The sons kept notes of his advice.

Robert was getting weaker and needed more medication. A nurse was hired and she advised the family that soon he would need morphine. That would be the beginning of the end.

Rebecca called often but Helena did not tell Robert. She knew he would not be pleased.

Helena and Robert talked a lot and he always ended his conversations by advising her, "You must be strong and hold down the fort!" He also told Helena that he was never sorry about his decision to make her his wife. She brought him happiness and he would always love her.

Katy announced that she was pregnant again. Robert and Helena cried. They were so happy. Katy hugged Robert and said, "If it will be boy, we will name him Robert."

That night Robert asked Helena to bring in two glasses of cognac for them to celebrate. He was very pleased and said to Helena, "Not too shabby, four grandchildren!" He fell asleep with a smile on his face.

The next day the whole family congratulated Max and Katy. The grandchildren prepared a play for Robert. The little show was enjoyed by all.

Robert was very tired by the end of the day and said he was going to bed early. When Helena left his room he was fast asleep. The nurse sat on the easy chair reading by the small lamp. Helena did not want to leave that night. She had an uneasy feeling.

Helena decided to call Rebecca at 2:00am. It was 8:00am in the morning in the U.S. She was alone upstairs. Rebecca was surprised by the phone call and said, "It is the middle of the night in Germany, is everything okay?"

Helena answered, "I just wanted to hear your voice." She told Rebecca about Katy's pregnancy and the funny show the kids put on. They had more small talk which made Helena feel better.

Six o'clock in the morning someone knocked on Helena's door. It was the nurse. "Robert passed quietly, in his sleep," said the nurse. "He did not suffer, he did not know he was dying."

Helena cried out loud. The housekeeper came running. They all ran back to Robert's room. Helena through herself on him. The nurse called the sons and they came immediately. They tried to lift Helena from Robert, but she did not let them. She held on to Robert, her tears flowed, she did not bother to wipe them.

Helena did not remember how she found herself on a chair surrounded by her daughters-in-laws. Max tried to explain to her that the doctor was on his way to issue the death certificate and the funeral parlor was coming to take Robert's body.

Katy and Monica's parents were called. The priest just walked in and said a few kind words to Helena. She did not know what he was saying. The nurse had given her some medication to control her hysterical crying.

Katy took Helena upstairs and helped her dress. She was so gentle with her. She had her wash her face, combed her hair, and kept repeating, "It will be okay, we will take care of you."

They picked up Robert's body. Helena was not aware how much time had passed, but Monica's parents were already there and Katy's family just walked in. They all said something to her, but Helena could not understand anything. Everything was hazy and she could not see anything clearly. The nurse was next to her and Helena asked her not to give her any more medication.

Someone handed her a glass of tea. It tasted good and she asked for more. Slowly Helena started feeling herself again. She asked Sarah to help her take a warm bath. Helena put her hair up in a bun and found a navy blue dress to put on. She did not have a black dress.

Helena went downstairs and embraced both of her sons. All three were crying and the boys pleaded, "Please Mama, stay strong, it will be okay."

The church was full of people. Helena was surprised. It looked like the whole town was there, including the new rabbi from the small synagogue.

At the gravesite it was the same, crowded with people. The service was brief. Helena wanted to stay a little while longer and her sons stayed with her. Each of them had their own thoughts.

Upon returning home, Helena made her excuses and went to her bedroom. She changed her clothes and sat at her desk. She wrote a note to the local paper to thank all the townspeople who came to pay their respects. She said it meant a lot to her and her family.

Helena called Rebecca. Rebecca had already spoken with Max. Her daughter begged her to come and recuperate in her house. Helena agreed. She asked Max to make the arrangements. She wanted to go within the month.

All the legalities and the reading of the will was taking place in a week. Helena stayed close to her grandchildren. Katy was feeling fine and Helena promised that she would be back before the birth of the baby.

Helena did not want to join her sons for the reading of the will but they insisted. The attorney read a very brief, written will. Robert left all to his sons and their offspring. The will said that Helena was to be supported and she could stay in the family house.

On her return from the lawyer's office, Helena realized that she would be at the mercy of her sons for the rest of her life. This reinforced her feeling that she always had. She never belonged to this family. But she created this family, she was the mother. She accepted this bitter truth. Money was not important to her anyway. She would leave for the U.S. in three weeks.

The house was empty without Robert. Helena did not know what to do with herself all day. It was just her and the housekeeper. She did not want to impose on her daughters-in-law by visiting all the time. She could not concentrate on reading a book. The only place she wanted to be was with her daughter. She busied herself gathering gifts and some small trinkets from her house to bring to her daughter. Sam loved elephants and there was one in Helena's room made of silver. She would bring this to Sam. Helena was looking in her jewelry box for something to bring for Lilly. She found a little necklace with a ruby. Helena thought that would do.

The next thing to do was something she never imagined she would ever have to do. She had to ask her sons for money. She did not want to come to the USA without a penny. She visited her sons one evening and reminded them that she would need some cash in U.S. dollars. Max asked how much she would need and Helena answered, "You have been in the States. You know how much I will need."

Two days later Max handed her a thick envelope and said, "If you need more money, I will have more transferred to the States." She thanked him and put it away. She did not open the envelope in front of him.

Her sons asked that she not stay away too long. For the first time that she could remember they told her they needed her, and not to forget them. Helena was moved.

CHAPTER 48

Helena was on her way. It was a long flight but she did not mind. She felt free. The envelope she received from her son contained thousands of dollars. "How generous," thought Helena.

Upon arrival she retrieved her suitcase and held on to her tote bag. At the exit she saw Rebecca, Alex, Sam and little Lilly running towards her with open arms. She never felt so much love from anyone. She hugged her precious girl and whispered in her ear, "I missed you so much."

Finally they were home and Helena entered Henry's room. She felt warmth in his room. She unpacked and put the elephant on a shelf with the necklace next to it. Rebecca had placed fresh flowers all over the room for her. Helena did not know where to keep the money. She finally placed the envelope between her nightgowns. Rebecca needed to take her to the bank to open an account. She slept like a newborn.

The first thing Helena saw when she opened her eyes in the morning was Lilly coming into her bed. Helena took her under the covers and kept her close to her. They watched cartoons together until Rebecca came to get them for breakfast.

Rebecca prepared an Israeli morning meal. An omelet, finely chopped vegetables, farmer's cheese with toast and the best coffee. Sam told Helena about his school, his friends, his soccer practice, and then he became sad.

Sam said, "You know, grandmother, my grandpa loved soccer."

"I know," said Helena.

And then the surprised Sam asked, "Did you know my grandfather?" Helena nodded.

Upon the first Shabbat the family went to the synagogue. Helena prayed for Robert. The next day Helena would give her presents to the kids. She took the elephant to be polished. It made a rattling noise, as if there were small stones inside. She was surprised that she had never heard it before. Helena examined the statue and there was no opening anywhere on it. Then she saw it. The trunk of the elephant had a groove and it turned until it opened. What fell out took Helena's breath away.

Crumbled pieces of yellowed, dry paper and four large diamonds with a brilliant shine fell from it. This must have been hidden there for a very long time. It had just stood there in the antique cabinet most likely for hundreds of years. Helena shook out all the pieces of paper, closed the trunk of the elephant, cleaned the silver and put away the diamonds. She would rent a security box in the bank and put it in Rebecca's name. But first she would have the diamonds appraised.

The next morning Helena gave the kids their gifts. Sam loved the elephant and Lilly said that the necklace was just like one that a princess would wear.

Helena showed the diamonds to Rebecca and she was shocked. She thought they must be very expensive. She would give one to David to be appraised. Helena said the diamonds would be for Rebecca and the kids for their future. Somehow, Helena felt the diamonds belonged to her and she had not even a touch of guilt.

David took one of the diamonds to the diamond district on the lower East side to be appraised. When David returned that night, Helena could not wait to hear what he had to say.

David, in a monotone voice, said "Close to $200,000."

He stretched out his hand to return the diamond to Helena, and she said, "Sell it."

Within a few days, David brought the money to Helena and she placed it in the safety deposit box. Helena turned to Rebecca and said, "Now I won't have to ask my sons for money." Rebecca did not know what she meant, but did not question it.

All this was forgotten in a day and Helena just enjoyed the pleasure of her stay. Rebecca took her mother everywhere, to school for drop-off, food shopping, cleaners, dancing lessons and little league practice. Helena loved it. She was tired at the end of each day, but it was good. As they ran around doing the errands, they talked about everything. They were making up for lost time.

Their conversations took a serious tone when they spoke about the Witkowskis in Poland. Of course they could not go there. Helena asked if Rebecca remembered the years she spent with them. Rebecca said she did, but not that much. She remembered a lot of love towards her and she would love to see them again. She also told her mother that her father still had some valuables with them and maybe one day they would be able to retrieve them.

The time was passing quickly. Helena communicated with Katy and learned she was doing well. Her due date was in three months. She spoke to her sons and all was good at home.

Home. Helena did not know where she belonged. She only knew that from then on she would share her time equally in both places. She would never abandon Rebecca again. Nor would she abandon her sons.

At night, as she lay in bed, Helena was thinking that life passes so fast. She was a grandmother to four boys and a girl and soon another grandchild would be born. Six lives, she thought. Would they remember her when they were grown?

Helena sat with Sam and Lilly and explained that she had to return to Germany. She told them that as soon as their new cousin was born she would return. The kids were not happy about this. They knew their grandmother could not stay with them all the time but they wished she could.

Rebecca tried to explain to her mother that soon she would not be able to hop from one place to another. Helena agreed and said quietly, "As long as I can do it, I will. Once I cannot travel, I will stay here with you."

Helena was packing for her return. She was not happy about it, she did not miss the family in Germany. This made her feel sad. She could not understand her feelings or lack thereof. She could not justify why she did not miss them at all.

* * *

The flight back to Germany was bumpy and unpleasant. Finally back with her sons and grandsons, they were all gathered around her and all seemed happy. She had brought the kids gifts from the United States. Katy was getting big and her sons looked so much like their father, and behaved like him too. They were serious, no nonsense and straight to the point. So very German.

Helena asked if she could keep the cash they gave her so that she did not have to ask them each time for money. They agreed.

Back in her bedroom, Helena looked around and realized she did not have that happy feeling of returning home. Sleep did not come. She tried hard to nod off but to no avail. The next night she would take a sleeping pill. She thought it interesting that she did not have to resort to a sleeping pill while at Rebecca's.

Helena received a call from Sarah welcoming her back. They spoke for a while but Sarah did not know with whom Helena stayed in the states. She only knew that Helena traveled around. Sarah said she was coming one month before the baby's birth. Helena told her she would be happy to see her.

Helena placed a call to Monica's parents. They had a short but friendly conversation.

Sarah arrived, all smiles, bearing gifts for all the kids. She hugged Helena. Katy was getting bigger by the day and was counting off to her due date.

Sarah said she would stay with Helena for a while. They had late tea in the living room. Sarah was telling her tales about her family. It was obvious that she wanted to entertain Helena. Helena could not tell her anything of her own past. She wanted to but knew she could not.

After one week with Helena, Sarah moved into her daughter's house. As much as Helena liked Sarah, she was glad to be alone.

But being alone was not good for her at all. Helena could not find a place of comfort. The house was so big. Helena asked the housekeeper to eat with her in the kitchen. She could not sit by herself at that big dining room table. Helena and the housekeeper were reminiscing about years past, when the kids were small.

Helena's sons were living so close, yet felt so far away to her. They were busy with their own lives and kids. They usually returned from the office late at night and went directly home to enjoy their own families. Helena noticed that every time she saw them, their smiles disappeared. When Helena asked why, Albert simply said, "Every time we see you, we remember our father is not with us anymore."

"How is that fair to me?" thought Helena.

Helena asked that Sarah let her know when it was time for Katy to leave for the hospital, even if it was the middle of the night.

The next morning Max knocked at the door, all happy, and said, "Mom, you have another grandson. His name is Robert."

Helena hugged her son, got dressed and went with him back to the hospital. The baby looked exactly like his brother and his cousins. Helena asked Sarah why she did not wake her up. Sarah answered, in a whisper, "I was told not to, sorry." That hurt Helena and she left the hospital with a bitter feeling.

After a few days Katy returned home. Helena went to visit but stayed only a short while. The christening would be in a month. Sarah left for her home and would be back for the christening.

Helena spoke with Rebecca almost every day. Rebecca asked if she and her kids could come for the christening. "Of course," said Helena. Helena informed her sons that Rebecca was coming for the event. The brothers looked at each other.

Max said, "We are very busy and now with the new baby, this may not be such a good time."

But Helena answered, "Rebecca is coming and she will stay in my house. If you are too busy, you do not have to visit."

Her sons withdrew immediately and promised they would do their best to welcome Rebecca.

Rebecca would be arriving the following week. The housekeeper was happy that the house would be full again.

Albert went with his mother to pick up Rebecca and her kids. Little Lilly was clinging to Helena. Albert never saw his mother behave as warm to a grandchild as she did with Lilly.

That evening they all visited with the new baby, Robert. The daughters-in-law made plans with Rebecca to have the kids play together and get to know each other.

They all noticed that Helena behaved differently with Sam and Lilly than she did with the rest of the grandchildren. Katy did question Helena about it but Helena denied it. She responded that they were her guests and she wanted them to feel welcome. But in her heart, Helena knew it was true. She, herself, could not explain it. It was just the way she felt.

The visit continued pleasantly. Helena's sons were very kind, just like their father. The decision was made to be nice, and so it was. Helena knew it did not come from their hearts. Rebecca appreciated how nice everybody was to her and Helena did not correct her.

The time came for Rebecca to leave. The housekeeper cried. She came to love Sam and Lilly. It was most surprising that she never questioned who Rebecca and the kids were to Helena. She probably knew and she was smart not to talk about it.

Once they left, the house was very quiet. The only noise was from the housekeeper cleaning every corner.

Helena wanted to see Kurt. He was home with a cold. He was six years old now, very bright. As they were reading a book together, Kurt asked, "What is Jewish?" Helena asked who told him this word, and he answered, "My cousin Sam."

"So what did he tell you?" questioned Helena.

"Well, he was confused," answered Kurt. "He thinks that I am Jewish. But I do not know what that means. Being Jewish."

Helena answered, in a choking voice, "You are right, Sam was confused."

At that moment Helena understood why Robert opposed bringing the families together and why her sons did not want to maintain a relationship with their sister. Helena thought Kurt would forget this and it would end for now, and then thought maybe he would ask his father.

Helena promised Rebecca that she would be with her within the next two months, just in time for winter.

Helena meandered through each room of her house. The furniture, the silverware, the valuable statues and paintings, even the silk drapes were all here before she came to the house. Helena did not choose any of it, she did not buy any of it nor did she bring anything of her own with her when she came. She never made any decision on how to decorate this house or change it. She lived there over thirty years. She had been a wife and mother to the heirs of this property and yet nothing there belonged to her.

Helena had a talk with her sons. She thanked them for the nice reception they gave their sister. She informed them of her return trip to Rebecca and she told them she would be staying through the winter. She told them she did not need any money, she had enough from the last visit. The only thing she asked of them was to continue to pay for the housekeeper. Her sons agreed. Max was going to make the travel arrangements for his mother but he did complain about the length of her trip. Helena just shook her head and said, "You won't really miss me."

Helena spoke with Sarah and the Schultz family. She asked that they visit the kids more often. They needed loving grandparents. She spoke with her housekeeper and told her about her plans. She thanked her for her service. Helena was prepared for her longest absence from her sons and her home.

Helena and the housekeeper were very busy preparing the house for her long absence. All the furniture had to be covered, the silver had to be wrapped and stored and the kitchen needed to be cleaned out. Helena helped as much as she could but she tired quickly. This surprised her.

Helena spent a lot of time with her grandsons, her four perfect grandsons. The youngest one, Robert, was developing nicely. Katy lost her pregnancy weight and she looked well. Monica and Katy lived in perfect harmony raising their sons. They had each other for company and did not look for outside friendships. From time to time they did entertain, but it was mostly business related. The investments that Robert made in the United States turned out to be very profitable. Helena was delivering some documents to an office in Manhattan. She was finally packing for her trip.

Helena took a few pieces of jewelry to give to Lilly. She found a little lion made of silver to bring to Sam. She shook it and she laughed to herself.

Her flight was late in the evening. Helena was packed and spent her last few hours with her grandsons. Her sons returned from the office earlier so that they could all have dinner together. Afterwards, both her sons drove her to the airport. It was a very unusual goodbye. They hugged. Helena cried. Her sons kept repeating, "Do not forget us, Mama."

CHAPTER 49

Helena fell asleep on the flight. Rebecca and David were meeting her. The kids were in school when she arrived. Slowly, Helena unpacked.

Henry's room felt so welcoming. She sat on the couch looking at the garden. She did not know how long she was there. She was thinking there was no one walking on the streets. How quiet it was in the suburbs.

Rebecca came to her room and asked if she wanted to come with her to pick up the kids from school. They arrived at the school and Helena saw all the young mothers waiting for their children.

First Lilly came out. She noticed Helena and came running and screaming, "Grandma, grandma, you are here. I am so happy." She stayed in Helena's arms for a long while. Sam came next, but he was more reserved. He gave her a kiss and a hug and said how glad he was that she was with them.

Alex came from work with David and they all had dinner. They shared all their news and activities of the day. It was very lively and noisy and friendly. Helena loved it. Later in the evening Helena gave the kids their gifts. Sam said, "I will cherish this elephant and lion all my life." Lilly said, "Me too."

Every morning Helena woke up early, with the housekeeper, to prepare breakfast for the family. Helena loved to try new recipes and going to the super market was a treat. Rebecca wanted to take her mother sightseeing, but her mother was happiest staying at home.

Winter came in all its glory. The light fluffy snow fell all night. In the morning everything was covered in a white blanket. It looked beautiful. The kids had a snow day from school and they were jumping with joy. They all put on their warm coats and boots and went out to build a snowman. Helena had so much fun. She felt like a young girl.

That same evening Helena had a sharp pain in her left temple. It did not last too long but was extremely painful. Helena did not say anything about it to Rebecca. It probably would not happen again, she thought.

Helena spoke with her sons. She asked them to send new photos of their kids and they promised. They were having a very harsh winter back in Germany. They also said the grandchildren were missing her. It was good to hear.

David was a frequent guest at Rebecca's home. Every time he had a chance he spoke to Helena about Henry. It was a great surprise for Helena to hear all the achievements made by Henry. She was pleased to hear that people admired and appreciated Henry for his talents. Helena knew that Henry was very smart but she did not have enough time with him to fully know the man. Rebecca was always so proud of Henry. He was a good father and for that Helena was so appreciative.

At night, Helena sat down to compose a special letter to her daughter. She wanted to express something that had been on her mind for a long time. In the letter, she asked to be buried in Jerusalem next to Henry. She asked that Rebecca tell her German family that her body had been cremated, and to send "her ashes" to her sons so that they could bury them in their family vault. Helena knew how deceitful this was, but her whole life had been a big deception. Helena wondered if Rebecca would do this.

Now that Helena wrote her request, she felt an ease in her soul. She would give Rebecca this letter in a sealed envelope to be opened upon her death. That night Helena slept well, worry free and happy to be with her daughter.

Helena cooked for the kids. They loved her thin schnitzels sprinkled with sesame seeds, her vegetable soup and the sponge cake she baked. Rebecca was very caring to her mother and Helena tried to be the mother that Rebecca never had.

The sharp, short pain in her temple returned and Helena knew she had to tell Rebecca. Her daughter made an appointment with a neurologist immediately. They sat in the waiting room and Helena saw how distressed Rebecca was. The nurse called her name and they both went into the examining room. They first took her blood pressure, and sure enough, it was dangerously high. The doctor suggested a hospital stay for a few days but Helena begged to go home. She would do whatever was necessary at home. The doctor instructed Rebecca on what had to be done and what medication had to be taken.

On the way home, Helena was trying to put Rebecca at ease. She promised she would do all that the doctor requested and that she would be okay. The kids were instructed not to bother grandmother too much. The housekeeper got a list of foods that should be prepared. Helena just remembered that this was how Henry would have behaved. Right away they jumped into action. Rebecca was definitely her father's daughter.

Finally, alone in her bedroom, Helena was questioning her feelings. She was not afraid of death but she did not want to be paralyzed by a stroke and be a burden to her children. She would religiously take her medication and see her doctor in a month. After a few days she felt much better.

David stopped in one day and asked Helena if she would like to tell her life story. It would be presented to the same audience that Henry had spoken to. Helena answered with a strong, definitive "No. That will never happen," she said.

Lilly followed Helena's steps all the time and was saying, "Please sit down, grandma. You are sick and you must rest." She was Helena's heart.

Alex was traveling to Europe on behalf of his company. He would be away for a week. Rebecca did not like it. She was afraid that this was a prelude to an overseas job. Rebecca loved her life in the United States and did not want to move anywhere else.

The appointment with the doctor was approaching.

The physician was not pleased. Helena's blood pressure was still very high. He would prescribe stronger medication to see if it would help. Helena was disappointed. She begged Rebecca not to say anything to her sons, and Rebecca promised.

The new medication made Helena sleepy and lethargic. She hated feeling that way, but after a short while her blood pressure was much lower. Now Helena had to make a choice. Should she sleep away the rest of her life or live as much as she could. She needed to speak with her doctor.

They went back to see him again and Helena was told, in a simple way, "If you do not continue to take this medication, you will be at risk for a stroke."

At home, after dinner, Rebecca spoke to her mother. Helena was very surprised at what she had to say. "Mom, this is a decision that you will have to make by yourself. I will respect your choice," said Rebecca.

Helena made her decision. She would obey the doctor's advice, but not all the time. She promised herself that she would not think about this anymore. She would live her life as much as she could.

Winter was ending and Helena could see the first signs of Spring. The doctors did not give her permission to fly. Helena would have to tell her sons why she was not returning home.

Max and Albert decided they would come to visit her in the States. First came Albert. He was thirty one years old now, very handsome, tall and trim. Helena cried when she saw him. He brought her drawings and clay animals made by the kids.

That evening Albert spoke with Rebecca and she told him everything about Helena's condition. Albert stayed for a week. They took walks and they sat on a bench, even though the weather was still cold. When saying goodbye to her youngest son, Helena knew she would never see him again.

Within the next two weeks, Maximilian came to see Helena. She was picturing him as a little boy. She was a stranger in a strange place when he was born. At that time, he was her only happiness. Now she saw in front of her a sturdy man of thirty four, a father of two sons himself. He hugged her tightly and looked at her with his worried blue eyes.

Maximilian was great with Sam and Lilly. He did not want to leave the house. Helena prepared his favorite foods. They talked about his kids and what his hopes were for them. Max said that everything was different without his father and now his mother had been gone for so long. He had to return home. He parted with his mother, sobbing like a little boy. It was very painful for Helena to see this. She promised herself that she would call very often and talk to them very often.

Helena took her medication faithfully for a week. She needed to sleep and forget the painful goodbyes she had with her sons. She was resigned to her fate. She was sixty years old but felt much older.

Helena's emotional life had been difficult since the war broke out and she was tired. She felt she did not have much to contribute to the life of her children or grandchildren anymore. She was resigned to her fate.

Alex mentioned a possible job offer in France but Rebecca did not agree to it. She did not want to go anywhere. Rebecca was comfortable in her suburban community; she had a social circle, and the children were thriving. The money was not an incentive to uproot.

Helena remained in Westchester with her daughter. She spoke to her sons and grandsons in Germany very often. She played with Lilly constantly and had long discussions with Sam. She loved cooking for the family and actually enjoyed herself.

The summer was unusually warm and they had very little rain. Helena spent her time outdoors as much as she could. She read a lot and loved American television programs.

Rebecca took short trips with her children. She did not stay away any longer than three days at a time. She was afraid to leave her mother alone. David always stayed with Helena when her daughter was away. He spoke to her about the politics of the world, about the achievements of Israel and about the Communist Bloc. Helena could listen to him all day long.

As she sat in the garden, Helena could see the start of the yellowing of the leaves. Her favorite time of the year was fall.

The grandchildren returned to school and were there most of the day. Helena made herself available as soon as they returned home. Their favorite food was always prepared for them. She inquired about their day and asked if they had homework. Rebecca was trying hard not to show her worrying face. But knowing that her mother was a walking time bomb made her feel helpless and anxious. She wanted to be next to her mother all the time. She just wanted to be there and hold her hand till the end.

Helena went on living her life in peace. She was content. The fall was in its full glory. The colors of the trees were vibrant. The winds moving the leaves created a most pleasant sound and Helena loved sitting on the bench just watching this miracle of nature. Helena realized that all the major events of Helena's life took place in the fall.

Helena spoke to her family in Germany that morning. They were slowly getting used to her absence. Sarah called and asked if she could come and stay with her for a while, but Helena refused. She claimed she was not feeling well, and said maybe she could come sometime in the future.

CHAPTER 50

It was an evening like many others. Dinner with the kids, a little reading, and bedtime. In the morning when Rebecca did not see her mother in the kitchen, she knew why. She told Alex to take the children to school and return home immediately. He also sensed a crisis.

Once Alex left the house, Rebecca and the housekeeper entered Helena's room. Helena looked as if she were sleeping. There was a calm look on her pale face and a slight smile. Rebecca touched her mother's forehead. It was cold.

Helena was dead.

Rebecca let out a cry. The housekeeper embraced her and they just stood there helpless. Alex returned and found them in the bedroom. They had not moved an inch.

The first call Alex made was to David. He said he would be there shortly. Alex then took Rebecca out of the room. They all sat in the living room waiting for David. Rebecca was not crying anymore. She just sat there frozen.

Finally David arrived. He spoke quietly with Rebecca. He told her later in the afternoon a casket would arrive at the house with people from the Chevra Kadisha. This was a Hebrew word for the people who prepare the body for burial. That night there was a direct flight to Israel and the casket would be taken to the airport. Alex would stay home with the kids. David and Rebecca would escort the casket on that flight. Rebecca nodded and thanked him.

David persuaded Rebecca to go to her bedroom and pack a few things. He did not want Rebecca to see her mother being carried out of the house. She knew. She stayed in her bedroom until the housekeeper came in to tell her it was time to go to the airport. Alex took the kids to their friend's house after school and then returned home to say goodbye to Rebecca. He told her to be strong. David gave Rebecca a pill on the flight that put her to sleep.

Upon their arrival, there was a limo to pick up David and Rebecca which was followed by the hearse carrying Helena's body. In Jerusalem, at the cemetery, everything was prepared for them. There was a Rabbi, and Joseph and Moshe were present. A plot was dug adjacent to the resting place of Henry, so Helena's body could be buried next to Henry.

The Rabbi asked Rebecca what was the name of the deceased. Rebecca answered, "Liliana Wise Kopel, survived by a daughter, two sons and six grandchildren."

David had already ordered a monument and he and Rebecca returned to Tel Aviv. They took the next flight back to the States.

Upon her return to the United States, Rebecca called her brothers. She told them of the death of their mother and that the body was cremated immediately. She said this was Helena's wish. Rebecca told them she would come to Germany to bring her mother's ashes for burial. The urn was made of marble and it was permanently sealed. .She also was bringing them the death certificate. Little did they know, the sealed urn contained only sand. Rebecca was departing the next day. Alex accompanied his wife to Germany.

Max was waiting for them at the airport. He hugged Rebecca and asked her a lot of questions. He also asked if it was okay with her to have a service in the church.

"It's okay, but I will not attend," said Rebecca.

The church was almost empty. Just the family, the extended family, the household help and the priest were in attendance. The local people of the town had never embraced Helena because they thought she was Polish, and did not attend her service.

Sarah was almost inconsolable. She was saying, "I had so much more to tell her, and I never did."

They all proceeded to the cemetery where the Van Klaus family had a huge mausoleum. The urn was placed next to Robert Van Klaus's casket. The priest conducted a prayer and they all left.

The next day the local paper had an announcement of Helena's sudden death.

Albert saw Rebecca at a meeting he requested. He said that he and his brother wanted to discuss the inheritance from their mother. They wanted to share it with her.

Rebecca thanked him and told him, "Whatever you feel is appropriate will be okay with me."

They all parted friendly and promised each other to remain in touch.

Rebecca and Alex were on the way home to their life and their kids. Rebecca felt numb. She felt sorry for herself. She had a very short time with her mother. Alex and Rebecca still had not determined what to tell the children. They had not come up with the dialogue.

Sam knew what happened. David explained it to him already. Lilly was another matter. Rebecca told her that her grandmother was in heaven together with her grandfather and they were happy.

The housekeeper had already gathered all of Helena's clothes. She packed them in a large plastic container and put it in the attic. She only left three small perfume bottles on the dresser.

When Rebecca entered the room it was clean and looked lifeless. The only reminders of the occupant of the room were the photographs of her father and mother in an old antique frame and the lingering smell of her mother's perfume.

Within a few weeks, Rebecca received a very generous check from her brothers. She gave the check to David to be donated to the largest hospital in Jerusalem. She knew this would please her mother.

Rebecca stayed in touch with her brothers, but less and less as the years passed.

Rebecca and Alex continued to live in the United States. Their son and daughter both married. Rebecca just had her first grandchild.

* * *

AUTHOR'S NOTE

Thank you for purchasing and reading Parallel Lives. I'm extremely grateful that you chose my book, and I sincerely hope you've enjoyed reading it as much as I've enjoyed writing it.

If you liked the story, I would love to hear from you. I hope you will take a minute to leave a short review on Amazon. Reviews from readers like you make a big difference in helping new readers find stories like Parallel Lives. Your help in spreading the word would be greatly appreciated!

LENA ROTMENSZ

CPSIA information can be obtained
at www.ICGtesting.com
Printed in the USA
FSHW022028250820
73299FS

9 781983 359170